MARIAH MUNDI
AND THE GHOST DIAMONDS

Also by G. P. Taylor

Praise for *Mariah Mundi: The Midas Box*

'When Harry Potter hangs up his wizard's cloak, booksellers will be looking to G. P. Taylor's *Mariah Mundi: The Midas Box* to keep the cashtills ringing.'
BBC News

'It really is wonderful, wonderful stuff . . . *Mariah Mundi* surpasses Potter on just about every level there is. Highly recommended.' *The Bookbag*

'The book that combines the big story of C. S. Lewis and the plot of an Indiana Jones movie. We could genuinely be looking at the book series that will replace Harry Potter at the top of every child's wish list.'
BuddyHollywood Review

Praise for *Shadowmancer*

'The biggest event in children's fiction since Harry Potter.' *The Times*

'The adventure unfolds at a vivid and breathless pace.' *Observer*

'*Shadowmancer* is flying off the bookshelves as if a wizard had incanted a charm on it.' *Herald*

'A magical tale of vicars and witches.' *Daily Telegraph*

'A compelling and dark-edged fantasy . . . highly recommended.' *Independent*

Praise for *Wormwood*

'*Wormwood* is breathtaking in scope . . . an extraordinary achievement told by a master storyteller. The book is, quite simply, marvellous.' *Guardian*

Praise for *Tersias*

'It is, in a word, brilliant. Colourful, dramatic, relentless, accessible to children – and more frightening for their parents.' *Scotsman*

'The plot hurtles along carrying the reader from one cliffhanger to the next.'
Daily Telegraph

G. P. Taylor

MARIAH MUNDI
and the
Ghost Diamonds

faber and faber

First published in 2008
by Faber and Faber Limited
3 Queen Square London WC1N 3AU

Typeset by Faber and Faber Limited
Printed and bound in the UK by CPI Mackays, Chatham ME5 8TD

A CIP record for this book
is available from the British Library

ISBN 9780–571–22646–7

2 4 6 8 10 9 7 5 3 1

MARIAH MUNDI
AND THE GHOST DIAMONDS

[1]

Paradise

THE man walked nervously in and out of the long, dark shadows. He followed the alleyway that led from the harbour up the Customs House steps and into an old street of narrow cottages. His wet feet left a trail of footprints across the stone steps. He wore his long coat tightly wrapped about him and kept his head down as he strutted on. With his cane he marked out each step. He kept a black, gloved hand to his face, as if to hide himself from the world. A spot of blood trickled from the fingers and across the back of the glove. The man coughed as he walked and looked back and forth to see if he was being followed. A door opened, a cat was thrown into the street, and the door slammed again. The man paused for a moment and tried to look inside the house without being seen.

Peeking through the misted glass he could see two children huddled beside the fire. To one side was a man slumped in a chair, his head lolling from side to side like a dying fish gasping for breath. The children at his feet raced two beetles across the fire hearth, not knowing they were being intently watched.

'Shall these be the ones?' the man asked himself in a voice of gravel.

'Too small . . . Not enough meat to fill a louse,' he replied as he gathered up his coat even tighter and walked on. The man turned into Princess Street and walked as far from the light of the inn as he could. Above him he could see the outline of the church that had stood on the hill for a thousand years, and beyond that the silhouette of the castle.

'This way,' the voice inside urged him on as he took the first step up the hill. 'I know there'll be one this way . . .'

Not far away, Mariah Mundi stood on a narrow flight of stone steps that led from the churchyard, through the alleyways and ginnels, and eventually to the harbour far below. He looked older than fifteen short years. Mariah was tall, thin, with a mop of black hair that curled and curled like thick brambles upon his head. In the glow of the gas lamp, the steps looked as if they were the glistening back of a serpent that had coiled itself through the town unbeknown to anyone.

He blinked. Above his head the gas lamp spat and bubbled in its green metal casing that held four panes of thick glass. It coughed and hissed as the flame burnt brightly. He waited and looked out across the rooftops below. With the golden tip of his little finger, Mariah traced the pattern of the lamps upon the far bridge that straddled the ravine and led his eye to the Prince Regent Hotel. Four towers reached up and touched the dark clouds that were swept in from the sea. Every window of the Prince Regent was lit, and even at that great distance, Mariah could hear the chords and swirls of the orchestra that played each night for those who cared to dance.

He shrugged his shoulders, pulled up the collar of his coat against the wind and took a fob watch from his pocket. Mariah looked at the golden hands that dragged themselves across the oyster face. In his mind he counted the seconds and listened as they kept pace with his own heart. He stared again towards the

Prince Regent, the grand hotel where he had gone to work as a magician's apprentice. It loomed from the sea as if every brick had been placed one on top of the other by a giant. Mariah remembered his first day, when he had arrived from the Colonial School for Boys in his five-pound suit and with his writ of worthiness. He had the golden tip of his little finger to remind him of the Midas Box.

In the dark churchyard, the clock on the high tower began to strike the tenth hour. The wind screamed through the dark streets below. It rattled the locks on the tall terraced houses of Sepulchre Street and slammed the gates to the backyards one by one.

Out to sea, just off the harbour mouth, Mariah could see the broken bones of a ship, the rigging of its foremast billowing in the swell. In the months that had followed the mysterious sinking of the SS *Tersias*, rumours had abounded. Some had said that it was the work of the Kraken, a hideous sea creature that would drag ships to the bottom of the ocean. Others had argued that, in the age of reason and exploration, nothing could be further from the truth. Just beyond the breakwater, the funnel of the stricken ship poked from the waves and even at high tide served as reminder of the night it sank.

No one had dared go near the wreck. Several bodies had been washed ashore on the fine sandy beach below the Prince Regent Hotel. In great secrecy, they had been quickly taken away and buried before anyone could see what was wrong with them. It was the talk of the town. The *Evening Chronicle* had, for once, faithfully recounted the night of the disaster with eye-witness reports. It had even mentioned that one of those who had drowned had been turned to gold, with a look of terror upon his face as if he had seen the devil himself.

This was fervently denied by the Mayor, Inspector Walpole of the town police and Joseph Peabody, the magistrate. Despite their feeble protestations, the people of the town at the end of the railway line believed that since the sinking of the SS *Tersias*, gold was being given up by the sea.

At every high tide for several days following the sinking, almost the whole of the town turned out to see what would be washed ashore from the wreck. Children ran after the breaking waves that pulled back into the undertow. They grabbed the rolling rocks and shells and tapped them against their teeth to test for gold.

On one particularly dark night when the sea was high and beaten into a great swell, an old man with long fingers and no shoes had found a golden fish. It was as if it had been frozen in time, its mouth wide open. He had dragged the petrified creature across the sands to the pawnbrokers on Quay Street and even at that late hour had beaten upon the door to wake the shopkeeper, who pronounced that it truly was made of the finest gold he had ever seen.

Inspector Walpole had seized the fish as evidence. He had chipped at the metal creature with the point of the sharp knife he always carried on his belt and gouged out a golden eye. This had been then placed securely in the top pocket of his grubby gabardine. Walpole had then picked his nose and muttered something to the small, fat detective who lurked in the darkness of the pawnbroker's shop. With that, the fish was snatched from the pawnbroker and was never seen again. The snivelling Inspector made promises over the protestations of the man that he would get what was rightly his, but then he wiped his nose on the sleeve of his coat and he and the fish vanished.

When the storm of that night had given out, the beach was strewn with pieces of gold. It was as if creatures never before seen by the human eye had been chiselled from the seabed, turned to gold and thrown on to the beach by the waves. Cockles, mussels, seaweed and several prawns had been miraculously transformed into beautiful and shining objects of desire. Each one was made of solid gold.

Then, as soon as it had started, it was finished. The sea beat against the coast but gave nothing more. The crowds dwindled and streets emptied. From Christmas to skipping day nothing else had been found. The wreck of the SS *Tersias* broke up in the waves leaving only the foremast and blackened funnel as a reminder of its grave. Those who combed the beach looking for gold had now gone. In the pub at the bottom of Paradise Hill, talk of treasure had all but ceased.

Mariah had heard one man saying that he thought the Kraken would have taken every ounce by now and hidden it far out to sea. His companion, a younger man in thick breeches and sea boots, had muttered into the froth of his beer that all was not right with the world and it was surely coming to a fateful end.

As he listened to their words that night, Mariah had smiled contentedly. He gripped the badge in his pocket and ran his fingers back and forth over the words etched in the metal. He knew them by heart: *Bureau of Antiquities*. Mariah had tapped the golden tip of his little finger against the metal. It was something he felt he couldn't get used to. It was a part of him, joined seamlessly at the knuckle, gold and then flesh. He wondered how his flesh and blood had been turned to gold, but he had seen it with his own eyes. The Midas Box had left its mark, and Mariah had been touched by its power.

Now Mariah wanted to stand before the whole town and tell them everything. He could answer all their questions, tell them the truth about the gold. It was a feeling that was bursting in his chest and he wanted to scream out. Every time he heard someone talking about the gold from the SS *Tersias* he wanted to boast how he knew, how he had been the one to see the box work its magic. He knew that the Midas Box was making the gold. Once every day, as it was tossed by the currents, it would open up and shine brightly on all that was near. Mariah knew that it was still out at sea, just waiting to be washed ashore.

Every time he looked at his right hand it reminded him of the fight with Gormenberg in the Prince Regent. The Midas Box had burnt with a brilliant light and transformed Gormenberg's hand to gold as well as the tip of Mariah's little finger. He knew that Gormenberg was now dead and would never return. He also knew that such a wonder as the Midas Box would never just vanish, and that soon its power would slither back into the world.

A man and his gold may soon be parted, Mariah had thought as he left the smoke-filled pub. Sacha had followed on behind, chuntering to herself that Mariah should stop wearing the glove to cover his hand; either that or have the finger chopped off and melted down.

Now, as he looked out over the town, he waited for her at the top of the steps. Sacha had been gone for fifteen minutes. As Mariah huddled against the wall, under the gas lamp, the clock on the church tower gave its last chime of the tenth hour.

'Where have you been?' Mariah asked as Sacha's shadow broke across the steps.

'It was me dad – he's had too much again.' She sighed as she spoke, reluctant to say any more.

Mariah knew not to press her any further. Sacha was feisty, like the small terrier dog that he would watch on the pier end chasing rats. She would snap out her words, screw up her eyes and give him that look. He in turn would smile, change the subject and say no more.

'Best be getting back,' Mariah said as he put the glove on his hand and waggled his fingers so that the glove pulled tight against them.

Sacha saw what he had done. She looked at him. 'How long can you keep that to yourself?'

'Jack Charity knows of it,' Mariah said as he walked on, counting the streetlights that lined the alleyway.

Sacha followed two paces behind, her long coat with its bright silver buttons dragging on the cobbled steps.

'It's growing more and more. I've seen it, Mariah. More of your finger is turning to gold.'

'Not that much,' he said briskly, not wanting to think that soon his whole hand could be solid gold. 'Just a bit. Taken six months to grow to the knuckle. It'll stop there – I know it.'

'What'll happen when it's your whole hand and then your arm?'

'Won't get that far, Jack Charity said –'

'He's a soldier, not a doctor. What does he know?'

Mariah said nothing. He twisted the tip of his finger in his hand. She was right – more had turned to gold. 'If it grows any further I'll have it taken off. There's a surgeon in London, Charity said he would write to him.'

'It's not much use to you, is it? Might as well get rid of it before you end up like that bloke Walpole found on the beach. They said he had staring eyes and an open mouth. That he'd been frozen to gold in the middle of a scream.'

'Who told you that?' Mariah asked.

'Quadlibett . . . in his sweet shop. He hears everything,' she said as she danced on ahead of him down the glistening steps. 'Same thing happened to that sailor as to your finger. That Gormenberg would have done it.'

'He's dead. No one could have survived that wrecking. I saw the Kraken reach from the sea and drag the ship down . . .'

Mariah stopped suddenly. He looked ahead. Sacha was gone. The alleyway was empty. She had been there just a moment before – but now he was alone.

'Sacha . . . Sacha,' he said nervously as the hairs on the back of his head stood bristly tight. 'Stop playing, we have to get

back to the Prince Regent – Charity said to be back for eleven,'
he pleaded, as if he thought she were hiding from him in a
game of hide-and-seek.

There was no reply, not a sound. The alley was completely
empty. Mariah took three paces to the exact spot where she had
been. Set into the wall so that it could hardly be seen was a
small gateway. It was made of wood, with flaking green paint,
and was surrounded by the damp brick wall. It swung gently
from one hinge; the other was rotted through with sharp flakes
of rust. On the wet ground, wedged against the frame, was a
silver button. It shone in the lamplight like a small moon
ripped from the sky. It was the same as the one upon Sacha's
coat.

'Sacha,' he said again, this time just above a whisper. 'Are
you there, girl?'

All was quiet. Mariah pressed his hand against the wooden
gate and pushed slowly. It opened without a sound. He shuddered as a cold chill ran through him like a knife. Stepping
through the entrance he found himself in a small yard stacked
with lobster pots. It smelt of the sea and dead fish. The yard led
to another passageway and then in the distance to another
street. Mariah could see the amber reflection of the gas lamps
shining from the window of a house at the end of the alley. All
was quiet. The wind had ceased its squalling, yet he felt he
wasn't alone. Something, something near, made him gulp,
swallow hard and hold his breath. Mariah had felt the same
when he had searched the tunnels of the Prince Regent for
Gormenberg. He verged on panic – he wanted to run and shake
the shivers from his back.

Hanging from the walls of the yard were bundles of kelp
weed tied with string. The long, dried sea palms rustled in the
breeze. Mariah looked about him. The roofs of the houses that
made up the yard cast crossed shadows against the walls.

Behind him, the gas lamp from the alleyway shone in through the half open door that swung slowly back and forth, flapping like the wing of a dying bird. There was still no sign of Sacha.

'You there?' he asked impatiently as he pulled the glove tighter against his hand. 'Stop messing with me, Sacha. This isn't hide-and-seek.'

Mariah stopped and listened. He was sure that somewhere very near Sacha was hiding from him in some strange game. She had done this before and thought it fun; it was part of her character to hide and then appear with a smile on her face.

There was a loud crack - it happened without warning. Suddenly, from the gloom, a stack of fishing pots fell to the ground, blocking the door to the alley. A rat jumped from the ground, leapt on Mariah's shoulder and then off into the darkness. Mariah turned as Sacha was thrust from her hiding place. She fell forwards as she stumbled in panic.

'Run! Run!' she screamed just as Mariah fell against another stack of mouldy pots.

There was a slither of metal on metal; its sharpness grated as a sword was drawn. In the glimmer, Mariah saw the flash of a long blade and a dark figure in the shadows. A gloved hand hit out, smashing him in the chest and knocking him to the ground. Sacha leapt over him to make her escape.

'Get out!' Mariah shouted to her as he jumped to his feet.

The blade slashed, just missing his face and striking a hail of sparks against the wall. The dark figure stepped forward; its face was disguised by the mournful grimace of a gold theatrical mask, tied to the head with a long, bloodied rag. The man wore a long black coat, tightly wrapped about him. It glistened with beads of silver liquid as if he had spilt mercury upon it. In that moment, Mariah saw the eyes of his attacker staring coldly at him. They were blank and unblinking. It was then that he realised that the eyelids had been burnt from the face and the villain's eyes were set in a wrinkled mess of horrific scars tinged with gold.

Seeing the attacker lift the blade again to strike, Mariah grabbed a lobster pot from the ground and held it like a shield. The blow came once more and sliced through the weave of the net stretched across the bent spars of wood, narrowly missing Mariah's face. Mariah quickly threw the pot with all his strength as he looked for a way of escape. The attacker stepped back as the net cage struck him on the shoulder.

'Damn you, boy!' the voice of the man said as if in pain. 'I'll run you through!'

There was something familiar in the man's voice. It was as if Mariah had heard it before.

'Try me,' Mariah said coldly. All emotion drained from him as his throat dried quickly.

The man struck again and again. With each blow Mariah jumped out of his way as the sparking steel crashed against the wall of the yard. Another blow severed several thick strands of seaweed above Mariah's head and smashed through the narrow fall pipe that came down from the roof. The man let out a gasp, as if he was tiring and out of breath. He stood panting. He stared at Mariah through red, bloodied eyes that appeared to glow in the faint glimmer of the gas lamp.

'Someone else . . . has to . . . die,' the man panted as he held his chest with his gloved hand. 'It should have been the girl – but you'll have to do…'

'Have to hide behind that mask, do you?' Mariah said as he edged his way towards the broken pipe near his feet. 'Take it off and then you can kill me. I have to see your face before I die.'

'If it were so simple – but what hides my face is but part of my flesh, a divine joke, retribution for a past life.' The man gurgled his reply in a deep, gravelled voice.

'Then I shall not die,' Mariah said as he quickly grabbed the metal fall pipe and pulled it from the wall. There was a crunch as the metal tore away from the stone wall. He twisted and spun, swirling the pipe as if it were a long bludgeon.

The man lashed out time and again with his sword. Mariah parried the blows one by one. The man fell back into the deep shadows. Mariah struck a blow, not knowing where it would land, and the man gasped in pain. The dull thump of metal on metal rang out like a dampened bell. Mariah struck into the darkness again and again. The metal pipe thudded as the man growled in anger.

Then came a sudden, sharp, snapping punch that leapt out of the shadows and struck Mariah in the face. He felt his legs buckle beneath him. The sound of the world deadened and the night grew even darker. From far away he heard what he thought was the shrill call of a police whistle. It echoed through the streets nearby. Soon it faded into the enveloping darkness that numbed his fingers and wrapped itself around him.

As his memory of the world faded, Mariah could feel himself being dragged slowly along the wet ground and his arms and legs being pulled uncomfortably. He was aware of someone tearing at the collar of his shirt and ripping at the fabric with a cold hand. The sound of a button that had popped from his coat and danced upon the stone flags came again and again. Mariah thought that he could hear the man muttering in some strange tongue words he could not understand. It was as if he was invoking long-dead creatures to come and help him in his preparations.

Then there was nothing. No sight or sound – just deep blackness. It reminded Mariah of a dream he once had where he was locked in a room all alone. It was black as pitch, but Mariah knew there was someone hiding just out of reach. He could hear their breathing and smell the dirty scent that stenched around him.

He was unaware how much time had passed or how he had got to where he now lay. Mariah felt Sacha's hand on his face as she lifted his head from the ground. He was aware of someone else talking and Sacha trying to speak even faster than usual. His eyes opened slowly and for the first time he could feel the throbbing of the wound to his face.

'You're all right, lad,' said the deep voice of the man that cowered over him. 'Getting Doctor Merewether – he'll see to you.'

Mariah looked up. All he could see were the bright collar buttons of the man's uniform shining above him.

'Where is he?' Mariah asked.

'Gone,' replied Sacha gently. 'But you're alive. I thought he killed you.'

'Did you see what he looked like?' Constable Lancing asked as he tried to lift Mariah to his feet.

'Had a mask and a cane that became a sword,' Mariah muttered.

'Grabbed me in the dark and told me to be quiet,' Sacha gabbled, her voice singing the words faster and faster.

'Second time tonight,' Lancing murmured in reply as he thought aloud. 'The other lass wasn't as lucky – found her on Silver Street, what was left of her.'

[2]

The Hotel of Dry Bones

IN the lobby of the Prince Regent Hotel, a large circular fan in the shape of an ornate ceiling clock spun slowly around and around. From the heights of the vast gold vaulted ceiling it gently swirled waves of hot air that had been brought from the boiler far below through miles of ducting pipes. Sacha opened the door to the hotel and waited whilst Mariah went inside, holding his now swollen face.

'Best get Captain Charity,' she said as she disappeared amongst the crowds of people all dressed in their finery and awaiting the start of the midnight ball.

Mariah waited and then took three paces to a large leather armchair hidden from view by a gigantic aspidistra plant. He eased himself into the seat and sighed. He thought of how the Prince Regent had changed since the time of Gormenberg. As he watched the flames in the hearth of the large stone fireplace opposite, he listened to the chamber music echoing along the vast corridors from the gilded concert hall that overlooked the bay.

Since Captain Jack Charity had bought the hotel for a song, it had become the place to be seen by the best in society. Kings and princes, politicians and actors had swarmed from across Europe to spend at least one night at the Prince Regent Hotel. They had sampled the delights of the mud baths, the hot bubble spas and of course the galvanised bathing machine. Some had even taken to having their bodies wrapped in seaweed. They were then heated gently until the weed shrank tightly. Occasionally even the most vigorous of men would scream – but as this was all in the cause of good health, their complaints didn't last for long.

It was as if the changes had been meant to be, the working out of some natural destiny. Bizmillah the magician had left the Prince Regent on the night Gormenberg had been drowned at sea, and the hotel was now in the hands of the man who had once been the friend of Mariah's father and who had become Mariah's godfather. There would be no more of Bizmillah's magical tricks involving the illusion of cutting people in half. This was now left to Mariah, who had been given the task of performing each night in the grand theatre. His performance had been a great success. Rabbits had miraculously appeared from hats. Pigeons had materialised from thin air and two white ferrets had been trained to fight in his trousers. Giant puppets would dance on invisible strings, each one made in the image of Mariah. They would fight and dance, spinning until they disappeared, and Mariah himself would then appear, forced through the air by a gigantic steam ramrod that would vanish without being seen.

His most spectacular illusion was that of the sub-aqua escape. Sacha would tie him in chains and lock them with brass fetter locks and then, with a bag over his head, Mariah would be submerged in a glass tank. Time and again he would escape drowning and appear unharmed before the watching eyes.

All was well. The bones of Otto Luger that Mariah had found in the cellar had been neatly packed in to a silk blanket, placed in a small oak chest and buried in a quiet corner of the churchyard. Mariah remembered that it had rained that day. Water had dripped relentlessly from the bare branches of the oak trees. Captain Jack and Mariah had been the only mourners apart from Mr Mapleton, the shrew-like clerk from Dunlop, Fraser and Jenvey, solicitors to the late Otto Luger.

Mariah had been unable to take his eyes from Mapleton. He had twitched with every word he spoke and sniffed at the end of every sentence. A forest of hairs seemed to grow from the tip of his nose and hold the clerk's small, round spectacles in place. Whilst the box of dry bones was lowered into the deep hole, Mapleton had rubbed his hands and clicked his shrewish fingers nervously.

'Don't like death – all seems a bit too final,' he had squeaked. 'No one seems to be able to come back and tell us what it is like.'

'One man did and *I* trust all he says,' Captain Charity had said hurriedly as he patted Mariah on the back and turned to walk away.

Mariah had followed, leaving Mapleton at the graveside with his dark thoughts. It had been then that he had seen Grimm and Grendel, the two private detectives who had worked for Gormenberg. They had tried to hide beside a single tall oak. They looked out of place at the funeral. Grendel had a pink scarf that nearly touched the floor wrapped around his neck, whilst Grimm had just blankly stared at the moping Mapleton. Mariah had later asked Charity what they had been doing. Charity had laughed and told him they would do themselves more harm than anyone else, and from that day they had never been mentioned again.

It was as Mariah daydreamed that someone caught his eye. Through the stems of the aspidistra, he saw a man in full military uniform warming himself by the fireplace. He was tall and elegant, with a large moustache that had been waxed into the shape of an eagle's wings. In one hand he carried a black hat laced with the feathers of a tropical bird. Twisted gold brocades fell from the shoulders of his uniform and three gold stars emblazoned each lapel.

But it was not the manner of his dress that caught Mariah's attention. At first he wasn't sure, but as he looked, he realised that the thumb on the man's left hand looked as if it were made of solid gold.

'How?' he asked himself, as he tried to get a better view without being seen.

The man appeared to be waiting for someone, and tapped the golden thumb against the rim of his hat. It glistened in the light from the row of gas filaments set in the crystal holders above the fireplace. He then paced up and down, taking several steps each time and with great military precision turning and pacing again.

Mariah sank back in the shadows so as not to be seen and hoped that Sacha would not return with Captain Charity until he had seen what the man with the golden thumb was doing and who he would meet. From far away, he heard the Chinese battle gong as it tremored through the hotel. It called everyone to the midnight ball and the vast buffet of ice carvings, plated meat and swirled curd and chocolate.

The man didn't move, but nervously looked this way and that and glared at the fob watch that he pulled from his pocket.

'Baron Hoetzendorf – I am sorry for my lateness,' Captain Charity said as he approached and held out his hand in welcome. 'There is a matter of importance to which I have to attend – perhaps we could meet after the ball?'

'It should be now, Captain,' the Baron insisted. 'I have waited long enough and tomorrow the ship will be here.'

'This isn't the time or place, my dear Baron. Later. I promise.' Mariah saw Charity put his finger to his lips as if to signal to the Baron to say no more. Then, without speaking, he picked three strands of fallen hair from the Baron's shoulder and brushed the jacket with his hand.

'Very well, later it will have to be.'

The Baron put on his hat and briskly swaggered towards the midnight ball and the clanging of the battle gong. Captain Jack Charity turned slowly and looked in to the shadows. It was as if he knew Mariah had been there all along.

'Sacha tells me you're hurt,' he said, stepping towards the armchair.

'Walking wounded,' Mariah replied as he leant forward to show Charity the extent of the bruise that ran down the side of his face.

'You'd both better stay in the hotel until the lunatic is caught. I fear there is more to this than just the random attack of a madman.'

'They said he killed a girl on Silver Street. He was seen and they gave chase but he leapt the wall of a house and onto the roof as if he had fire on his heels,' Mariah said excitedly.

'They'll be saying it's the work of Spring-Heeled Jack – that or the devil himself. Did you get a look at him?' Charity asked.

'He was wearing a mask, just like the one on the wall in the theatre. It was tied to his face with a tattered bit of cloth.'

'Anything else?'

'He smelt . . . He smelt sweetly of something like gunpowder and lamp oil mixed with perfume – and he was quick with his fist.'

'You're getting old, Mariah. Slowing down so even old men get you with a punch,' Charity joked, laughing.

'Not so old that I couldn't give you a good hiding,' Mariah said. 'One thing. The man you were speaking to – who was he?'

'Why do you ask?' Charity said.

'Nothing . . . He just looked . . . nervous.'

'He's Austrian, and says he is recovering from an accident and has come here to rest,' Charity replied. 'Yet I have never seen the man rest for a minute. This morning he sent a message that he required to speak to me before midnight.'

'Seems –' Mariah stopped what he was about to say.

'You could do me one thing, Mariah, if you are feeling well enough?' Charity asked.

'What?'

'You could keep an eye on him for me. You and Sacha. Just make sure he doesn't get into any *difficulties* . . . He'll be at the midnight ball – watch him from the balcony and let me know who he speaks to.'

'Does this have anything to do with the Bureau of Antiquities?' Mariah asked as he felt the badge in his pocket.

'Possibly, but it is best we don't mention it just yet. A ship arrives tomorrow – the *Irenzee*. It is the private yacht of a rich American. Since the news of its arrival we have had too many strangers from all parts of the world book in as guests. I fear a meeting is to take place, a gathering of importance, and we need to find out why.'

'So it *is* the business of the Bureau,' Mariah replied.

'It is too much of a coincidence for an Austrian general, a Russian commander, an American Ambassador and an emissary from the Emperor of Japan all to be *so* unwell that they have to take refuge in a hotel beside the sea,' Charity said as he rubbed his chin and stared at the flames. 'The waters of the spa may be appealing and the galvanised bathing machine may work wonders, but I fear there is another reason why they are here.' Charity reached into his pocket and pulled out a small leather case. 'You may need these – you have seen them before.'

Instantly, Mariah knew what he had. There in the leather case were the divining spectacles that Grimm had once used so well to search for them when they had escaped from the Prince Regent. Mariah knew of their power to track someone for days. He held out his hand expectantly.

'Diving spectacles,' he said as he took hold of them, pulled them from the snakeskin case and looked at their strange design. 'But I'll need something of the Baron's if you want me to follow him – that is how they work, isn't it?'

'Then you may need this,' Charity said, and he carefully showed Mariah the three strands of hair he had taken from Hoetzendorf's jacket. 'Be careful, Mariah, it could all be quite innocent but I have a feeling there will soon be trouble,' Charity whispered as he turned to walk away. 'If anything happens let me know. And next time, *try* to duck before someone hits you . . .'

Mariah didn't have time to reply. Charity was gone in an instant and vanished in the crowds of people making their way to the midnight ball. Mariah got up from the chair and stood by the fireplace. He looked at his face in the mirror and admired the bruise as if it were a trophy of war. Then, for the briefest moment, he was frozen to the spot. He couldn't move, his arms and legs were petrified. There, in the reflection of the mirror, as if the figure was behind him, was the face of the masked man. For a fleeting second, Mariah saw the bloodshot eyes and drivelling mouth half hidden behind the golden mask of tragedy.

When he looked again, the face was gone. All he could see was the chair and the large aspidistra billowing from the brass pot. Mariah turned. His eyes searched the shadows for the faintest trace of the man. There was no one. Quickly he put on the diving spectacles and looked about the hallway. He tuned each lens with the dials on the side of the frame. The colour of the room transformed from purple to blue and then to red as the frequency changed.

In the corner of the alcove where he had been seated was the slightest trace of blue ectoplasm. It coiled like a smoking miasma. Suddenly it twisted in the air like a whisping serpent about to strike. Mariah watched as it seemed to dance to the distant music of the orchestra, and then the snake suddenly disappeared.

Mariah took the spectacles from his face and put them back into the box. Searching the alcove, he looked for a way of escape. He was sure that the face of the man had been real, that it wasn't just his imagination. Frantically he tapped the wall for any sign of a secret door. Mariah knew the man could only have vanished so quickly from the hallway by such a device. He pushed against the plaster and ran his fingers along the low picture rail. There was nothing.

'What you doing?' Sacha asked as she sneaked up behind him. 'I've been watching you for ages. Lost something?'

'Someone . . .' he replied in a stony voice. 'I saw the man who attacked me. I was looking in the mirror and he was there behind me. I saw his reflection. When I turned he was gone. He couldn't have got away, he had to hide somewhere.'

'How could he be here?' Sacha asked. 'He would have been noticed.'

'What if he's more than a man – what if he's a ghost or something?' Mariah blurted his words as if in a panic as his mind raced to find an explanation.

'Then we'll find him – can't be worse than fighting Gormenberg.' Sacha froze as she spoke the words. They had come to her mouth without thought – to say such a thing was ridiculous, she thought to herself, as the vision of being captured by Miss Monica and then seeing Mariah kill her in the nitrogen tank flashed through her mind. 'We could do it – couldn't we?' she said, her voice breaking with uncertainty.

'If he's killed once, he'll kill again. He said to me, *Someone else . . . has to . . . die.* He'd already killed the girl and wanted to do it again. It was *you* he was after, Sacha.'

She looked at Mariah and gulped back her tears. 'He just appeared, came from nowhere. One minute I was in the alley and the next he had dragged me into the yard. He held me so tight that I couldn't breathe – he put a stinking rag to my face – I wanted to sleep.'

When the police had arrived they had been bundled onto the back of a cart and taken straight to the Prince Regent. Sacha had not had the time to say or even think anything about what had happened. She began to shake with nerves as the realisation that she had been in the hands of a monster came to her.

'It was chloroform,' Mariah said. 'I knew what it was but couldn't think of the name. We used it at school to experiment on rats. It would kill them, they would go to sleep and die. It's a smell I can never forget – reminds me of death.' He shook his head as if to rid himself of the memory. 'Mister Soubeiran would take it all the time. Sniff it on a rag and then grin at us before falling asleep at his desk. It sent him mad in the end. I would see him from the window of my classroom, hopping around the school grounds as if he were a giant rabbit. That man was going to put you to sleep and then –'

'I don't want to think about it,' Sacha burst in angrily. 'Captain Charity said he had a job for us and you'd tell me about it. What is it?'

Mariah didn't speak at first. He knew she wouldn't be listening. Taking her by the arm, he walked with Sacha along the grand hallway with its gold pillars and twisting staircase towards the midnight ball. The music grew louder and the passageway more crowded. All the while he looked for the man in the mask.

'You can go to your room if you want,' he said, wanting her to take the words in kindness.

23

'And wait for him to come and get me? No chance. What did Charity want us to do?' she asked again, this time hoping for a reply.

'To spy on an Austrian Baron and tell Captain Jack who he speaks to. That's all we have to do,' Mariah said quickly as he fumbled with the badge in his pocket and remembered the words of Isambard Black, Master of the Bureau of Antiquities.

'Remember, Mariah,' Isambard Black had said on the night he had left the town by train for London soon after Gormenberg had drowned. 'You do not choose the Bureau, the Bureau chooses you.'

Mariah could not and would not forget. Aldo Rafden, he was told, had formed the Bureau of Antiquities, a hundred and fifty-three years before. He was an explorer, collector and government spy. To those who knew him, he was a scandalous thief who loved nothing more than finding something precious and taking it for himself. He had plundered the tombs of the East and put the loot on display in Bloomsbury. Rafden had a particular interest in the mummified remains of animals and had filled his displays with dead cats so that the whole museum looked like a charnel house.

The sole purpose of the Bureau, as it was known, was to find those mysterious objects of power and legend that were only spoken about in whisper. Often, what the Bureau found was so secret that people would never dare mention it in public or claim to know of its whereabouts, and through the years the Bureau had searched out many things. Isambard Black had told Mariah, over a plate of fish and chips in the Golden Kipper, that even the Holy Grail was now in the possession of the Bureau and that this object of legend was in itself quite unremarkable.

'It was made of pot and looked like a herring jar,' Black had said as he picked a large fishbone from his teeth. 'And as for the philosopher's stone, we discovered that in the possession of a woman who lived in Edinburgh and spent all her time writing ditties in restaurants.'

Now, as Mariah led the way to the balcony, Black's words excited his imagination. He smiled at Sacha and squeezed her hand as he would always do at times like this.

'All we have to do is keep an eye on him, that's all,' he said as he opened the door and stepped inside a velvet-clad opera box that overlooked a large dance floor.

'How will we find him?' Sacha asked.

Mariah didn't need to answer. There, twenty feet below was Baron Hoetzendorf in the arms of a rotund lady in sparkling shoes. It was obvious from her vice-like grip upon the slender Baron that this was his wife. She was at least two feet taller than him and three times as large. The woman was squeezed into a gigantic corset that gripped her as if she was about to explode. Despite her great size, she was extremely nimble and danced like a demented squirrel. Baron Hoetzendorf didn't really dance: any chance of his feet touching the ground was frustrated by the invincible grip of his gargantuan wife in her tight corset.

Watched by Sacha and Mariah, the Baron was lifted from the floor and swirled back and forth by his wife as if she were a child playing violently with a disliked rag doll. From the pained look upon his face, Mariah presumed that Hoetzendorf was about to faint – either that or be violently sick. As the music shrilled to a crescendo, Madame Hoetzendorf danced faster and faster, keeping immaculate timing. Then, as the music stopped, she let go of her husband, who fell to the floor unsure as to where he was.

'Better not be seen,' Mariah said, wanting to laugh as he settled back in the shadows to keep watch.

[3]

De Incendiis Corporis
Humani Spontaneis

T HE hour passed slowly. The midnight ball was incredibly
crowded and incredibly dull. Keeping the Baron under
surveillance was quite simple, as it appeared that Madame
Hoetzendorf insisted that her husband dance to every tune. At
times they were the only couple upon the dance floor. She
dragged her beleaguered mate from corner to corner and back
again, not caring how many guests were trodden under her
incredibly large feet. Straining through one eye, Mariah
formed the opinion that she looked like a mad rogue elephant
stampeding across the veldt. As the night progressed, fewer
and fewer guests dared to go near to the Baron and his wife for
fear of being crushed to death.

From the safety of the balcony, Mariah looked on. Occasionally he would allow his eyes to close as the music droned and
moaned and the lateness of the night brought on a desire to
sleep. Sacha had wrapped herself in the thick red velvet curtain
and yawned continuously as she propped her head against the
gilt banister. She tried to smile at Mariah, but he didn't notice.

Just as Mariah was about to fall asleep, he saw the Baron
slipping away from his wife. She wasted no time in picking a

small, reluctant man from a nearby table and dancing him to the centre of the ballroom.

'He's gone,' Mariah said with a start that woke Sacha. 'The Baron has left the ball.'

Mariah didn't wait for Sacha to reply. He ran from the balcony box and down the staircase. Sacha followed as best she could, unable to keep pace with him. He ran faster and faster as he jumped the treads two at a time.

He was soon inside the kitchen. Taking a shortcut through the crowds of waiters who were huddled in a small anteroom, Mariah sneaked towards the two large doors that led from the back scullery into the ballroom.

This was a route known only to the staff; guests could never find their way through the labyrinth of tunnels, passageways and corridors that ran amongst the thick walls and under the floors of the Prince Regent. From the kitchen it was just a short way to the ballroom. The corridor was dark and had thick, beaded curtains at each end. Each of the hundred strands rattled against the others like the tail of a snake; they clattered against the walls and gently moved in the cold draught. Mariah shuddered as he walked through the first curtain. The light grew dim and the air chilled. He counted the steps as he always did; it kept his mind from thinking what could be hiding in the shadows. Sacha was nowhere to be seen. He knew that if he was to find the Baron then he couldn't wait for her to catch up.

Mariah took the last pace towards the ballroom door, his footsteps echoing about him. In his mind a voice told him that he was not alone. He brushed aside a strand of the beaded curtain and stopped to listen. All he could hear was the rattle of the beads against the tiled floor, the sound of babbling waiters from the kitchen, and the distant whirring of the steam generator that gave life to the hotel. Taking the brass handle, he pulled open the door and peered inside the ballroom. Amongst the crowds of people he could see Madame Hoetzendorf waiting for the one-o'-clock gong that would announce the night buffet. She was several feet from the door, at the head of a long queue that slithered around the golden columns and out of the ballroom doors.

Everyone awaited the coming of the supper with great anticipation. It was the highlight of a night at the Prince Regent. With great ceremony, a tall man in a frock coat and black tie made his way across the ballroom and onto the stage. He pulled back the curtain to reveal a large Chinese gong. He preened himself and, taking the felt hammer, struck the gong firmly.

'Ladies and gentlemen,' he said in a high-pitched and squeaky voice. 'The night supper!'

The huddled waiters left the anteroom and stormed into the ballroom ferrying large trays of cold meat and oysters, which they laid on rows of tables bedecked with swans and antelopes carved from ice. Inside each carving were the frozen bodies of small green frogs that glistened like the lights of a Christmas tree.

There was a burst of applause as everyone gathered looked on in delight. Mariah stepped inside the room to search out Hoetzendorf. The waiters in their fine purple jackets lined with gold braid formed a peculiar procession, circulating amongst the guests with trays of arachnid-like canapés.

In the heat from the myriad gas lamps the frozen statues were already beginning to melt. Miraculously, one by one, as each frog was exposed to the air it came back to life and jumped from the table and across the floor.

Mariah could see Baron Hoetzendorf standing on the far side of the room. He was alone. Mariah edged his way around the ballroom. The Baron twisted his fine moustache and tapped his fingers against the brim of his hat.

A waiter in an unusual white jacket walked directly to the

Baron carrying a small silver tray with a selection of neatly cut sandwiches. He offered the tray to the Baron, who clumsily attempted to tuck his hat under his arm and take a sandwich at the same time. The hat fell to the floor, and the waiter handed Baron Hoetzendorf the silver plate and bent down to pick up his hat. The Baron greedily ate three wedges of cheese and bread. He twitched his moustache as he swallowed, as if they tasted quite bitter. He then ate another and then another, until the plate was empty.

The waiter handed the Baron his hat and bowed before walking out of the main door and disappearing from view. Mariah looked on. A tall man in a pink waistcoat spoke to Hoetzendorf politely as Mariah struggled to hear what was being said. It sounded foreign, and not a language that he could understand. The man handed the Baron a small scrap of paper. He looked at it momentarily, smiled, folded it neatly and put it in his coat pocket.

Hoetzendorf then turned and briskly walked towards his wife, who had taken up residence amongst the trays of chocolate gateaux. She was helping herself to a seventh portion of a particularly large slab of cake when something made her turn and look at her husband.

There, in the middle of the dance floor, Baron Hoetzendorf had begun to shake uncontrollably and froth at the mouth. He gripped the tight collar of his uniform and pulled at the buttons as he gasped for air. Mariah quickly realised that the Baron was extremely unwell. As a crowd gathered around him, Hoetzendorf shook and shivered and then his face changed colour. First it took on the shade of a winter sun and then quite violently turned bright purple. The Baron gasped and gasped for a breath that could not be found, and then pointed a finger as if towards someone standing before him.

The grand Madame began to scream and nimbly rushed

towards her husband. Reaching out, she took hold of the Baron by the hand. He let out a faint moan and, to the awe of the spectators around him, began to smoke from the ears. His mouth opened as if to speak, but instead of words, blue flames danced from his tongue. Instantly he caught fire. Within a second he was completely engulfed in a cold blue flame. The Baron momentarily glowed bright red and was then surrounded by thick swirls of white smoke.

Madame Hoetzendorf screamed even louder as her husband disintegrated before her eyes. The fire burnt intensely but without any heat. As the Baron was consumed, particles of bright silver dust were blown upwards, as if he were an erupting volcano. His wife pulled fearfully away, dislodging his shaking hand from his vanishing body.

'Herman! Herman!' she shouted as she shook the smouldering dead hand back and forth. Her husband then suddenly exploded, showering the screaming guests with a fine silver powder.

It was too much. Madame Hoetzendorf fainted. She hit the floor with a loud bang that shook the polished parquet. She quivered, rolling on the floor like a Chicago moll, and then whimpered faintly.

Apart from the hand and his Napoleonic hat, all that was left of the Baron was a pile of grey ash. Everything else had completely combusted. A soft rain of dust gently fell on the cowering guests, who by now had formed a large circle around what was left of Hoetzendorf.

Mariah pushed his way through the crowd and stared at the remains.

'Get Captain Charity!' he screamed to a waiter who stood mesmerised by what he had just seen.

The waiter didn't move, but remained petrified and trembling as he held the tray of drinks rigidly in his hand.

'Get Charity!' Mariah shouted again.

'Spontaneous combustion,' said the tall man in the pink waistcoat who had been talking with Hoetzendorf. 'I have heard of it many times but have never seen it.'

The man bent down and from the pocket of his waistcoat took out a silver magnifying glass. He began to examine the remains just as Captain Charity pushed his way through the guests.

'Captain Charity,' said the man in a Mordovian accent. 'Strange that this should happen tonight. Hoetzendorf had asked to speak with me, but I never got the chance.'

'Mister Pugachev, I wouldn't touch that,' Charity replied. 'Ladies and gentlemen, this has been a terrible accident. I suggest you all go to your rooms.'

No one moved; it was as if everyone was frozen. The circle of guests closed in even tighter around the ghoulish spectacle.

'It is quite safe – this cannot happen again,' Charity said. 'But you must go back to your rooms. The police have been called and will soon be here.'

Captain Charity didn't finish what he was about to say. As he spoke, Pugachev began to cough and splutter. His eyes welled with tears as he choked on the air. Pugachev tore at his clothing and fell to his knees. He reached out to Charity with an open hand as he tried to speak.

'It's the same as before,' Mariah said as a thin plume of smoke emanated from Pugachev's nostrils. 'Stand back, he'll explode!'

Panic broke out in the room. People screamed and ran. The emissary of the Emperor of Japan began to shake violently and scream in fear as hundreds of people rushed towards the door in a vast stampede. Mister Pugachev crawled towards Mariah, reaching out for help.

'Beware . . . Under the iron sea . . . That's where you'll find the answer,' he said over and over.

His words were edged in the same blue flame that had consumed Hoetzendorf. In seconds he was engulfed in a silver cloud and had erupted like a volcano. Then, just as Pugachev exploded into a fine dust, the Japanese emissary screamed even louder. Mariah and Charity both turned at the same time. The man gripped his stomach as if something inside him was trying to escape. There was a sudden flash of blinding light as he too disintegrated into dust.

'Get out, Mariah,' Charity hollered as the gas lamps began to fade.

Mariah ran for the door. He could see the crowds gathered on the other side. The lobby was filled with people hiding behind furniture in fear that someone else would explode. Charity pushed him from the room and slammed the large doors firmly shut behind them.

'Best stay this side, Mariah – don't know what is causing them to explode.'

'Spontaneous combustion – that's what the man said.'

'That is something I do not believe in. Once, perhaps – but three times, never.'

As soon as Charity spoke there was a scream from the doorway of the hotel. The American Ambassador was wedged into a compartment of the revolving door that led out to the street. Mariah ran towards him with Charity close on his heels.

'Stand back! Everyone out of the way!' Mariah said as he leapt over two old men in badly fitting wigs who were hiding behind a leather sofa.

'Mariah – no!' shouted Charity as he tried to grab him and pull him back.

He was too late. Mariah landed a yard ahead and ran towards the revolving door. There, trapped like a squashed fish, was the American Ambassador. He was wedged firmly against the glass panel unable to move. Too fat to get through, the Ambassador moaned and groaned as three men outside the hotel attempted to push him back inside.

'Leave him!' Mariah shouted as he noticed the Ambassador's wife stuck in the same compartment and hidden in the folds of his extra-large coat. 'He's stuck.'

Stuck he was, and from the colour of his face he was about to explode. Before he could be set free, the Ambassador smoked, smouldered, erupted and then exploded. The glass from the door was blown into the street as the lobby of the hotel was filled with wisps of grey smoke, silver dust and fragments of the Ambassador's ten-gallon hat.

The eruption of yet another guest sent the hotel into a greater panic than before. Guests jumped from the downstairs windows and ran into the streets. Others hid and refused to come from their rooms. Waiters threw down their trays and barricaded themselves in the kitchen. The lobby emptied quickly, leaving Mariah and Charity to examine the scene.

They could find no trace of the American Ambassador or his sparrow-like wife. All that remained was a tiny shoe with a gold buckle.

'Will there be any more?' Mariah asked as he picked the shoe from the carpet and looked inside.

'It was murder,' Charity replied cautiously. 'Tell no one of what Pugachev said to you.'

'Under the iron sea? He was talking rubbish,' Mariah replied.

'I wish he were,' Charity said as he brushed the dusty remains of the Ambassador from his jacket. 'It was *Irenzee* that he tried to say. It's the ship that arrives tomorrow. It could be the key to what happened here tonight.'

'I saw him talking to the Baron. He gave him a piece of paper. He told you he'd never spoken to him.'

'They were old friends – Pugachev's mother was Austrian. I

opened a letter he sent to her yesterday saying they had met.'

'What killed them?' Mariah asked as yet more guests stormed down the steps of the Prince Regent and into the street.

'It is more *who* killed them. Inspector Walpole will soon be here. Think before you speak to him. That man has wanted to see the back of me for many years and I wouldn't trust him an inch. Think before you speak.'

Mariah took a final look at the pile of grey dust where the Ambassador had stood. He picked several small shards of glass from his jacket and as he turned to the lobby saw that it had filled again with guests wanting to leave.

'What shall we do?' asked the weasel-like receptionist as she clambered to stop them from leaving.

'Let them go. It's a cold night and there are no trains until the morning. Perhaps they'll enjoy a night on a park bench. I'll be in my office.' Charity looked steely-faced and tried not to show a glimmer of emotion. He suddenly felt as if he were in the jaws of a tightly sprung lion trap and that there would be no escape. One death would be mysterious, two a cause for concern, but four in the same night and from the same symptoms shouted conspiracy. He looked at Mariah as he closed the door behind him and was angry with himself for allowing Isambard Black to recruit the boy into the Bureau of Antiquities.

'Nowt but a lad,' Charity said under his breath as he crossed the large office to the desk by the fire.

Outside the office, Mariah looked out for Sacha. For some reason she had not followed him to the ballroom and now she could not be found. Mariah waited by the revolving door and kept the guests that were left away from the pile of ash that was the late Ambassador and his wife. He knew this was the best place to find Sacha; she would have to come this way if she wanted to get to her room in the tower.

With one hand, he picked the skin from his lip until it was sore. The thought of the masked murderer plagued his mind. He couldn't get away from what he had glimpsed in the mirror. Mariah wanted to go to the mirror and stand before it and see if the vision appeared. This time he would be ready – he would turn as soon as the mask appeared and see if the man was real or just a figment of his imagination. Nothing was certain, he thought, as more guests packed their luggage and speedily left the hotel.

It was then that a tremor struck the whole of the Prince Regent, as if there had been an earthquake in the bay below the hotel. A vast sound set the foundations of the building vibrating and shook every bone in Mariah's body. It was like the amplified groan of a whale.

'Look!' screamed a waiter from the balcony bar. 'It's a ship.'

Captain Charity ran from his office.

'Quickly, Mariah. It's the *Irenzee* – a day early.'

Everyone rushed to the windows that overlooked the harbour and the bay. There, setting anchor in the calm waters, was the biggest vessel that Mariah had ever seen. It shone silver against the sea and had three tall masts which each appeared to be fitted with the blades of a windmill. A steam funnel came out of an illuminated bridge in the centre of the ship and to the rear was a large phosphorescent spotlight that not only lit up the ship, but also cast a dark shadow across the town.

Mariah was pressed against the window glass by several thin, prune-like spinsters all dressed in mourning black. One tried to push him out of the way so she could get a better view. She smelt of seaweed and muttered under her breath about the disgraceful behaviour of young people. The spine of her whalebone purse pressed into Mariah's back until he could take her persistent irritation no more.

Charity dragged him to one side, opened the door to the

balcony and stepped out into the cold night air. Far below, the ship began to glow as more phosphorescent lights were illuminated. Charity handed Mariah a small brass telescope through which he could clearly see the ship in great detail. He scanned the decks, but could see no crew; in fact he could see no one at all.

Even the bridge of the ship was empty. The blades on each mast rotated slower and slower until they finally stopped. Then the ship's horn blasted again, sending a shock wave through the water and shaking the Prince Regent. One by one the rotor blades folded into the masts. In turn each mast folded back into the deck of the ship. The funnel slowly contracted back into the roof of the bridge, and beneath the ship the sea began to glow bright red as if the sun was about to rise from beneath it.

The sharp, sword-like bow of the *Irenzee* came out of the water like a scimitar facing towards the town. The ship's powerful searchlights quizzed back and forth and lit up the Prince Regent with their blinding light.

'Why has it come to a place like this?' Mariah asked Charity as the two watched spellbound.

'Zogel is a powerful man. I saw him once in Africa. On the day he arrived, his gifts changed the lives of so many people. He took away their contentment and gave them misery. Zogel showed them a new world and a desire to have what they could never get.'

'What does he do?'

'Charms people – and then like a spider sucks their juices until they have nothing left. Wherever the Bureau is involved, Zogel is not far behind. Some say he is the richest man in the world and yet no more miserable wretch have I ever found. He is an inventor. But, the things he invents are designed to kill people. Kill them as quickly as possible.'

Mariah stared at the *Irenzee*. The searchlights still dashed back and forth across the town, lighting up the roofs of the houses and frightening great flocks of seagulls into the night sky. He thought that even in its beauty there was something quite menacing about the ship. Mariah slowly lowered the telescope and looked at Charity.

[4]

Inspector Walpole

AN hour later Inspector Walpole arrived at the hotel.
Captain Charity had asked Mariah to wait for Walpole and
show him immediately to his office, but Mariah had spent the
time looking at the Irenzee and wondering where Sacha had
gone. The longer she was away the more his concern grew. He
had even used Charity's brass telescope to scour the faces of
the crowds of people who had gathered on the long seafront to
look at the ship. She was nowhere to be seen. He knew that it
wasn't like her just to vanish – Sacha was always there.

Walpole banged his hand repeatedly on the bell on the desk
in the lobby. From what Mariah could hear, the man was not in
a good mood.

'Walpole – Inspector Walpole,' he snapped at the elderly
receptionist who was just finishing a plate of mussels. 'I'm here
to see Charity about the explosions.'

'I've been asked to –' Mariah said as he came face to face
with the Inspector. The shock of seeing Walpole was evident on
the boy's face. He had never seen a man like this before.

Walpole was seven feet tall to the inch. In his long, thin fingers he gripped a rolled umbrella that in his large hand looked

as if it were made for a child. On one finger Mariah could see a gold sovereign ring, and etched into its face was what looked like a square and compass. Mariah had seen the design before, on the front door of the house opposite the Prince Regent. Every Thursday evening he would watch as men jumped from their carriages and scurried up the steps as if they did not want to be seen. When he had asked what went on in the house, no one would tell him.

'A society of secrets,' Rhamses the chef had said in an unguarded moment. Mariah asked nothing more but from the porthole of his tower room he always watched the strange visitors to the ramshackle Athol House across the square.

'I want to speak to the organ grinder, not the monkey,' Walpole barked at Mariah as he stared at him. 'What are you looking at? Never seen a policeman before?'

Mariah gulped. Apart from Walpole's incredible height, long pointed nose, thin face and greasy hair, the man was also incredibly thin with a neck like a giraffe. In the middle of his throat he had a large Adam's apple that bobbed distractingly up and down with every breath he took.

No less alarming than Inspector Walpole's appearance was his suit. It was bright green, pinstriped, and made of thick Irish tweed. The jacket was belted around the waist and the trousers stopped three inches above the man's ankles. This made him look as if he had grown to an incredible height in a short period of time.

'Here, take this and do something useful,' he snapped. He handed Mariah a porkpie hat with an exceedingly greasy rim and a leather bag with a brass handle. 'Now, where's Charity?'

Without a word, Mariah led Walpole to the office. He knocked and then entered. Charity sat at the large desk in front of the fire. It reminded Mariah of when he had first seen Gormenberg. In all that time, nothing had changed.

39

'Inspector Walpole, thank you for coming,' Charity said as he stood from his chair.

'Don't talk rubbish, Charity. I'm here because I have to be and nothing more. Keep the pleasantries for your guests – well, the ones you have left,' he said with a snigger and a grunt at the same time.

Charity didn't reply. He nodded for Mariah to sit down on the chair by the door. Walpole looked at the boy and grimaced.

'Is *he* staying?' Walpole asked as he hung his umbrella over his arm and fiddled with the gold ring on his finger.

'Mariah is my assistant – whatever you want to say can be said in front of him.'

'Then you'd better be telling me what's going on. The streets are already full of stories that people have been involuntarily exploding and erupting, like –'

'It's true,' Mariah interrupted. 'I saw them all. They burst into flames, exploded, and turned to dust. The American Ambassador was trying to get out of the hotel through the revolving door with his wife . . .'

'People don't explode, boy. People don't burst into flames and turn to dust. It's not normal.' Walpole stared at Mariah with one raised eyebrow as if to tell him to shut up.

'They exploded. Baron Hoetzendorf then Mr Pugachev, the emissary of the Emperor of Japan and the American Ambassador . . .'

'Typical. Foreigners never die normally,' Walpole said under his breath.

'Important guests, and their deaths will have consequences, Inspector Walpole, consequences.'

'That they will. I have to find out if it were natural consequences or murderous consequences.' Walpole stopped and stared at Mariah as if he was inspecting every inch of him. 'You're the lad from the Paradise murder aren't you? Attacked by the masked man – the one who mysteriously got away.'

Mariah nodded and instinctively touched the wound on his face. He didn't like Walpole. The man smelt of snuff and the smoke of the herring shed.

'Left you something to remember him by, did he?' Walpole quizzed, his eyebrow raised even higher than before. He picked a strand of tweed from his jacket with his knife-like fingers and then said, 'Strange, that. We have five deaths in one night and the only factor that links them all is that this young Mariah is near to everyone. Gets me thinking, as an officer of the law, that you are an interesting fellow. Gets me thinking that you may know more about all this than you're letting on.'

'I was at four of the deaths, Walpole. Does that make *me* interesting?' Charity asked, knowing where Walpole's mind was taking him.

'It makes you both interesting. Since we were boys I always knew there was something not right with you – going off to your fancy London school, joining the army, being a hero.' Walpole sounded bitter. His nose twitched as he spoke and little strands of spittle formed at the corner of his mouth.

'Not his fault,' Mariah butted in angrily. He hadn't realised that Walpole had known his godfather for all those years.

'Leave it, Mariah,' said Charity. 'Theodore Walpole has always been the same. He was born an hour after me and has chased me all of his life. Did you ever know that my father sent me away because of you, Theodore? You made my life a misery and the Colonial School could never be called fancy.'

'That's what *you* say – always good with your words. Never knew what real work was – fopping around in all your gold braid – someone to wait on you hand and foot.' Walpole stopped and thought for a moment as if remembering a pleasant memory. 'I recall – I almost forgot – wasn't your father worried that some ruffians who were never found strapped you to the pier at low tide? Couldn't they hear you screaming for help from the other side of town?'

Charity didn't reply. He knew the memory well. It had haunted him often. Seven boys in sacking hoods tying his hands, dragging him across the harbour mud, strapping him to the wet arches of the far pier. The smell of the cold water rising about his neck as he had managed to spit out the gag and scream.

'Must have been quite frightening – would scar any normal boy for life,' Walpole quipped casually.

'Did you come to find out why these people died or just to insult Captain Charity?' Mariah shouted at Walpole.

'I take it he's another one of your Colonial boys, is he, Jack? Too big for his boots if you ask me – but nothing a good hiding wouldn't sort out.' Walpole snivelled as Charity cast a glance to Mariah bidding him to be quiet. 'Cat got your tongue, Mariah? Run out of words, have we?'

'I think, Theodore, that you should do the job you came to do and not say anything more,' Charity said as he walked to the door and opened it for the Inspector to leave.

'Don't worry, Jack, I'll be about my business and you about yours. Doubtless we'll meet up – and perhaps . . .' Walpole paused for a moment as he looked about the room and snivelled his words. 'Perhaps you may even have to come and speak to me in *my* office. Can't promise anything as snug as this, but at least the prison beds are comfortable.' Walpole wiped the strands of spittle from his mouth. 'Now, Charity, I think I should be looking at the remains of these foreigners. Can't leave the American Ambassador blowing away down the street, can we?'

Walpole left the room; he ducked under the door as he snatched his hat and leather bag from Mariah. Charity and Mariah followed on as the Inspector went to the revolving door to look at what was left of the Ambassador and his wife. The

Inspector got on his knees and examined the grey powder, then, reaching inside his leather bag, took a silver snuffbox and very carefully filled it with some of the remains.

Throughout all of this he never spoke. One by one he did the same to the other piles of powder that were once the emissary of the Emperor of Japan, the Russian diplomat and finally Baron Hoetzendorf. It was only when he was finished that he asked Mariah exactly what had happened.

Mariah remembered what Charity had said about not saying too much. He was brief and to the point, explaining to the Inspector all the events prior to the spontaneous combustions. Throughout the questioning, the Inspector eyed him warily as if every word he spoke was a lie. At one point he asked Mariah to empty his pockets on the table. Mariah refused – the only thing of value was his badge for the Bureau of Antiquities and that he would show to no one without good reason. Walpole had then asked Charity for a list of everyone at work in the Prince Regent that night.

'Is it murder?' Charity asked as Walpole put aside his investigations and closed his bag.

'Well, it's not normal – how many people have you ever known burst into flames and explode? A rather sudden way to depart the world, wouldn't you say, Charity?'

Charity nodded as Walpole took his snuffbox from his pocket and laid a line of silver powder across the back of his hand. Mariah smiled as he realised that Walpole was about to inhale a good sniff of the late American Ambassador.

Walpole put his hand to his nostril and with the seasoned relish of a snuff addict inhaled deeply. The dust vanished as if sucked into the vortex of a tornado. Walpole winced immediately. He screwed up his face and pinched in the end of his nose. He took the silver snuffbox from his pocket, flipped the lid and looked inside. To his horror he realised his mistake.

'Dyargh – snyam – asspew!' The Inspector sneezed. His greased and curtained hair shook wildly. The gush blew what remained of the American Ambassador into his face. Mariah looked away as if to search for something on the floor. Charity folded his arms and gritted his teeth. 'Not funny, Charity, and given half the chance I'll wipe that grin from your face.'

Walpole brushed the American ashes from his bushy eyebrows, folded the lid of the snuffbox and slipped it quickly into his pocket. He set off at a pace along the corridor towards the revolving door. With every step they could hear the man chunter and moan. As he turned to step through the door he looked back.

'I'll find out what killed them, Charity, and then I'll be – ASSPEW!' He sneezed again and dropped the leather bag to the floor. 'I'll be back . . .'

Walpole left the Prince Regent hurriedly.

'He thinks it's me,' Mariah said to Charity.

'He *wants* it to be you – there is a difference. Walpole and I have been at war for most of our lives. There is something in his heart that hates me and everything I stand for. If he has half a chance I'll be in that new prison of his.'

'What killed them?'

'Whatever it was, it kept them from speaking to me.' Charity looked solemn as he pulled three notes from his pocket. Each was written on the headed paper of the Prince Regent. The embossed crown on each note sparkled in the gaslight. 'They are all virtually the same, Mariah. They all wanted me to meet with them before the arrival of the *Irenzee*. Even the emissary of the Emperor said he needed to speak. Each one said they had something of interest to the Bureau of Antiquities.' Charity looked back and forth along the corridor, not wanting to be overheard.

By now, the lobby of the hotel was virtually empty. A last

party of guests dragged their cases to the door in a desperate attempt to escape the epidemic of spontaneous combustion. Outside, a small coach waited to take them to the station.

'Did they say what?' asked Mariah.

'Nothing that they would commit to paper, but I know it has something to do with the coming of that ship to the town. I'll search their rooms and see what I can find. You look for Sacha – we'll need her help.'

'She's been missing since before the explosions,' Mariah said quickly as he racked his mind as to where she could be.

'Then better you find her. I'll meet you in my office in an hour.' Charity looked at his fob watch. 'Back here at three – then we'll have some breakfast and get some sleep.'

Before Mariah could reply, Charity had opened the office door and had gone inside. The boy stood in the corridor and looked to the lobby. For a moment he thought about where to look for Sacha. From far away, near to the entrance of the Prince Regent theatre, Mariah heard the whirring of the steam elevator. He walked quickly and just as he arrived at its sliding grille doors, the elevator stopped and the door slid open.

Mariah stood back, expecting someone to step from within. But the elevator was empty, apart from a silver button. It shone in the bright light, and something about it was familiar. Mariah stepped inside the elevator and, wedging his foot against the door so it couldn't close, picked up the button. He read the inscription around its rim – *The Prince Regent*. The words stood bold against the metal. He looked at his coat – it matched. There were the torn threads in the place where it should be.

It's mine, he thought, the one I lost tonight – but how could it be here?

From several yards away he heard the sound of a wooden panel opening slightly. It creaked like a whisper or the cry of a mouse. It was the type of sound that should not have been heard, one that would normally have gone unnoticed. Mariah listened. The sound came again.

Edging his way from the elevator, he slowly slid foot by foot along the wall of the corridor until he reached the alcove opposite the fireplace. The noise came again, this time as if someone was dragging a heavy burden through a narrow entrance. There was a clatter and the dropping of a latch. Mariah looked into the mirror to get a glimpse of whoever was there without being seen. There was no one. The alcove was empty. All was as it should be. There was the ornate mirror above the large fireplace. The leather chair was just where it always was and the gigantic aspidistra had not moved.

Mariah crouched down so that his reflection could not be seen. He crawled around the corner of the lobby and into the alcove. Then he noticed the smouldering embers of the fire, which looked like several slices of stale bread without the crust. The bread seethed and burnt in a peculiar way, and as every thin slice turned up at the edges and scorched in the heat, spirals of smoke began to appear from each piece. The smoke grew deadly thick to the point where the chimney could not contain it any longer. It spewed from the fire like a dense fog that crept along the floor until Mariah could no longer see the carpet.

The fireplace soon disappeared in a pall of smoke as the lobby began to fill with the oozing smog. Mariah stood up and looked above the small, dense cloud that had formed around him. He could see that as it radiated from the fireplace it grew like a gigantic ball of fog. Fearing he would be completely engulfed, Mariah got onto the table, but as he did so he noticed that the smoke clung to him in tendrils. It was as if he had stepped into a large spider's web and that each strand gripped him tightly. The smoke stuck like glue and began to coat his hands with thin grey gossamers like strands of hair.

Mariah pulled his hands from the smog. The strands stretched and strained and then began to tighten, pulling him back deep within. He leapt from the table, hoping the force would pull him free. The tendrils stretched and stretched as he landed on the far side of the cloud, and then they suddenly snapped.

From deep within the fireplace, Mariah could see the embers begin to glow brighter. They seemed to take the form of a face in the thick mist. The ball of smog oozed out even further. The fire began to roar like a furnace as the heat melted the paint of the far wall and singed the strands of the aspidistra. The smog came towards him as if it were a reaching hand.

Mariah stepped back as it came closer like spilt treacle. From the fireplace he heard the sound of crackling, as shards of purple sparks jumped from the haze and struck the high ceiling like tiny firecrackers.

He stepped back even further. The door to the steam elevator was open. Mariah looked towards the increasing smog and knew soon he would have no way of escape.

The fire hissed and fizzed as more sparks jumped from the purple flames and then suddenly the cloud ignited. Mariah jumped into the steam elevator, slammed the grille door and frantically pressed the first button he reached. For a moment the elevator remained deathly still as the treacly smog began to ooze in through the grille door.

There came a loud explosion. Every smoking tendril burnt bright blue. The steam elevator dropped suddenly as the smog burst into cold flames that scorched the walls. Mariah was in free fall. The steam elevator dropped like a stone and then stopped with a sudden crash.

Above him Mariah could hear the roar of the fireball coming closer as it chased him down the shaft. The elevator was stuck between floors and Mariah was engulfed in complete darkness. There was a shuddering crash and a bright, blinding flash of light and then all went black as if he were in the centre of the earth.

[5]

Pestiferous Piscis

FOR several minutes Mariah lay in the dark elevator. Above him, the roof crackled as the explosion subsided. There was a small electric light hidden beneath a brass plate in the wall. It flashed into life and then glowed dimly. The neon bulb flickered on and off and then seemed to regain its power and burnt brightly. Mariah could smell the charred wood that encased the elevator. He got to his feet, brushed off the grey dust that covered his clothes and pressed every pearl button on the panel by the grille door.

There was a judder as the steam elevator sprang to life and slowly dropped floor by floor to the deep basement far below. It was as if it didn't have the strength to go higher. The thick metal rope uncoiled itself creakily. As Mariah leant against the handrail he noticed a brass plaque lower down the wall. In small black letters was the word EMERGENCY. Mariah pulled back the door and looked inside. There, to his surprise, was an axe and a phosphorescent torch. He took the torch, unscrewed the base and unwrapped two cubes of white gum from their silver foil. He had seen Charity do this many times. Mariah placed the phosphorescence into the torch, pulled the

49

cowl over the lens and waited. He counted another twenty-six cubes stored in the base of the hand lamp. It was enough to give him three hours of light. Mariah slid the torch inside his coat and pulled the axe from the two spring fasteners that held it tight to the wall. It jumped into his hand, the wooden shaft smooth against his skin. Mariah waited for the elevator to stop.

After several minutes it came to a grinding halt. Mariah could smell the sea and feel the chilled cavern air. He knew he was deep inside the hotel, deep in the dark depths where Gormenberg had kept his oyster lagoon and a gigantic crab had kept guard. Since his death, all had been left as it was. The doorway had been sealed and the elevator stopped from descending to this depth.

'Must have been the explosion,' Mariah said in a whisper as he slid back the grille door and stepped outside. 'Shouldn't have come this far down.'

His soft words echoed faintly in the silence. The steam elevator sighed as if it could go no further. Mariah took the torch from his coat and pulled back the cowl. It burnt brightly, lighting a long tunnel that led to a flight of stone steps. He walked on; his feet crunched the chalk limestone pieces beneath his feet. The steps took him higher, every one cut from the rock, the chisel marks clear to see in the torchlight. He walked on.

After ten minutes of hard climbing, Mariah stopped. He was hopelessly lost. Desperately he tried to remember the time he had been here before and how to retrace his route back to the Prince Regent. He closed his eyes and forced himself to concentrate. All he could see was the mist and the face from the fireplace. It was no use – he would just have to keep walking.

Mariah turned several more landings chiselled from the rock and eventually walked the length of a steep corridor. He knew he was getting further from the sea. The smell of salt water and the cold chill had subsided. Mariah shone the torch along the tunnel. In the distance he could make out what he thought to be an iron door, like the vault of a bank. In a minute he stood beside it. The door was rusted, corroded by the salt air. Sticking into the rock on both sides was a long metal bolt that had fused into the clasp. Mariah smashed at it with the axe. It gave way easily. He pulled on the door. At first it wouldn't open. He pulled harder and the creaking hinges gave way. The door then opened.

For a moment, Mariah couldn't believe where he was. There in front of him was a wall of water at least twenty feet high and the width of a room. It was held in place by a sheet of glass that looked to be a foot thick and was braced like a window with girders of steel.

From the door, two steps led down to a metal gantry that went off to his right. As Mariah walked along the gantry he looked inside what he knew was the back of a gigantic seawater aquarium. It was built underground, beneath the bridge that spanned the deep valley between the Prince Regent and the drinking spa a mile to the south of the town.

Every Sunday Mariah had come to Titus Salt's Aquarium and Pleasure Palace to see the fish that had been caught in the German Ocean. The most unusual would be displayed for all to see. Once he had paid an extra penny to view a shark with two heads. He had watched the fish for an hour, as it couldn't decide which way to swim and fought against itself in discontent. Within the week it had died, to be replaced by an electric eel that would spark as it lunged against its reflection in the thick glass.

Every week there would be something new, something strange and ever more exotic. The Aquarium was lit in perpetual gaslight. A vault of steel supported the road above with gigantic perpendicular arches like the inside of a vast Hindu temple. Each one was encrusted in thick green paint and in the centre of the Aquarium was a long row of skylights covered in moss.

Beneath the skylights was an ice-cream stall that sold hot waffles and jam. Sacha would always insist on buying one to eat on the way back to the Prince Regent. The woman who owned the stall had a thin beard of long black hair. He could tell that she knew he couldn't take his eyes off her, wondering if she curled the tip or if it just formed itself into a natural point beneath her chin.

Mariah knew where he was. All he had to do was get to the front of the exhibits, follow the tour route to the end of the long room and push his way through the turnstiles. From there he could easily get back up the hill to the Prince Regent and within the hour would meet Charity back in his office.

He opened the door at the end of the gantry and stepped into the long room. As on any Sunday it was brightly lit and the fish were swimming in their tanks – but there was no other person but him. To his left was the ice-cream stall. It was shuttered and covered in a candy stripe canvas shawl. Quickly he closed the door and set off to walk the hundred yards to the turnstiles and then out of the Aquarium.

It was as he passed the third piscary that he suddenly felt he was being watched. He turned and saw no one, yet he had the unnerving feeling that someone or something was staring at him from close by. Leaning against the glass, he looked back and forth along the illuminated avenue of fish tanks – there was still no one. The Pleasure Palace was empty. There was not a sign of Titus Salt or his dog.

Sacha had told him that at night they slept in the small office that was cut into the ground like a cave. Titus would curl up with the dog and the day's takings. It was said that if Titus caught anyone in his Pleasure Palace they would never be seen again. When Barcus Dobbs, a notorious villain, had robbed the

52

Pleasure Palace, Sacha had said that he had disappeared and the fish had eaten well on him for many days.

Mariah didn't want to meet with Titus Salt. He listened intently to the gurgling sound that came from the large pipe that ran around the entire building. He looked up at the large temple arches hung with vines. Small oriental birds danced silently through the leaves that wrapped themselves around each arcade.

Then he felt it – a sudden, sharp tap against the glass just above his left ear. It happened three times and then stopped. Slowly he turned, expecting to see old Titus with his face pressed against the glass.

Mariah shuddered. There, staring at him through thick plate glass, were the red eyes of three large fish. The tank was in darkness and yet each fish glowed and emitted a blue essence of light. It followed their outline as if they were electrified and lit from within. What made Mariah stare in disbelief was their size – each fish was at least six feet in length. Their tails swished back and forth effortlessly in the cold dark water as they weaved in and out of the long strands of seaweed.

The smallest fish stayed by the glass and looked at him. It appeared to follow his every movement. Mariah raised his hand to the glass. The fish in turn moved towards it. They stared eye to eye – each examining the other for the first time. Mariah smiled, and to his amazement it looked as though the fish smiled back. It shuddered and changed colour from blue to purple and then to red. Mariah wondered from which sea these fish had been taken and how they had come to a place like this. At the base of the tank was a hand-painted sign pasted carelessly to the glass: *Piscis Humanis – please do not feed.*

As Mariah looked closer, he was sure that the fish had the face of a man. Not a completely human face, but similar in many ways. The eyes, nose and mouth looked as if they had been pulled back over the creature's head, as in a caricature. He tapped his finger twice on the glass – the fish tapped back with the tip of its nose. It then came close to the glass and in the lamplight Mariah could see it clearly for the first time. The creature looked as if it had a human eye. It stared mournfully, and an array of gills fluttered just behind what looked like a small but very human ear.

There was a sudden swirling of the water as the other fish darted frantically back and forth and shone from blue to red. It was as if they were trying to warn Mariah and signal some coming danger. The smallest of the three banged against the glass, its head shining so brightly that it lit Mariah in a red glow. Then, as quickly as they had appeared, they were gone.

It was then that Mariah heard the tap-tap-tap of metal heels against the stone floor. The footsteps echoed through the Pleasure Palace. He was unsure from which direction they came.

'Who's there?' a voice shrieked from the other side of the arcade. 'I know you're there – the dog's got your scent.'

Mariah froze as the words of Titus Salt echoed through the arches under the glass roof. He could hear the growling of the dog from nearby. Looking through the mouldy green tank opposite, Mariah could see the misshaped reflection of old Titus. It shimmered in the gaslight, and made him look ten feet tall with a hunched back and long staff. The dog appeared to be as big as an elephant as the glass reflected its image through the murky water.

Mariah had seen Titus many times before. Even in his great wealth, he was a man of miserly temperament. Never would he buy a new coat, but would rather stand at the door of the Pleasure Palace in his crumpled top hat and fingerless gloves. Titus would collect the pennies and check each one by biting them in his teeth. Then he would hide them in a leather bag he kept around his neck. He was a man of two voices. One was kept for thrilling the Sunday crowds with tales of his adventures at sea: it would lure the young girls with all his talk of adventure, it was croaked and yet kind, tinged with the rasp of tobacco but always welcoming. The other was harsh and bitter – kept for those who would try and sneak in without forfeit. Then old Titus would shout and snarl as Grub would bark and snap wildly at their heels.

Now, Mariah could hear Grub sniffing at the floor as he searched for his scent. The dog began to growl as it sensed him nearby.

'Better come out now – before we get ya!' Titus shouted. There was a hint of hesitation in his voice. It was as if he wasn't sure who or what he was searching for.

Mariah watched him through the glass of the fish tank. He knew that he could not be seen as the light that shone through was behind Titus Salt. The dog sniffed as it walked along. Mariah stood motionless as he wondered how he would escape. There was a gentle tapping on the glass behind him. He turned and there was the fish. It shone red and then turned to blue before it darted upwards to the top of the tank. Mariah looked up. There above the tanks was a long feeding gantry that could just be seen from the ground. It led the length of the arcade to the gates that led out to the street.

The fish frantically swam up and down as if pointing Mariah to his escape. There, cut into the metal frame of the tank, were six neat footholds. Quickly Mariah climbed from the ground up the side of the tank and onto the gantry. The fish swirled about in the water beneath his feet, and from it pulsed the most beautiful white light. Its head broke the surface and looked at him. For a moment Mariah was mesmerised. In the twilight, it looked as though he was staring into the eyes of another person. He smiled and lowered his hand to the water. The fish shuddered as he stroked the tip of its nose.

'Thank you,' Mariah said in a whisper.

The words echoed around the arcade as Grub began to bark.

'I know where you are!' Titus shouted as he ran and cracked his stick against the floor. 'You'll not be having my money – the dog'll be having you!'

In a panic, Mariah began to run. The gantry shuddered and shook with each step and vibrated the water below. He crossed one tank and then another and another as he ran the length of the glass avenue towards the exit from the Pleasure Palace. All the time he could hear Titus and his dog chasing him.

'You'll not get far, not from Titus – I know where you're going and you'll not get that way – 'tis locked.' He sounded old and out of breath as he wheezed each word. 'Get him, Grub! Rip him to bits, tear him to pieces . . .'

Mariah leapt over a small gap above a tank of silver fish that skimmed the surface. Suddenly the air around him was filled with silver darts as fish leapt from the water and flew. They jumped and dived. One snapped at his ear with sharp, needle-like teeth. It bled quickly and profusely.

Getting back to the gantry, Mariah ran on. It was as if every piscary contained an even stranger creature than the one before. As he ran on he could see the deep waters beneath him and hear Titus and Grub catching up on him.

'There's no way out. Just give yourself up and face the consequences,' Titus shouted above the ravenous barking of his dog. 'I'll spare you, if you give yourself up.'

Mariah thought he sounded insincere. There was smug laughter in his voice. From where he was he could see the long shadows of Titus and Grub dancing on the wall at the other side of the Pleasure Palace. They were getting closer.

'Come out and I'll open the gate and let you go,' Titus said, jangling a set of keys on a thick chain. 'Just be gone and that'll be that – understand?'

Mariah now knew that Titus Salt had no idea where he was hiding. Grub sniffed at the stone floor that ran the length of the arcades. The dog had lost the scent. The lad crouched down on the gantry, keeping himself as close to the long metal walkway as he could. A drop of blood dripped from the bite to his ear and splattered in the water below. It scented the water with a bloody infusion. Mariah looked down. The tank was crystal clear. He could see the rocks and crab shells that littered the bottom of the tank. He couldn't see a single creature.

Titus drew closer step by step, until he and the dog were underneath him. He could see their shadows in the water below. He pressed himself closer to the gantry, trying to hold his breath for fear of being heard.

Titus Salt looked in to the tank, his eyes searching every inch. Grub whimpered, as if there was something here he did not like.

'Wise old dog,' Titus said as he stroked Grub's neck. 'Didn't like getting this one – always knew it would be trouble. There was wickedness in its eye – that's for sure.'

Titus spoke as if he had forgotten he was chasing an intruder. He cupped the grubby, half-gloved fingers of his hand against the glass so he could see inside.

'Don't like things that hide in the dark. Look at them crabs, never stood a chance, sucks off their shells and gouges out the innards.' He paused for the briefest of moments as in his heart he regretted buying the beast that hid away in the shadows of the fish tank. 'Can't be . . .' Titus looked up. He could make out the outline of a man on the gantry. The water shimmered on the surface, but he was sure that he could see someone twenty feet above him.

'There he is, Grub!' Titus shouted as he banged his fist against the glass in delight. 'Got you now, lad – get yourself down here.'

Unseen to them both, something stirred in the far corner of the piscary.

Mariah looked down through the crystal-clear water and could see Titus and Grub far below. He looked along the gantry and quickly measured the race he would have to run to get to the end and down the steps before they would capture him. Without thinking he leapt to his feet and set off at a pace. The gantry shook back and forth. After just two strides there was a sharp thud from below. At first he felt no pain and then a sudden burning tore into his skin. He tried to move his leg but was held fast. Reaching down, he took hold of what he at first thought was the head of a snake that had wrapped itself around his ankle.

Suddenly from the water came another and another. They lashed at him like long strands of thick, barbed rope as they took hold of every part of his body.

'No!' Mariah screamed as the beast rose from the water and began to envelop him with long tentacles.

'Quickly, Grub – the octopus has him!' Titus shouted at the dog as he ran to the steps that would lead him to the gantry.

Mariah couldn't move. The octopus had quickly wrapped itself around him and was squeezing him to the gantry. His face was squashed against the metal slats and dragged closer and closer to the water. He stared down and the beast stared back at him as it snapped its bird-like beak.

'Stay still!' shouted Titus Salt as he ran along the gantry towards Mariah. 'Let it think you're dead – just until I get to you.'

Mariah could hear Titus getting closer. The old gantry moaned and twisted with his weight. The octopus sniffed at him as it slowly unwound its tentacles. Then, without a sound, it pulled him slowly into the water. Instinctively Mariah gripped onto the gantry for as long as he could, but the octopus was wrapped around him and he could feel its heart beating against him and its beak gnawing against his shoulder.

'Steady, lad,' Titus said as he drew closer. Mariah could see the man's shadow cast across the water. He saw him raise his walking staff like a spear and take aim. There was a crack like lightning. Mariah felt the octopus suddenly tense itself. The water filled with black ink. The creature shivered. The crack came again and again as Titus Salt beat his stick. Grub howled like the gates of hell had been opened and heaven was about to be vanquished.

'Back! Back!' shouted Titus as he hit the creature again and again.

Mariah could feel his fingers giving up their hold as the water sucked him down.

'You'll not be taking him this time,' Titus shouted at the beast. 'Not from old Titus Salt.'

A hand reached down and took hold of Mariah by the locks of his hair just as he vanished under the water.

'Now you belong to Titus Salt and he will have his pound of flesh,' the man jeered as he dragged Mariah from the water.

[6]

Titus Salt

MARIAH woke up with the smell of his smouldering trousers fresh in his nostrils. Instinctively he reached out. His hands felt the leather of the large armchair in which he had slept the last hour. As he opened his eyes he could see the chiselled roof of a small cave. In the corner by a wooden chest that looked as if it had been nailed together from pieces of driftwood was a black stove. It burnt brightly and lit the room, and resting on the top was a simmering kettle of water. He looked at his smouldering trousers and steaming boots and watched the vapour rise in spirals. His face felt sore, the salt water stung the wound on his cheek and now he could feel burning in his neck. Mariah rubbed his hand around the collar of his shirt. He could feel a circular blister just under his chin. It was sore and stung as if he had been scalded.

From the top of the fire stove, a long black chimney went up the rock wall and into the roof. His eye followed it higher until it disappeared in the rock. From what he could see, Mariah knew he was in a cave, a small, neat cave cut into the rock.

There was no sign of Titus Salt or Grub. Mariah was alone. He turned around and to his surprise saw that the tiny door was open. He could see the back of the ticket booth where Titus would stand and collect the money. He knew this was Titus's office. He had seen the small doorway behind the ticket booth every time Sacha and he had come to the Aquarium to look at the strange exhibits on wet Sunday afternoons. Mariah had always wanted to know what it was like inside. It was different to what he expected. He had always thought it would have been bigger, grander and more in keeping with an entertainer such as Titus Salt.

Now as he waited for his clothes to dry he looked around eagerly. Next to the wooden chest was a table on which sat an old oil lamp with a dirty brass handle. On the far side was a small bed cut into the rock just above the floor. It was strewn with an old blanket, a felt cushion and a large book with a leather clasp. The floor sloped towards the stove and in the furthest corner was a pile of logs and black sea-coal that had been picked from the beach. Mariah pushed himself forward in the leather armchair to get nearer to the fire. He thought of how he would escape and what Titus Salt could do to him.

'Still here?' came a voice edged with a slight chuckle. 'Thought you'd have run off as soon as you woke.' Titus ducked through the doorway carrying a small silver tray piled with meat and cheese. 'Had to get this from the pantry – don't keep it in here in case of the rats. Don't like the idea of rats, never did. Remember when I was a sailor, rats were the things I hated the most. Found one once in my trousers – don't know how it got there.'

Titus sighed as if he had remembered something wonderful that he would never see again. He smiled at Mariah, his two gold teeth shining in the light of the oil lamp.

'That thing could have killed you. More importantly it could have killed me. Should have left you to it – and I wouldn't have had to feed it for the week.' Titus laughed again as he put the tray on the ground by the fire and took the simmering kettle and poured coffee into two cups that he took from a long shelf behind the door.

'You don't have to tell me who you are,' he said softly in his best Sunday voice. 'You are Mariah Mundi. I've heard all about you. Quite a lad I hear and all.' Titus spoke quickly as he sat on the ground next to the fire and cradled the steaming pot mug in his gloved hands. 'Can't understand why you have to break in here. I've seen you often enough with that lass of yours – so, what were you doing?'

'You going to kill me?' Mariah asked as his lips tightened and he made ready to leap from the chair and run.

'Why should I do that?' Titus asked calmly as he eyed the lad from head to foot as if he knew what Mariah was about to do.

'Barcus Dobbs. Didn't you kill him and feed him to the fish when he stole your money?' Mariah said, trying to hide his fear of the man.

Titus began to giggle. He juddered in mirth as if he were electrocuted.

'Did you think I killed Barcus Dobbs? All that I got of him was a patch from his trousers as old Grub tore his pants from him. He ran from here half naked. Wouldn't do his repute any good if people found out that Titus Salt's dog had ripped off his pants and he was frit of the beast. Cried like a baby, surprised you didn't hear him from that fancy hotel of yours.' Titus sipped from the cup and filled his mouth with cheese. 'The man is hiding and the rumours of his death do him good. Dead men can't do no wrong and it suits him to be dead. Suits Inspector Walpole too.' Titus chewed frantically as he spoke and looked eagerly at Mariah. 'Leads me to ask – what you doing here?'

'I . . . I was looking for someone. There's an entrance through a metal door. It was all rusted and it came out behind the fish tanks.' Mariah stared at Titus, unsure if he would be believed. Titus rubbed the stubble on his chin and pouted like a fish.

'Thought that had been sealed up long ago,' he said thoughtfully as he smiled at Mariah. 'Otto Luger had that done when he took over the Prince Regent. Was going to be a way for the guests to come from the hotel, but Otto had other ideas.' Titus stopped and looked at Mariah. 'What happened to your face? That looks like it wasn't the octopus that did that.'

'It was a man in Paradise, a man in a mask, he'd killed a girl.'

'So it's true. Thought it was just gossip.'

Mariah told him all that had happened. The exploding Ambassador, the fire and Inspector Walpole. Titus listened without interrupting. He nodded and grunted as he and Mariah shared the cheese and meat and swigged the coffee from the pot until there was none left.

'It's as if they were murdered one by one and Walpole thinks it's Charity or me that did it. He said I was at every murder last night and that makes me a suspect,' Mariah said as Titus listened.

'Trouble is, Mariah, the Prince Regent should never have been built. Some say it's cursed. I told them but they never listened. There's a salt cave and a hot spring – that's where they get the heat from for that generator. Keeps me awake half the night with its rumblings. Luger was breeding fish. I don't know how or why but some of the things were so strange he got rid of them straightaway and the others, the ones that weren't bad, he gave to me.'

'*Piscis Humanis*?' Mariah asked.

'People fish . . . Them as well. Far too clever *and* they look at you as if they know what's in your head. When Luger brought them here I thought he was having a laugh. Looked as if they were people covered in scales.'

63

'Luger brought them?' Mariah asked.

'In that lagoon of his were all sorts of things that shouldn't be. I sneaked in there one night and saw more than I should – that's why he blocked up the door. He didn't want Titus Salt knowing what he was up to.'

'What sort of things?' Mariah asked.

'It was as if he were doing experiments. Some of them fish looked like cats and dogs with gills and fins – cross breeding, new creatures. Most of them died or went mad. The *Piscis Humanis*, as he called them, they lived and grew and grew. Now look at them – glow in the dark and look at you as if they know better.'

Before Mariah could reply, Grub growled. The dog then sat by the fire and slept. Mariah talked and talked as Titus listened. His face appeared to grow softer, less furrowed and more at peace. They laughed together as Titus joked about the octopus and how Barcus Dobbs had thrown the money back at Titus when Grub had taken hold of him. He told Mariah of his life at sea and how he had always wanted to own such a place as the Pleasure Palace.

'I knew it would be mine one day,' he said as he ate more cheese. 'I have these *visions*. I can see things that haven't happened – always had them – the seventh son of a seventh son, that's me. Sometimes they just come to me as I'm working. It's as if I see the possibility of the future and I can choose if I'll walk that way or not.'

'Fortune telling?' Mariah asked impatiently. He had seen so many charlatans on the promenade who said they could see the future. Charity called them rogues and scoundrels, not to be trusted. Mariah had agreed.

'More than that lad. It's as if there is a perfect plan for your life. A plan to prosper you in all things. Sometimes I get to see what's coming. Sometimes I see it and then make a mess of it and it never happens. I knew I would have this place. I knew that Luger was a bad thing. I knew I would meet you.'

'What do these *visions* look like?' Mariah asked.

'Sometimes it is just a picture or a glimpse of a person. If you're blessed you see it as if you're watching actors on a stage. More often than not I just hear things of what will come, like distant whispers.'

'Are you talking to the dead?' Mariah asked. He had once seen a man on the corner of Garibaldi Street who said that those who had died told him everything. They never spoke to him of the horse and cart that had killed him the next day.

'Never speak to the dead. What do they know? Best listen only to that which will bring life, young Mariah,' Titus replied as he finished the last piece of cheese.

The kettle and tray were soon empty and the fire in the stove dimmed. Mariah sat back in the leather chair.

'I thought you to be a wicked man, but you're different from that,' he said as Titus took a handful of sea-coal and stoked the fire. The flames flickered on the chiselled wall of the cave. Mariah looked about him; he liked the place with its threadbare rug and old leather chair. It was warm and smelt of the sea. It was everything he had never had and reminded him of a night he'd once spent with his father as they camped by a fire on Hampstead Heath.

'We're all different underneath, Mariah. I heard things about you – but you're not the lad they said you would be,' Titus replied. 'Jack Charity will be wondering where you are, you best be off. Next time you come in here through that door – shout my name and I'll know it's you. Keep away from that octopus. Nasty beast, would kill you if it got the chance.'

'So I can go?' Mariah asked.

'Unless you want to swap that room of yours for a bed in this cave?'

'Can I come back?' Mariah asked.

'Whenever you want. My special guest.' Titus got to his feet and shook the cold from him. 'Not many people like speaking to me. Like you they have listened to too many stories of what I am supposed to be like. I just wish they would find the truth. Judge not lest you be judged, Mariah. That's what it says in my book and that's how I live, me and my house serve that and always will. A fine principle for life.' Titus stopped speaking and listened. It was as if he could hear something that only he could hear. He looked as if he were staring through the rock and into the night sky. 'Sure you don't want to stay until morning? I have a feeling, Mariah. All is not well with this world and you're in danger.'

'Have you seen something?' Mariah asked.

'No lad, just heard it. I heard a child crying as if they were locked away in a dark room without any light. Someone has got them and they're afraid. They were calling out – calling your name.'

'Who was it?' Mariah asked as Titus listened again and stared like before.

'Not a good thing, Mariah. Don't go near the castle. I can see its shadow cast across your life. Stay away from the ship in the bay.'

'What can you see?' Mariah asked, sure that Titus Salt wasn't telling him everything that was in his vision. Titus stared at the roof of the cave, his eyes flickering like the flames of the fire. He seemed to be watching an invisible performance played out in mid-air. He followed the meanderings of his imagination with the tip of his finger as he drew their movements in the air.

'There's a fog coming, a mist you can't see with human eyes. It'll cover everything and everyone. There are two people who want to see you dead. Each for a different reason.'

'Why?'

'Be careful. Visions don't tell you everything. They're like a dim mirror. If we talk too much about them we fill them with our own words and not what we're given – best leave it at that, Mariah. Watch yourself, I can do nothing to help you. You'd better get going. Keep to the lit streets. Tell Charity you met old Titus Salt and lived to tell the tale.' Titus spoke quickly as he tried to push Mariah through the door and into the Pleasure Palace. 'Can't be staying here all night. You're dry now and the octopus didn't kill you. You'll have to go and go quickly.'

'You've seen Sacha, haven't you?' Mariah blurted out his words. 'Where is she?'

'Can't be sure it's her. Can just hear her voice calling you . . . You best be off now, lad.' His voice was edged with a panic as if he was helpless to control what he saw in his mind.

'Where is she?'

'It's a dark place – that's if it's her – could be anyone. You best be gone.'

'She went missing just before the people started to burst into flame. I thought she had left and gone to her room.'

'Might not be her. I could be dreaming all this and none of it is true,' Titus said as his head bobbed like a madman.

'Could be that you can see more and won't tell me,' Mariah replied as he tried to stand his ground.

Grub growled by the fire stove as they raised their voices.

'I'll not leave until you tell me everything you can see. It's my life and I need to know,' Mariah shouted.

'Do you think it would help you for one moment if you could see what I can see? If it is your friend then she is in a very dark place and one from which she will never escape.' Titus pushed Mariah through the door and into the long avenue of the Pleasure Palace. It was icily cold as a breeze blew in through the open doors from the sea.

Titus Salt stopped and looked as the doors swung back and forth on their hinges.

'Didn't leave the doors like that,' he said as he quickly pushed them shut and slid the bolt on one side to hold the door in place. 'Best if you go by the turnstile. Keep to the road and up the steps by the bridge. Don't speak to no one until you get to the Prince Regent. Grub, here lad.' He shouted for the dog, and it came to him quickly. 'Go and see, lad – find them.'

'It could have been the wind.'

'Slipped the bolts whilst we were talking, did it?' Titus replied as he looked in to the gloom of the Aquarium and listened out for Grub as the dog quickly scented a trail. Titus thought it too much of a coincidence that the doors should be open on the very night that he was visited by Mariah Mundi.

'What about Sacha?' Mariah asked.

'If I see any more I will tell you.'

'Promise?' Mariah insisted.

'I'm beginning to think they were right in what they said about you,' Titus said as if distracted. 'You don't take no for an answer. Very pushy, doesn't know his place. I promise. Now be gone, Mariah, and be blessed . . .'

Titus pushed him through the metal turnstile and once he was on the outside, he turned a brass handle in the wall and locked the gate.

'Tell Charity what I saw. He knows me, knows my ways. Keep safe. Remember, Mariah, beware the ship.'

When Mariah turned to say farewell, Titus Salt had vanished. It was as if he had been a part of his imagination, a make-believe friend who would come and go as he pleased. The wind blew cold from the sea and blasted salt and sand against his face. On the high bridge above his head, the gas lamps flickered. The waves crashed against the beach and the Prince Regent looked as if it were a vast ship that had struck the cliff.

In the bay, the *Irenzee* glimmered like a city of gold. All around it, the sea glowed a phosphorescent green as if it were alive. Mariah listened to the seabirds squawking above him as they circled the high towers of the hotel. He looked up the path that led from the Pleasure Palace to the hotel. An old vagrant slept on the bench under the gas lamp. He was wrapped in newspaper with a bag over his face to keep out the wind. Mariah had seen him there before. All was well, he thought as he shrugged the warning of Titus Salt's vision from his shoulders and set off up the path. He thought of Sacha and wondered where she could be. Visions . . . He thought about them over and over, and whether Titus Salt could see the future or know where Sacha could be.

The sea wind blew against his back as old, dry leaves rustled down the path. He passed by the terrace of shops next to the side of the museum and looked inside the windows. On the bench underneath the gas lamp the tramp slept on, oblivious to his presence. Mariah gave him a fleeting glance as he looked at all the fine things that were on display. In the shop at the end of the terrace were tall jars of pickles, sweets of every description and strange devices that when attached to string would spin up and down. There were candy sticks and running hoops hanging from the ceiling. Mariah had never noticed the shop before. He had walked the terrace many times on his way to the museum and then on to the Pleasure Palace, but this time, for some reason everything in the shop window drew his attention. It was as if every item was magically illuminated.

There, right in front of him, was a small clockwork train that ran in and out of the window display and disappeared into the dark recesses of the store. It spurted steam that came from the tiny funnel and fascinated Mariah. The lights of the carriages reflected against the glass like a million diamonds every time it rocketed by the window. He stood and watched as all around him the wind blew spirals of sand from the beach and the waves beat against the shore.

For some reason, Mariah turned. He didn't know why he did just at that moment, but something caught the corner of his eye. The first thing he noticed was that the tramp had gone. The man had packed up his newspaper bed and disappeared into the night. Still, Mariah had the feeling that he wasn't alone, that someone was watching him from nearby. He swallowed hard; he wanted to run but fought the urge with all his might. His legs twitched like a racehorse ready for off as he felt the panic rising in his chest.

Run, Mariah . . . The thought came again and again. His instincts told him to bolt from the place as fast as he could. From all around him it appeared that the darkness was closing in on him and the very night itself was his enemy.

To his right was a flight of stone steps that led from the terrace up to the bridge and then on to the Prince Regent Hotel. A gas lamp flickered on the corner, casting a black shadow under the bridge.

He began to run, knowing that if he could get to the top of the steps he would be safe. Mariah tried to count the steps to keep his mind from thinking of what could be there in the darkness. He wasn't afraid of the dark – he told himself this again and again as his sprinting feet barely touched the sidewalk. Yet as he ran, Mariah had the feeling in his stomach that if he stopped for just one moment it would be the last thing he ever did.

He got to the steps; the gas lamp lit his face. He could see the lights of the ballroom of the Prince Regent. Mariah sighed and wanted to laugh. He shivered with relief and shook his head like a wet dog.

'Stupid boy,' he said to himself as he got to the top of the stone stairs.

It was then that five silver coins rolled from the shadows and down the steps. They chased each other as they bounced and clattered on the stone. Mariah froze as they jangled down and down into the dark shadows.

'*Mine!*' said a sharp voice that snarled as if to snatch the coins. Suddenly, Mariah felt someone grab his wet coat.

[7]

Spring-Heeled Jack

MARIAH was pulled to the ground by a heavy hand and dragged down the steps away from the light and into the shadow of the bridge. His face was gripped, then smothered by a stinking leather glove. He tried to scream as he gulped helplessly for breath.

'Don't do anything stupid, boy. Me and you need to chat, me and you have unfinished business,' the man said through a tight black shawl that was wrapped about his head. 'I nearly had you and you got away, but now things will be different.'

Mariah was thrown to the ground. The man stepped back and pulled a long black handle of a swordstick that was hidden in the wall behind him. Slowly, he unwrapped the scarf from his face. In the half-light, Mariah could see that the man wore a mask.

'It's you,' he said, his voice shaking.

'And you will never have the chance to know who I really am. All I can say is that I thought you would be a far better adversary than you have been. One so clever – yet so easily captured.'

'Tell me why I should die,' Mariah demanded as his mind raced for a way of escape.

'Because, Mariah Mundi, you have been chosen – you are the sacrifice.' The man laughed as he spoke. Mariah pushed himself against the wall and waited for him to strike. He knew he had one chance. Wait until the man drew back the sword, then just as he was about to strike run as fast as he could. It was his only option, the only way he could escape. What would he lose if he failed, he thought to himself as the seconds felt like a fear-filled lifetime.

The man took off the glove from one hand, pushing it roughly into the pocket of his coat. Mariah could see a gold ring glinting upon his finger.

'It isn't something I like to do,' the man said as he smoothed the blade between his finger and thumb. 'But it has to be. Don't hold it against me, it's for the good of the world.'

'What good would it be for me to die? I am but a poor boy.'

'Poor perhaps, but important just the same. There has to be another death tonight and then five more and my task will be over.'

As the man spoke, Mariah thought there was something familiar about his voice. It was as if he had heard it before. He could not think where, but every word he spoke reminded him of Gormenberg.

'Seven?' Mariah asked.

'Like the stars of that great constellation, seven. It is a complete number, perfection, total perfection.' The man paused for a moment as if he were distracted by a faraway sound.

'I know your voice – but who are you?'

'I have many names, Mariah. Hiram Duegaurd, Louveteau . . . Now I am known as Packavi – but it will be of no use to you. For you are a cowan – a dog – a builder of walls that will be torn down – just like your life.'

'Riddles and nonsense,' Mariah muttered as he made ready to bolt from the man.

'Find the meaning of my name and you will find me, but for you it is too late.'

Mariah saw him hesitate as the sound of a falling stone clanged against the metal beams of the Spa Bridge that spanned the ravine.

Packavi pulled a golden fob watch from his pocket and flicked the glass cover. The purple light of the illuminated watch face lit his mask. The man paused, turned to Mariah and raised the swordstick.

'If you give in to the steel it will be over far quicker and with far less pain than you would expect,' he said, his voice cold and without emotion.

'Speed the day,' Mariah replied as he saw movement in the gloom behind Packavi.

'Who for?' asked Titus Salt, who stepped from the shadows, Grub at his side. 'Set to him, lad!'

The dog growled like a choking demon as it paced towards the man with its teeth bared.

'Stand aside and let Mariah go,' Salt shouted at the man as the dog stood its ground.

'Two dogs and one master?' Packavi asked as he stepped closer to Mariah with the sword cane raised above his head.

'Grub will snap it from your hand before you can strike – take your chance and be gone.'

'I'll take the boy – dead or alive,' Packavi shouted as he lunged for Mariah.

Mariah dived out of the way as Grub leapt like a wolf and took hold of Packavi by his hand. The dog tore at the glove, ripping it from him. It lunged again, gripping him by the coat and pulling him back and forth. Packavi, recovering from the attack, began to fight back. He dragged the dog into the darkness as if its gnawing upon his arm had no effect and he was immune to the pain. He struck the creature with a blow from his once-gloved hand. Grub recoiled and snarled, ready to strike again. Packavi flicked the crown on the cane handle, scattering a glittering white powder in the air. All at once it exploded in a blinding flash that cracked like a whip and burnt the eyes.

The dog howled like a transforming werewolf as Titus Salt staggered to take hold of Mariah.

'Get him, Grub!' he shouted to the beast.

'Titus, I can't see – I'm blind,' said Mariah as he stumbled in the darkness, his hands held out like those of a blind man.

'It'll soon return, it's just the explosion, close your eyes and cover your face.'

'Where is he?' Mariah asked.

'Gone, Mariah. We are safe,' Titus replied as he took hold of him by the hand and led him into the light.

'He would have killed me,' Mariah said softly as they sat on the bench where the tramp had slept.

'I saw him, that's why I came. I had a vision of you in danger, more than before. I knew he would attack,' Titus said calmly.

'Your vision saved my life,' Mariah said.

'It may not always be that way, Mariah. I saw your friend, Sacha. She must be found.'

'Where do I start?' he asked.

'At the Prince Regent,' Titus said as Grub dropped the tattered remnants of the glove at his feet.

'I wish this was all that was left of him,' Titus said as he picked the glove from the floor.

'But it will lead us to him,' Mariah replied.

'Grub cannot trace a scent as well as he could.'

'No, but I can,' Mariah said as he took the divining spectacles from his pocket. 'These will find him.'

Mariah held the glove to the spectacles and tuned in the device. He looked under the bridge. Even in the dark shadows,

Mariah could see the fading red footsteps of Packavi. It was as if they had just been made.

'This way,' Mariah said as he gave chase.

'It's not safe, Mariah – he could be waiting for you.'

'Grub will tell us if he is nearby,' Mariah replied as he strode on, following the footprints upon the path.

Soon they had left the shadow of the bridge and had followed the narrow winding pathway that clung to the cliff and led below the Prince Regent. In the bay, the *Irenzee* glowed at its mooring. A single searchlight flitted across the water as if it hunted for the crest of each breaking wave. Mariah followed the glowing footprints down the path and through the ornate gardens that hung to the side of the cliff. Grub sniffed at his feet and barked for Titus to keep pace.

It was as they approached a large willow tree growing out of the rock that the footprints stopped. Mariah tuned the diving spectacles more intensely and looked over the edge of the path to the garden below. There was nothing. It was as if Packavi had leapt from the pathway into thin air.

The vapour from the footprints began to fade. Grub sniffed at the roots of the tree.

'Nothing here, lad,' Titus said in a whisper that sounded like a groan. 'Must have jumped from the cliff and into the sea.'

'I should see something, some trace of him – but the footprints stop right here and there is nothing more.'

'Let me see you back to the Prince Regent – I can't let you alone tonight, not with him still about.'

From the far side of the bay, the church clock beat four heavy bells to mark out the hour. Mariah searched the pathway for a sign as to where Packavi could have gone.

'There must be something here,' he said as he yawned and tried to keep his eyes from closing. 'He can't just disappear.'

Grub began to growl. He shuddered and shook the fur on

the back of his neck. It stood on end as if he had been spooked and could see someone invisible to the human eye. Mariah looked up into the branches.

There was a crash, and a crack of steel upon the ground. Packavi dropped to the ground and then sprang on fiery heels above their heads. He landed several feet away and drew his swordstick.

'Think you could gain the better of me, Mariah Mundi?' he boasted as he slashed the blade back and forth. 'There will be a time when I shall come back for you and you will not escape. You will never know the time or place, but sometime in your future, somewhere near I will be waiting.'

Packavi appeared to twist where he stood and spun on one leg as his coat swirled about him. Mariah took off the divining spectacles and stared. In an instant, Packavi leapt backwards from the path and somersaulted through the air before disappearing over the cliff. He was gone as quickly as he had appeared.

Mariah placed the spectacles on his face one more time. A faint trace of red vapour hung like a birthday ribbon in the air. Packavi had vanished into the night.

'Spring-Heeled Jack,' Titus said quietly. 'I've heard of him before. Can jump higher than a house and no man can catch him. Never thought he'd be here, never thought I'd see him with my own eyes.'

'He's a murderer,' Mariah said angrily as he thought of his own fate. 'And one who wants me dead.'

'Best be off, lad. Not safe to be here in the dark. Never heard of Spring-Heeled Jack being out in daylight – best stick to the day and leave him the darkness.'

'I have to find Sacha and find her before the morning.'

'You'd be better telling Charity and seeing what he thinks.'

'But –' he protested.

'Where would you start to look? Best if you go back to the Prince Regent and start there. I saw her in a black place – dark and cold – that's all I can tell you.'

They walked up the steep pathway to the door of the Prince Regent. Grub followed on behind. Titus waited until Mariah had gone in through the glass door. He waved as he went inside, the images of his vision burning in his mind.

Mariah walked by the reception desk. Mrs Mukluk was sleeping, her head cradled uncomfortably in her hands. Behind her, the service lights of several rooms flickered urgently for her slumbering attention. She dozed on, occasionally snorting like a large sea lion.

'What kept you?' asked a voice from behind him.

'Sacha?' Mariah said as he turned to his friend. 'But I thought –'

'You ran off,' she said indignantly. 'I couldn't find you. So concerned to do the business of the Bureau of Antiquities that you forgot all about me.'

'I came looking for you – met Titus Salt – he had a vision – said you were alone - a prisoner.'

'Drunk, the feckwit's always drunk. I'm no more a prisoner than you,' she said scornfully.

Mariah looked at her. He knew there was something wrong: it was the way she spoke, her voice was not the same. It was as if she was keeping something from him. Mariah knew her every movement: the raised eyebrow she would give in discontent – the smirk of a hidden joke – the stare at the insanity of a guest. These were the secret things they would share. Never a word would need to be spoken. Mariah could tell what was in her mind by her look.

'Titus said you were in trouble.'

'Trouble? How can I be in trouble here? I've been watching the guests leaving.'

Mariah glanced at her long boots; they were edged in beach sand with a white salt stain about the ankle. Now he knew she was hiding something from him.

'Been far?' he asked, hoping not to show his reason for asking.

'I was here all the time – why are you so worried?'

'He tried to kill me again. The man in the mask. I *did* see him in the hotel, I know that now, he was here. Titus saved me from him.'

'How could he be here?' she asked quickly.

'He knows how to get into the hotel – I know he does,' Mariah snapped at her.

'Then you better find him. I've had enough of today. You seem to have forgot that he attacked me as well. All you seem to care for is yourself and your stupid Bureau – don't think things happen to other people, do you, Mariah?'

'Why do you think I have been looking for you?' he asked as she screamed at him.

'You can't look for someone who isn't lost – I have been here all the time, I never left. It was you who went off, you who got attacked again. Would be better if you'd just stayed here.'

'We'd been asked to look out for Hoetzendorf,' Mariah argued.

'You'd been asked, not me. I just get dragged along, it's always the same.' Sacha stamped her feet as Mrs Mukluk raised a sleepy eyebrow and stared out from the reception desk.

'They were all murdered, exploded before our eyes,' Mariah protested.

'I saw it all, Mariah – where do you think I was?'

'Lost – Titus said you were in a dark place.' Mariah replied.

'He was wrong – very, *very* wrong,' Sacha said as she turned to walk away. 'It's late and I need to sleep. You can play your games and run about for the Bureau but I am going to bed.'

'So you say you've been here all night?' Mariah asked as she walked off and Mrs Mukluk chuntered in her sleep.

'Say? Say? Are you asking me if I'm lying? Just spit it out. Why should I lie about being elsewhere? What have I got to hide from you?' Sacha slammed her fist against the wall in anger. She was red-faced and ready to fight.

'There is sand on your boots. You said you'd been here all night – but you have a salt stain and sand on your boots and don't tell me that the hotel has sprung a leak.'

'It's from before,' she said flustered. 'Just forgot to get it off.'

'Looks like you've been in the sea . . . or in the cellar,' Mariah replied, knowing she would explode in rage.

To his surprise, all Sacha did was take a deep breath and smile. She twizzled the tips of her hair with her fingers as she looked at him and nodded. Inside she wanted to scream, she was furious, but she tapped her finger ten times upon her folded arm and then ten more for good measure. They stood looking at each other, waiting for the other to break the silence.

'I don't have to tell you everything, Mariah,' she said calmly as she turned again to walk away.

'I just want to know where you have been,' he said as he followed on behind.

'I came looking for you when you ran off – then there were the explosions and I couldn't find you and I have been here ever since.' Sacha spoke softly, as if she didn't want to hear her own words.

'So you haven't been on the beach or in the cellar?' he said, knowing she was lying to him.

'No . . . Neither place.'

'And that's your last word?' Mariah asked, not wanting to believe she would lie to him and giving her the chance to tell him the truth.

'My last word,' she said softly as she walked away.

Mariah watched as she walked off along the corridor towards the stairs that spiralled to the top of the hotel. He waited until she was gone from sight and then followed on behind. He got to the mirror where he had seen the reflection of Packavi. Mariah checked the alcove once more for any sign of a way of escape. He then examined the fireplace where the substance had exploded. There was no damage at all, just a faint charring of smoke upon the wall. It was as if the explosion had chased him and him alone.

He didn't know what to do. For the first time since Captain Charity had taken over the Prince Regent, Mariah felt threatened. It had been a safe place, a sanctuary, a castle and fortress. Now he believed the bastion had been breached and the enemy was somewhere deep within in its heart.

[8]

Dedalus Zogel

AS dawn broke over the sea, Mariah dressed quickly and slipped quietly from his room. He ran down the spiral staircase taking the treads two at a time. Beating out the call for breakfast, the Chinese gong echoed through the chimneys and up the shaft of the steam elevator. It was as if the building shuddered with every beat and yet sounded empty. Turning from the staircase, Mariah walked along the outside balcony and across the sun terrace that overlooked the beach far below. In the bay, the *Irenzee* looked bigger in daylight than it had the night before. It towered from the water and looked as though it stretched across half the bay. Several fishing boats circled the ship. They were minuscule at its side and dwarfed by the height of the ship.

There was a low rumble that shuddered the water. It trembled the flat calm as from within the ship the sound came again. Three tall masts began to slide upwards from within as the funnel extended from the bridge. Every movement of the vast ship juddered the sea, and for the first time Mariah saw several men on its deck. Even from that great distance, he could see them running back and forth as the ship's masts grew taller and the funnel stretched to the sky. Then came an even louder rumble. It sent the seabirds squawking from their roosts and up into the morning air. A sudden blast from the ship's horn rattled all the windows of the Prince Regent and a gigantic cloud of smoke blasted from the ship. It hung in the still morning air.

'Thought it was the end of the world,' Charity joked as he stepped from the restaurant and onto the balcony of the hotel. 'I also thought we had a meeting last night.'

Mariah flushed red and looked away. 'I didn't want to see you – it happened again.'

'What?' Charity asked.

'I got lost under the hotel and found my way into the Pleasure Palace. I met Titus Salt and . . . and on my way back the man attacked me.'

'Mariah, I need to know these things,' Charity exclaimed, scowling.

'I would have told you but I felt a fool – I argued with Sacha and could think of nothing else.'

'I should have been told. There are some things that even you cannot handle by yourself.'

'I'm an agent of the Bureau just like you,' Mariah argued.

'Even more reason why you should tell me. Did you see much of your attacker?' Charity asked as Mariah looked out to sea, unable to talk face to face.

'He told me his name – said he was called Packavi.' Mariah spoke sullenly.

'*Packavi* . . . Are you sure?' Charity asked in disbelief.

'Packavi – I can't forget it,' he answered.

'The world turns on such a name. He plays games with us. That is not a name but a condition of the heart. All he tells us is that he knows the wrong he does. A *peccavi* is one who has sinned and seeks confession. He will not rest until many are dead – he is a master of a dark art, sworn that anyone who hears his secret must be killed.'

'How do you know?' Mariah asked.

'I have met his kind before – prophets of a society so filled with secrets that they can only be found out by their own words. They infest every echelon of our world and cannot be trusted. They are the power behind the power and even Queen Victoria is helpless against them.'

'But Packavi is one man,' Mariah protested.

'One man he may be, but there are many who whisper in his ear and give him his words.'

'Titus said . . . Titus said he was Spring-Heeled-Jack,' Mariah said nervously as if the mention of the name would invoke the creature.

'A monster of the imagination and the penny dreadful – but he is more than a creature from a comic book, that man is a cold-blooded killer.' Charity spoke in a harsh whisper as he gripped the rail to the balcony as if to squeeze the life from it.

'He said I was to be a sacrifice.'

'Then we shall frustrate his purpose. You must not leave the hotel – and stay above stairs,' Charity replied.

'But I think he is already here. I saw him in the reflection in the mirror. Then just as I searched for him, some bread in the fire exploded. I think he did it.'

'Then we will double our guard and be sure that you are kept safe. I will contact Isambard Black – he will know what to do.' Charity looked out to sea. 'It has not been a good day for the Prince Regent. Most of the visitors are gone and already there are rumours in the town that we are killing our guests.'

'And Inspector Walpole believes we did it,' Mariah added.

'Then we shall find the culprit and prove to the lanky genius that we are innocent,' Charity said, trying to make light of the dire situation.

'Does he really hate you so much?' Mariah asked. 'You could see it in his face. His eyes twitched when he spoke to you and he looked so . . . so –'

'Jealous?' Charity asked.

'Yes.'

'Believe it or not we were once good friends. Then he began to change. He would joke about me and then those jokes turned sour. His mother died on his seventh birthday. I remember it well. They had Italian ice cream and real soda. Everyone was gathered around the table. She started to laugh and laugh and then turned purple and suddenly collapsed face down into the birthday cake just as he was about to blow out the candles. He never smiled again.' Charity bit his lip earnestly.

It was then that the balcony shook with the moaning of the foghorn from the *Irenzee*. It rattled the windows, and several slates slipped from the roof and fell to the beach below. On the side of the ship two large doors began to open, level with the sea. Then from inside the vessel slipped a long, narrow steam motor launch.

'We have a visitor,' Charity said as he pointed to the craft which sped quickly across the water. 'I received a telegram this morning saying he would be checking in to the hotel for a week. Dedalus Zogel, the richest man in the world.'

'He's coming here?'

'And you shall welcome him, Mariah.'

The vessel cut through the still sea, leaving a trail of black vapour in its wake. It sped towards the harbour, gaining speed by the second until the bow was clear of the water. Suddenly the engine stopped and the boat glided to a halt as it pulled up by the harbour wall. Mariah watched as a small procession left the vessel and one by one walked slowly up the harbour steps to a waiting carriage.

'Quickly, Mariah, come and welcome our guest,' Charity

85

said as he strode towards the door of the restaurant. Mariah followed. He stopped momentarily and looked back out to sea. A maroon fireball shot into the air from the ship and exploded above the Prince Regent. It filled the morning sky with plumes of red and blue smoke as if to herald Zogel's arrival on dry land.

'The man is a fool,' Charity muttered loud enough for Mariah to hear.

Mariah walked through the restaurant. He smiled to the small cluster of guests who had gathered around the long table to snaffle a pile of hastily prepared pancakes.

'We'll be leaving at eleven,' one of them shouted to Charity as he walked by. Charity ignored the small man in the tight waistcoat. 'We're not staying here to be blown up.'

'Pity,' Charity replied as he walked on.

'We could all be killed,' the man protested at Charity.

'Chance would be a fine thing,' he replied as he pushed open the doors and walked into the lobby.

'What's he doing about it?' the man asked Mariah, waving his finger under his nose.

'It's a matter for the police,' Mariah replied

'Then where are they?' the man asked abruptly as he jumped up.

'They'll be here at eleven.'

The man sat back and tugged at the buttons on his waistcoat and then pulled on the long strands of hair that grew from under his ears.

'I'll tell them all I know. I saw everything – poisoned they were, poisoned, and to think I nearly ate the same food as they all did.'

'The same?' Mariah asked as he stopped and turned to face the man. 'They all ate from the same tray?'

'I tell you, every one of them and no one else. I watched

them. Wondered why they were getting special treatment. Thought it was Captain Charity's way of keeping in with them. Saw the waiter come in and visit each one. First he served that American Ambassador, then the other two and finally the mad German with the fat wife. Then they began to explode. Saw it. Watched it and believed it not . . .' the man spluttered.

'Who served them?' Mariah asked.

'A waiter – a Prince Regent waiter in a white jacket and black trousers.'

'That wasn't a Prince Regent waiter – not dressed in that way,' Mariah said as he tried to remember the face of the man he too had seen in the ballroom.

'But –' the man said as Mariah walked off, not waiting for him to finish.

'Captain!' he shouted as he followed Charity along the lobby.

Charity stopped by the newly mended revolving door. In the dark hours of the night it had been completely replaced before any more guests could complain about the pile of dust that was once a large American and his wife.

'It *was* murder. I don't know how or why but I think I can prove it,' Mariah said.

'Keep it to yourself,' Charity whispered. 'Best not let these things out just yet.' Charity smiled as yet another guest stormed by and jumped into a waiting carriage.

'Did you know the men who died?' Mariah asked as Charity went through the door and on to the wide steps that fronted the road.

'I had met each one. Bureau business – that and the war.'

'Then, why should someone want to kill them?' Mariah asked.

'That, my dear Mariah, is a mystery that by the hour becomes more intriguing.' Charity could say no more. At that very moment a long black carriage with six horses and three grooms drew up at the front of the hotel. A photographer in long breeches and a flat cap quickly set up his tripod and waited for the occupants to jump out.

A steward blustered his way from a cart that had followed behind. He took hold of the door handle and threw down the folding steps from beneath the carriage. The man then opened the door.

'Mr Dedalus Zogel,' he said in a pompous voice as he bowed.

There was a flare of bright white light as the flash powder prepared by the photographer exploded. The man in the doorway of the carriage held a pose and when the smoke had cleared he stepped to the ground.

'Spectacular,' said the photographer in approval.

The man was six feet tall with long black hair that was tied tightly behind his head. In his hand he carried a peculiar hat that looked as if it was made of straw. The man had an extravagant moustache that swept around his mouth and under his chin. A thick beard swept about his neck like a scarf. Covering one eye was a golden monocle hung from a thin leather strap. Without him even speaking a single word, Mariah knew instantly he was an American.

'Captain Charity,' the man said in a warm voice that echoed the smile on his face. 'So good to see you again.'

'Mr Zogel.'

'Please call me Dedalus – after all, we'll be seeing a lot of each other.' Zogel's smile widened even further as he thrust out his hand. 'And who is this fine boy?'

'Mariah Mundi, my assistant,' Charity said as he turned away from Zogel.

'An assistant, Captain? He looks so fine I should be stealing him from you.' Zogel said as he reached out his hand and patted Mariah on the head as if he were a small dog. 'I shall enjoy my stay here. I expect the best – for the best.' Zogel drooled the words in an accent from south of the Mason-Dixon line. 'You know, boy,' he said as he turned to Mariah, 'I'll double the pay Charity gives you if you work for me.'

'It's more than money, Mr Zogel,' Mariah replied. 'This is like a family business.'

'Well, boy, I always get what I want and never give up trying – so if you ever get let down, Zogel will be there to pick you up . . .'

Mariah smiled and gave a slight bow. Something about the man reminded him of Isambard Black. Mariah bowed again. It was all he could think of to do as Zogel took off his buckskin gloves and slapped them across the back of Mariah's head.

'In with the cases and be careful – they're all made from alligator, caught them myself,' Zogel blustered.

'You chose the Prince Regent rather than stay on your yacht?' Charity asked as he followed the procession up the steps and into the hotel.

'If I could think of another way of travelling I certainly would. I hate the sea, it's an abomination on the mind – and I have heard so much about this place I wanted to see it with my own eyes. Is it true you still have a galvanised bathing machine?'

Mariah stood back as a stack of alligator-skin cases were unloaded from the carriage and the cart that followed. A small man the size of a child gave particular attention to all that was happening. He would nod and moan at the stewards, pointing to cases and bags and muttering under his breath. The man was half the size of Mariah and perfect in every way. He wore a neat black suit, white shirt and black tie. On his feet was a pair of sparkling black boots that looked as if they had been made for a large doll. He stopped and stared at Mariah.

'You gonna help or just stand there?' he said in a foreign accent that sounded like nothing Mariah had heard before. He pointed to an alligator bag on the sidewalk. 'Pick up the case and take it inside – and don't drop it.'

Without thinking, Mariah did what he said. The case was light and felt as if there was something moving inside – something slithering as if it wanted to escape.

'Be careful, boy. That is my case,' the man said as he walked closely behind.

'Do you go everywhere with Mister Zogel?' Mariah asked out of nervousness.

'Why do you want to know?'

'Just seems like you do,' Mariah replied, wishing he had never spoken.

'I go everywhere and do everything for Mister Zogel. Nothing happens without me knowing – does that answer your prying question?'

Mariah nodded. He could feel his face turning red as the man stared at him.

'They call you Mariah, yes? That is the name of a girl?' he asked.

'It was the name of my father's best friend. My parents named me after him.'

'There is much in a name. Mariah makes me think of a little child that needs its mother.' The man laughed as he spoke. 'I am Lucius Nibelungen – see, that is a good name, a powerful name.'

'It's this way,' Mariah said in reply as he walked ahead with the alligator case. 'You're on the third floor, I'll show you the way.'

Mariah led the procession higher and higher up the stairs. Lucius began to drag far behind, each step for him like a mountain. The stewards followed briskly. Some stacked the cases on their heads and carried them up the stairs without the slightest complaint. Lucius moaned at every turn until they reached the final landing. Mariah opened the door that led along the hallway to the room.

'This is it,' he said as he walked along.

The door to the suite was already open. Dedalus Zogel stood in the window looking out to sea towards his ship. He had wrapped himself in a black bearskin coat and donned his large straw hat.

'It's the biggest one in the world, Mariah. Come and see,' he said, pointing to the *Irenzee*. 'Five hundred feet long and near-ly two hundred high – and it's all mine. Yet I turn green when-ever it sets sail. Fancy that!' Zogel drawled in a voice that spoke as if he'd never left the Carolinas.

Mariah didn't speak but put the case on the floor and turned to leave. The procession of servants, stewards and hangers on began to fill the room. Finally Lucius Nibelungen walked through the door.

'Is everything to your liking, Mister Zogel?' the dwarf said as he pulled on the cuffs of his shirt and straightened his tie.

'Perfect, perfect,' Zogel replied as he took a snuffbox from his pocket and lined the powder on his hand and then sniffed deeply.

'And you have a view of the *Irenzee*?' Lucius asked as he fussed about the cases as if he searched for something.

'In direct communication, Lucius,' he replied casually as he slipped the fur coat from his shoulders and let it fall in a heap on the floor.

Mariah stood still, not knowing what to do next. He felt trapped and yet wanted to see what would happen. Zogel turned, reached into his jacket pocket and slipped a large white five pound note from his wallet.

'Take this, boy. Told you I would pay more than Captain Charity – consider it a down payment on our future relation-ship.'

Zogel held out his hand. Mariah saw a gold ring on his finger identical to the one worn by Inspector Walpole. The design of a square and compass was set in a bed of diamonds.

'Like the ring, do you?' Zogel asked. 'I love diamonds – it's my hope to own every diamond in the world.'

'It's interesting,' Mariah replied.

'Seen one like it before?' he asked.

'Never . . . not ever.' The lie slipped easily from his lips without him feeling a twinge of remorse.

'You could have one just like this. You can't buy them – they are given. Given on oath. Work for me and it'll be the first thing you get – that's a Zogel promise.'

Lucius coughed. 'Mister Zogel has to rest – it's been a hard day. Goodbye, Mariah.'

[9]

The Towers

THROUGHOUT the day the black cart went back and forth from the Prince Regent to the quayside. It drudged through the rain as it brought more and more cases for Dedalus Zogel, Lucius and their servants. The dwarf stood at the door of the hotel and checked each delivery against a parchment list that he ticked with a quill pen. As more cases arrived, more guests left. A large crowd had gathered in the square outside the hotel. Many had come to watch the richest man in the world unload his belongings; others had heard the street-corner rumour that Captain Jack Charity was poisoning his guests and that they had all begun to explode.

By three in the afternoon, an old man in a plaid suit had filled a tray of vials with fire dust and sold them as the remains of Baron Hoetzendorf. He entertained the crowd with the story of how he had seen the Baron explode before his very eyes and that this dust was proof of the first case of spontaneous combustion.

By four o'clock, another man began strolling up and down with a sandwich board while proclaiming at the top of his voice that the end of the world was coming and that eventually everyone who didn't believe would explode in divine rapture. He stopped at every turn and shouted 'We're doomed!' before walking off and repeating his protestation again and again. By evening, the only people staying at the Prince Regent were Zogel and his intriguing entourage.

Outside the crowds grew troublesome as even more people came to see if the cold fire would consume more guests. The photographer waited, flashgun at the ready, in the hope of catching a picture of someone about to spontaneously combust and shower the crowd with fiery dust. As the rain drizzled, disappointment grew.

Mariah waited by the door and peered outside. He kept one eye on the crowd and the other on the lobby. Mrs Mukluk slept as usual. She snored loudly and gasped for breath and every now and then belched in her sleep. Mariah looked out for Sacha. He had seen her once that day. She was quiet and didn't speak. He had tried to smile, but she looked away and when he spoke she grunted a curt reply. Every time he went near she just turned away. It was as if something lay heavy on her mind. It was more than the argument of the night before – it was just as much her fault as his – he would wait, he said to himself . . . Mariah wanted to say that he was sorry but couldn't think how. He said the word in his mind but somehow it could not come to his lips. It had always been the same – a stiff lip in everything. At the Colonial School he had never been allowed to say what was in his heart. 'Feelings are for girls,' the headmaster would say to any boy with the merest glistening of a tear. 'Boys of the Colonial School keep these things to themselves – we are men of the future – the Empire . . .'

No matter how much it hurt or what the pain was, Mariah had been told to keep it locked away and this is what he had done.

Sacha had never been that way. You could tell her heart from the look on her face, he thought as he looked at the crowd and listened to Mrs Mukluk's high-pitched snoring. That afternoon Mariah had prepared the theatre for the evening performance. Sacha had loaded the cannon, filled his magical jacket with rabbits and pigeons and set the trap door. Before he had a chance to apologise she had gone. He had looked for her throughout the hotel, but she was nowhere to be found.

The Prince Regent was ghostly empty. As Mariah's magical performance had been cancelled when the last guest had left, he had nothing to do. He had taken the disappearing pigeons and the vanishing rabbits and put them in their cages and now waited like everyone else to see what would happen. It was as if the hotel had suddenly become another world. Zogel was a remarkably quiet guest; he stayed in his room and had not been seen since his arrival. His servants saw to everything and even tasted his food before he would eat it. Lucius, however, appeared to be everywhere. Once he had checked in all the cases and trunks, he walked every corridor of the hotel. He had even come into the theatre and for a while had watched Sacha and Mariah as they worked silently.

It had been there that Mariah had noticed something strange about him. Whilst watching them, it appeared that Lucius was in the habit of talking to himself. He muttered wherever he went and could be seen to be listening to a voice that only he could hear. He would stop as he walked and then look up, listen and mutter a reply. Mariah thought him to be quite mad.

Now, as Mariah watched the door, he saw the dwarf appear in the lobby. Lucius was alone. This was unusual as he was always escorted everywhere by two servants who walked a pace behind. He stopped for a moment by the grand staircase, and looked about him.

Mariah quickly stepped into Mrs Mukluk's office so he could not be seen. He listened to the small footsteps as they crossed the lobby. The door creaked as a blast of cold night air blew in. It slammed shut as Lucius stepped outside. Mariah looked at the sleeping Mukluk, who by now was sprawled over the desk. He took a sheet of paper from the letter rack by her head and scribbled a note that he folded neatly and pushed under her nose. Then he grabbed a bellboy's coat from the back of the door and slipped out of the hotel.

It was cold, but the rain had stopped and the night sky was clearing from the west. Lucius was walking briskly towards the town. Mariah followed him down by the Market Vaults and along Sepulchre Street. He began to feel uneasy. Charity had told him not to leave the hotel; Titus Salt had said leave the night to Packavi. But now he was walking through the empty streets as he followed Lucius, even though with every step his mind told him to go back. Thoughts of Packavi flashed in his memory as the voice of the assassin plagued him again and again.

Mariah thought it strange that the man should go this way. There was nothing here to be seen. The road didn't lead to the harbour, and yet from the speed he walked Lucius obviously knew where he was going. Soon they had begun to climb the steep hill from the town to the castle. It led through even darker, narrower streets. The houses were jammed so tightly that not even the night sky or the stars could be seen. Each doorway had a shadow, every passageway some terror.

Mariah stopped, as the urge to turn back grew more intense. It nagged at him like an aching pain. Far ahead he could see Lucius turn the corner. Mariah heard the gate to the cemetery creak slowly open. Taking a deep breath he followed on, keeping to the shadows. As he approached a passageway he would wait, look into the blackness and then dart across, sure a hand would dive from the darkness and take hold of him. But as he went on his fears began to calm. He smiled and shrugged his shoulders, scolding himself for being afraid. All he knew was that he had to find out what Lucius was doing.

Very soon he got to the entrance of the graveyard that surrounded the old church. The gateway was draped in thick strands of green ivy that hung like ropes from the bars of the railings. Mariah twisted the brass handle, pulled slowly and slipped inside. Lucius was nowhere to be seen. The pathway ran up a gentle slope. A solitary lamp cast a dim light upon the path and the tall gravestones. Dotted here and there were stone sepulchres that looked like peculiar small marble houses.

He listened; in the distance he could hear Lucius talking. The voice echoed from grave to grave, so that Mariah could not understand what was being said. Mariah crept silently through the tombs.

There, in the shadow of the lamp, by the wall, was Lucius. He was kneeling by a grave, one hand upon the stone, the other tracing the name carved in the surface: OTTO LUGER.

Mariah wondered how Lucius could know of Luger and why he should want to visit his grave. He tried to get closer to listen to what he was saying. Lucius stopped and looked up as if he had heard a noise. Mariah cowered behind the door of a tomb.

'Who is there?' Lucius shouted. 'I know someone is there – you have not done a good job of following me.' He took a small pistol from the pocket of his coat and pulled back the firing hammer. 'If you don't come out, I will shoot.'

Mariah was trapped. He pushed the door of the tomb. It opened with a jolt and a hiss of stale air.

'I know where you are – I can see your shadow,' Lucius said as he walked warily towards him. 'Come out.'

Mariah slipped into the tomb – it was cold, dank and smelt of the meat cellar at the Colonial School where Felix had once locked him overnight in amongst the hanging carcasses.

From outside he could hear Lucius speaking. Mariah had no

time to close the door of the tomb. Quickly, he climbed over the lid of an old coffin on the topmost shelf and slid down the side against the wall.

'This is your last chance – come out or I will shoot,' Lucius said.

Mariah heard the tomb door slide further open. Stone grated on stone as it was pushed wider. He lay deathly still, not wanting to breathe.

'Very well,' said Lucius as he peered into the darkness. 'If you want to play games . . .' The door to the tomb grated shut and the metal catch dropped into place. 'See if you can follow me now,' Lucius said as he walked away.

Mariah was in complete darkness. He waited until he was sure that Lucius had gone. Then as quietly as he could he pulled his way from his hiding place and slid over the lid of the coffin and onto the floor. He pushed at the door to the tomb: it didn't move. He tried again, this time forcing it as hard as he could – there was nothing. He sat on the floor and wondered what to do next.

He thought of Felix and the night he had been trapped in the meat cellar at school. The hours had dragged slowly by and Mariah had got colder and colder. It was only when he had been locked in the cellar for five hours that he had discovered how to escape. He had taken the edge of a copper penny and prised open the screws on each hinge and opened the door. Mariah felt inside his pockets now – they were empty.

Blindly, he felt around the tomb – there must be something he could use, he thought as he reached out. Stacked on either side were three coffins, each on a separate shelf. At the farthest end of the tomb was a solid wall, at the top of which Mariah noticed a faint chink of light. He climbed on the shelves and braced himself astride the coffins. He could feel a draught upon his face. With the tip of his golden finger he began to dig at the crumbling plaster between two slabs of marble. It came away easily and the light grew brighter. Within a minute he could see the street at the far side of the graveyard. There under the gas lamp was Lucius.

It appeared that he was waiting at the bottom of the drive-way that led up to a boarding house just below the entrance to the castle. Mariah could see the four towers and large front door. Lucius walked up and down as if he were waiting for someone.

It was then that he heard the sound of a carriage on the cob-bled street. It was old and rattled as if the wheels were about to drop off. As it came into view, Mariah could see that it was being pulled by one horse. It walked slowly as if it cared not when it would arrive. The carriage stopped and a man got out and opened the gate of the boarding house and stepped inside. Lucius followed and together they disappeared into the dark shadows of the trees.

The carriage turned and slowly trundled into the night. Soon, Mariah could hear it no more – he was alone.

He could see a stack of coffins at the side of the tomb, each with a name and date etched into a brass plate on its side. He read them one by one and felt as if those inside could hear his thoughts. Mariah tried the door again – he wanted to scream, but knew that if he was found he could not explain why he was there. He thought that Lucius might come back and shoot him dead. He shivered.

'Should never have come,' he said to himself to break the silence. 'Should have stayed in the Prince Regent.'

There was a sudden noise from the graveyard as the gate opened. Footsteps followed quickly as three men ran up the path. There was a thump against the door of the tomb.

'Listen here,' a voice said outside. 'We shares what we get – equal like.'

'We shouldn't be doin' it – 'tis wrong, it is,' said the voice of another.

'They're dead and dead men can't tell tales and dead men don't care if we pick their pockets and snatch their jewellery. I was told she was buried in a gold necklace and that's enough to keep us all for a month.' The man laughed as he spoke.

'Remember, we take them out one by one and open them up. Take what they've got and be gone. If anyone comes we split up and meet at the Merchant Inn – and if you get caught say now't.'

'What if they come and –' said a voice quietly.

'What if who comes?' the man asked.

'Their ghosts,' the other replied. 'I've never robbed the dead before.'

'Dead is dead – they can't come and get you,' said the man, and then there was a loud crack as he forced the lock from the tomb door. 'Quiet now – we have work to do and money to spend.'

'What if they –'

'Shut up and push on the door – look, a knife wedged under here.'

There was a scraping sound as the knife was pulled from under the door. Mariah knew the men were grave robbers and he didn't have time to hide. He stepped back and waited for the door of the tomb to open.

'I knew her,' said the man feebly. 'She had a tongue as sharp as a razor and she wouldn't like this.'

'She's dead – dead, do you understand?'

'But –'

'Money is money and at least the dead don't put up a fight. Give me the lamp.'

The door to the tomb opened slowly. Mariah quickly rolled in the dust and stretched out on the floor by the side of an old coffin, stiffening himself like a corpse.

'Look – the cheapskates even put one in without a box. Grab him by the feet and make sure he doesn't fall apart,' said the man as he cast the lamp across him and turned away.

Mariah felt someone take hold of him by the toes of his boots and begin to drag him from the tomb. He kept his eyes tightly shut as his face brushed against the side of a man's leg. It smelt of fish, beer and horses. In seconds he was dragged outside and laid on the cold stone.

'This one's fresh and a young 'un,' said the man as he shone a lamp on Mariah's cobwebbed, dirty face.

Three men gathered around and looked down at him.

'Poor lad, to die at that age. Fancy coat, brass buttons – sell that, get a fine price.'

'We'll go inside and get another – when we find the old lass we can get that necklace and be off.'

Mariah could feel the man pulling at the buttons on his coat. He tried not to breathe. A hand slipped inside his coat and made him jerk.

'He's . . . He's –' Before he could finish, Mariah leapt to his feet. 'ALIVE!' screamed the man in fear as he saw the boy coming to life before his eyes. 'I told you – quick!'

Mariah stared at the man, who stepped back towards the tomb. Two faces appeared through the narrow doorway. One mouthed several words without a sound. The man in front of Mariah held out the lamp as if to protect himself.

'Back, demon child,' he said, his voice quivering. 'Be gone and leave us be.'

Mariah stepped forward and held out his hand towards him. The light shone and glistened on his golden finger.

'Is it gold you want?' Mariah asked in a croaking voice as if he were dead. 'Then gold you shall have . . .'

A hand seized the man and dragged him in to the tomb. Another fumbled for the door and, grabbing the steel brace that held fast the hinges, pulled it shut before Mariah could get any closer.

'Leave us be, demon! We'll take nothing from here – just go!' said a muffled voice from inside the tomb.

'And you'll do this no more?' Mariah croaked as he wedged the lock firmly shut.

'Never again – just let us live, we meant you no harm,' the man squeaked.

'I'll watch you from now on and when you sup in the Merchant, sat by the peat fire nice and warm, I'll be there, watching you . . .'

'Trust us – we'll not do this again!'

'Very well. I have spent an eternity in that tomb and you shall spend one night. In the morning you shall be set free.'

'No! You can't leave us – not in here – they're dead.'

'You would have taken what they had but are not prepared to pass the night in their company? Shall I join you?'

'No,' squeaked the man. 'We are content in our predicament. Leave us be and torment us no more.'

'I shall be gone, but in the dark hours you will never know if I am there or not.' Mariah secured the door with a piece of marble and before leaving banged three times upon the wall. 'Heed my words,' he said in as miserable a voice as he could muster. 'I'll be back . . .'

In three steps he was away from the sepulchre. Mariah walked the path to the road and looked up at the boarding house where Lucius had gone in. He read the sign that hung above the gate: *The Towers*.

High above him he could see a light in a room with a blind drawn at the window. The flames of a roaring fire flickered boldly and cast the shadow of a man against the canvas. Mariah opened the gate and stepped into the garden. Later the door opened and Lucius stepped outside. As he did so, he buttoned up his coat and pulled his collar. A man followed close behind.

'Zogel will not regret this,' the man said.

'But will I regret this?' Lucius asked. 'I am not so bothered what Mister Zogel thinks. He enjoys what he has, and in that I care for him. If you cross me then you will know about it.' He drew his thumb across his throat as if to cut it with a knife.

'Business is business, my dear friend,' the man said, 'and it is in our mutual interest that all goes well. I have taken steps to ensure that we will get what we want. I have someone in authority who is bound to help us.'

'Then do me one thing to prove yourself,' asked Lucius quietly.

'Anything.'

'There is a tomb in the graveyard. The one by the gate. Inside there is someone who followed me. He is locked in. Make sure that he never escapes.'

'I will do it tonight. My men shall see to it,' the man replied.

'See to it yourself, see to it yourself.'

[10]

Bloodhound

THERE was a frantic banging on the door to his room. It shook the walls and in his sleep he could hear Captain Jack shouting his name. The banging came again, louder and louder, shaking the plaster from the cracks in the ceiling. He tried to wake himself but his mind clung to sleep like a warm blanket.

'Mariah, wake up! Sacha is missing,' Charity barked.

The words echoed as Mariah leapt from the bed and turned the key in the lock. The door opened and Charity stepped quickly inside. He closed the door behind him as if he wanted no one to hear what he would say. Mariah looked surprised.

'Where were you last night?' he asked Mariah.

'I followed Lucius to the Towers – he isn't what he seems to be – he has a plan,' Mariah replied as he rubbed his eyes.

'Was Sacha with you?' he asked quickly.

'I saw her in the afternoon,' he said, trying to think of the day before.

'She's gone, everything has been taken from her room and her father has no idea where she is. He came this morning asking to see her – said it was important.'

Mariah paused before he spoke. He looked about the room. 'We argued – I thought nothing of it. It could be my fault.'

'What in heaven should possess her to leave and take everything with her?' Charity asked, as Mariah quickly got dressed.

'She'd lied. On the night Hoetzendorf and the others were killed I lost Sacha. When I got back I found her and asked her where she had been. Her feet were covered in sand and her shoes had salt marks. She said she hadn't left the hotel. I knew she was lying – I knew there was something she didn't want me to know.'

'What could be so important?' Charity asked.

'Titus salt said he had seen her. That she was in a dark place. It was a vision he'd had,' Mariah replied.

'Doesn't mean to say he is right. Titus is a seer – especially when full of gin.'

'I believed him. He saved my life and he'd seen that in a vision. Do you think someone could have taken her?' Mariah asked as he fastened up his shirt and brushed his hair.

'All I know is that it will take a great deal of explaining if the police get involved.'

'Then I'll find her – I'll ask Titus to look for her.'

'Zogel has asked to see you,' Charity said. 'He insists on you taking his breakfast.'

'Then he will go hungry. I have to find her – it's my fault, whatever has happened to her.'

'And where would you start? Do you know something that you are not telling me, Mariah?'

Mariah stopped. He didn't know where to start looking for her. She could be anywhere. Sacha could have gone and found another job. Just because she had left didn't mean she was in any kind of danger. It was then that he saw the divining spectacles on the table by the bed. He picked them up as a thought came to him.

'I could find her with these,' he said as his face lit with antic-ipation. 'Even at this time, surely there should be some trace of her.'

'And what would you use? Her room is empty and swept clean. It's as if she has never been there at all,' Charity said impatiently through clenched teeth.

'Do me one thing,' Mariah said. 'Take Zogel his breakfast and let me look for Sacha. Just this once?' he pleaded as the guilt grew in his heart.

'Just this once,' Charity said with a smile. 'But you will come and see me before you do anything else – and this time don't leave the hotel.'

'I promise,' Mariah said as he pulled back the drapes from his window and let in the cold morning light.

As Charity took the steam elevator, Mariah went straight to Sacha's room. The door was open and as Charity had said, it was swept clean. The floor was brightly polished and there was not one speck of dust. As he searched the cupboards and the wardrobe he thought it was as if she had never existed. Gone was all sign of his friend, all trace.

Mariah sat on the bed with his head in his hands. 'You could have told me you were going,' he said out loud as if she was in the room. He waited but there was no reply. He stared at the floor. A large black beetle crawled from under the floorboards and skittered across the shiny floor. It ran along the side of the wall towards him. Mariah followed it as it ran, wondering how fast it would be if it were the size of a man.

Just then he saw something that caught his eye. Had the bee-tle not just run over it, he would never have noticed. There, on the floor, were two small holes where once were nails that pinned the board. Six inches to the left, near to the bedside table, were two more empty nail holes. As Mariah looked even closer he could see that the varnish had been scratched away.

Mariah reached down and rattled the floorboard. It was loose. Within a minute he had lifted it from its place, and beneath he found a black silk bag tied with a length of gold braid. He quickly lifted it from its hiding place and placed it on the bed. He untied the string and tipped out the contents.

Mariah was surprised by what he found. There, scattered on the bed, was a handkerchief, a small bracelet, two gold coins, Sacha's favourite scarf and a postcard of the Towers Guest House.

He looked at the back of the card. In scrawled black letters were the words: KEEP SILENT – MEET ME TONIGHT. The mark on the stamp clearly said it had been posted on the pier two days before. Mariah had no idea who Sacha would meet, and 'keep silent' meant nothing to him. He wondered why she should keep this secret.

What he did have was her scarf and he knew that the diving spectacles would work on this alone. Mariah wrapped the scarf around his neck and put all the other items back in the bag and then in his pocket.

Taking the divining spectacles, he flicked the frames onto his nose and tuned in the device. He could see nothing in the room: there were no faded twists of essence and no invisible footprints. It was only when he looked towards the door that he saw the faintest trace of where Sacha had been. Impressed upon the wood were the imprints of Sacha's legs as if she had been thrown against it with great force. Kidnapped, he thought, as he searched for more signs of her abduction.

Mariah followed on. In the hallway by the entrance to the steam elevator was another imprint: it looked as if the side of her head had been pushed against the wooden floor. He pressed the button and heard the lift far below, juddering and shuddering as it came closer. It stopped; Mariah opened the gate and stepped inside. He pressed the express button for the ground floor and held tight. Sacha's essence was everywhere. Whoever had taken her had met with a struggle. The elevator was covered in red smears that could only be seen with the divining spectacles. It was obvious that there had been a fight.

The elevator descended quickly and in two seconds the grille door of the lobby opened. Dedalus Zogel stood in front of the door, arms folded.

'Thought you'd be bringing me breakfast?' he asked as he stared at Mariah through his gold monocle.

'I had to –' Mariah couldn't think of what to say. He could see by the look on Zogel's face that he wouldn't believe any excuse.

'Zogel gets what Zogel wants, boy. If I ask for you to bring me my food then I expect to see you.'

Mariah was about to reply but the words jumbled in his head. He took off the divining spectacles and put them in his pocket. Just as he was about to speak the door of the hotel burst open.

'Is he here?' asked Inspector Walpole, who was clutching a piece of paper. 'I want to see Captain Charity now.'

Mrs Mukluk woke from her sleep. 'Who shall I say wants to speak to him?' she asked, as if she had heard everything said whilst she slept.

'In his office, is he?' Walpole asked as he pushed by Zogel and Mariah and set off along the lobby to Captain Jack's office. Two constables and a scruffy old man in a tweed coat pulling an overweight bloodhound on a long leather leash followed Walpole. The dog sniffed as it went, drooling spittle on to the Persian rugs. 'Charity! I need to see you, Charity,' Walpole shouted excitedly.

Captain Charity stepped from his office before Walpole could break down the door. He looked at each man in turn before he spoke.

'Unusual way to carry out your business, Inspector?' he asked.

'Not when evidence drops through your letter box,' Walpole replied, shaking the piece of paper in Charity's face and hardly able to contain his excitement any longer. 'Arrived not but an hour ago, delivered in the first-class mail and look, it was posted last night.'

'That Her Majesty's Mail has surpassed itself in their delivery is always a cause for great celebration,' Charity replied as he stepped back from Walpole, who was now hopping on the spot.

'Not when you read what its says and see what it contains,' Walpole said as he showed the envelope to Charity and neatly pulled out what looked like an old piece of stale bread. 'Hexogenamite! Hexogenamite – I had it tested and it truly is. And let me read this: *Search the Prince Regent and you will find even more – and the man who did it.*'

'Congratulations. And what may I ask does it have to do with me?' Charity asked.

'That's how you killed them. I knew you'd done it and now I have the evidence. This is the most modern of explosives and it would take a military man to know how to use it. You are the killer. Nothing like a bit of old hexo to get rid of your enemies and it doesn't matter that they were foreign. You can't use that as an excuse. Foreigners are not exempt from the law of murder – not even Frenchmen,' Walpole replied as he sniffed the explosive with his quivering nostrils.

'Be careful you don't explode,' Charity said.

'You should know, Captain. Can you tell me how it was done?'

'I am not your man – look elsewhere and stop wasting my time,' Charity replied angrily as he stepped back into his office and slammed the door.

Walpole banged on the door as Mariah and Zogel looked on.

'I have a warrant to search the hotel. Mister Brough has brought his finest hound. Burgho was used to track the villain in the Whitechapel murders,' Walpole said as the fat hound slavered on the rug, 'and he'll soon find any hexogenamite you have hidden.'

The office door opened suddenly. 'Then let him look for it – be my guest. I only have eleven guests in the hotel so please frighten them away as well. Put me out of business – that's your plan, Inspector Walpole. I can see the glee upon your face.'

Walpole nodded to Brough to bring the hound. Charity stepped aside as the man took the dog into the room. Zogel and Mariah came closer. Captain Charity watched as the hound sniffed the floor and then the furniture. It knocked over the lamp by the fire as it nuzzled under the rug. Walpole looked on, rubbing his hands.

'Won't take long, Charity – we'll have it soon.'

'You speak as if you already know where it is,' Charity replied.

'Did I not read that to you? How could I forget?' he said as he held the note to his face and peered down his long nose.

'Then I shall await my fate in the restaurant. Please tell me when you leave,' Charity said as he nodded for Mariah to follow.

'Do you think they'll find something?' Mariah asked as they sat at a large round table by the balcony.

'Of course, Mariah. It is not just Lucius who has a terrible plan. Walpole will find more hexogenamite and I will be arrested.' Charity handed Mariah a large bunch of keys. 'Take these and run the hotel until I return. I made provision for this with Dunlop, Fraser and Jenvey – they have all the papers.'

'Did you do it?' Mariah asked.

'I had every reason to kill each one. If Walpole finds that out, then he will have a case against me.'

'But did you?' he asked again.

'No, Mariah. I would do no such thing. Believe me. I couldn't believe they should all come here at the same time – on the eve of Zogel's arrival. It is as if it was planned by a greater hand than mine.'

'What would be a reason to kill them?' he asked.

'It is best if you do not know what they have done and what they intended to do. Beware the power behind the power, that's all I can –'

'So, Captain Jack Charity – innocent until proven guilty?' Walpole said as he burst into the restaurant, unable to keep his smirk of contentment from erupting across his face. 'How do you explain what the incredible Burgho discovered in your office?'

'More hexogenamite hidden under the floor?' Charity asked as he got to his feet.

'So you confess?' Walpole asked as he waved a large bag in the air. 'Twenty slices of hexo – enough to blow up the hotel.'

'You look for the wrong man, Walpole, and deep down you know it's not me. How do I know it's not stale bread?'

Walpole didn't speak. He walked smugly to the fish tank and looked in through the thick glass. Breaking a piece off one slice of hexo, he dropped it into the tank. 'Watch this,' he said as a large codfish swirled around it and then snapped at the hexo suddenly.

They waited . . . and they waited. The fish swam back and forth looking for more food. Walpole broke off several more pieces and dropped them in the tank.

'I wouldn't do that, Inspector,' Charity said as he stepped further away.

'What you doing to my fish?' Rhamses shouted from the kitchen door as the Inspector dropped yet another piece of explosive into the tank.

'Proving a point – shut up and wash the dishes,' Walpole replied without even looking to see who had spoken.

'Not a wise thing to say,' Mariah replied as Rhamses stalked across the restaurant holding a large copper pan.

'What are you doing to my fish?' Rhamses insisted as he got nearer.

'Waiting to see them explode,' Walpole said with a snigger.

'You kill my fish?' Rhamses said as he grabbed the bag of hexo and sent the pieces spilling across the floor.

'I'll have you arrested,' Walpole said as he struggled with the manic chef who was attempting to beat him with the copper pan.

In the tank, the large cod began to cough and choke. It swam faster and faster around the tank and then suddenly stopped. Its eyes bulged and several large bubbles erupted from its mouth. Without warning a small halibut exploded – then another and another. The cod floated to the surface and turned on its back. Rhamses dropped the pan to the floor and scooped the fish from the water with a large green net that hung from the side of the tank.

'Look what you have done to him,' the chef said as if pleading for the life of the fish.

Walpole looked in to the wood-framed net with its carved frieze of ornamental frogs. The fish stared back at him as it drowned in the air.

'This is your fault – you are a killer,' Rhamses said, vehemently excited.

'But you cook them – pull them from the tank and fry them at the table,' Walpole protested feebly as the cod began to expand even more.

Just as the chef was about to speak, the fish exploded. It was blasted into a thousand pieces of steaming sushi. Walpole took the force of the explosion. He was strewn with fish guts that hung from the brim of his hat like so many glistening Christmas decorations. His face was splattered with blood, and a large fin hung from his cheek like a Chinese fan.

'It – is – dead,' Rhamses said dramatically as he looked at what remained of the net with tears running down his lined face.

'Told you it was hexogenamite,' Walpole gloated as he got to his feet and picked the innards from his hat and grabbed the remaining explosive from the floor. 'This means you are under arrest for murder, Captain Jack Charity.'

'You make a mistake. I am not the one guilty in this.'

'I found the stuff in your office and I have a letter naming you,' Walpole replied as he took a pair of iron handcuffs from his pocket.

'Doesn't a murderer need a motive?' Mariah asked in his defence.

'That was also in the letter. Why don't you tell him, Jack?'

Charity shook his head.

'He had good cause to kill each one of them. Three of them he had done battle with in Africa and the fourth wanted him court-martialled. Isn't that right, Captain Jack?'

'Don't listen, Mariah – he twists the facts to suit himself,' Charity protested as Walpole snapped the handcuffs on his wrists.

'You'll have a chance to say your bit in court – they'll hang you for this, Jack,' Walpole sniggered.

'He didn't do it!' Mariah screamed as Walpole led Charity into the lobby.

'If I wasn't taking him, I'd be taking you,' Walpole replied as the two constables, Mr Brough and his hound followed on.

'Remember what I told you, Mariah!' Charity shouted as he was led through the door and down the steps to the awaiting carriage. 'Look after the hotel and trust no one.'

Charity was slammed into the prison cart and the door locked. Mariah saw his face appear at the window grille in the door. Charity tried to smile but in his heart Mariah knew it was all in vain. He felt a warm hand on his shoulder.

'A lot of responsibility for a boy of your age,' Zogel said amicably. 'Good job old Zogel arrived just when he did. We'll have Captain Jack out in no time and until then *I'll* be here for you just as I said.'

Mariah looked up and smiled as he gulped and held his quivering lip with his teeth.

Walpole stared at them from where he stood on the pavement. He smiled at Mariah. 'Better be about your business, lad. Well, what's left of it.'

[11]

Ectoplasm

MRS Mukluk slept at her desk. Her snoring was quieter than usual. Mariah listened to the chiming of the grand clock. It was louder, brighter and clearer than he had ever heard it before. It was then that he realised that the hotel was completely empty and the sound of the clock and the snoring of Mrs Mukluk was not being drowned out by the constant noise of the guests, the whirring of the steam elevator and the gurgling of the galvanised bathing machine three floors below.

As he walked along the lobby from Charity's office towards the entrance desk he looked into the empty restaurant. Rhamses sat alone at a long table with his head in his hands. His chef's hat lay crumpled in front of him next to a small brown paper bag.

'They've all gone,' the chef said as he heard Mariah's footsteps. 'Left me to deal with that madman upstairs and his leprechaun assistant. None of them would stay. Not after they saw the fish explode – said they would be next – too dangerous.'

'So did the chambermaids and the waiters,' Mariah replied. 'It's only you, Mrs Mukluk and me that are left. That's if you . . .' He was unsure whether the chef was also planning to leave.

'You can trust me,' Rhamses replied. 'It'll take more than a few exploding guests to get rid of me. I promised Charity that I would always be there when he needed me. You can't let a friend down – not when he's done so much for you.'

'Known him long?' Mariah asked as he looked at the large fish tank filled with dead fish.

'He was my Captain in the army – went through many a fight together. Brought me here and he gave me a job at the Golden Kipper when I needed one,' he said as if Charity had rescued him from a terrible fate. Rhamses then opened the paper bag and looked inside. 'Shouldn't have this – picked it up when Walpole took him away. Hexo – powerful stuff.' Rhamses tipped the broken pieces of explosive on the table and nudged them cautiously with the tip of his finger.

'Won't it explode?' Mariah asked.

'Not this stuff. This is gelignite and carbide. One thing I can tell you is that it's home-made.'

'How do you know?' Mariah asked as he picked a lump from the table.

'It's the wrong colour. This has been made to look like bread. That's how they were killed – someone made them a hexogena-mite sandwich. Once eaten they would have several minutes to live before they exploded.'

'Into dust?' Mariah asked.

'Into dust,' he replied. 'When I saw Walpole kill my fish I realised what it was then. One thing I do know is that the Captain wouldn't do it. Not even if he did have a grudge. He's the kind of man to see you face to face – not his style, doing things cunningly.'

'Don't know what I'll do now, Rhamses,' Mariah said as the weight of the world crushed his heart. 'I feel as if it's all coming to an end.'

'You can't be running off when things get bad,' said the chef as he tidied the explosive back into the bag and handed it to Mariah. 'Be careful with that stuff. Sometimes you have to stay and fight. If Charity didn't do it then we'll find out who did.'

'But I can't run this place on my own,' Mariah replied as he put the bag in his pocket.

'And you won't have to, not with me and Mrs Mukluk to keep an eye on you. Zogel's easily pleased and the leprechaun does his food. We could even take in more guests – that's if they don't think they'll explode with my cooking.' Rhamses tried to laugh as he spoke.

There was a sudden and shrill buzzing of the reception bell. It went on and on as at the same time every telephone in the hotel began to ring. The sound filled the halls and corridors of the hotel as if a million calls sounded at once. Mrs Mukluk slept on, completely unaware. Mariah ran from the restaurant to the front desk. She was in her usual place with two thick strands of cotton wool wedged in each ear and for some strange reason an even larger strand wedged in her right nostril.

Mariah switched off the bell and picked up the receiver.

'Hello, Prince Regent Hotel,' he said as politely as he could, never sure that the telephone could be trusted.

There was no reply. Mariah listened, sure he could hear the faint sound of someone breathing, and then there was a sudden click as the line went dead.

'What you doing?' Mrs Mukluk asked in a surprised voice as she woke from her sleep.

'Did you hear the bell?' Mariah asked.

'Of course I'm well – if I wasn't well I'd be in bed.'

'The telephone was ringing – well, every one in the hotel rang at the same time.' Mariah said as he pulled the wool from her ears.

'Impossible. Can't be, not in a month of Tuesdays,' she

117

replied as the cotton wool in her nose blew back and forth like the pendant of a small Baltic state. 'Only way that could happen is if someone was ringing from the Captain's office and he's in prison.'

The telephone rang again. Mariah and Mrs Mukluk stared at the receiver as it jangled and clattered on the desk. Mrs Mukluk hesitated, her hand reaching out and then darting back.

'Would you?' she asked as the cotton wool dangled from her nose and the light for room 237 flashed on the board. 'It'll be that awful Mr Lucius, he always snaps at me and mutters under his breath.'

Mariah reached out and took hold of the telephone. 'Hello, Prince Regent Hotel.'

'Mariah?' the voice sighed. 'You sound tired – working hard, are we? Mr Zogel invites you to his room to look at the *Irenzee*. It has been illuminated just for your enjoyment – *now*.'

There was a sudden loud click and the telephone went dead. He knew it was Lucius. The voice was cold and sharp like broken ice.

'Don't look so worried,' Mrs Mukluk said as she saw the frown on his face. Mariah placed the ivory receiver back on the brass cradle. 'You fret too much, Mariah. Sometimes life seems to be dark and lonely, then all will change.' Without thinking, she reached out to touch his face and then suddenly pulled her hand away. 'He's only trying to be nice – since Captain Jack was taken away.' She spoke softly and tried to smile in between yawning and forcing her eyes to stay open.

'That's the trouble,' Mariah said as he watched a spider run over Mrs Mukluk's grey hair. 'I don't know what to do. Sacha has gone, Captain Jack is locked away and the business is ruined.'

'I know Sacha well enough and that girl won't be far. She has a temper like her father. And we all know Captain Jack killed no one. How things change in the time it takes for the sun to set,' she said in a trying-to-be-wise voice with another mouthful of yawn. 'Doesn't have to stay bad just because it is bad. I remember when my son Twink was your age. Always thought the worst of everything. Worried just like you – left home twenty years ago and I haven't seen him since . . .'

'Really,' Mariah replied not knowing what she was talking about.

'Still,' she went on as she rattled a small packet of powder in front of him. 'Doctor Cornelius has seen me right and now I don't worry at all. Told me to get some rest and find a job.'

'Zogel wants to see me. Do you think I should go?' Mariah asked.

'No harm in finding out what he wants,' she yawned. 'Not a guest in the hotel apart from him so it would be polite to call in. Business as usual, that's what the Captain would want.' Mrs Mukluk yawned again and struggled to keep awake. She held up her head with the palm of her hand and rested her elbow on the desk. 'While you're gone I'll have a little nap – been a long and tiring day. Twink could come home tonight and I wouldn't want to be too tired to wish him well. It's been twenty years,' Mrs Mukluk said with a lopsided smile.

Mariah took the steam elevator to Zogel's floor. He opened the gate and turned left. The corridor was empty and yet he felt he was being watched. It was always the same, whenever he was alone he felt as if a pair of eyes burrowed into the back of his head and tried to read his thoughts.

He remembered the first time that it ever happened. It was his fifth birthday. He had been taken to visit Gladius Garveenie, an elderly relative and the inventor of the four-wheeled penny-farthing cycle, who lived in a large house on the edge of Hampstead Heath. At some point Mariah had wandered off to explore the corridors and rooms on the floor above the morning room where his aunt was having tea. He knew he had been away for some time as the sun had changed its position in the sky, and as he wandered the empty rooms he suddenly realised he was lost.

It was as he walked into a large, grubby room with shuttered windows and cobwebbed frames that he had the intense feeling that someone or something was standing behind him. At first he dare not look and as the sensation grew more intense, to the point of him wanting to scream, Mariah had turned. For a moment he thought he had caught the slightest glimpse of a man in the shadows of the corner of the room. A voice within that sounded like his father told him to run. Mariah had broken into a gallop and blindly fled from the room. By chance he had found his way to the stairs and as a servant had reached out to take hold of the screaming child he had leapt the balcony and fallen to the floor below. As he looked up, he was sure in his own mind that he had again seen the man from the room. Now, whenever he was alone and walking in such a place, he felt he was being watched and sometimes even followed.

Mariah counted the numbers on the doors of the suites as he walked, hoping to distract himself from the feeling of being watched. 209 . . . 213 . . . 215 . . . 217 – as he passed the door he heard a noise inside the room. It sounded like someone had coughed and cleared their throat in a long moan. He stopped and looked back along the corridor and shivered. The sound came again, and this time it was as if he could hear someone shuffling with old feet across the wooden floor in carpet slippers.

He tapped lightly on the door three times and waited. The noise stopped. He tapped again.

'King's Suite, 217,' he said to himself as he read the name plaque and stared at the brass number on the dark stained wood, realising this was the suite where Baron Hoetzendorf had stayed. 'Hello,' he said softly – hoping he was alone and knowing the room should be empty. 'Do you need anything?'

There was the sound of a glass falling and smashing on the floor and the rattling of a wooden sash window opening. Mariah tried the door. It was locked.

Taking the master key from his pocket he placed it in the lock and slowly turned the lever. The lock snapped open and the door jumped an inch. He pushed slowly and could see the glow of the light from the window that overlooked the square at the front of the hotel.

The door opened by itself. Mariah stepped inside. He looked behind the door and then to each corner of the room. He kept to the wall as he checked under the bed and behind the sofa. By the window was a low mahogany table. All was just as the Hoetzendorfs had left it before they had gone to the midnight ball. A pair of fine leather shoes was on the hearth of the fireplace. A jacket was laid across the back of a chair and Madame Hoetzendorf's glasses were on the dressing table.

On the table by the window were a scattering of printed letters on squares of card that formed a circle of the alphabet and on the floor was a broken glass. The window was open and a breeze blew the drapes across the table, scattering the letters on the dusty wooden floor.

Mariah quickly shut the window and slipped the bolt in place. 'Must be the wind,' he said out loud to break the spell of silence that locked his nerves deep within and made him shiver. He looked up and saw the mirror above the fireplace. It reminded him of Packavi and as he looked at the glass he expected him to appear in the dark reflection.

As Mariah looked about the room he realised that everything was slightly out of place, as if someone had moved the furniture and had not put it back as it was. On the table by the bed, next to a half full glass, was a leather glove. Carefully, Mariah picked it up and without thinking slipped it on his hand to try the size. It was soft and well worn and as it touched his skin he realised it was still warm. Mariah quickly took it from his hand and stuffed it into the front of his coat. 'Someone was here,' he whispered to himself without thinking.

He stepped from the room as fast as he could, pulled the door firmly shut and turned the lock. He stood for a moment and listened and then looked along the corridor. In four paces, Mariah turned the corner on to the landing outside Zogel's door.

Outside room 237 was a tall man in a blue uniform with gold braid on the shoulders. He was as tall and as wide as the door, with a white cap pulled tightly over his shaved head.

'What do you want?' he asked quickly, sneering at Mariah.

'Lucius has invited me to see Mister Zogel,' Mariah answered.

'Why should Mister Zogel want to see you?'

Mariah didn't have time to reply. The door to room 237 opened and Lucius stared out in to the dark hallway.

'Took your time, Mariah. Mister Zogel doesn't like to be kept waiting,' Lucius said as he ushered him inside and led him into the sitting room.

The room was lit with several candles placed on the mantelpiece above the fireplace. It was cold and breezy as the night air flooded in through the open windows. Mariah noticed that all the furniture had been rearranged and a bed sheet now covered the gold mirror that hung on the far wall. Zogel sat in a large leather chair wrapped in a gigantic bearskin coat as he puffed on a fat cigar.

'Good to see you, Mariah. Hotel still doing business?' Zogel wheezed as if someone held him by the throat.

'You all right, Mr Zogel?' Mariah asked.

'He's fine, none of your business,' Lucius chided him quickly before Zogel could answer.

'The boy can see I'm not well, Lucius. You'll have to forgive him, Mariah. We've been together for a long time and he thinks he's my nursemaid.' Zogel coughed as he spoke. 'If truth be known, that's why I'm here. I have all the money in the world but lack one thing that makes it all worthwhile. I thought I may find what I need here at the Prince Regent, but since Captain Charity is locked away it looks as if I have searched in vain.'

'What did you want?' Mariah asked.

'Heard the water here could do me some good – that and the galvanised bathing machine and the seaweed pie.' He sighed loudly as he puffed on the cigar once more.

'You need your medicine, Mister Zogel. Send the boy away and get some rest,' Lucius insisted.

'I got the *Irenzee* ready just for him. Come, Mariah. Look at what I have for you to see.' Zogel nodded as he spoke. In the corner of the room another man in a blue uniform lurched from the shadow. Mariah stepped back as the man took two torches from the side table and signalled to the ship. There was a sudden, powerful and blinding explosion of bright light as the searchlight flashed its reply. It blistered the darkness of the room, momentarily turning night to day. The frame of the window smouldered in the heat. 'They are ready,' Zogel said quietly as the servant stepped back. 'Look at the ship, Mariah – what a spectacle to see.'

Mariah looked on as the *Irenzee* began to change colour and the sea around it began to glow. First it shone gold and then white and then turned to blue. It was as if the colours pulsed from deep within, like a heartbeat in the depths of the ship.

'What more could you ask for on a night like this?' Zogel asked as he smiled.

'It's amazing – how can it do such a thing?' Mariah asked, as the light from the ship got brighter.

'That's a secret, and one that many would pay a fortune to know. But watch this,' he said as he pointed out to sea.

It was as if he gave an unseen command. There was a blast of the ship's siren as the foremast was raised from the deck and the funnel appeared from the roof of the cabins. Then the ship suddenly vanished and the sea was empty.

'Imagine a whole navy that could not be seen, Mariah. What an invention that would be – they could sail up to an enemy and destroy them completely, as if they were attacked by ghosts . . .'

Mariah wasn't listening. His eyes searched the sea for the *Irenzee*. Where there had once been a vast ship was now just an open stretch of water.

'Where did it go?' he asked.

'You are the magician's apprentice – you tell me,' Zogel wheezed.

'Too much excitement. You'll have to go,' Lucius said nervously, as if he didn't want Zogel to answer. He took Mariah by the arm and began to drag him to the door.

'Lucius,' Zogel said as if to tell him to stop. 'It's good for me to have company and Mariah is now a powerful young man – he is in charge of this magnificent hotel.'

'But you need to rest,' Lucius insisted.

'I'll have eternity to rest and while my heart beats I will enjoy myself,' Zogel said as he waved for Mariah to come closer. 'It's a trick of the light, Mariah – the ship is just where it was but we cannot see it.'

'You could show him in the morning Mr Zogel,' Lucius persisted as he tugged at Mariah yet again.

'Perhaps you're right, and Mariah will need all my help if we are to free Captain Charity,' Zogel said reluctantly as he flicked the remains of the cigar through the window and watched the red embers fall like a shooting star. 'You best be going – and by the way, whatever I can do to help you, just ask.'

'Do you think we can get him from prison?' Mariah asked as the dwarf pulled him from the room urgently.

'We can try, Mariah. I believe a man to be innocent until proven guilty and from what I know of Charity he is not a man who would blow up his guests,' Zogel replied slowly as he turned and slumped back in his seat wearily.

'Wait for a moment,' Lucius snorted at Mariah. 'He needs his injection.'

Lucius disappeared into the next room and quickly came back with a small leather case. Opening the case he produced a glass syringe fitted with a short needle. He rolled back the sleeve on Zogel's arm and injected the brown liquid deep within the skin.

Zogel lolled his head back and forth and groaned as the linctus seeped through his veins.

'Now it is time for you to go,' Lucius insisted. 'Mr Zogel will be well in the morning and will help you then. Now is not a good time.'

He spoke quickly; his words were as sharp as his eyes. Mariah watched Lucius take out the needle as he walked towards the door.

'Mr Zogel wouldn't want you to see this – he is a private man. You must tell no one,' Lucius insisted.

As Mariah opened the door to leave he looked back for one last time. In that moment, as Lucius was talking quietly to Zogel, Mariah saw what looked like long strands of thick mist circling the chair in which Zogel now slept. In the darkness of the room, they whirled this way and that, weaving in and out of the legs of the chair. Like three long grey snakes, they swirled about Lucius, who gave them no attention. They were similar in every way to the longs strands of mist he saw when he used the divining spectacles, and like the ghostly serpent he had seen by the fireplace. This time they seemed to be pouring from Zogel himself, as if his soul was oozing from his nose and mouth as he slept. Just before he slipped from the room, Mariah looked again, and whatever it had been had, in an instant, now completely vanished.

[12]

Grimm and Grendel

IN the long, dark passageway outside suite 237 there was a definite feeling of gloom. The guard stood silently and didn't even speak as Mariah left the room and quietly closed the door. As he walked down the hallway, Mariah had the urge to look back to make sure he was alone. With every other step he turned his head and looked over his shoulder.

In his heart he felt a sense of foreboding. As he walked, all he could think about was finding Sacha and getting Captain Jack from prison. He felt alone and didn't know where to start. He shrugged his shoulders and tried not to step on the lines in the carpet.

As Mariah walked towards suite 217 he began to feel his stomach twist and churn. He didn't want to go by the door. The thought of walking to the far end of the hotel and going down the stairs filled him with dread. Mariah looked back. The passageway was empty and silent. In the distance, a small amber light illuminated the doorway to the steam elevator. It glowed warmly in the cold, dark corridor. From far behind, Mariah heard a door slam shut and then footsteps. It had to be Lucius or one of Mr Zogel's guards – the hotel was empty and all the guests had gone apart from Zogel and his entourage. Mariah turned to look but could see no one.

Before he knew it, he was outside suite 217. Instinctively he tried the handle just to make sure it was still locked. To his surprise it opened. He looked inside, peering in the dim light. Strangely, the room was tidy. The lettered cards that had been scattered across the floor were now in a neat pile on the coffee table. The drapes were drawn and everything was just as it should be. There was also a faint smell of perfume and tobacco. Mariah fought back a welling fear. Rooms don't clean themselves, he thought, as he looked at the clothes that had been spread across the room now hanging neatly from the rail.

There was another waft of the perfume. It smelt of apples and roses and clung to the roof of his mouth with its sickly sweetness. It was as if it came from behind the heavy green drapes that were pulled tightly across the window.

Mariah was about to step forward and peek behind them when a sudden thought made him look down. He had caught something out of the corner of his eye, or knew instinctively that all was not well. There at the bottom of the curtains were the tips of two polished black shoes. They stuck out from the fabric as if a man hid on the other side in the bay of the window. Mariah didn't know what to do. Everything within him told him to run.

In desperation, he grabbed a long candlestick from the sideboard near the door as he crept closer. He held his breath as he raised the weapon above his head ready to strike. He took two more steps and then with all his strength aimed a single blow at the drapes. There was a soft thud as the candlestick struck against the velvet, and then nothing . . .

With one hand he cautiously pulled back one side of the curtain. There on the floor was the pair of shoes, placed in such a way as to show the place of someone hiding. It was then that the door of a large mahogany wardrobe burst open. A figure leapt across the room. Mariah jumped back and dropped the candlestick and as he was pushed to the ground he caught a glimpse of a man running from the room.

He got to his feet and ran as fast as he could. Far ahead he heard the thudding of footsteps on the floor. In the shadows he could just make out a figure running. He chased after it, not thinking of any danger. The figure turned and pushed open the doors to the metal stairway used by the servants. They circled down and down. Mariah followed, avoiding the swinging doors, into the darkness. He could see nothing. Far below he could hear footsteps clattering against the metal treads. Whoever it was ahead of him knew their way, he thought as he followed on breathlessly.

There was a flash of light from the landing below as a door opened. Mariah ran on wanting to see the face of who had been in the room.

'Be it anyone but Packavi . . .' he said to himself as he ran.

Mariah got to the door and pushed against it. For some reason it would not move. He pushed again and heard the jangling of chains holding it fast. Quickly he ran to the landing below and, taking the steam elevator, went up one floor. He could see that the door to the stairs had been chained and bolted on the outside.

'They know this place,' he said as he looked along the landing but could see no one.

Mariah waited for a moment to get his breath, hiding in the doorway to a room. He listened for any sign of the man. All was silent but for the rumbling of the steam elevator and the whirring of the generator as it sucked the steam from the earth to power everything in the hotel.

On the carpet by his feet was a neatly folded handkerchief that looked as if it had been placed for him to find. Taking one corner he held it to the light by the steam elevator. There, embroidered into the silk were the initials C.V.B. Mariah could think of no one with a name to match and, taking the divining spectacles, he tuned in the device and looked along the passageway.

As if looking into another world, Mariah could see a trail of vapour footsteps. They swirled in red and green threads of mist and from the way they danced from the carpet, he knew that they had just been made. He followed. The divining spectacles caused the whole of his sight to glow bright green. There were marks upon the floor that could not be seen by human eye but easily gave away the trail of the man.

Daring to go faster, Mariah trotted and then ran. The vapours grew brighter as if each step had just been taken. They twisted and turned along the labyrinth of corridors until they came to an open window high above the beach.

Mariah looked out, above a safety ladder that stretched far below as a way of escape. He stared down as the wind blew against him. In the dark of the night he could vaguely see a shadowy figure drop from the ladder to the promenade below.

Reluctantly he followed, fearing to look down and tightly clutching the rusted metal ladder that swayed back and forth with each step he took. His hands shook as he went as fast as he could. The vapours of the man swirled about him like a thicket of barbed stems. Again he could smell the sickly sweet fragrance of apples and roses. It hung in the air as if it clung to the bricks of the building.

Soon Mariah was on the promenade. The trail was easy to find and wound in and out of the bathing machines that stood in rows like candy-striped houses stuck on horse carts. A track of red footprints led up the steps of one machine, in through the door and then out the back and onto the beach.

Far ahead he could see the man running towards the pier.

Mariah knew he was too far behind to catch him and thought he could do nothing if the man was Packavi. He slowed his pace to a walk and watched the man disappear amongst the fish huts and oyster stands. Ahead, he could see the lights of the Golden Kipper and beyond that the harbour. It brought the memory of Sacha and Captain Jack and the nights they had spent together eating fried fish and wedges of potato and onion.

In the time since he had left the Colonial School, it had been those nights in the Golden Kipper that he had treasured the most. It was the closest he had felt to having a family. Sacha would laugh as Smutch told stories of the sea and Captain Jack would sit and shake his head in disbelief at the tales of such an old man.

Somehow all this had been lost after the Captain had taken over the Prince Regent. Mariah had seldom seen Charity smile, and laughter had become a stranger in his company. It was as if some dark thought weighed down upon him and Mariah could do nothing to help his misery. If he could shift the sands of time and go back in some machine to those nights he would. For so long at the Colonial School he was a stranger to happiness. This was something he now sought in friendships – but never found.

Now, as he strode through the sand and spray from the cold sea, friendship was all he wanted. Whatever it took he would carry on to the end. Life was not worth living unless he made things right again, he thought as the wind whipped his face. Even in this adversity, he believed that nothing would stop him. His mind was fixed on finding Sacha and seeing Charity free once more. But even in that thought he hoped that future circumstance would change what they had all become, and as he walked on he began to cry. They were tears of deep remorse, anger and helplessness. He thought of his mother and father and all he could see was their bodies covered by African sand with vultures flying overhead. He didn't know their true fate, but his imagination had created this as their end.

The divining spectacles continued to show him the tracks of the intruder in suite 217. Soon Mariah had crossed the sand, walked the length of the pier and passed the Golden Kipper. In the upstairs restaurant he could see a man and a woman dining by the window. They held hands in the candlelight and looked at one another. In the doorway of the ice-cream parlour a man slept, wrapped in newspaper and oblivious to the world around him. Next to him an alleyway led from the harbour into the old town.

On the corner, a Peeler stood in his cape keeping watch. He smiled at Mariah as he passed by.

'Bit late in the night for a lad like you to be out,' he said as he rubbed the whiskers on his face.

'On my way home, Constable,' Mariah said. 'Off to Paradise.'

'If only I could find it myself,' the man snorted as he tapped the brim of his helmet with a gloved finger.

Mariah walked into the darkness of the alley, leaving the light of the harbour far behind. The divining spectacles led on; the vapours were stronger and more intense, as if the intruder had waited for Mariah to follow. He could see no one and walked slowly and as quietly as he could. It grew darker as the houses stacked themselves upon each other to form peculiar catacombs of yards, fish sheds and sleeping rooms. There was noise everywhere: children were crying, dogs barked and men shouted. And there was the foul stench of the cess that trickled through the streets to form small streams that led to the sea.

He walked on for five minutes until the houses grew larger and neater as the hill got steeper. The higher you lived the cleaner the air and quieter it became. On each side of the road were tall buildings with fine iron railings. Higher still was the shadow of the old castle with its broken battlements. Set into the castle wall was a long brick house with a grey slate roof.

The street was empty. Every few yards were gas lamps that lit the road ahead. On the sidewalk were the telltale signs of the intruder that could only be seen with the divining spectacles, allowing Mariah to see clearly the footprints that he followed. From the way in which they were spaced it looked as though the man had a limp or that one of his legs was shorter than the other.

The trail led up the hill, through the churchyard, across the street and through the gates of the Towers. Mariah waited by the high wall and looked up at the dark house. The high, pointed roof was etched against the night sky. The wind blew wisps of clouds and rattled the branches of the trees like sabres ready for war.

As he waited, a light came on in the same room as before when Lucius had visited. A figure came to the window, looked out and then pulled down the blind against the glass. The clock in the church struck midnight. As if reminded by its calling the man came to the window and looked out yet again.

It was then that Mariah heard the rattling of the wheels of two carriages, as if summonsed by the clock. They came closer, driven quickly along the stone road. As they approached, he could see that the horses were draped in black with feather plumes upon their heads. The first carriage had glass sides that reflected the doors of the fine houses in the light of the gas lamps.

He could now clearly see that this was in fact a hearse and mourners' cart. The driver was dressed in black with his scarf pulled across his face. The hearse turned into the driveway of the Towers and disappeared amongst the trees. The mourners' cart followed on. Its windows were shuttered so that no one could see inside.

'No one would be buried at this time,' Mariah said to himself as he crouched in the shadows to get a better look.

From the long garden of the Towers in the shadow of the palm house, Mariah watched the small procession come to a halt. The door to the house opened, bathing the hearse in a golden light. It shone brightly as a servant came and stood at the threshold holding a carbide lamp. No one spoke. Three men got out of the hearse and they and the driver took a small coffin from the back and carried it through the high doorway.

Then the door to the mourners' cart opened and out stepped two strange women. The first was small and quite rotund, the other very tall and very thin. Both were dressed in long skirts and tight jackets that squeezed them at the waist. They appeared to be quite ungainly and uncomfortable. The tall woman kept on shrugging her shoulders as if to shake the jacket from her back. The first thing that Mariah noticed was that they could hardly walk in their shoes. It was as if each one was filled with glass. The women tiptoed painfully towards the door, holding each other's hand.

'Stupid idea,' the tall one grunted as her fat companion fell to the gravel drive. 'Why do we have to do this?'

'So we're not discovered,' the other squealed as she attempted to stand straight and talk at the same time.

'If we're discovered dressed like this we'll –'

'It worked – we got the body and now she's with us, and we'll be waking the witch,' her friend interrupted quickly as she bowed to the servant at the doorway before they both vanished inside to be consumed by the golden glow of the light.

The door was slammed shut. The garden was drenched in darkness and the grey-blue shadows of the moon returned to cast gnarled hands across the shingle drive. Mariah waited in his hiding place. There was a familiarity about the voice – he had heard it often before. Quickly Mariah realised that despite their macabre disguise the two women were in fact Grimm and Grendel, so-called detectives . . .

As he waited, the light of a downstairs room shone above his head as the shutters were drawn back. He crept closer through the overgrown plants and under the canopy of gigantic hog-weed that grew up like a forest of trees at the side of the gravel drive. Mariah could hear muffled voices. They jabbered in the room above him as the shadows fell against the glass.

'We can't keep her here,' Mariah heard Grimm say.

'Not for the night – it is not safe,' he heard another voice say.

Mariah crept even closer. To the side of the window was an old ornamental pot stand. It was covered in ivy and dead Virginia creeper and looked like the wizened head of an old man. Taking hold of the fall pipe that ran from the roof and down the wall, Mariah put his foot on the stand and looked through the side window of the room.

From where he stood, he could just see Grimm standing by the fireplace. On the other side of the room was Mr Grendel. He was reclining in a shabby leather sofa with his petticoat around his ankles and his large bare feet stretched out towards the fire. The room was brightly lit by lamps and candles that flickered against the walls. The flames of the fire changed their faces constantly from black to red as they bathed them in light and shadow. In the corner by the door was the coffin that had been brought from the hearse. The lid had been removed and the body removed.

'Bet you never thought you'd ever travel like that – did you, girl? Not when you were alive. Think of the privilege to see the inside of a coffin before you are dead,' Grendel said as he snivelled and rubbed his swollen feet.

Mariah couldn't see who he was talking to. The room was large and filled with old furniture; all he could think was that in the far corner of the room was the girl.

135

'Cat got your tongue?' Grendel asked when there had been no reply.

'She has a gag in her mouth, Mr Grendel – it is impossible for her to talk and you were the one who placed it there so you should know.' Grimm spoke curtly as his shadow crossed the window just where Mariah was eavesdropping.

'She could mutter or mumble. Very impolite just to sit there in silence staring at me with those sorrowful eyes. It's not as if we're going to kill the witch – just keep her until her father does what we've told him and then she'll be free.'

'Would have been different with Gormenberg – at least he knew how to treat a prisoner,' Grimm replied in a melancholy voice. 'If you tell anyone where you've been, girl, then you won't be going home to your father, understand? See, Mr Grendel, that's how you get them to reply – nodding away, she is. She knows what we mean.'

'But does her father? If he doesn't do what we've asked him then the Templar will not be a happy man,' Grendel said.

'He'll do it. He has to – that's if he wants to see his precious again,' Grimm snapped as he paced the room.

'But why did we have to dress like this?' Grendel shouted.

'How else could we snatch her from the street? You are the most well-known face in the town apart from the church clock. Anyway, I quite like it. It makes me look –'

'Stupid, that's how they make you look – like an overgrown owl,' Grendel replied as he shrugged his shoulders.

Mariah edged his way closer and closer to the window to see if he could see whom they were talking about. He stretched one leg from the jardinière and the other to the metal railings that ran under the window and down the cellar steps. One hand gripped the narrow cracks between the stones, the other held to the strands of the creeper that covered the front of the house. Leaning out as far as he could, he peered around the stone mullion.

From where he was now perched he could see Grimm and Grendel clearly. Grimm stood with his back to the window, shadowing whoever was sitting in a winged chair that had been pushed into the far corner of the room in a small alcove. Grendel slouched on the leather sofa near the fire. They were both dressed in the most ludicrous costumes Mariah could ever imagine and looked as if they had modelled their look upon the most cantankerous of creatures they could find. Grendel had painted his face with rouge and lipstick, whilst Grimm swished his posterior closer and closer to the flames of the fire. His bustled dress whooshed back and forth like the feathers of some gigantic fat bird.

Mariah leant out even further to see who was in the chair. With a sudden crack the jardinière snapped and fell from its stand. Mariah fell, and as he did he clutched the top of the mullion and hung in mid-air like a startled monkey, his face pressed grotesquely against the glass.

The sound echoed around the house. Grimm turned with a start and stared him in the eyes as Grendel jumped to his feet.

'MUNDI!' they screamed together as Grimm stepped back in complete surprise, the shock wrinkling his face like an old Aunt Sally.

'Get him!' screamed Grendel as he searched the room for his shoes to give chase.

As he hung from the mullion, Mariah saw Sacha for the first time. She was bound and gagged and looked at him with frightened eyes.

'Don't let him escape!' Grendel screamed even louder as Grimm jumped out of his way and stepped onto the fireplace, his dress wafting in the flames.

Mariah looked down to the drop below. A line of sharp black railings ran the length of the window and followed the steps to the cellar door. They pointed fearfully upwards to where he dangled precariously, holding on to the stone mullion with stretched fingers.

He looked into the room and saw Grendel run to the door. Sacha twisted in the chair as if she was trying to escape, whilst Grimm fought to extinguish the flames that now leapt from the back of his dress.

'I'm on fire!' he screamed as he rolled on the floor to put out the burning mass of bolsters and crinoline.

'Quickly, Grimm, before he escapes!' Grendel shouted as Mariah saw him leave the room.

Outside, in the chill night air, Mariah could feel his fingers stretching and slipping from the stone. He looked at Sacha through the misted glass and tried to smile as he clung to life. He heard the bolts on the front door being opened one by one as the sound of Grendel's commotion billowed from the hall-way. A chink of bright light broke the darkness of the garden. Mariah looked down into the black pit of the cellar steps. Unable to keep their grip any longer, his fingers slipped from their hold and Mariah fell into the blackness.

[13]

Paradise Mislaid

IN less than a few seconds Mariah hit the floor at the bottom of the cellar steps and slumped against the rotten wooden door. It smashed open, giving way quickly as he fell forward into the pitch-black room. It had a stench of damp wood and rotten apples. From outside he could hear Grendel screaming for Grimm to come to his aid as he skipped across the gravel drive in his short stiletto heels. In the blackness Mariah scrambled to his feet as fast as he could and looked for somewhere to hide. He knew he could not be caught. There would be no bargaining for his life, and now his eavesdropping had even put Sacha in jeopardy.

He stumbled over a pile of broken chairs and an old bicycle with one wheel. Grendel's shouts drew ever closer and now Mariah could hear that more people had joined the chase. Blindly he stumbled on, not knowing where to run. He searched the walls for a doorway but was unable to see even a hand in front of him. The blackness swirled around him without a single piece of light to show him the way. Mariah fell against the wall as his foot caught in the spokes of the bicycle wheel.

Footsteps came slowly down the cellar steps as the swinging of a lantern reflected off the walls.

'He must be down here,' Grendel said sharply as he stood at the door, hesitating to enter the vast cellar that stretched out in the gloom before him.

More footsteps echoed down the steps. Mariah hid in the darkness and waited as Grendel held the lantern above his head and peered into the vast dome-shaped room.

'How can we find him in there?' he asked as Grimm scurried inside the cellar.

'We have to look for him. Should have known he would come looking. How do you think he found us?' Grimm asked as he kicked over an old perambulator by the door.

'Never know with that boy. We should have finished him when we had the chance last time. I knew Monica wouldn't have the guts to kill him. You should have done it, Grimm.'

'I'll do it now if I find him,' Grimm replied as he drew a revolver from a purse he had strung over his shoulder and pulled back the hammer with a loud click.

Mariah could hear Grimm's footsteps getting closer. He twisted his foot from the wheel and moved as quietly as he could, slithering along the floor.

'I can hear him, Grendel,' Mr Grimm shouted as he aimed the pistol and fired a shot in the dark.

There was a sudden flash as the bullet blasted from the gun, then a deafening explosion as the bullet ricocheted around the cellar, bouncing from the floor and embedding itself in the wall behind Grendel's head.

'That could have killed me, you fool!' Grendel screamed as he got up from the floor. 'It missed me by an inch.'

'He's there,' Grimm insisted as he picked his way through the debris of boxes and old wardrobes that filled the cellar.

'And so am I – and I don't want you to forget that when you

fire the gun,' Grendel moaned, worried that the only person Grimm would shoot would be him.

'Stay by the door – he can't escape again,' Grimm replied as he drew closer and closer to where Mariah was now hiding in a stack of rolled carpets.

Mariah held his breath. He could feel Grimm close by. There was a scent of roses and sweet apples. Grimm didn't speak as he searched for him in the dim light of the lantern that Grendel held by the door.

Grimm could see nothing in the faint light. The cellar was cold and foreboding. He listened hard, hoping to catch the briefest clue as to where Mariah was hiding. He stumbled forwards in the dark, the rolls of carpets tumbled about him like falling trees. Mariah was curled up at his feet like a rat frightened to move.

'Are you sure he came this way?' Grimm asked, hoping he would have to look no more. 'He can't be here – nowhere for him to hide.' As he turned to move his foot pinned Mariah's fingers and pressed them into the soft earth floor. Mariah knew he could not call out in pain.

'I . . . I heard noises.' Grendel hesitated before he replied.

'So he might not be here at all?' Grimm asked as he stepped from Mariah's hand and made his way through the cellar and back to the light.

'I just thought –'

'Just thought he could be here?' Grimm replied with obvious annoyance as he bustled by Grendel in his burnt dress and scorched camisole.

'He fell from the window,' Grendel protested.

'But not in here,' Grimm replied earnestly.

'Perhaps not . . .' Grendel said.

'Perhaps he ran off back to the Prince Regent,' Grimm said quickly as footsteps came down the steps.

'Then *I* would have seen him,' said a voice from outside the cellar.

'Inspector Walpole – how nice of you to come,' Grimm flustered.

'Having trouble?' Walpole asked as Grimm hid the gun in his purse.

'Just a burglar,' Grendel replied. ' But he appears to have . . . disappeared.'

'Can't have anyone burgling the Towers – what would the Templar think to that?' he asked.

'Dismayed, Inspector Walpole, he would be dismayed,' Grimm said feebly.

'He would indeed, and he wants to speak to you upstairs,' Walpole said.

'But we have to find him – he could still be hiding,' Grimm protested.

'He wants to see you and he can't be kept waiting,' Walpole snapped as he went on. 'I'll have one of my men stand guard. If your burglar tries to escape then we shall have him. Time is pressing in our task and we cannot let anyone distract us from it. If he is here he will do us no harm,' Walpole said as the cellar door was pulled shut and the bolts slid across.

Mariah sat in the darkness and listened as the procession of footsteps climbed the cellar stairs. He felt in his pocket for the phosphor torch that he always carried in his jacket. Just as he was about to charge the lamp he heard the sound of leather soles on the gravel outside the cellar.

Following a small chink of light he made his way to the door and pushed against it. It was stuck tight, the bolts barring his way. He followed the walls around the cellar, hoping to find another way out – there was nothing. Then, just as he was about to give up in despair, his hand felt the jagged corner of the brickwork. There was a strong draught that sucked air from the room, and he was sure that high above he could hear voices.

'A chimney,' he said to himself as he felt his way into the large alcove where the kitchen range had once stood.

From above him he could hear the whispering of voices and the crackling of the fire. He knew that the chimney would be wide enough to take him, but was unsure if there would be any way of escape from the roof. The walls of the alcove were smooth brick, with damp plaster hanging in places.

Mariah ran his hands to find a finger-hold and just as he was about to give up came across a narrow crack in the wall. He pulled hard and wedged his feet against the sides of the alcove as he reached up. Step by step he made his way higher. Within six feet the smooth brick gave way to coarse stone, which made it easier to climb. The walls became hotter as he got nearer the room above and the voices became louder. He could hear them speaking clearly.

'If he comes out of the cellar door, then one of my men will be upon him,' Mariah heard Walpole say.

'And what about the girl?' Grimm asked.

'Take her to the castle and we'll keep her there until her father does what we have asked of him,' Walpole replied.

'And if he does not?' said a voice that Mariah had not heard before. It sounded cold, dark and edged with gin.

'Then, sir . . . she will have an accident and be found below the bridge,' Grendel said slowly.

'If her father won't help us then we cannot succeed. I have come too far for all this to fail,' the man said in his gruff voice.

'Sir, you should not worry – I would do it myself, but I have my position in the town to think of,' Walpole grovelled. 'Mr Grendel or Mr Grimm should help us out of our predicament.'

'I hope they will, I hope they will. Has Mr Lucius reported to us?' the man asked.

'He is with Zogel,' Walpole replied.

'Then all is well at the Prince Regent. I was disturbed when I was searching suite 217. I think what we are looking for is still there. See to it that it is found immediately, Walpole,' the man said as Mariah heard heavy footsteps cross the floor.

'And what of the boy – Mariah Mundi?' Grimm asked slowly, as if mentioning the name would be a bad omen.

'Kill him. At your first opportunity, kill him,' the man said in a matter-of-fact way as he left the room.

There was silence; all Mariah could hear was the crackling of the fire logs. He climbed higher. The walls of the chimney grew so hot that soon he could barely touch them. They were drenched in soot that covered him like a fresh fall of black snow.

'Better get the girl and take her to the castle,' Mariah heard Walpole say.

'I'm not going dressed like this,' Grendel replied.

'Shame,' Walpole scolded. 'I thought you looked . . . fetching.'

'Then I'll look fetching in a suit and tie with shoes that fit,' Grendel snapped back as he stamped from the room.

'I hope your friend can be trusted in this, Mr Grimm. I employed you because you were the best detective in the business and I don't want to be let down. When her father does what we want him to do – I expect her to fall from the heights of the castle to the sea below, understand?' Walpole said quietly.

'Kill her anyway?' Grimm asked in disbelief.

'Loose ends, Mr Grimm, loose ends,' Walpole replied. 'She'll talk and the secret will be out.'

Sliding his hands into the sleeve of his coat, Mariah pressed on silently. He didn't know what to think – he couldn't believe an inspector of police would be prepared to kill. What Walpole had said was repeated over and over in his mind. Loose ends . . . All Sacha and her father were to Walpole were loose ends.

Smoke filled the chimney until it grew thick and choking

black. Mariah climbed even higher until he got to the open fireplace of the room above. Slipping through the mouth of the fireplace he was soon in the room. It was cold and empty and the moon shone in through frosted windows. For a brief moment he caught his soot-stained reflection in the glass.

Mariah listened by the door. He could hear the complaining of Grimm and Grendel below. He twisted the handle and, pulling gently, knew the door was locked from the outside. It was then that he heard footsteps on the stone tiles of the hallway. They were crisp and bright and edged with steel. The front door opened and then shut suddenly. Mariah looked out of the window and in the dim light saw the tell-tale figure of Inspector Walpole walking down the drive and into the night. By his side was a tall man and in the man's hand was a silver-capped walking stick. There was something about him that was familiar: Mariah knew it was the man he had followed from the Prince Regent.

Mariah watched the two men until he could see them no more. It was as if he stared at a vast puzzle that made no sense. He picked at each piece in his mind but could find no connection between them. He had found Sacha and knew he would have to help her escape – but he could not think of a way of freeing Charity from Dean Prison. Now he knew that Walpole was willing to kill, Mariah realised that unless Charity was set free by any means he would face the gallows.

Below, the hearse and the mourners' cart were still in place on the corner of the house by the cellar steps. Mariah could see the shadow of a Peeler waiting beneath the window. Quietly, he slipped open the sash and looked outside. To the left was the low roof of the palm house. Mariah looked at the Peeler who leant against the wall with his arms folded.

In one silent stride, Mariah was on the roof of the palm house, keeping as low as he could. Within a minute he had shinned down the drainpipe and was in the overgrown garden. Soon he was deep amongst the giant hogweed. He knew these plants well. At the Colonial School there had been a game where new boys were beaten with their barbed stems. They would blister in the sunlight, leaving extraordinary scars for many weeks. Mariah quickly lost this thought as he crawled through the undergrowth until he could see the door to the house. He knew that if they were to take Sacha to the castle they would have to go that way and he would be ready.

From his hiding place he could see the Peeler by the steps. He wondered how Walpole should be involved in such a crime as kidnapping Sacha. Who would believe him? Who would believe the evidence of a lad like him against an inspector of police? Mariah knew he needed something that could not be doubted; his word alone was not good enough.

As Mariah waited underneath the enormous leaves of the hogweed, he realised that this had now become a matter of life and death and his own life would be changed for ever. Not only had Walpole arrested Captain Charity, but now he planned the death of his best friend and her father. Whatever was to happen, Mariah knew he could not fail in his task.

It was then that the large oval-topped door of the Towers opened slowly. A thin face peered out and looked back and forth. Then, without waiting, a regal procession of black-clad undertakers in elaborate top hats carried the coffin from the house and placed it in the hearse. Grimm and Grendel followed and slipped quietly into the mourners' cart. The carriages turned around the large araucaria tree in the centre of the drive and slowly processed along the gravel towards the gate.

Mariah waited until the hearse had passed by and then followed, keeping pace with the mourners' cart. He weaved in and out of the trees until he neared the gate.

The carriages clattered on the road as they gathered pace.

Mariah ran on in the shadows, keeping to the high wall that edged the road. He breathed hard as the horses began to slow on the steep hill towards the castle. Far ahead he could see the light from the gatekeeper's fire. It shone against the locked doors of the outer tower that guarded the bridge spanning the deep ravine of the castle dyke. Mariah knew that the carriages would be allowed inside and that he could go no further.

The mourners' cart rattled from side to side on the blunt stone cobbles. Mariah ran as hard as he could and, taking hold of the back of the cart, jumped aboard and hid himself in the luggage rack.

'What was that?' he heard Grimm ask Grendel.

'Was nothing,' Grendel replied as the carriage jolted from side to side.

Mariah kept silent, hoping the carriage would not be searched, hoping more that he would not be found. He pulled the tar rug over him and curled as tightly as he could in the pit of the rack. Soon the horses began to slow down as they approached the gate.

'Who comes at this time?' shouted the gatekeeper through a small arrow-slit in the wall.

'Grimm and Grendel, detectives,' shouted Grimm in reply.

'Watch out for the dogs – they run loose and will eat a man given the chance,' the gatekeeper said.

Mariah heard the large door open slowly, creaking on its hinges. The carriage rolled on slowly, the wheels slipping on the smooth stones that that lined the road from the outer tower across the bridge and up the steep hill to the castle keep.

The deathly procession didn't stop. The gate closed behind them with a clatter and a long iron bar was slid across the doors.

'Mariah Mundi will trouble us no more in this castle,' Grendel said as the carriage struggled up the hill.

'I have no more concern for Mariah Mundi. I need to talk to

147

you about something – something important,' Grimm said tentatively to his companion. 'I do not like the circumstances of this night.'

'Speak plainly, Mr Grimm,' Grendel said as Mariah listened.

'This is not the place, nor is it the time. But we should speak soon – for I am afraid of what we shall be asked to do.'

'What we have to do is look out for ourselves. That which does not destroy us makes us stronger – has that not always been our motto, Grimm?'

'But I am afraid it is we who shall be destroyed. We are employed by a power that I care not at all for. Gone is the enjoyment, Mr Grendel, gone. We are detectives, we are select. But now we are henchmen for *him* – a man who wears a mask to hide his face.'

'He pays us well,' Grendel replied as the carriage came to a sudden halt.

'But what shall we pay in return?' Grimm asked as the door to the carriage opened and the cold night air gushed in like the chill of a death. 'Is there no help for the widow's son?'

'It's already too late for us, Mr Grimm. The tide has turned on our lives and the water is about our throats,' Grendel said, sensing his companion's hesitation. 'We shall have to see this to the end no matter what, and when it is done we can be free of it.'

'Having met *him* – I think we will never be free,' Grimm said as he stepped from the carriage into the dark night.

'Enough, enough,' Grendel whispered so as not to be overheard. 'We take the girl to the guard house and leave her there. We wait until her father does what is required and then let her go – what could be more simple?'

'That would have been good enough, but now, my dear friend, things have changed. Walpole wants her dead – thrown from the cliff and into the sea – and her father is to be killed as well,' Grimm replied as they walked behind the coffin. 'He called the girl a "loose end", and I fear we too may be loose ends that need to be tied up – and it is from what height that bothers me . . .'

[14]

The Cellist

MARIAH waited until the only sound he could hear was the wind whistling amongst the chimney pots and around the broken-down castle walls. Some time before, he had heard the footsteps of the men dressed as undertakers as they removed the coffin from the hearse, and he had heard too the church clock strike the third hour of the morning. Under the tar rug in the back of the mourners' cart, Mariah huddled as tightly as he could to keep out the cold. It bit at his fingers and stopped him from thinking.

It had been his hope that the undertakers would return and the procession would leave the castle and he could escape. At any moment he thought the door to the guard house would open and the carriages would slip quietly away and into the night.

Mariah waited and waited. Then, just as he began to feel that they would never come, a door opened. He peered from under the canvas and saw four men cross the yard. They had changed from their top hats and dark coats and were now dressed in the suit of Peelers.

'Police?' Mariah said to himself, unable to keep the words in his mouth. From his hiding place he could see that one had three sergeant stripes on his arm that glistened in the moonlight. None of them spoke as they got onto the hearse. With a sudden jerk the mourners' carriage set off. He knew that he would have to wait until he was out of the gate and then he could leap for freedom and get help.

Even before he had finished the thought, the sudden, dark and terrifying realisation came to him that there was no one to help. Charity was in prison, Sacha was captured – he was alone. The carriage trundled on down the hill. Mariah heard the driver call to the gatekeeper. The brake of the hearse squealed as it was held against the hill that led down into the town. Then, without warning the mourners' cart stopped suddenly. The driver jumped to the ground and turned the carriage. He could then hear the horses being unstrapped and led away. They were still inside the castle.

Quietly, Mariah pulled back the canvas cover and peered out. It was dark; the carriage was beside the wall of the castle. He could hear the driver talking close by. The sky was full of thick silver clouds edged in moonlight. They blew quickly from the north, tumbling as they rolled across the sky. He knew he would have to escape. The driver could return at any time and find him hiding there. Then it would be too late both for him and for Sacha.

There was laughter from the shadows. Mariah heard a door open and shut suddenly. All was then quiet. He slipped quickly from his hiding place and, keeping to the wall like a sewer rat, made his way from the gate. The hill was steep and the pathway strewn with rocks. Built into the wall, some way off was a large brick building with a slate roof. It was bleak and windowless. A single chimney blew smoke out to sea. He knew this was the guard house and that inside was Sacha.

Indescribable desires within him made him want to steal her

back right there and then. All he wanted to do was take an army and beat down the door and fight for her. He knew how she would look and what she would say and could even hear her voice in his head. They would stand back to back and fight – just as they had done before, and she would bellow in her Irish accent that he loved so much. Then they would escape and run – she a yard faster than him, running like a wild horse that would never stop.

With these thoughts flooding his mind, he stalked the walls. In a few moments Mariah stood by the guard house where it was built into the castle wall. There was a small stone privy with a flat roof. The door was shut tightly, the paint flaked from the wood by the beating of the wind. High above, under the eaves, was a solitary window lit by a candle. Mariah could see that it was a ship's brass candlestick made in such a way that it would always keep the candle upright, even in the most violent of storms. It sat, out of place, on the window ledge, and behind it – in shadow at first, but then clearly illuminated by the candle – was Sacha. She was looking out of the window. She lifted both hands to her face and cupped her cheeks, covering her eyes for a moment. Mariah knew she was crying. It stirred the anger in his heart, which beat in his chest loud enough to burst his ears.

It was then that from nearby, Mariah could hear the mournful sound of a cello. It played and then stopped and then played again. It was as if whoever commanded the instrument gulped for breath at the end of each line of music. Still it went on, giving the night a feeling of warmth and unreality. The music came from within the guard house and could clearly be heard in the cold night air.

Mariah climbed the privy wall, onto its roof and then onto the outer wall of the castle. Far below were the harbour and the lights of the town. In the distance, he could see the Prince

Regent. It looked dark and empty, silhouetted against the sky. From the sea came a haar mist, thick and black. It ran through the streets like the fingers of a witch casting a cauldron spell. It hugged the cobbles and covered the sea, leaving the *Irenzee* like a steel island in the bay.

He had soon climbed onto the long roof of the guard house, where he rested against a warm chimney pot. Then, crawling across the slate, he made his way quietly to a solitary skylight cut into the roof.

In the room below he could see the light of the candle and the flickering of a fire. Whatever was to happen, he knew he had to get inside and find Sacha. But before he could move again, the door to the room opened and Grimm stepped inside. He carried a tray and on the tray was a solitary cup. It steamed, the hot brown liquid bubbling in the pot mug. He placed the tray upon the table by the fire and without speaking left the room.

The church clock sounded the fourth hour of the night and was echoed by the foghorn of the lighthouse that warned of the coming of the haar mist. Mariah cast a glance to the town below. The dense fog had filled every street to the rooftops and had walked every alleyway like a myriad of ghosts haunting the dark places. It was thick and impenetrable like the flank of a dark, faceless, invading army.

Below him, Sacha had gone to the table and taken the cup in both hands. Mariah looked down and saw that she held it more for the comfort of its warmth than the brown liquid she did not want to drink. He watched her for a moment, wondering how he could gain her attention without her screaming. She was still dressed in the uniform of a magician's assistant. Her long black trousers and black jacket were dirty and creased from her confinement in the coffin. Mariah could only see Sacha – but he didn't know if she was alone. Grendel could be keeping guard inside the room, or somewhere very near.

Sacha stared into the mirror above the fire. Mariah could see her reflection. She looked angry and cold. She shrugged her shoulders and screwed up her face, then sipped the broth. Mariah gently tapped the glass with the tip of his golden finger. Sacha didn't move. He could see her eyes look about the room as if she wasn't sure what she had heard. He tapped again.

Slowly and carefully, Sacha put the mug of broth on the fireplace and turned from her reflection. She looked about the room and then, just as he tapped for a third time, she looked up. Mariah gestured for her not to speak. Sacha went to the door and listened and then, taking a chair, she lifted the catch on the skylight.

'Where did you go to?' he asked in an angry whisper.

'I went nowhere – I was kidnapped,' Sacha said quietly as the wind blew into the room.

'Give me your hand – I'll pull you out,' Mariah said as he reached down for her.

Sacha stood on the chair and reached upwards, taking hold of his wrist. Mariah pulled and pulled but couldn't lift her any further.

'It's no use,' he said as Sacha dangled above the chair before he let her go and she fell to the floor with a loud thud.

The sound of the cello stopped momentarily. It was as if the player had heard the thud and listened to hear if the sound might come again. Mariah thought quickly and then slipped in through the window and dropped quietly to the floor. Without speaking, he stood on the chair and slipped the catch back on the skylight and then looked about the room. It was warm and plain, with a bed by the window, a fire and a blanket box. There was a small parlour chair by the fire and an old rug. Hanging from the ceiling were coils of rope and rusted lifting blocks.

'I have to get you out of here,' he said desperately.

'They'll let me go. They have me for a while and then –' She stopped as the words stuck in her throat as if she didn't want to say what her father had to do.

'I know. It's your father,' Mariah replied in a whisper.

'If you get caught here it'll make things worse. They'll just keep me for three more days and then I'll be gone.'

'For good,' he said without thinking. 'I heard Grimm and Grendel – they won't let you go.'

'But they told me – my father, he . . .' She flustered her words as she looked to the floor.

'Will turn another blind eye?' Mariah asked impatiently.

'It'll be no harm – it's just money,' she argued.

'They're going to kill you and your father. I heard them talking and Grimm has been told to throw you from the cliff and then have your father killed – even if he does help them. We have to get you away from here tonight. Things have changed – Captain Jack has been arrested for murder, the Prince Regent is empty and all the guests have gone apart from Mr Zogel.'

'Doesn't mean they'll kill us,' Sacha argued in a faint whisper.

'If Walpole is involved in all this then it is serious business, Sacha.'

'But not to die for?' she asked.

'Whatever they are planning to do involves your father looking the other way. Whoever is behind this has the power to involve the police and to fit up the Captain for murder. So don't think they won't kill you.'

Sacha looked at the fire as the sudden import of Mariah's words came to her.

'We'll not get out, Mariah,' she said suddenly. 'Grimm and Grendel are downstairs, and if we did get out of here then we wouldn't get out of the castle.'

'There's always a way, Sacha – whatever.'

There was the sound of footsteps on the wooden stairs outside the room. They seemed to walk in time with the music from the cellist as he bowed the strings far away. Sacha looked at Mariah.

'It's Grimm. Hide!' she said quickly.

Mariah hid in the blanket box by the bed. The door opened and Grimm stepped inside.

'There's been a slight change . . . of plan,' he said, stuttering over each word. 'Things are moving quickly and –' He stopped speaking and sniffed the air like a water rat. 'I can smell something . . .'

'It's the fire,' Sacha said as she tried to yawn.

'Not fire I can smell,' he said as he sniffed about the room. 'It's the smell of the night – cold fog – grass and mischief. It's the smell of a damp dog warming itself by the fire.' Grimm looked wildly about the room. 'You got someone here?' he asked.

'Who could I have here with the door locked and you and Grendel downstairs. My father won't like this Mr Grimm – he knows I am here.'

'He thinks you're at the Towers and I don't care what he thinks,' Grimm said as he sniffed even more. 'There's someone in here – I can smell him.'

Grimm sniffed closer and closer to the large blanket box at the foot of the bed. His eyes searched for the tiniest clue that all was not right. He ran his stubby finger along the floor and then across the lid of the box.

'Who you got hiding here?' he asked Sacha as she took a pace towards the fire. 'I can see from your face that you're hiding something or someone.'

'You're mad, Mr Grimm – who could I hide in this room? How did they get by you?'

Grimm looked up. There, dangling from the catch of the skylight, was a small piece of fabric torn from Mariah's coat.

Grimm looked at the chair nearby and saw footprints in the dust.

'Doesn't take a great detective to see that – does it?' he asked as he pointed to the footprints. 'Came in through the window on the roof – you must have let him in – and is now hiding in this box.' Grimm took a pistol from the pocket of his coat and aimed it at the long, thin box. 'Makes an ideal place to die – can just bury him in that – eh, Mariah Mundi?'

Grimm spoke as if he knew who was hiding in the blanket box – gone was the discontent from his voice.

'There's no one here,' Sacha pleaded. 'I had just opened the window to get some air – you can smell the sea.'

'Footprints – torn cloth – the stink of fear,' Grimm gloated. 'Come out, boy, and let me see your face once more.'

There was no sound. Sacha stared at where she had seen Mariah hide. Grimm waited, pistol at the ready. He pulled back the hammer until it clicked, ready to fire.

'Last chance, Mariah Mundi – last chance!' Grimm shouted.

'He's got a gun – come out, Mariah!' Sacha insisted.

Grimm kicked open the lid of the box and pointed the pistol within. The box was empty.

'He was here,' Grimm said as he looked about the room. 'So why did you trick me?'

'I never . . . I thought –'

'He can't just vanish, can he?' Grimm asked as he turned his back to the bed.

Sacha stared in disbelief. Rising from the shadows in the corner of the room, like a spectral ghost, was Mariah. He picked the washing jug from its stand and quietly followed Grimm across the room as he walked towards Sacha. He stalked him step by step. With each pace he drew closer until he was within a distance to strike.

'You going to tell me where he's gone?' Grimm asked,

unaware he was being followed. 'Tell me or it's going to hurt – hurt very badly,' he said, pointing the gun at her. 'Sadly for you, Miss Sacha, there has been a change in plan. There are powers that believe you shouldn't live beyond this night. Get your things – we are going on a short journey.'

Grimm didn't finish what he was about to say. As the man spoke, so Mariah struck. It was a single blow. Hard, fast and aimed to the back of Grimm's head. There was a dull thud and then the sound of splintering pot, which exploded into a thousand shards. Grimm slumped to the floor with a dreary groan.

'Told you they would kill you,' Mariah said in the way he always did when he thought he was right. 'Best be taking this,' he went on as he took the pistol from Grimm's still hand.

'How did you get out of the box?' Sacha asked. 'I saw you hide in there.'

'Easy. I *am* a magician's apprentice,' Mariah replied, finding himself smiling for the first time.

Grimm groaned and tried to lift his head from the floor.

'We'll never escape,' Sacha said as Grimm tried to get to his feet. 'There are men downstairs and we'll never get out.'

'We have no choice,' Mariah replied as he stepped over Grimm's body, knocking him to the floor yet again. 'There must be more than one way from this place.'

'They brought me up the stairs – but there was a landing off to the right. There is a barrack room below with a mess hall to the side – that's all I could see when they took me from the coffin.'

'Then we'll go this way,' Mariah said, pointing to the long hallway that led from the open door to the rooms in the attic of the guard house. Mariah stepped out of the room and took a last look at Grimm. He appeared to be unconscious, his face buried in the rug by the fire. Sacha followed on. Just as she was about to step outside a hand grabbed her by the ankle. She turned and saw Grimm clutching at her leg. He seemed unable to speak and mouthed words she could not understand. Sacha tried to shake him free. His grip became tighter and tighter.

'Mariah,' she said under her breath hoping he would hear. 'Quickly! Grimm has me . . .'

Mariah came back into the room and quietly closed the door. Grimm moaned, trying to remember how to speak.

'Get off her, Grimm,' Mariah said as he held the gun to his head.

Grimm just smiled, unsure what was happening, knowing only that he had to keep the girl where she was.

Mariah looked up, took a coil of rope from a hook on the ceiling and prised Grimm's hand from Sacha, and then he tied the man up as tightly as he could. Together they coiled the rope around the detective until he was like a fat wasps' nest and unable to move. Grimm's head lolled from side to side as he dribbled down his cheek.

'Leave him here,' Mariah said as he pushed Grimm onto the bed and then wrapped him in the thick blanket. 'Stay where you are, Mr Grimm,' Mariah whispered in his ear, 'and if you ever try to kill Sacha – you'll have to kill me first.' Mariah stuffed a corner of the blanket in Grimm's mouth. 'Until we meet again . . .'

Grimm smiled and winced at the same time. It was as if he couldn't understand what Mariah had said.

Closing the door behind them, Mariah and Sacha crept onto the gloomy landing. It was lit by a smoking oil lamp above the furthest doorway. Mariah could smell fermenting cabbage and lamb stew. Far below he could hear snoring and the crackle of a fire and from somewhere nearby the sound of the cellist playing on and on. He wondered why so late at night, and why no one had told the player to stop. The sound was haunting and sent a chill through his spine. It reminded him of the music he would hear as he passed old Bloomsbury churches with black carriages outside and crying people. It was sullen and joyless – and it came from behind a door on the landing.

'Who can it be?' Sacha asked as they got nearer to the door.

'We can't chance to find out,' he replied as he passed the door and noticed that the key was on the outside and the bolt slid firmly shut. 'Whoever is in there is a prisoner.'

'We could set him free,' Sacha said as she stopped and glanced at Mariah. He walked ahead along the hallway. She knew she had to look in the room. She knew she had to turn the key, slide back the bolt and look inside. It would be so easy, she thought. She looked again as Mariah stopped and turned to see where she was. Sacha saw him shaking his head, his eyes wide and his words apparent in his face. She turned the lock, slid the bolt back with her long fingers and pushed against the door.

For a brief moment the music stopped, and then it started again. Sacha stared into the darkened room. The light from the lamp in the hallway cast a shadow across the cell. It was cold and without a window on the world.

'Who's there?' she asked softly as the cello continued to play.

Sacha was aware of Mariah standing nearby.

'We can't do this,' he said softly, the words warm against her face. 'We have to go, alone . . .'

Mariah pushed the door wider. There, in the shadows of the room with his face to the wall, was a man. He was sat with his back to the door, the neck of the cello pressed against his left shoulder. At his feet was a walking cane and a rolled cape. There was no fire, no light, nothing but the cello and the chair. The man ignored their presence. He played on frantically. The music grew faster and faster. Sacha wondered how his fingers could touch the strings. It was as if a hundred hands picked out the tune.

'Beautiful,' she said forgetting where they were.

The music stopped suddenly as the man dropped the bow to the floor. It was as if her words had brought it to an end. In the darkness, they saw him turn to them and smile. Then, as the light was cast upon his mask, Sacha screamed. She had seen the man before. He had gripped her tightly and squeezed out her breath as if to kill her.

'Packavi – the slayer,' Mariah said in disbelief.

Haar Mist

P ACKAVI jumped towards the door and grabbed Sacha by the cuff of her jacket. Mariah panicked and fired the gun. Two loud explosions rattled in the room and in surprise the masked man let go.

Sacha pushed Mariah from the room ahead of her and had the presence of mind to kick the door shut behind them. Mariah turned the lock and slammed the bolt.

The house burst into life. Packavi banged and screamed upon the door, calling Mariah by name. From the rooms below came the sound of men shouting. Grendel's voice carried upwards, shrill and cold. He screamed loudly for Grimm as he woke from his sleep. Footsteps then pounded on the three flights of stairs. Grendel ran ahead, blaring for Grimm as he wondered who had been shot.

Sacha and Mariah ran the length of the landing towards the light. The stench of fermenting cabbage grew even stronger. At the end of the corridor was a small window that looked out over the castle wall. Mariah could just see the lighthouse on the end of the pier. The mist surrounded it, with only the light showing above the fog. It gave bursts of bright light that shone over the top of the clawing mist as if from the summit of a mountain looking down at the clouds.

Mariah opened the window, took out his handkerchief and threw it onto the wall below. It caught on the overgrowth of leafless bramble stems that grew from in between the old stones. Sacha wondered what he was doing. She could hear the footsteps beating their way up the stairs. She knew that at any moment Grendel and his men would appear and they would be captured. To her annoyance, Mariah calmly put his footprint on the window ledge and then pushed her through a small doorway that led under the eaves. Outside, the window flapped back and forth as they hid in the dark. The footsteps got closer. Doors banged. Men shouted. Grendel prowled the corridor until he found Mr Grimm.

'Who did this?' they heard him scream. 'Then he shall be caught,' Grendel said, replying to the answer they could not hear.

Sacha and Mariah stayed silent, crouching under the roof and covering themselves in a discarded hessian sack.

The door of Packavi's cell rattled on its hinges with his manic beating. As he went by, Grendel checked the lock and pushed the bolt deeper within its keeper.

'It's not your time,' Grimm said apologetically as he walked behind, rubbing the rope marks on his wrist. 'We are to keep you here until *he* says you can go out again. Don't worry, Mr Packavi – it will be soon.' Grimm's voice trembled.

'*Now* is the time,' Packavi shouted through the crack that ran the length of the door. 'The boy is here and I have seen him – let me out to finish what I have to do.'

'Silence!' Grendel screamed as he stamped his feet against the dusty floorboards that ran the length of the attic corridor. 'If we find the boy we will give him to you – now be silent.'

Packavi stopped banging upon the door of his cell. The music started again as swiftly as before.

'He will have to be let loose – regardless of what the Templar may think,' Grendel chuntered as he walked along the passageway.

'But look at what happened,' Grimm replied. 'Too many, far too many . . . And now the boy has a gun. What shall we do?'

'Do?' Grendel asked as he took a magnifying glass from his coat pocket and examined the marks on the open window. 'Do? We shall do what we always do, Mr Grimm – we shall investigate and when he is found he will be punished.'

'And the girl?' Grimm asked with a hint of hesitation.

'*And* the girl – if that is what the Templar requires then that is what he shall have.'

'But I'm not sure if it would be a good thing,' Grimm said as he pondered what was ahead.

'Money, Mr Grimm, money – nothing more, nothing less, and this shall be our last employment. Think of it, Mr Grimm – we could leave this place and live in San Francisco – imagine that – we could be whoever we wanted to be . . . True to ourselves and amongst our rightful companions in life . . .'

'It's when I look at my hands, Grendel – even though they tremble I see them covered in blood, and it's not my own, but the others'.'

'Poppycock, Mr Grimm. It's your imagination. Let us find the clockwork monkey Mundi and his companion and despatch them with great haste. There is a ship that leaves Liverpool in five days – we could be upon it and gone for ever.'

'We could just let them go.'

'No!' screamed Grendel as if his companion had said too much. 'Look. The window. Footprints. There,' he said, pointing below to the luminous handkerchief blowing in the breeze. 'That is where they have gone. Quickly!'

Grendel pushed Grimm back along the landing. He didn't notice the small doorway cut into the wooden panel. Inside,

Mariah and Sacha sat in the darkness. They didn't speak. Mariah held Sacha's hand and felt the soft skin of her fingers.

They listened as the footsteps ran along the landing and then down the stairs. A door opened to the yard outside the guard house and voices carried through the window. Men shouted in pursuit and the barking of a large dog filled the cold night air. From the small cell along the corridor the sound of the cello carried on.

They waited until they could hear nothing but the music.

'They're searching the grounds,' Mariah said quietly as he heard the faraway call of the dog.

'How will we get away?' Sacha asked. 'The castle wall is too high to jump from.'

Mariah crawled to the small doorway that opened onto the attic landing. He opened the door just a crack and peered outside. The lamp above him cast a long shadow to the stairway.

'We'll take our chances, Sacha. If I get caught, you can't go to the police. Just get out of the town and don't come back,' Mariah said as he helped Sacha from under the eaves.

Silently they passed Packavi's cell door. The music played on. Turning the stairs they crept to the floor below. It was one large room with beds on either side and in the middle was a large stove with a blackened kettle that steamed away. At the far end was an open door.

They quickly crossed the wooden floor. The door led down two flights of steps into a mess hall below. On the stove in the corner was the pan of lamb stew and fermenting cabbage. A long table ran the length of the room that was lit by two oil lamps. The tiles were spread with straw and, hiding in the corner, a solitary rat watched as they crept through the room.

'How will we get out? Grendel and his men will be waiting – and they have dogs,' Sacha said as Mariah searched the room. 'What are you looking for?' she asked.

'A key – ammunition – anything,' he replied as he emptied a jar of stale biscuits on the table.

It was then that Sacha saw two small folding doors inlaid into the floor by the stone fireplace. On one was a metal clasp the size of a fist, and above it was a rope fitted with a pulley block. A thick iron hook dangled from the rope just above their heads.

'There's the cellar,' she said as the barking of the dogs drew closer. 'I heard my father talk about it – rumours of a way out, a tunnel from the castle to the town.'

'There must be another way,' Mariah snapped without thinking as he looked for a way of escape from the guard house. 'The windows,' he said, pointing to the narrow cuts in the stone walls that were barred with iron rods.

'They're coming,' Sacha said as the sound of Grendel and the search dogs came closer. 'We can't stay.'

The door opened. The night rushed in. Grimm, Grendel and two soldiers with dogs walked slowly into the mess hall. Without them even noticing, the shutter on the cellar lowered into place, not quite closing. Sacha peered up into the room through a tiny gap. Grimm slumped into a chair by the fire, out of breath and complaining about the cold. The dogs circled and turned, then lay down at his feet.

'They would never have got over the wall,' Grendel said as the two soldiers took off their coats and went upstairs. 'They must still be in the castle.'

'I care not for all this, Grendel. They are better gone, better gone, I tell you. Too much trouble and for no return. A madman in the attic and a girl on the run – am I bothered?' Grimm moaned and spat out the words angrily as he took off his shoes and rubbed his feet.

'Her father will do what we say – if he doesn't then he'll be swimming to the bottom of the ocean,' Grendel replied as he took a swig from a small bottle of green linctus.

From her hiding place, Sacha watched his every move.

'I don't enjoy this any more, Mr Grendel. If we knew why then it wouldn't be so bad. But we are kept in the dark, Mr Grendel, in the dark. Do this, says Walpole – do that, says Walpole – and we do it without question. I preferred it when we were solely matrimonial detectives – matters of the heart, that's where we should have stayed. Intrigue has its disadvantages.'

'It pays well – tickets to San Francisco, Mr Grimm, a new life.'

'Then let's leave tonight – forget all this and go now.'

'I'm staying, staying until we have done the job. I want to see the end of Mariah Mundi and Jack Charity. I want that satisfaction. If Walpole is right then Charity will be tried for murder and the boy as his accomplice and whatever Templar wants from suite 217 will be found.'

'What could be so special that *he* would be prepared to see the downfall of the Prince Regent so he could have it?' Grimm asked as he toasted his toes against the flames and watched the steam rise from his socks.

'Something so wonderful that he would be prepared to take the building apart brick by brick – that's what he said to Walpole, brick by brick,' Grendel said excitedly as he paced the room.

'And what of Packavi?' Grimm asked.

'A distraction, a smokescreen, and an assassin, Mr Grimm. The Templar knows best and we should not contradict him in any –'

There was a sudden thud as the cellar door dropped into place. A dog by the fire growled as a spiral of dust billowed in the air.

'The cellar!' they said together in the sudden realisation that they were being overheard.

Grendel dived for the handle to lift the flap just as the sound of the sliding bolt screeched loudly as inside Sacha locked the two doors.

'Quickly, Grimm, get me something to open the doors,' Grendel said as he pulled on the handle in vain.

Grimm looked up and, seeing the block and tackle dangling above, untied the rope and let it fall. It crashed onto the doors missing Grendel's head by an inch as it rushed past him.

'Could have killed me,' Grendel shouted as the dogs barked and the soldiers ran down the stairs.

Grimm slipped the hook through the door ring and began to pull on the rope. Soon the soldiers and Grendel took hold. The rope quickly tightened in the pulley and the doors to the cellar buckled against the thin bolt.

Sacha and Mariah stared at each other.

'This must be the place my father told me about, there must be a tunnel – if only we could find it,' Sacha said as the doors above her head began to splinter and Grendel's screams grew louder.

Mariah took the phosphor torch from his pocket and unscrewed the cap. There were three pieces of white, salt-like lumps that he knew when placed in the chamber would give light. Taking one small piece he put it into the lamp and screwed on the lens.

'It has to be somewhere nearby,' she said as she held out her arms and the light from the torch burst on her face.

The cellar went on into the distance and faded into black as the vaulted roof arched above their heads. The walls dripped with damp that formed rivulets of green fungus hanging down in long beards.

Grimm and Grendel shouted for them to stop as they battled against the doors. By now, someone was hammering against the wood with an axe, and splinters fell into the cellar. Ahead of Mariah was a stone wall. He shone the torch. There in the corner he noticed a small alcove. It was made of the same stone but in the beam of the light looked different. A draught of air wafted a long cobweb that blew like a tantalising finger.

'That has to be it,' he said as the axe crashed through the door and Grendel's face appeared above them.

'Mariah Mundi – it *is* you,' said the detective as he stared at him upside-down through bloodshot eyes. '*And* his lovely sweetheart – how quaint.'

'Get back, Grendel – I'll shoot,' Mariah shouted as he aimed the pistol and shone the lamp in Grendel's face.

'So brave – so talented – so stupid,' Grendel said as he tried to force his head through the hole and the barking of the dogs grew louder.

Mariah didn't hesitate. He aimed the gun, closed his eyes and squeezed the trigger. Grendel screamed as he pulled his head back, knowing what was to come. The blast echoed through the guard house as the bullet exploded from the gun. Grendel slumped back on the tiled floor, holding his face.

'My nose, my astonishing nose!' he shouted as he held his face. 'Monkey boy has shot me.'

Grimm pulled Grendel's hand away. The bullet had taken the tip of Grendel's nose from his face.

'Get Packavi, Mr Grimm,' Grendel cried as he got to his feet and mopped his face with his handkerchief. 'Send in the dogs and the madman. Mundi has three bullets left – one for each of them and then we'll have him and I shall have my pound of flesh.'

'The madman and the dogs!' Sacha said as they ran towards the alcove.

'Don't worry, Sacha. There will be a way out of this,' Mariah said hoping she would believe his foolish words.

Once in the alcove, they found the entrance to the tunnel. It had been clumsily built into the wall and fell quickly away as it ran down to the town. Mariah shone the torch ahead of them. The dangling cobwebs formed dark shadows on the walls like a crowd of onlookers moving back and forth in the murk.

Sacha coughed on the choking fumes. 'What is that?' she asked.

'Firedamp,' Mariah replied. 'It's a gas, we can't stay here – too dangerous, it could explode.'

Even in the tunnel were the traces of the haar mist. It seeped through the drains above and crept through the narrow fissures between the large stones that formed the walls. The mist filled the bottom of the tunnel so that it looked as if they walked through clouds. It swirled about them, forming ghostly hands that reached up in the fading light of the phosphor torch. They slipped on the wet stones as they walked, their feet crunching on broken bones and the carcasses of dead rats.

It was only at the edges of the torchlight, just where the shadow met the brightness, that Sacha could see them. From every crack in the wall, every crevice and fracture, Sacha noticed tiny pink and red eyes staring at her. They glared as she walked by and they sniffed the air. The noise of scurrying and scratching echoed in the darkness. The higher up the wall, the bigger they seemed to be, and the deeper they walked into the tunnel more and more appeared – *rats*!

At first Sacha didn't want to admit they were there. Her father forbade her to say their name for fear that misfortune would fall upon them. If one came into their house they would salt the walls and pour vinegar on the floor and ask St Anthony to rid them of it. Every boat in the harbour was the same and no captain would put to sea if one were seen.

Sacha had been told a story that once, long ago, when her father was young, a boat had entered the harbour with a cargo of masts for the shipyard. In its hold there had been a plague of rats. In the dark of the night the hordes had jumped for the shore and swam in the tide.

At night they attacked the grain store and ate the salt fish, and worst of all they bit the children. From All Angels to All Souls time they had cursed the town. The bailiffs had called for a wanderer to banish the plague. He had come with his burning cross, shaken his bag of bones and chanted from the castle cliff. The rats turned and ran into the sea. Like a seething carpet, they drowned in the waves and took with them their pestilence and even the mention of their true name. Never were rats to be talked of in the town at the end of the line.

'Long-tails,' Sacha said reluctantly as more and more of the creatures began to run about her feet. 'Long-tails.'

'Rats, Sacha. Nothing to be afraid of,' Mariah replied as his words echoed through the tunnel.

From far behind they heard the commotion as the doors to the cellar were ripped from their hinges and the barking of the dogs grew nearer.

'Run!' Mariah said as they were set in the chase.

'They'll soon catch us – we can't outrun them,' Sacha replied.

'Then let them eat bread,' said Mariah, and he took the bag of hex from his pocket and scattered its explosive contents on the floor and down the stone walls.

'What is it?' Sacha asked as the rats fought one another hungrily.

'Hexogenamite – the explosive that killed the general,' he explained. 'When they eat it they will explode and we don't want to be here when they do.'

Together they set off running down the tunnel. The haar grew thicker and the phosphorus lamp weaker. It became just a dull glow that could hardly cast a shadow in the mist. Soon they had snaked their way deeper and could hear the sound of the sea. They spoke a little as they ran, Mariah telling Sacha of all that had happened at the Prince Regent. He coughed out the words whenever they stopped to look back.

Suddenly, the barking of the dogs as they gave chase went deathly still, as if the dogs had found something. Then it came: a sudden, low rumble and a flash of bright light as if it thundered above them. The tunnel began to tremor and roar. Coming towards them was an immense black, burning cloud of gas. Roaring and snarling as it gathered pace and scorched the damp from the walls, it turned into a vast, all-consuming ball of fire . . .

[16]

Ghosts

MARIAH pushed Sacha to the floor of the tunnel. 'Cover your face!' he shouted as the roar came closer and all around them the methane gas began to explode. 'Wait until it is past.'

There came a sudden rush of air as the fire sucked its life from the tunnel below. It was as if they were in the centre of a whirlwind. The fire-flash cracked above their heads like a thunderstorm as it blew away the mist. Sacha buried her face in Mariah's coat and covered her ears. The light was intense and as hot as the sun, burning the back of her hands. Then there was silence, a long and lasting silence. It was eerie and still, with not a single sound.

The phosphor torch rolled back and forth on the floor of the tunnel where Mariah had let it fall. Their shadows were cast against the roof of the tunnel and moved from side to side. They lay together, knowing they had to wait.

Mariah looked back to where they had just come from. It was obvious that the rats had exploded and ignited the gas built up in the tunnel. He knew that if Grendel had been near then he would surely be dead. Nothing could have survived the blast.

As he was about to tell Sacha his thoughts, he heard the first sound. Beginning like a whimper, it turned into the lament of a hound crying at the full moon. Then came marching steps in time with the ticking of a clock. Heavy footsteps edged in steel beat solidly against the stone slabs. The click of a cane hit the middle beat between the footsteps as someone strode confidently towards them through the darkness.

Mariah shone the faint beam of the torch up the tunnel as he wondered who had survived the explosion.

'We can't stay,' Sacha said as she began to run.

Mariah followed and, taking one last glance behind, saw a dark figure coming towards him.

'Packavi,' he said as he heard the drawing of the swordstick. 'Run, Sacha, run!'

They bolted headlong down the slope. Behind them the footsteps came on just as before. They neither quickened nor slowed, marching at the same steady pace, but strangely never seemed to get further away.

The tunnel curved. Mariah and Sacha were halted by a fall of rock. They climbed over the stones, Mariah pushing out several large blocks so they could get through. The footsteps came nearer and were now joined by the whimpering of a large dog that sounded as if it were being held back from the chase. Packavi had no light, but walked as if he could see in the dark.

On the other side of the rock fall, Mariah and Sacha ran on. When they had gone half a mile the tunnel narrowed so that they could not walk side by side. Mariah went ahead, using the dim phosphor torch to light his footsteps.

It was then that the tunnel stopped. Several thick metal bars formed a gate that appeared to be embedded in the ground.

'What do we do now?' Sacha asked as the sound of Packavi's footsteps drew even closer.

Mariah tried to lift the gate. It moved several inches and then slipped back.

'Here,' he said handing Sacha the torch. 'Cover the lens until I tell you and then shine it up the tunnel – I have one last surprise for Packavi.'

Sacha was about to do what he asked when she shone the torch through the gate. There, on the other side, was a long handle that came from the wall.

'That's it,' she said as her eyes lit up. 'That must be what controls the gate.'

Mariah pushed his arm through the bars, trying to reach the handle. His fingers could just touch the metal but he couldn't take hold.

All the while, the footsteps behind them trudged ever closer. Mariah pushed harder against the bars. His fingers stretched out. Taking the gun, he hooked its grip over the handle and began to pull as hard as he could. The handle began to move slowly and as it did so the gate lifted up inch by inch.

'Help me Sacha,' Mariah said as his hand stretched from the pistol.

There was a sudden lurch of the bars that snapped his grip on the gun. It fell to the floor on the other side of the gate. The pistol slid down the short slope and into the gutter, out of reach of Mariah's outstretched hand.

From out of the darkness they could hear the clatter of Packavi's footsteps. They came closer step by step.

'He's almost with us!' Sacha screamed as Mariah fought to push the gate higher.

'Get underneath,' Mariah said as he pulled on the gate and lifted it several more inches from the ground.

Sacha slid on to the floor and squeezed herself under the sharpened bars. With one hand she grabbed the pistol. She pushed as hard as she could to get through and as she did so she shone the torch back into the darkness. There, standing quite still and watching quietly, was Packavi. At his feet was a large snarling dog.

'Behind you!' she screamed at Mariah, who turned to face the killer.

'Never thought it would end like this, not in such a squalid place,' Packavi said as he let go of the leash that held the dog close to him. 'You killed the other beast with your little trick – very clever, Mariah Mundi, the great detective and agent of the Bureau of Antiquities.'

'Why do so many have to die, Packavi?' Mariah asked as he pressed himself against the bars of the gate and slipped his hand back towards Sacha.

'You would never understand – your sort seldom do. It has more to do with the construction of the universe than just wasted lives. The Prince Regent is the *sectio aurea*, built to a golden principle. You, Mariah, stand in our way –'

'*Our* way?' Mariah asked as he took hold of the pistol from Sacha's hand.

'I don't act alone – but that would be telling you both too much, for even in death you could still tell tales.'

'But the Prince Regent is just a hotel – why should it make you want to kill?' Mariah asked quickly as he held the gun behind his back and gently cocked the trigger.

'It is built on a grand design, to the principle of Fibonacci, by a great architect. You would not understand its significance. It is only when you take to the air and see it as a bird that its power can be understood.'

Packavi twisted the swordstick in his hand as if he made ready to strike.

'You're mad – and *dead*!' Mariah screamed as he pulled the gun from behind him and fired shots through Packavi's black coat and crisp white shirt.

There were three dull thuds. Mariah watched as Packavi fell backwards, the mask slipping from his face. The snarling dog at his side cowered away. Packavi staggered to one side, gripping his chest. He turned to Mariah, who stood motionless, wondering what he had done to the man.

'I knew you wouldn't shoot me in the head,' Packavi said as he picked the bullets one by one from his chest. 'And I am thankful for my metal jacket.'

As Packavi spoke he pulled open his shirt. There, like the skin of a bronzed statue, was a contoured breastplate of metal. Around the heart were three small indentions where the bullets had struck.

'Now it is your turn,' Packavi said as he stood upright, twisted the handle on his swordstick and stepped forward.

Without warning, he lunged at Mariah with the sword. The blade glanced against his sleeve and through the bars of the gate. Mariah stared eye to eye with the man. He could feel his breath against his face. Sacha pulled the handle of the gate, which suddenly and with great force was catapulted into the roof. She pushed Packavi back and grabbed Mariah. He fell backwards through the opening as she slammed the handle as hard as she could. The blade came again and again as the gate fell, snapping it from Packavi's hand. From out of the darkness the dog leapt towards Mariah. It forced its head through the gap between the bars and took hold of his arm. It twisted and turned, pulling at the fabric of his coat with its jagged teeth.

Packavi picked himself from the floor and laughed.

'Thought you'd get away?' he asked as he took the broken blade from the floor and examined it closely. 'Still enough to finish you, Mariah Mundi,' he said as he looked at him.

The dog held fast, pulling Mariah through the bars as it growled. Sacha struggled to hold on to Mariah. All she wanted was to pull him away from Packavi.

In the twilight of the phosphorus torch, Packavi sharpened the broken tip of the sword against the stones. Seeing what was to come, Sacha reached into Mariah's pocket and took a broken corner of hexagenamite and thrust it into the dog's mouth. It coughed momentarily and shook its head, then let go of Mariah's arm.

Packavi screamed. 'No! You will not escape!' he shouted as he thrust the sword at Mariah.

Sacha pulled Mariah from the gate, forcing him to the ground as the broken sword came towards her face. She grabbed Packavi by the wrist and held him fast as she kicked out at the handle of the gate.

Above them they heard the quick spinning of the winch and the turning of the gears as the counterbalance dropped. The gate shot to the ceiling, lifting Packavi from his feet and pinning his arm against the ceiling. He dangled like a marionette above them. Packavi was trapped, pinioned by the metal bars to the ceiling above.

'Don't think I won't get free!' he screamed as the dog began to choke.

The beast growled, foaming at the mouth. It shook its head from side to side as if to free itself from the invisible grip of the hexagenamite. Slowly the dog began to expand before their eyes as if it were filling with gas. It howled as it bolted into the darkness, and when it had gone just a few feet it exploded. There was a shower of silver dust as the animal evaporated.

Packavi dangled above them, pinned by his arm to the ceiling of the tunnel, his feet inches from the floor. Sacha shone the torch in his face.

'You are so lucky, Mariah Mundi,' he said. 'It will have to end soon.'

Mariah and Sacha looked up. In the torchlight they could see that the mask had been pushed to one side. The face beneath was hideous and grotesque, a caricature of a human form. It was etched in gilt, every line of the man's age lined in metal on the skin.

Hanging at Packavi's side was his arm. Mariah looked at the gloved hand and saw that the wrist shone in pure gold.

'I've seen this before,' he said to Sacha as he pulled the glove from Packavi's fingers.

There beneath was a hand made of solid gold. Its fingers were gripped like a fist, as if they had been formed purposely around the handle of the sword.

'Just like the tip of your finger,' Packavi moaned. 'It is not only Mariah Mundi who was caught with his hand in the Midas Box.'

'How do you know of that?' Mariah asked.

'We haven't time,' Sacha insisted as she began to drag Mariah away.

'I need to know, Sacha, I need to know,' Mariah replied as he stared at the gilded face.

'It's useless, Sacha.' Packavi laughed, the sound of his voice echoing in the dark tunnel. 'Mariah Mundi is like a fish caught on a hook. He will not be happy unless he knows everything. See – you only have enough phosphorus for another few minutes and then all will be in darkness. That doesn't bother me. I have lived in dark places for so long my eyes are as good as any creature of the night. But you Mariah, how you cling to the light. I could tell you things about yourself that even you don't know. You are a pawn in a game that surrounds you – and you are more important to its outcome than you would ever imagine.'

'Don't listen to him, Mariah – we have to go,' Sacha said.

'What do you know of me?' he asked.

'I know that it was not by chance that you were brought to this place. The Prince Regent is your destiny,' Packavi replied. 'Just let me go and I will tell you everything.'

Mariah looked at Packavi and then to Sacha. He thought for a moment, his desire torn in two.

'Grimm and Grendel – they'll be here soon,' Sacha persisted. 'They sent him in because they knew you had a gun – three bullets, that's what they said. They'll think you've killed him and they'll come after you – we can't be waiting here, Mariah.'

'I have to know,' he said as he took hold of the handle to drop the gate from the ceiling.

'Set me free, Mariah, and I will tell you. Things about your parents – your life at the Colonial School – everything – how Charity will betray you. The Bureau of Antiquities cares little for you. All you are to them is bait in a trap . . . Set me free – I can do you no harm.'

'Don't trust him, Mariah – it's a trick,' Sacha said as she tried to pull him away.

Mariah looked at her and smiled. 'I have to know the truth. You know your family and I need to know mine. What harm can he do us on the other side of the gate?'

'That's right, Mariah. What harm can I do you here? My weapon is broken and my desire to kill you has gone. I see so much of you in me – I was once an agent for the Bureau and I can see from your heart that you seek enlightenment. Let me go, Mariah, and I promise to help you.'

Packavi pleaded as he dangled from the iron bars. He looked sad and pathetic. The mask hung from its silk straps about his chin. Half his face was edged in gold, the other scarred beyond recognition. He smiled at Mariah.

'And you will tell me everything and want nothing in return?' Mariah asked.

'He's not to be trusted,' Sacha said again and again as she could see her companion's heart turning towards Packavi before her eyes.

'Everything, everything . . .' Packavi said in a voice of cold steel. 'I know things of you that you wouldn't believe. Gormenberg – the Midas Box – Isambard Black . . .'

'You know of Isambard?' Mariah asked as his hand edged towards the handle.

'Know him well, and his brother Perfidious. I served with both of them,' Packavi said quickly. 'Just let me go and I will tell you more.'

Mariah took hold of the handle. Sacha grabbed his arm as she screamed at him. 'You can't do this – he's a killer!'

'Nothing so dull, my dear girl. I am an assassin for a worthwhile cause – I never kill for the sake of it.' Packavi laughed.

The handle fell in an instant. There was a sudden rush of air as the gate slid from the roof with a snap. Packavi dropped to the floor. Then the gate halted suddenly, half open.

'No!' screamed Sacha as she saw Packavi reach in to the back of his coat and pull from his belt a long thin knife. His eyes flashed from her to Mariah and then to the gate. He got to his feet. In the blink of an eye he dived towards the gate. Mariah stood mesmerised, unable to move, as he realised he had been betrayed by his own curiosity.

In that second Packavi was forcing his way under the gate. Mariah pulled the handle yet again. The gate shot to the ceiling and crashed against the stone. It showered them in fragments of dust and rock as up above the turning cogs whirred furiously. Packavi got to his feet and held out the knife.

'Stupid boy,' he said as he cut the air with the blade.

Sacha tried to drag Mariah away but he held his ground in front of the man.

'I gave you a chance,' Mariah said as he pulled the handle once more.

The gate crashed to the ground with an incredible force. Packavi was crushed beneath it. He lay motionless as the bars pinned him to the floor, one either side of his body.

'Is he dead?' Sacha asked, taking her hands from her face and shining the torch upon him.

'He's still breathing,' Mariah said as he brushed aside the discarded mask and looked at Packavi's face. 'I think I know this man, he seems so familiar.'

'Perhaps you do,' said Grendel a few feet away. 'Isn't it time you ended all this?'

'Run!' Mariah shouted as the detective reached through the bars and easily took hold of the handle.

'The trick, Mr Grimm, is to flick the handle without the gate pinning you to the ceiling – isn't that right, Packavi?'

'Your humour is wasted, Mr Grendel,' Packavi replied as he pushed against the bars with the strength of several men. 'And Mundi and the girl flee into the darkness.'

'We shall not follow, Packavi. We shall wait our time. We were delayed by news – news that changes the task ahead . . .'

Mariah and Sacha couldn't hear what was said. Their feet clattered against the stone as they ran off. Mariah knew that soon Grendel would move the handle and the gate would smash into the ceiling and Packavi would be free. Then they would follow, track them through the tunnel until it reached the town. All he knew was that they had to reach the Prince Regent.

The tunnel twisted and turned as the light from the phosphorus torch grew dimmer by the yard. Ahead in the murk they could see that the passageway narrowed and was blocked by a small doorway. It was made of thick, studded wood, braced with straps of metal. It was old and blackened by years of smoke and strewn with dank cobwebs. In the middle of the door was a lock, and in the lock an iron key.

Sacha put her ear to the door and listened.

'I can hear running water, sounds like a stream,' she said as Mariah turned the key as carefully as he could.

The door opened, the hinges groaning with rust. Mariah peered through the doorway into the cavernous room beyond. A set of iron steps led up from the door and across a narrow sewer to a passageway on the other side. A tall iron ladder ran up the wall to the street above. It was held in place by rusted bolts that precariously gripped the metal to the stone. Through the grates above their heads came a fall of steam-damped soot. It fell like black rain in time with the hissing of a large steam engine.

'It's the railway station,' Sacha said as an engine moved above them, shaking the ground like an earthquake. 'This tunnel must be two miles long.'

'But what good would a tunnel from the castle do coming to here?' Mariah asked as he locked the door behind them and put the key in his pocket so that no one could follow.

'How do you think the Ghosts get the stuff from the town?' Sacha asked.

'Ghosts?' Mariah asked.

'Smugglers – Vackans – Night Hawkers,' Sacha replied as she stared upwards at the long shaft of light that came from the grate underneath the platform. 'We call them Ghosts as they're not supposed to exist – well, everyone knows they do, but we don't speak of them.'

'So why do they have a tunnel to the castle?' Mariah asked as they crossed the bridge.

'The whole town is full of them, they go everywhere. My father said there is a fortune hidden. Ghost Diamonds. Lost for ever when the gang were caught and hung for what they'd done. Told no one – they were even promised to be let off if they said where the treasure was, but even on the gallows they kept silent. If *they* were not going to have the Ghost Diamonds, then no one would.'

'Ghost Diamonds?' Mariah asked as they reached the ladder.

'Biggest in the world,' my father said. 'Worth millions of pounds. Brought in on a ship from Holland – packed in casks of honey and wrapped in tar blankets. Seven diamonds, each as big as a fist.'

'The tale of an old fishwife,' Mariah replied as he shook the ladder to see if it was safe.

Crumbs of plaster fell from high above as the ladder rattled.

'I'll go first,' he said as he took the first faltering steps up the ladder. 'Wait until I am halfway and then follow me.'

Above them, the early-morning train came into the station. Mariah pushed the grate and presently they were both underneath a long line of railway carriages. Thick steam blew about them as they made their way silently along the inspection pit to the rear of the train. They could see the feet that pounded upon the platform, eager to be about their business. Some walked barefoot, others were brightly shod in crisp leather boots with neat buckles. Women scurried on tall heels and children wore galoshes against the wet. Soon they followed on. Mariah walked ahead of Sacha as if they didn't know each other. They slipped quickly through the gate and into the street.

The town was still lit by gas lamps as they scurried through the alleyways towards the Prince Regent. The dawn refused to break and a chill wind blew large drops of cold rain from the north. As they turned the corner towards the hotel they could see the *Irenzee* at anchor in the bay. The haar mist had gone, the lights of the ship shone in the water, and from beneath the waves the sea appeared to glow blood red.

[17]

The Blood Eye

THE Prince Regent was deathly still and Mrs Mukluk was fast asleep. She was sprawled across her desk with her face pressed against a carved paperweight in the shape of Queen Victoria. In the lobby, Rhamses sat in a large chair with a newspaper over his head and his feet on a small table. He didn't move. The sound of muffled snoring emanated from under the neatly ironed pages of the *Evening Gazette*.

Sacha smiled at Mariah as they quietly walked by.

'Food?' he asked, his stomach creaking with pain.

'Sausages,' she replied as the thought of them made her mouth twitch with sheer delight.

The kitchens were empty. Everything was stacked neatly away. The breakfasts for Zogel and his entourage had been prepared and left on four silver trays. All they needed was hot water for the urn of tea and there would be nothing more to do.

Mariah set about making breakfast and listened out for the telephone to ring for room service. He knew Mrs Mukluk would sleep through the ringing of the bell as she did most mornings until the daytime receptionist woke her up and sent her off to bed.

'So, all the guests went away?' Sacha asked as the sausages fizzed in the large flat pan.

'When the General exploded, I think they wondered who would be next. Some lasted out the night, then Captain was arrested for murder and everyone decided to leave – all except Zogel and his servants.'

Sacha said nothing in reply as she picked a sausage from the pan with a silver fork and walked to the long window overlooking the bay. She thought for a moment and wondered about her father.

'He's not really that bad,' she said on the spur of the moment.

'Who?' asked Mariah as he tipped a pile of mushrooms in with the sausages.

'My father . . . I sometimes don't know why he gets involved with the Ghosts. He told me he took over where someone left off, as if it was part of the job.'

'Stand for nothing, fall for anything. That's what Professor Bilton would always say. What do you think they're bringing in?' Mariah asked.

'It'll be from that ship and when it's gone all will be right again,' she said.

'The *Irenzee*. It belongs to Mister Zogel – he's a millionaire, what would he be doing smuggling?'

'Where did he make his money? You have to start somewhere and sometimes old habits die hard – that's what my father would always say.' Sacha paused for a while as she ate her sausage and picked another from the pan. 'What was it like at that school of yours?' she asked.

'Cold,' Mariah said curtly.

'Is that it – just cold?'

'Cold food – cold beds – cold hearts. You could never make a friend for fear they would give away your secrets. That's what the Colonial School was all about. Preparing the sons of Englishmen for foreign service.'

'The Prince Regent isn't foreign,' she said sarcastically. 'Couldn't really call this town tropical, could you?'

'It's where I was sent. Professor Bilton said I had a job to do here,' he replied.

'I bet you regret coming here.'

'It was the best thing that ever happened to me – I met you . . . and Captain Jack.'

'Packavi said you were important – here for a reason.'

'It was a lie. You were right. Just wanted me to open the gate. Never should have listened. I've spent all my life searching for answers to where my parents are. When someone tells you that they know, you'll listen to whatever they say.'

'So what are we going to do?' she asked as she ate yet another sausage.

'Sleep. Tell Rhamses he's in charge and then sleep. Zogel should be easy enough to look after. Funny thing . . .' Mariah paused and looked about the room as if he was checking that no one was there. 'His servant – that poison dwarf Lucius. I saw him go to the Towers and then when I found the man in suite 217, that's where he went to as well. That's how I found you. Who lives there?'

'It's been rented out ever since –' Sacha stopped before she finished her words.

'Since what?' Mariah asked.

'Since nothing . . . Can't talk about it. They say it'll happen to you if you mention it,' Sacha said quickly in broad Irish. 'You'd never understand and I'd be an eedjut to tell you. Superstition. My mother would have me keep my mouth shut.'

'You were kidnapped and taken there. If we knew the name of the man who rented it then we would have an idea who is behind all of this.'

187

'It's not a man – well, not *one* man anyway. It's a sort of gentleman's club. They meet across the road in Athol House – you
must have seen them?'

'That's it,' Mariah exclaimed as if struck by a flash of genius.
'It all begins to fit. Walpole had the ring on his finger. It has the
same symbol as what's above the door of Athol House. Rhamses told me they kept everything secret. Do you know what
they do?'

'No one knows what they do or what they are called,' she
said quickly. 'Not even my Father. They used to meet at the
Old Globe Inn, and then they moved to the Athol five years
ago. They must be important, the Queen's son came to dinner
with them – that's why this hotel is called the Prince Regent.'

'So Packavi was right, the Prince Regent is more than a
hotel.'

'My father wanted to become one of them – he said it would
help his job. A man called Tyler said my father was a Fenian and
they gave him the sign of the blood eye.'

'Blood eye?' Mariah asked as he stared at the fried egg that
spat in the fat pan.

'Blood eye,' she said sullenly. 'A bull's eye, freshly cut and
wrapped in a silk handkerchief. It's what they give you when
they don't want you. Not a gentleman, they said. Too Irish,
they said. I'm sure they thought he would blow the place up in
an act of revolution. What would Tyler know? The man's a
greengrocer on Bar Street. I told him they weren't worth the
fuss but he wouldn't listen.'

'Did your father say what they did in Athol House?' Mariah
asked.

'Secrets. That's all he would say – secrets. They would go to
Athol House and stay for the night. I even tried to watch them.
If you stand on the wall in the alleyway you can see inside.
They all march about and chant. There's a meeting tonight,

we could keep watch and see who goes there. Can't stand secrets.'

Mariah nodded in melancholy agreement. 'Then where were you the other night after the combustions?'

'I told you. In the hotel,' Sacha replied as her eyes said she would take the conversation no further.

'Why did you have salt marks on your boots and sand on your clothes?' Mariah asked.

Sacha didn't reply. She turned from Mariah and looked out of the window to the ship.

'You'd been out of the hotel. It was easy to see it. So why did you lie to me?'

'I didn't lie – I told the truth,' Sacha said as she stared through the glass at the cold sea.

'I looked everywhere for you. I thought you'd been captured. That's what Titus Salt told me.'

'Titus Salt, what does he know?' Sacha scolded. 'Fish in the tanks and fish in the head, that's all Titus Salt has got.'

'He can see things – he knew you were in danger. Knew I was too. It's as if he can see the future. Saw you in a dark place all alone – that's when you were in that coffin.'

'Did he tell you anything else?' she said furiously as she turned to face him. 'If you must know, and I don't think you do, a man in a black suit called at the kitchen door looking for me. He left a message saying my father wanted to see me by the pier – that he was in trouble. I went straight away. There was no one there. I looked for him and when I got back you saw me. I felt stupid and didn't want to tell you. I didn't think it mattered – you're not my keeper. All you were thinking about was exploding Americans and Bureau business. I could see it in your face. You're like a dog with a rat. Once you get your teeth into something nothing else matters, Mariah. Did you ever know that about yourself?'

'It *was* Bureau business,' he replied.

'That's your excuse for whenever you want to leave me out. Never seem to want to take a girl with you. Didn't I help you enough when we fettled Gormenberg?'

'It's not true.'

'It is and you know it.'

Just as Mariah was about to reply, the bell sounded at the desk. Mrs Mukluk roused herself from her sleep and could be heard talking. Sacha left the kitchen and minutes later returned clutching a folded piece of paper.

'A telegram,' she said quietly, 'and I'm sorry. I have to see my father and warn him what they're going to do. In three days he'll be of no use to them and he'll be found floating at the bottom of the castle cliff.'

Sacha handed Mariah the telegram and left him alone in the kitchen. She walked into the dining room and sat at a bare table and stared about the room. It seemed desolate, like an empty jungle of parlour palms and mahogany chairs. She tried to imagine it as it had been before, with laughter, music and the screaming of the chef at all the waiters. Sacha's dream was broken as she heard footsteps on the wooden floor.

'It's Captain Jack,' Mariah said as he walked through the door, his eyes searching for one word of hope in the telegram. 'They've refused bail. He's been remanded to Dean Prison on a charge of murder. He wants to see me.'

'You can't go,' she cried out as she stood up and put a hand on the table to steady herself. 'Walpole will find out that you're at the prison. Grimm and Grendel will catch you. Mariah, you know too much.'

'But I have to go. Captain Jack wants to see me,' Mariah replied.

'Then we'll go together,' she said quickly.

'You can't. I go alone. If we were both to be caught then what

190

good would that do?' Mariah insisted. 'We have to get Jack from prison. I have to prove he didn't kill those people. It's all been set up. Walpole said he found explosives in Jack's office. I think Packavi planted them. Either him or the man I chased from the hotel. Don't tell your father just yet. He will be safe for three days. And Grimm and Grendel will want to find you. Stay in the hotel. I'll tell Rhamses, and speak to no one.' He blurted the words and set off to walk from the room.

'What if they find you?' Sacha asked.

'Then it's over, we have lost and we'll never know what they were going to do,' Mariah said as he turned to face her. 'Ask Mrs Mukluk to send a telegram to Isambard Black. You will find the address on a silver card on the desk in Captain Jack's office. If we fail then he must know what has gone on.'

'What shall I say?' she asked.

'Tell him . . .' Mariah stopped speaking and thought for a while. He looked at Sacha, his eyes saddened by circumstance. 'Tell him Mariah Mundi is held in the balance – he will know what is meant by that.'

'And if you are caught?' Sacha asked.

'Then take your father and leave the town. Go to the Claridges Hotel, room 13, and you will find Perfidious Albion – the Bureau will keep you safe.'

'I'm not going to run, Mariah. They can't force me from my home.'

'They won't force you to go, Sacha. They will simply kill you. Whatever it is that they are doing is worth more than our lives. Captain Jack said that these people are a power behind the power and that not even the Queen can stand up to them. It isn't the government that runs the world but these people. They are the sworn enemy of the Bureau of Antiquities and will do whatever is in their power to see us destroyed.'

'So they are the government?' she asked.

'They are the power behind it – that's all the Captain would say.'

Mariah turned to leave. As he reached the door he stopped and looked at Sacha.

'Keep the wind on your back,' she said as he smiled at her.

'Sacha, I have always wanted to say this but dare not for fear it would burden our friendship . . . I . . . I –' Mariah struggled for the words.

'What?' she asked.

Mariah said nothing more. He gave a faint sigh as he lost the courage to say the words. Turning quickly, as he tried to hold the image of her in his mind, he walked into the lobby and towards the door.

'Mr Mariah! Mr Mariah!' shouted Mrs Mukluk, surprisingly awake.

Mariah kept on walking, his face set to what he had to do. He pushed open the door and strode down the steps into the cold morning air.

'Going far?' asked a voice from somewhere nearby.

Mariah turned. At first he saw no one, but then, almost out of sight behind the tall Corinthian column that held up the portico bearing the name of the Prince Regent, was Lucius Nibelungen. He had changed from the dark suit that he always seemed to wear and was now garbed in a miniature fur coat with a fox's head for a collar. Lucius smiled at Mariah and tapped his walking stick against the marble steps of the hotel.

'Mister Lucius, I thought you would be with your master,' Mariah said politely so as not to attract suspicion.

'Master? I have no master. The tail wags the dog, Mariah, the tail wags the dog.' He grinned as he spoke and for the first time Mariah saw that his mouth was entirely filled with gold teeth capped with ivory.

'Is Mr Zogel well?' Mariah enquired as he began to walk on.

'He's sleeping, as he will for most of the day. He is not the world's best traveller. Are you going far? Perhaps I could walk with you, I could get to know the town.'

'I . . . I go for supplies,' Mariah said, hoping to dissuade the dwarf from coming with him.

'Well, let me at least walk you to the end of the street. I think I will go to the castle today. It seems to be such a nice place. Have you ever been?' Lucius asked inquisitively.

'I prefer Titus Salt's Aquarium and Pleasure Palace. It has fish of all descriptions and monsters from the deep, Mister Lucius,' Mariah replied as he walked on with the dwarf following him as quickly as he could. The square outside the hotel was empty. A small horse and carriage was outside Athol House. The driver was nowhere to be seen as the horse pulled against the weight strapped to its bridle.

'Shame all the guests have departed. How can you pay the bills without any customers?' Lucius asked.

'I charge those left twice as much,' Mariah replied.

'Will you consider selling the hotel?' the dwarf asked as he picked a hair from his nose with his tiny fingers.

'Not mine to sell. Captain Charity is the only one who can decide that.'

'Ah, yes. The one whose head is already on the gallows. No bail, I hear, and finally charged with murder. How did he do it, I wonder? And to think they found the explosives in his office. Quite a scoop of evidence.'

'Who told you?' Mariah asked as he stopped and glared down at Lucius.

'I asked the post boy, he had read your telegram and for a guinea told me what it contained.'

'Why do you need to know my business?' Mariah asked sharply as he fought the urge to punch the man to the floor. 'I thought you had brought Zogel here for his health, but –'

'Go on, Mariah. I could ask you the same question but I know you would treat me with a foolish answer. Dedalus Zogel is a man who admires things of beauty. This hotel is the most wondrous creation he has ever seen. Where in the world would you find a vista such as this? He doesn't have long for this world and for the right person – who treated him kindly – he would allow them to inherit riches beyond the imagination.'

'Life isn't having what you want, but wanting what you have. Riches matter not. Surely happiness and friendship are above the money in a man's pocket?'

'The ranting of a crow soaking up the sun, Mariah. One day you will understand the importance of money. Happiness will never end your hunger or put a roof over your head. If you had enough money you could free the man who you were going to see. Think of it. Selling the Prince Regent might be the only way to save your friend from the gallows.'

'You can't buy justice.'

'Justice?' Lucius laughed as he spoke. 'Justice is not blind. It can see the colour of money. Everything in this world has a price, as does every man. Be he a king, a pauper – even a judge. You can buy them all and the services they sell. Think about it, Mariah. Tell Captain Charity what I have said. A hundred thousand pounds and that is our offer. If he accepts he will be free by the morning. I will take care of all the arrangements.' Lucius looked about him as he spoke. It was as if he knew he was being watched.

'And what if he says no?' Mariah asked.

'There are those who will take it by other means. The Prince Regent is highly valued. Do not be surprised if it is stolen from your hands. We will give Charity a fair price – but some may not.'

'Who are they, Mister Lucius? You appear to know so much about this place and have only been here for two nights.'

'Every town is the same the world over. There are those who want to live out their lives and those who feel it is their divine right to interfere. Behind them are the ones with real power – power over life and death and complete in their subterfuge.'

'How can he trust you?' Mariah asked as they walked across the road and into Bar Street.

'That is where *you* have to trust me,' Lucius insisted as he felt the fur of his coat.

'I don't think a man like Zogel would want to buy this place for its beauty. He could have any hotel in the world,' Mariah replied as he took shelter from the wind and the bustle of the street in the doorway of a grocer's shop. The street filled with people going about the business of their lives. Women carried baskets of food as children played in the puddles of the night storm.

'You would be surprised by what Dedalus Zogel would want. In the last breaths of life a man can desire many things. Soon it will be his time to leave this world. He told me last night that his life was like a jigsaw with a piece missing. The Prince Regent is that final piece.' Lucius again looked about him anxiously and went on speaking quickly. 'Tell Jack Charity to make Zogel a happy man and sell him the Prince Regent. Let Zogel fight off the power seekers. He will still have the Golden Kipper and there are plenty of fish in the sea.'

'One hundred thousand pounds?' Mariah asked. 'And he will be free?'

'I can make you that promise.' Lucius shrugged the collar of his fox coat. He suddenly stopped speaking and started to walk off at a pace. He gestured quickly for Mariah to follow. 'Do not look, but we are being followed. I thought as much when we left the hotel but wasn't sure. Do not answer me but listen careful- ly. They will do whatever they can to stop you meeting with Charity. Now they have seen you speaking to me it has made matters worse. When I tell you to, run – run like the wind and never stop until you get to the prison. If they catch you before you speak to your friend than all is lost.' Lucius dropped several gold coins purposely to the floor. 'Now Mariah, *run*!' he said as a gaggle of children grabbed for the money and blocked the narrow street.

Without reply, Mariah set off at a pace. The wind blew his hair and the first drops of rain beat on his face. He dodged in and out of the people who filled the street and jumped the cages of squawking chickens that were stacked ready for slaughter outside the butcher's shop.

Taking a look back, he saw Lucius engulfed in a brood of brats hunting the cobbles for the gold coins. A man tried to push his way through, shouting as he stumbled over a pile of children eagerly snatching for the money. Mariah smiled as he ran, knowing that he would have a chance to get away.

From Bar Street he turned the corner and ran underneath the clock as it struck the hour. He followed the narrow alleyways until the houses were no more and the old pond came in sight. Before him, reaching up from the ground and surrounded by a high wall, Mariah could see the towers of Dean Prison.

[18]

Habeus Corpus

LOOKING up from the mud road at the tall gateway, Mariah felt that if he walked through the grand doorway of Dean Prison he would never escape. There was no charge on his life and he had committed no crime, but something inside, some bizarre instinct, told him that all was not well. He had the strangest sensation that he was a rat about to step on a gigantic trap that would snap shut and burst him in two. As he stood at the edge of a vast puddle of chalky water, he looked back towards the town. He could see the domes of the Prince Regent, the single spire of Athol House, the turrets of the Towers and above them the castle. It was as if they formed the points of a gigantic star that had been pulled from the sky and fastened to the earth.

In his hand he held the telegram. Already it was tattered and torn from the chase through the town. He opened it once more and read the words over and over. He looked back: the road was empty and he was sure whoever had followed him was nowhere to be seen.

Mariah couldn't stop thinking of Lucius and what he had done. In his mind's eye he could see him throwing the coins to the ground as the man who had been following them raced for Mariah. If Lucius hadn't done that, Mariah knew he would surely have been caught. Why? Mariah asked himself again and again as he looked up at the clock perched high above the gate and waited for it to strike the hour. He had followed Lucius to the Towers and knew that in some way he must be involved in whatever Walpole was planning, yet now Lucius had offered him a way for Charity to escape the gallows.

A sign on the door in faded black and gold letters said that visiting time would be over within the hour. Mariah walked to the door, took hold of the large brass handle and knocked. It gave a dull, empty thud that shook the wooden boards. A small shutter slid back and a pair of black squinted eyes stared at him.

'Yes?' asked the man from behind the door, his eyes blinking as if he saw the light for the first time.

'I've come to see Jack Charity, Captain Jack Charity,' Mariah said as bravely as he could, hoping his voice wouldn't crack.

'The murderer?' the man asked as he continued to stare at Mariah, his eyes searching every inch of his face.

'No,' he said sternly. 'The one who is the owner of the Prince Regent.'

The shutter was slammed quickly.

'A visitor for the murderer, outside, now,' said the voice.

The door to Dean Prison opened slowly. As it swung back on its great hinges it scraped the dirt from the courtyard. Mariah could see a tall building with a grey slate roof. Every window was barred and at every door was a guard. In the corners of the courtyard were large bloodhounds tethered to iron rings. They slept huddled in pairs, waiting for someone to escape. On one side of the prison building was a large wooden scaffold. There, hanging from a length of rope was a thick hessian sack. It was filled with sand and bricks to make up the weight of a man. It rested on a trap door.

The man with the black eyes ushered Mariah inside. He was the same height as Mariah and dressed in a neat blue uniform and small peaked cap. From his belt dangled a chain that went to the large hoop of keys he carried in his hand.

'Follow me,' he said with a nod and a twitch of his eye. 'The murderer is in here.'

As they set off across the courtyard, the door to Dean Prison closed behind them. Mariah gulped, fearing that he would never be free from the place and that Walpole would be waiting to capture him.

'Where are you taking me?' Mariah asked as the man walked ahead of him.

'To his cell – he's not convicted so we have to keep him away from the others.'

'Are there many people here?' Mariah asked, hoping to fill each footstep with conversation.

'Fifty, give or take a few . . . Can't keep track of them, they keep dying . . . or trying to escape. We had more but some were convicted and some were –'

His words were lost as the trap door on the gallows was snapped open and the sack fell with a loud crash, snapping the rope and bursting open on the floor.

'Good job that wasn't for real, eh, lad? Could have caused him a nasty injury. We would have to hang him all over again.' The man laughed. 'Through here and up the stairs.'

Mariah followed on as the guard opened countless gates and doors and walked up several spiral stairways. Everything smelt new. It was bright and shining and gleamed. It had the smell of caustic soda and reminded Mariah of nights spent in the infirmary of the Colonial School in front of the bright coal fire with toast and hot chocolate and the smell of carbolic soap.

There was not a single person in sight. Mariah followed the man along a gantry that looked down into a cavernous landing with cells on either side. Each had a solid metal door and each was painted in bright red with a brass number upon it. Far below he could see the stone tiles of the refectory floor and several empty wooden benches.

'Is Captain Charity the only one you have here?' Mariah asked as they walked up yet another spiral staircase and along another landing.

'Only the murderer in this block – only been open a week, paint's not even dry – he's our first guest. Just been built. We keep all the others in the old wing, but the murderer's special – Inspector Walpole said we had to keep him away from the rest of them and he had to have three guards all of his own. Not to escape is the murderer.'

'He's not a murderer,' Mariah said angrily in reply as they went through yet another door.

The guard stopped and turned to Mariah. He pointed an iron key in his face. 'If Walpole says the man is guilty then he is guilty and I won't argue. Guilty until proved innocent, that's what the law in this place is all about – you mark my words,' he said in his terrier voice as he screwed up his black eyes until they vanished in folds of wrinkled flesh. 'Now, if you want to see the murderer then don't argue with me.'

They continued in silence. Mariah counted the paces between the doors and watched as the guard used the same key in every lock. Soon they were in the highest part of the building. The roof sloped to one side as they walked under the eaves along a narrow passageway. There were only four cells on this corridor. Mariah looked down over the gantry to the floor far below.

The guard laughed. 'Fall from there and you'd know all about it. Still, you'd have a soft landing – so new, the mortar isn't yet set,' he said as he tugged Mariah. 'The murderer is in this one.'

The guard pointed to a cell without a number. He took his key and opened the door and led Mariah inside a small room. There was a stove in the corner with a metal chimney running up to the roof. Three men sat at the table playing cards. No one looked up as they searched for aces and kings and sipped at mugs of beer.

'This is the lad,' the guard said as he locked the door behind Mariah. 'Best be putting him inside.'

Mariah wondered what he meant. 'I'm here to see Captain Charity,' he protested as a guard got from the table and grabbed him by the arm.

'So you are, lad, and soon you will see him – but first I should let you know that you're here to stay.'

'I've done nothing – I just want to visit him,' Mariah shouted as he struggled to be free.

Another guard took hold of him as the door to the inner cell was opened and Mariah was pushed through the door.

'Go tell Walpole we've got the lad and the two of them are together,' the guard said as the door was slammed shut behind him and the lock turned.

'Mariah!' Charity said from the shadows of the dark cell. 'What are you doing here?'

'You sent a telegram asking me to come,' Mariah said as he looked at Charity.

'I sent nothing – I have spoken to no one,' he replied.

Mariah looked at Charity. He had been stripped of his clothes and dressed in the rude garb of a prisoner. His head had been roughly shaved and his face was bruised.

'They've hurt you,' he said as he touched the side of Charity's face.

'Nothing that is new to me – I have had far worse from better men,' he said quietly.

'I was tricked. I had a telegram. You asked me to come to

you,' Mariah said as he sat on the bed and listened to the faint laughter of the men outside the room.

'It was Walpole. For some reason he wants you prisoner as well as me. They only have two days left and then they must charge me for murder or let me go. I can't understand why he now wants you.'

Mariah took a deep breath and held Charity's hand. He told him of Walpole and the detectives, and Lucius and Zogel.

'So they had kidnapped Sacha and held her at the castle?' Charity asked.

Mariah continued his story until he had nothing else to say. As was his way he spared no detail until all had been said.

'Very well,' Charity replied as Mariah sighed with relief that he had told him at last. 'I suspect we will not get from this place with our lives. You said that those from Athol House were involved?'

'Sacha was sure in what she told me. It was they who had rented the Towers and Packavi said the Prince Regent could only be valued from the air,' Mariah replied, his hands shaking and face pale with concern. 'Why does Zogel want the Prince Regent? If you agree to sell he will set you free.'

'It would seem, Mariah, that we are caught in a war between two groups of desperate men. There is something in the hotel that they both want. If we agreed with his demands we would be rich but still in this place. Walpole is behind my imprisonment, but I am not sure if he was the one responsible for the murders.'

Mariah stood on the bed and looked out of the small window that let in the morning light. As he held on to the bars, he felt the paint sticking to his hands. He thought for a moment and then looked at Charity as if his mind had just exploded with delight.

'We could escape,' Mariah said quietly.

'There are guards and the outer door is also locked,' Charity replied.

'Down there,' Mariah replied. 'Out through the wall and over the roof. In their efforts to keep you here they have made one mistake.'

Charity looked on as Mariah took the silver badge of the Bureau of Antiquities form his pocket and began to scratch at the painted mortar between each brick. It was damp and crumbled away.

'It was something the guard said about this building. He said the mortar hadn't set and there is scaffolding on the far side.'

As Mariah scratched and scratched slices of damp lime fell like sludge from the wall. Charity looked on as the lad dug deeper until the first brick was free.

'We'll have to work fast, Walpole could return at any moment – when he knows you are here, his curiosity will not keep him away,' Charity said.

Within a minute they had piled several large painted bricks against the floor and there was a hole in the inner wall. Carefully, Mariah and Charity dug at the sandstone of the outer wall. The mortar fell away in their hands. Mariah lifted out a row of stones and handed them to Charity, who stacked them against the door of the cell. The raucous laughter of the guards covered all they did. Soon the wall was breached. There below them was the flat roof that led to the wall. Mariah slid through the aperture and dropped to the roof below. He was quickly followed by Charity. They ran close to the wall and then across the roof. Far below they could hear the guards as they shouted at the prisoners in the exercise yard. Within a short time they had reached the battlements of the outer wall and crossed the scaffolding from the roof to the wall.

'Where now?' Mariah asked Charity as they hid behind the

parapet and looked down to the mud lane and the fields beyond.

'There's no other way but to jump – you up for it?' Charity asked as he looked for any sign of prison guards. 'I'll lower you over the wall and then you'll have to kick away and drop – it's not far.'

Mariah looked down. There seemed to be a vast distance between the top of the parapet and the ground below.

'It looks so far,' Mariah said nervously as his stomach turned.

'By the time I have lowered you it'll only be ten feet. When you hit the ground roll over and get up running,' Charity said as he nodded for Mariah to stand between the brick turrets on the wall.

Mariah stepped back and slid down, his feet scrambling against the bricks. He closed his eyes as Charity held his wrists as he lowered him down. He dangled momentarily high above the ground and then Charity let go.

'No!' Mariah murmured in panic.

'Now!' Charity said as Mariah began to fall. He kicked out against the wall and dropped like a stone. The ground hit him quickly. His legs buckled and, like he had been told, he instinctively rolled to one side and got up and began to run. The shock of the fall still echoed through his body and all he wanted to do was drop to the floor and find his breath.

'Keep running, Mariah,' Charity said as he followed on. 'They could discover us gone at any time.'

As he spoke there was a whirring from the alarm of the prison as the siren blasted long and hard.

'We're discovered,' Mariah said as they crossed the fields towards the sea.

'They have the dogs after us, Mariah – we'll have to run hard.

As the sound of the siren began to fade, Mariah could hear the howling of the bloodhounds. The dogs sounded far away but desperate to give chase. Mariah ran on, a yard ahead of Charity. They crossed the fields and the streams until they reached the cover of the wood that clung to the cliff to the north of the castle. With every minute the barking grew closer.

'Into the sea, Mariah. It's the only way we will escape. We'll have to swim for it – the dogs will never track the scent in the sea. I know a way that they will never find.'

Charity led on as they ran from the wood and across the rocks to the sea. Soon they were swimming together towards the headland of the castle. The water seemed to take them along as Mariah struggled to keep afloat.

'Keep nearby,' Charity said as he slowed the pace of his swimming so that Mariah could keep up with him. 'Can't lose you here, not when we are so close.'

Mariah gulped for breath as a wave crashed above his head. He could feel the rocks beneath him as strands of kelp weed gripped his ankles.

'Where to?' he asked as he grabbed hold of a rock that jutted from the water in the shape of a large coffee pot.

'There,' Charity replied, pointing to the bottom of the high cliff that towered above them.

Mariah looked to the shore but could see nothing that would aid their escape. Most of the rocks were covered by the full tide, and at the water's edge a peculiar house had been carved from a gigantic boulder that had at some time dropped from the cliff.

Charity dragged Mariah from the sea and they hid between two large stones. From time to time he peered back to the wood. Even from such a great distance they could hear the barking of the dogs.

'Nearly there,' he said confidently as he smiled. 'This is the life, Mariah. Takes me back to the Sudan – takes me back . . .' His smile faded as he looked at Mariah. They both knew what he was about to say but couldn't.

'Will I ever see them?' Mariah asked.

'Never give up hope, Mariah. I believe your parents are still alive. Your father would never give up. That's what made him so special and I know he will find a way.'

Mariah gulped down the tears that stung his throat. He was wet and cold and in his heart of hearts had lost the will to fight. Even with Charity there he believed they would not succeed. In that moment he wanted a wave to come and snatch him from the shore and take him to the depths of the sea. He closed his eyes and gritted his teeth.

'Don't give up, Mariah,' Charity said. 'Not until your last breath. Goodness and truth are worth fighting for. Now, it's time.'

Charity went on ahead, keeping to the cover of the fallen rocks and the bushes that had grown in between. They climbed the steep cliff until they crawled into a briar of thorns cut through by what looked like an old badger track.

'This is the place,' Charity whispered as he slid into a large hole that appeared to have been dug by a stinking animal.

'But –' Mariah tried to reply as Charity slipped underground.

'Quickly!' Charity said as his face appeared in the shadowy entrance of the hole like a large fox. 'You will be surprised by what you see.'

Cautiously, Mariah slipped through the entrance of the tunnel and into the hole. He could feel the sides pressing in against him as he crawled on in the dark, and then suddenly he fell into a cave.

'What's this place?' he asked as Charity took a lantern from a small table and struck the wick with a flint and steel.

'Ghost hole,' Charity replied, holding his hands against the lantern for warmth. 'We'll never be found here. The hounds can track us to the door and think it's a set for badgers.'

'Ghost hole? Do you mean smugglers?' Mariah asked, as the light from the lamp grew brighter by the second.

'Precisely that, Mariah, precisely that,' Charity said as he blocked the entrance to the tunnel with a plank of wood. 'It's time for us to plan our war . . .'

The Mysterious Master Templar

IT was midday when the old butler with his bulging waist opened the door of the Towers and allowed Grimm and Grendel to make their way into the parlour. He nodded to each of them as they sheepishly crossed the threshold and walked along the hall before turning left into the room. The fire had been lit and burned brightly. The floor had been swept and polished and the house gave off the odour of honeybees.

Grimm and Grendel didn't speak. Grimm had the demeanour of a foolish child about to be reprimanded for a great folly. Grendel sipped on his linctus and didn't care. The green bottle was gripped firmly in his fingers and he wouldn't have minded if the world had come to an end there and then.

'*He* will be back soon,' the butler said as he fussed about the chairs as if they had to be placed perfectly before the arrival of his master. 'When he does arrive please show him the courtesy that his rank demands.'

Grendel grinned, showing his teeth like a large dog about to bite. It was as if something other than himself had control of his face. He winced regularly as his eye twitched and his cheek shook. Grendel knew it was the linctus; it always did that to him as it attacked his mind, but he didn't care. After all, he was thirty-six years old and in good health and had outlived his father by several years.

'Did he say why he wanted to see us?' Grimm asked nervously as he pushed his chair further from the heat of the fire.

'It's obvious, Grimm. They escaped, and Packavi went on a rampage – what else would it be about?'

'About whether or not I should continue to employ you,' the man said as he entered the room.

Grimm and Grendel stood up and gave a bow. Grimm shook slightly and Grendel twitched in deep agitation.

'Sir. What a fine day to see you, sir . . .' Grimm muttered, unsure as to what to say or do in the circumstances.

'Fine day, Mr Grimm? It is particularly cold and the wind is from the north and the sea is moderate. It is not a fine day.'

Grendel eyed the man through linctus eyes. It was the first time he had seen him in daylight. The man stood in his neat suit and sparkling shoes that shone as if they were tipped with diamonds. His waistcoat gleamed in silver and blue and around his neck was a tidy cravat. He was taller than Grimm and well fed, with a lock of white hair that fell over his brow.

'Do you think I could have some tea? My throat is parched.' Grendel asked without thinking, his thoughts emerging automatically from his twitching mouth.

'I think tea can wait, Mr Grendel. When I saw you last night you had the girl. When my butler woke me from a particularly comfortable sleep, he told me that you have lost the girl – and the boy, Mariah Mundi – and then lost him *again*.' The man took off his leather gloves and threw them on to the sofa. 'I give you everything,' he went on angrily, 'from the police to the army, and yet you cannot do something so simple as keep your hands on two children.'

'Hexogenamite,' Grendel blustered. 'That rascal blew up

the dogs, shot Packavi three times and would have killed us both. He's a maniac, demented and dangerous – not a normal child.'

'We didn't know he –' Grimm tried to add, desperate to say something.

'But still not a man, Mr Grimm – still not a man. I expected to have all these things coming to an end and now it seems as if it is just the beginning. You have let me down and the Society of Truth also. She was needed and so was he. When I left last night with Inspector Walpole all was well.'

'What is it that you are looking for in suite 217?' Grendel asked as he became mesmerised by the flames of the fire.

'That cannot be told to the likes of you. That is why I have to do the work myself and you are left in charge of the children.' The man warmed his hands by the fire. 'It is of such importance that it can be shared with no one. I was entrusted with the secret before Gormenberg died – he told no one else but me.'

'You told Walpole,' Grendel blubbered as he watched a particularly interesting flame.

'And he alone shall know. I have also taken care of Mariah Mundi – as we speak he is incarcerated in Dean Prison,' he said as he walked to the door and turned the key.

'How?' asked Grimm, unsure why they had been locked in.

'As soon as I had heard you had let him escape I sent a telegram to the Prince Regent. It invited Mariah Mundi to visit his good friend Captain Charity. The guards were well bribed and are lower members of the Society so I know they will do their job well – unlike some people . . .'

'What will you do with him?' Grimm asked, as doubts about his own future fuddled his mind.

'They will meet with a terrible accident. Charity will try to escape and as he does so he will be shot. Sadly and most tragically, the boy is shot accidentally – oh, how we will grieve his death, and I myself will walk before the hearse as a sign of respect. Then we will find what we are looking for in suite 217.'

'Doesn't Mr Zogel wish to frustrate our desires?' Grimm asked nervously.

'He may, for we do not see eye to eye and the matter is open to . . . negotiation,' the man said as he stood on one leg and rubbed the top of his shoe against the back of his trousers. 'I am a selfish man, Mr Grimm. I always get what I want. Gormenberg recommended you both to me and I hope he was right. I should hate to *lose* you.'

'I don't think we would ever be lost, we know the town well,' Grendel said as Grimm kicked him to be silent.

'I am glad you can appreciate the subtlety of what I say, Mr Grimm. I would even be prepared to offer you both membership of the Society of Truth – should you be able to fulfil my desires.'

'Gladly,' Grimm replied for them both, for by now the linctus had overwhelmed Grendel. His face took on the pallor of death, dark rings burnt the skin under his eyes and his face was drawn with pain. 'What is it that would be required of us?'

'You will die and be brought back to life,' the man said simply, as if it was a commonplace thing to say.

'Does it always work?' Grimm asked.

'Always – for those who are truly called. The Society of Truth is about leaving the cares of this earth behind. We act for the good – for fine and noble causes. We are guardians and we are the power behind the power. Do not fool yourself, Mr Grimm, that this world is run by governments and politicians, for it is not.' The man spoke sternly, staring Grimm deeply within his eyes. 'The Society of Truth provides presidents and prime ministers for the task. Since our foundation a thousand years ago we have grown in power. Every president of the Americas has been a Society man, and every prime minister of this island. Only the French stand for themselves. Even the city of Washington is built according to our divine principles, and so is the Prince Regent.'

'The Prince Regent?' Grimm asked, wondering why a society so powerful should bother with such a place as the-town-at-the-end-of the-line.

'Built by a great architect to the divine principle. It has a room for every day of the year, a floor for every month and a dome for every season. It points to our sacred city and can only truly be seen by the sea-hawks that fly above it. In all, Mr Grimm, the Prince Regent is a giant clock that marks the time for the Society of Truth.'

'So what happens when we die and come back to life?' he asked nervously.

'A simple ceremony. It will take place tonight and on my word you will be admitted. But remember – once the ritual is over you can never leave the Society. Some have tried and have not awoken on a new day.'

Grimm coughed as if to clear his throat as the man walked across the room to the window. He stared out across the town. Before him was the Prince Regent and in the bay below was the *Irenzee*.

'Such a strange way to travel. I always have thought that boats were never very good. I have a desire that one day we will master the air and be able to fly to wherever we desire. That would be a fine thing.'

'Some of us already do,' Grendel whispered to himself as he stared at a flame that appeared to have changed into the shape of a large bat. 'I had a dream that I saw the sky filled with sharp black sticks that beat against the clouds and caused the thunder. Then a ball of light crashed to the earth and raised up the sea so that the land was engulfed by water.'

'Do you dream often, Grendel?' the man asked as he pulled the blind across the window to keep out the light.

'Only when I am awake. I find sleep like death and do not wish to see either,' Grendel replied as he took another reassuring sip of linctus.

'Then,' said the man, 'I have changed my mind. Shall I take you both into my confidence?'

'That would be a fine thing, sir,' said Grimm, standing bolt upright as if summonsed by the King. 'A fine thing indeed.'

'Very well,' said the man as he went to the desk in the corner of the room and tapped on its side to open a secret drawer. 'I have here a plan of the hotel. What I search for was lost some time ago. You will have heard the rumour of the Ghost Diamonds?' he asked.

'Only in the Merchant Inn – late at night, when the old hag has stopped singing,' Grendel replied.

'Just a story, sir. I am sure of it,' Grimm said as he tried to make light of what he said. 'Seven men died for nothing – they couldn't tell where the Ghost Diamonds were, for they were not there in the first place.'

'A story, yes. A lie, no.' The man looked out of the window quickly and then pulled down another blind. 'Gormenberg knew of the location of the Ghost Diamonds and so do I . . . Help me find them and you –'

There was a banging on the door of the house. The doorbell jangled frantically. The beating came again. It was urgent and violent, a bare hand rapping against the wood. From outside the room they could hear voices raised in alarm as the butler opened the door and Walpole stormed into the house.

'Where is Master Templar?' he asked as his feet pounded against the hall floor.

A hand beat urgently on the locked parlour door.

'Master Templar! Master Templar, they have escaped!' Walpole shouted, out of breath.

'*Escaped?*' screamed the man as he unlocked the door and

dragged Walpole inside before the fire. 'Of whom do you speak, Walpole?'

'Char- . . . Char- . . . Charity,' he mumbled humbly as if the cold bit his lips. 'And the boy. The trap failed.'

'How?' the man asked sharply.

'We had them good and proper. Both together, just as you planned. I only have four Society men in Dean Prison and they worked well. We had the boy locked up with Charity and when I arrived they had gone. Dug themselves out of the place. Took out the wall brick by brick. They were chased to the sea. Couldn't be found. Hope they are dead,' Walpole said briskly as he sweated each word.

'Can you be sure?' asked the man.

'No, Master Templar. They were tracked by the blood-hounds to the sea and then lost.' Walpole looked at Grimm and Grendel as if they were responsible. He could see that Grendel had left this world and slept wide-eyed. Taking the snuffbox from his pocket he spread a line on the back of his hand and sniffed deeply. 'We should find the girl,' he went on. 'The blind eye should be turned tomorrow and then we can have done with them all.'

'And what of the Prince Regent?' the man asked.

'One of my detectives followed Lucius when he was talking with the boy – they don't know what was said.' Walpole looked at the Master Templar as if he wanted to say more but couldn't in the presence of Grimm and Grendel.

'You can speak. I have called them both to the Society of Truth. It will cost them more than their jobs if they break the oath,' he said, and he drew a hand across his throat as if it were a knife.

'Very well,' Walpole said as he looked at them both and sniffed the final fragments of snuff from his fingers. 'I think Mr Zogel is not to be trusted. His miniscule friend is playing a game with us and I think he would deal with Charity directly and cut us from the chase. All I know is that the dwarf talks about a Midas Box.'

'Why don't you trust him?' asked the man as he pulled the final blind on the window overlooking the Prince Regent.

'It was something Lucius said when he came to see you. I was hiding. I saw the Duegard – the sign of the brotherhood, the thumb drawn across his throat as if it were a knife. What man would reveal such a secret without asking?' Walpole asked.

'What is it you're saying?' the man asked.

'I don't trust him. There is something wrong in the way he is with Zogel. My men have been watching. It's as if Lucius is the one in control and Zogel just the puppet. On the pier, one of the sailors from the *Irenzee* told an informant that on the ship they only saw Lucius, and Zogel slept most of the time.'

'Perhaps he hates the sea?' Grendel quipped. 'I cannot stand sea nor dry land and am only comforted by my linctus. It stops the spinning of the world.'

'Perhaps all is not well with Zogel – there are rumours he is sick?' the man asked as he smiled at Walpole.

'That's not all,' Walpole went on. 'One of his men was arrested last night on a minor charge in the Merchant Inn. The beer spoke on his behalf and opened his heart. Whilst in the cells he kept on shouting that the whole town would soon find out why they were here. Zogel had him collected and taken back to the ship by his own guard before I could speak to him.'

'Do you think they know about the Ghost Diamonds?' the man asked uneasily as he paced the room.

'Whatever is known, Master Templar, our decree has to be completed soon. If we do not find what we are looking for then grand hail for us all and no help for the widow's son.' Walpole stood stiffly and raised both hands in the air to the Master Templar in the manner of giving him a secret sign.

215

The man didn't speak but answered sign for sign. He took his hand and drew it across his waist and then dropped his arm to the side and bowed.

'So be it, Walpole. So be it. Grimm and Grendel shall know of what we do. The Ghost Diamonds have to be recovered. I have promised that they shall be returned. For that, we will all be well paid.'

'I do this for different reasons, Master Templar,' Walpole replied ever so humbly as he stooped his great, thin frame like an old greyhound. As he did so he scowled at Grimm and Grendel, doing so in such a way that the Master Templar could not see him.

'That, Mr Walpole, is why I chose you. Your loyalty to the Society will not go unnoticed. And whilst we talk, what is our situation with Packavi?'

'He is still useful, Master Templar. His actions are a distraction from the work we do. There is a fear in the town that he will strike again. They think it is a phantom or Spring-Heeled Jack. We add to the rumours for our own good. I have had word from the police in London. They are to close the case on the Whitechapel murders on the understanding that Packavi will not return. He did well for The Society.'

'All in the service of the Queen . . . to keep her son's follies secret. Packavi makes me nervous. There is something about him that chills what is left of my soul. Should the situation change I would like him eliminated.' The Master Templar turned to Grimm and Grendel. 'In the meantime, we must find the Ghost Diamonds. For that, we need to have access to the Prince Regent Hotel. We cannot search properly with subterfuge or by the cover of night.'

'I could have the hotel closed down for reasons of evidence,' Walpole suggested as Grimm stayed silent, feeling like a spectator to an act of malice.

'Better still, Mr Walpole, could we not seize the building from Charity?' the Master Templar asked.

'How could you do that?' asked Grimm as his heart leapt nervously in his chest. 'It is not yours to take.'

'If he died tragically while trying to escape from a charge of murder, then he forfeits his estate. The Prince Regent can be seized. All we would need is a writ of Charity's death from the Mayor,' the Master Templar said arrogantly.

'But what he if wasn't dead and was just hiding?' Walpole asked eagerly.

'Then we must make sure that we find him and do away with our problem,' the Templar replied. 'We have to find the Ghost Diamonds and have them restored to their rightful owner. If we cannot do that in two days then it is the end of The Society of Truth.'

'And what if Zogel and the dwarf get in the way?' Walpole asked curiously.

'Then they too will meet the same fate as Captain Jack Charity,' he replied.

[20]

The Ghost Diamonds

DEEP in the cave, Mariah slept by the light of the storm lamps. Captain Charity kept guard by the entrance and listened to the sound of the sea as it echoed through the tunnel and into their hiding place. They had eaten well on a carton of ship biscuits and two mugs of Porto. The chase had exhausted Mariah and soon he had fallen asleep as his clothes steamed in the heat from the lamps.

He dreamed much. The faces of Grimm and Grendel merged with those of Sacha and Packavi. In his terror he imagined being caught by Packavi and as he raised his gun to kill the assassin, the bullets dropped onto the floor without the power of the blast. They then turned into spiders and ran quickly away, fearful of what they were meant to do. Mariah then tried to escape, only to find his legs took him backwards, closer to his attacker than he was before.

Charity watched him turn back and forth and moan in discontent as he dreamed. 'We'll get through all this,' he said to Mariah, knowing the lad couldn't hear his words and yet hoping they would reassure him. 'Then we can get all the answers for your life – perhaps then, Mariah, you'll have peace.'

It was as he spoke his final words that Mariah woke up.

'They're coming to look for us,' Mariah said sleepily, knowing they had to be the first words he said.

'Just a dream, Mariah,' Charity replied as he handed him another sea biscuit.

'I saw them. I saw them clearly. Grimm and Grendel were with Walpole outside the Prince Regent – they were nailing a writ to the door,' Mariah replied as he wiped the sleep from his eyes.

'Just a dream,' Charity said again.

'It was more than that. It was as if I was there. Walpole told them that the writ would do – until they could see Ebenezer Wolf,' Mariah said.

'Have you heard of the man they speak of?' Charity asked, quite bemused.

'Never before,' Mariah replied.

'Then your dream is of interest. Ebenezer Wolf is the Mayor. If this is more than a dream then it gives away what they could do,' Charity said as his mind raced with the thought.

'What?' asked Mariah.

'They intend to seize the hotel. Walpole can sign a writ of confiscation that lasts for three days, and after that the Mayor himself would have to agree and declare me dead. I would either have to appear to contest it or they could sell it by auction. Either way, they would have me.' Charity tried to smile. 'If your dream is true then it forces our hand. We should go to the Prince Regent and see for ourselves.'

'But they could be outside searching for us,' Mariah replied.

'We shall not see the light of day until we are safe with Mister Quadlibett in his fine sweet shop in the vaults of the Market,' Charity replied as he walked to the far wall and slid a wooden cupboard to one side.

There, as if it had been cut into the wall, was a sliver-like crack in the solid rock. It vanished into the side of the cliff.

'This has been here for a million years. It's a volcanic fault line, Mariah. It takes us to the tunnels under the town and to Mister Quadilibett's shop. This is the way the Ghosts would come and go and no one would ever see them.'

'You know a lot about the smugglers, Captain,' Mariah said. 'More than one only engaged in honest trade.'

'Then come with me and find out more. If your dream is something of the future we should not sit about in dingy circumstances.'

Charity took the lamp and led on. There were steps inside the fault that went higher and then turned. In the lamplight Mariah could see that each one had been cut from the rock by flat chisels. Some were worn where many feet had trod before them. Soon Mariah could smell the sea. The rough walls of the passageway that had been hewn from the rock gave way to smooth stones built one on the other.

From nearby Mariah could hear the sound of running water. He knew he was near to the town. Then all became familiar. He had been this way before. This was the passageway from Mister Quadlibett's Vendorium to the harbour. There was soon the smell of the baker's shop above them, filling the tunnel with a white mist of bread dust and the scent of fresh bread. In two turns he knew he would see the steps from the tunnel and there would be a door and then the storeroom of the shop.

'Does everyone in this town know of this place?' Mariah asked as he walked in Charity's shadow.

'There are a few who are familiar with what goes on,' Charity said softly as they approached the entrance to the shop.

'And the Ghost Diamonds – what is the truth of them?' Mariah asked.

'I know little of them. I was in Africa. From what I was told by Smutch, seven barrels were taken from a ship and brought into the caves. The smugglers had arranged to be paid the next night. When they went to the rendezvous, Inspector Walpole and the militia from the castle were waiting. The men were arrested.'

'But they didn't say where the diamonds were – they were offered a pardon, Sacha told me,' Mariah replied quickly.

'They couldn't say because they didn't know,' Charity said, his voice determined. 'Someone had gone to the hiding place and taken every barrel. All the smugglers thought they had done was bring in Porto. When Walpole began asking about diamonds none of them knew what he was talking about.' He paused momentarily and stared at Mariah. 'The men were murdered because of their own ignorance. They were double-crossed.'

'By who?' Mariah asked.

'I have heard it said that it was Gormenberg,' Charity replied as he took the steps to the secret entrance of the shop one by one.

'So why can't we look for the diamonds ourselves?' asked Mariah.

'We have to find out who killed the guests at the Prince Regent. I have a feeling that the two may be linked in some way. It was strange for Zogel to arrive the night they were killed.'

'He couldn't have done it – he was at sea on his boat,' said Mariah.

'Perhaps they were killed so they couldn't meet with him,' Charity replied. 'This was not just a chance attack. Everything was planned meticulously. If a meeting had been arranged between Zogel and the others, then someone was desperate to see it stopped and get me out of the way.'

'But Zogel wants the Prince Regent,' Mariah said.

'That is what his companion has told you. Zogel could have any hotel in the world and there has to be something far more that he wants than just another spa in a northern town on a craggy outcrop in the German Ocean. We need to be at the Prince Regent and I need a change of clothes.'

Charity tapped three times on the door and then waited before he tapped again. Mariah could hear shuffling in the room above. It was as if whoever was inside had to move large, heavy objects from the doorway. Charity smiled at Mariah, his face lined with the shadows of the lamp. It reminded Mariah of the day he had seen his father for the last time at Southampton dock before he had been taken to the Colonial School. There was something strong in his eyes. Mariah could see it easily. It was as if circumstances could not change the light within his heart.

'My father said the eyes are the window of the soul.' Mariah found himself saying the words out loud for no reason.

'Your father was right, Mariah. Always look at the eyes. In some they are dead and lifeless – as if the essence of the man has been robbed from him. In others they are alive with the fire of life,' Charity replied as he tapped again on the door.

'What will happen to us?' Mariah asked, fearing the worst but not wanting Charity to know how scared he really was.

'Never fear that which can destroy the body – only that which can take the soul,' Charity said. He dimmed the wick of the lamp, plunging the tunnel to a thick and murky black.

The door opened. A small candle flickered as the face appeared.

'Who is it?' asked a voice as the face stared into the darkness.

'Not ghost – but men of the sea – in business against the king with rum from far away,' Charity said, using the secret words of greeting known only to true Ghosts.

'And what name do the men have?' the voice asked as he held the candle higher.

'We have no name but that of our ship,' Charity replied.

'And what be that?' the voice questioned.

'Dignity and truth,' Charity said as he stepped forward.

'Can't be,' said the voice in fear, as the door was slammed shut. 'Dignity and truth are dead. It is the news of the town. Go away or tell me who you really are.'

''Tis I, Jack Charity. Quadlibett, open the door.' Charity pressed on the door.

'Back with you – I have a gun and I will use it. Charity is dead – don't joke with me,' Quadlibett replied like an angry rat, and there came the sound of boxes being stacked against the door.

'If I am dead then look at my face. You have seen it many times. I know you keep no gun so shooting me will be impossible,' Charity pleaded.

The door opened an inch. Mariah could see the large silver eye of Mister Quadlibett staring at them.

'I have never seen a ghost before – for surely you are dead. Every customer has told me this today and I have it written in the smudged ink of the *Evening Gazette*, newly arrived.' Quadlibett's voice trembled, truly fearful.

'Then touch my hand, Mister Quadlibett – give me hot chocolate and watch me drink and, most of all, fill it with sugar mallows and cover them with cream.'

'Even in death you still want food?' Quadlibett asked.

Charity shot his hand through the crack in the door and grabbed Quadlibett by the scruff of his jacket.

'Could a ghost do this?' he asked with a laugh as he twisted the silk scarf in his hand and lifted the man from his feet.

'It is you – but how? You have been seen – *dead*,' Quadlibett insisted.

'We are alive and will remain so with your help. I need a change of clothes and your silence.' Charity pushed his way inside with Mariah following on.

'Mariah Mundi – Captain Charity – alive, alive indeed,' said Mister Quadlibett with his silk cap pulled over one eye and the tassel bobbing back and forth. 'Great expectations, great expectations . . .' he went on as he opened the door. 'As soon as I heard of your escape I wondered if you would come here. Then I was told of your death. The town is alive with the news, but I must have powerful sight for according to the *Evening Gazette* you are both dead.'

'There are lies, lies, and then what is written in the *Gazette*. No greater work of fiction have I ever read.' Charity laughed.

'They say they have found a body on the beach, washed ashore – a prisoner from Dean Prison with a bullet in his back.'

'We are well, Mister Quadlibett. Hungry, but well. The man they discovered will be a poor unfortunate from the workhouse – proof positive of my death.'

'Inspector Walpole has confirmed it was you – he identified the remains, what was left after its beating against the rocks. It says so on the front page. There is also a photograph.' Quadlibett showed them both the crisp newspaper. On the front page was a sepia photograph that bore a dim resemblance to Charity.

'To disguise the fact it wasn't me. Doubtless the body will be the same height and age, a doppelgänger without a face.'

'But it is good to see the real Captain Jack so alive,' Mister Quadlibett said, offering his hand. 'I am so glad to see you and young Mariah. Just like old times.'

'And with old enemies, Mister Quadlibett. Grimm, Grendel and many others,' Charity said as his eyes searched the back room of the sweet shop.

'Then sit before the fire and we will plan what to do. It is late and the streets will be empty. They say that Spring-Heeled-Jack will strike again. No one dares to go outside, especially with the haar mist covering the town.' Quadlibett stopped and looked at Charity. 'I have to ask you one thing – to which I am already sure of the answer, but I need to know from you.' He paused before going on. 'Jack, did you kill those people? The ones who exploded?'

'Not I, never, but I know who did,' Charity replied seriously, his face sullen.

'Then I take your word and will help,' Quadlibett chirped as he flustered with his handkerchief. 'I get told many things in this shop. People confide in me.' He sighed. 'It's the candy, opens the mouth and heart quicker than gin.' Quadlibett looked at Mariah and then to Charity as if the presence of the boy forbade him from speaking. 'Some people . . . some people say they have heard things . . . alarming things, things without –'

'Be honest, Mister Quadlibett. Mariah knows much of what we do,' Charity said, realising that Quadlibett feared speaking in front of the boy.

'Very well. There are rumours, rumours that are fearful to believe,' Quadlibett said reluctantly.

'Go on,' said Mariah.

'They say . . . that you have found the Ghost Diamonds and that is why you had the people murdered. They say it is not a coincidence that the *Irenzee* came on the same night, and that you and Zogel are in concert with each other. More than that, Captain. They say you are Spring-Heeled-Jack . . .'

'A killer and a smuggler?' Charity asked.

'People like to talk and since your arrest they are talking about you. This town envies success – especially when it is one of their own that has done well. There are some who would like to knock you down to size and see you back on the pier gutting fish. It's jealousy, my friend. Now you have come upon hard times they are quite happy.'

'I've been given nothing and worked for all I have,' Charity replied.

'This is a small place and you have done better than most. I remember your father – he always worked hard. There are others who see what you have and turn green at the sight. Always remember that. Inspector Walpole has visited them all. They – to a man – would have spoken against you in court. Now you are dead. It complicates matters.'

'It also means that as far as Walpole is concerned I cannot be alive again and I am to be killed. Walpole knows I live and breathe and as we speak he will be looking for me,' Charity said with a hint of desperation.

'What have you done that could change the heart of the Inspector of Police? This is a conspiracy, Captain.'

'That it is. The reason is not yet clear – but will be soon.'

'What will you do?' Mariah asked.

'I need clothes, Mister Quadlibett. I have a suit at the Golden Kipper. Tell Mister Smutch it is for my burial – he will continue the rumour that I am dead. He could never keep anything to himself. Tell him that I am to be buried with my pistol and small brass telescope. I have a room in the loft. There's ammunition in the drawer of the cupboard by the bed. Bring it to me. Mariah and I have to plan our war.'

'War, on the streets of our town? I will be reminded in my heart of the fight against Napoleon. In the hour, Captain, you will have what you want. In the hour . . .'

Mister Quadlibett scurried like an excited rabbit from the room. He pulled his fingerless gloves upon his hands and took off his silk cap to swap it for a small, threadbare topper.

'You know where your favourites are hidden, Mariah. Help yourself.' Quadlibett smiled as he slipped from the candy shop into the candle-lit vaults beneath the market hall. 'Lock the door and pull the blinds.'

He disappeared from the shop. Mariah had followed him to the door and did just as he said. He turned the key in the lock and pulled the blind over the windows. All was quiet.

The hour passed slowly. The clock above the door ticked loudly. Mariah watched the second hand as it crawled across the white face. Charity sat in front of the fire, his eyes fixed and lips tight.

'What shall we do?' Mariah asked as the hour halved.

'I have a good mind to go alone. I can't take you to more danger,' Charity replied without looking at him.

'Impossible.'

'You are in my care, Mariah Mundi. Don't forget that,' Charity said.

'It's beyond your care. It was something Packavi said to me. He said there had to be another death and then five more and his task will be over. He said seven would be a perfect number, complete . . .'

'Seven? Are you sure?' Charity asked.

'He said I was to be a sacrifice and seven would die – something to do with the stars. When I found the man inside the Prince Regent, he was in suite 217.'

'Suite 217 was Gormenberg's apartment. That's it – I understand,' Charity said as if suddenly everything became clear. 'The Society of Truth.'

'What?' Mariah asked, not knowing what he was talking about.

'It all fits. It has to be them. That is why they want the Prince Regent, and finding the Ghost Diamonds is what they need to survive. That is why Gormenberg came here.'

'The Society of Truth?' Mariah asked.

'The power behind the power, Mariah. Never look at life with your eyes closed. Nothing happens in this world without them knowing. The Society of Truth is behind every war and disaster. The politicians may say we are sent to fight for freedom, but it is really for gain. I have known for some time that the Society of Truth put its men in positions of power. They then bring in more people from their society and so the rot spreads. They are like a plague, a virus that spreads its corruption. From the police to parliament they are all infected with the servile filth.'

'So Walpole – the sign on his ring – the Society?' Mariah asked.

'The mark of a minion. No one of real power would be so crude. Walpole is just a foot soldier for someone else,' Charity replied.

From outside the shop there was a gentle tapping on the glass. Mariah turned down the lamp before he opened the door that led into the shop. He quietly crossed the floor as the tapping came again. He peered around the screen and there, standing all alone, was Mister Quadlibett.

'Followed, Captain, I was followed,' Quadlibett gibbered with nervous excitement as Mariah let him into the shop. 'I think I gave them the slip in the haar mist but I am sure they know it was me.'

'Where from?' Mariah asked.

'From outside the Golden Kipper. Walpole's men are everywhere. I met Mrs Sacahvell the fish seller. She knows everything. She said they were out to catch Spring-Heeled Jack. They must think that old Mister Quadlibett is the suspect as two of his men set off after me when I got your clothes.' Quadlibett handed Charity a small brown parcel neatly tied with string. It was as cold as the night and brought the smell of the street and the strong odour of fried fish inside the Vendorium. 'I think I lost them in Sepulchre Street – not that I can be sure.'

There was a sudden spate of footsteps outside the shop. The door handle turned slowly as Mariah and Mister Quadlibett stepped back towards the storeroom.

[21]

The Mesmerist

THE door to the Vendorium sprang open. Two men in rough suits and dirty shoes stepped inside. They stood for a moment in their own dirt as the taller, scruffier man rubbed the day's growth of beard on his chin.

'We know you're here, Mister Quadlibett,' he said as he wheezed for breath. 'Saw you leave the Golden Kipper, we did. Police business – want to know what was in that parcel.'

The men waited for a reply. Mister Quadlibett walked slowly and elegantly from the back room into the shop, the tassel on his silk hat dangling over his face.

'Fish, fried potato and a side order of oysters,' Quadlibett replied. 'The Golden Kipper is the best place in the world for such food – here, would you like to try?'

Quadlibett slipped his hand around the door and unseen to the men, Mariah handed him a packet of fish, fried potatoes and oysters wrapped in brown paper.

'Parcel you was carrying was bigger than that,' the smaller man said as he rubbed the night dew from his nose.

'Double wrapped to keep out the night air – can't be eating cold fish can we?' Quadlibett replied as he offered some of the food to the two detectives. 'Must be serious business, hunting for fried fish. I hear haddock robbery is on the increase.'

'Funny,' said the small man in a droll manner as he looked about the shop and sneered at Quadlibett. 'Do you know Jack Charity?' he asked.

'Doesn't all the town?' Quadlibett said as he sucked on a fried potato. 'Sadly, I heard about his death. Here, I have it on the authority of the *Evening Gazette*, so it must be true. Never known them to get anything wrong. Why should you be asking about him?'

'Loose ends, Mister Quadlibett, snipping off loose ends,' said the taller man as he tried to look over Qaudlibett's shoulder and into the room beyond. 'What's in there?'

'Everything I own – my whole life. A bed, the good Book and a warm fire.'

'Can we see?' the man asked as he stepped forward, hoping that Quadlibett would get out of his way.

'Inconvenient. Especially as I am having my supper,' he replied, taking a mouthful of fish and oysters.

The man snatched the food from his hand, screwed up the paper into a ball and threw it to the floor. 'Supper's over, Mister Quadlibett. Now can we take a look?'

'I presume you are telling, rather than asking?' he said as he stood his ground and with a flick of his head flashed the long silk tassel into the man's face.

'You presume right – now get out of the way.'

'What are you looking for?' he asked as the man lifted him from the ground. 'That is where I live, nothing more –'

'We have instructions to find –' The tall man stopped and stared Quadlibett in the eye as he realised he had nearly said too much.

'I am not a mesmerist. There are no ghosts in my room, no spectre of the night, no phantom of death . . . I think you should –' Quadlibett was about to finish his words when he was thrown to the floor.

The man stepped forward and pushed on the door. There came a sound like the clicking of a ratchet. The burly detective stepped back as a masked figure in a fine black suit pressed a revolver into his forehead.

'This is a robbery,' said the man as he winked at Quadlibett without being seen by the detective. 'Move an inch and you're a dead man.'

The detective shivered. His companion looked to the door as if to run.

'Leave this place and I'll shoot you as well,' said the masked man as he held the pistol closer to the man's forehead.

The other detective froze and put his hands in the air. Quadlibett knew instantly that this was Captain Jack.

'You can't do this,' he said as he stared at the gunman. 'You didn't ask us if you could turn this place over – you from out of town? Them's the rules – we say who gets robbed.'

'Not tonight you don't – it's your turn. You,' he said to Quadlibett. 'Get up and take this rope. Tie them together and make it good and you won't get shot.'

'Please don't kill me,' Quadlibett pleaded as he snatched the rope from the robber's hand and with great delight began to tie up the two detectives. He pulled the rope as hard as he could until each squealed in great discomfort.

'Their feet as well,' the robber said as he held them at gun-point.

Quadlibett seemed to enjoy strapping the two detectives together. He disappeared into his room and returned with a large spool of gummed tape, which he proceeded to wrap around their heads until they could neither see nor speak. He continued to wrap them in the thick brown tape until they resembled two ancient mummies strapped back to back.

The robber pulled the mask from his face and gestured for Quadlibett to keep silent. Charity could hardly contain his laughter and Quadlibett smirked in deep mirth. Together they tipped the detectives from their feet and rolled them under the counter as they moaned vociferously.

'You,' Charity said to Quadlibett. 'In the back of the shop and give us all your money.'

Quadlibett scurried into the back room as Charity followed.

'One move from you, old man, and I'll kill you myself,' he said to Quadlibett as he slammed the door behind them. Charity then took a length of rope and wrapped it around his hand and then began to scrape it against the side of the fireplace until it split. 'Wait two hours,' he whispered as softly as he could. 'Then *escape* – tell them you were robbed and threatened with death. We'll be long gone. I'll lock you in and push the key under the door. Only unlock the door when they have been released – that way they will believe what you tell them.'

'How exciting!' Quadlibett trembled. 'If only I could come with you.'

'It'd be too dangerous,' Charity replied. 'Help Mariah onto my back. I only want them to hear one set of footsteps leave the Vendorium.'

Charity left the shop carrying Mariah on his back. He locked the door and slid the key underneath. Soon they were in the street. The haar mist was thick and cold. It gripped the street like an icy hand. They could hear the sound of carriages nearby but in the thick fog could see no one. The mist dulled the lights of the shops, sucking any brilliance from them and garbing their form in brackish dreariness. It was as if the whole town was covered in a deathly grey shroud.

Walking by the King's Arms towards the abattoir, they listened to the quiet conversation within. It was as if there was an expectation of something dreadful about to happen, as if every man, woman and child had been given a foreboding vision that there would be great misery upon that eve.

A man stood on the corner of the lane that led to the Prince Regent from East Bar. Mariah could just make out his dark outline in the gaslight. He smoked a pipe and leant against the wall. He held a brush in his hands and looked as if he had just finished washing the blood from the abattoir steps. He watched them closely as they passed by.

'Not an evening for a lad to be out,' he said as he chewed on the chalk stem of the pipe.

'Finished work,' Mariah replied, his head down.

'Spring-Heeled Jack will be out. Best get off, the pair of you. No respecter of circumstances is Spring-Heeled Jack.'

'That be right,' Charity replied in an accent that made him sound like a drunk Frenchman.

'All right for me,' the man went on. 'Don't think he'd be interested in an old butcher.' He took up his brush and swept the dregs of blood into the road.

The Prince Regent loomed ahead, rising out of the mist like a leviathan. The lights from the square cast a large shadow against the mist. Here and there, the haar swirled to form what looked like the transient shapes of whirlwind spectres that fleeted momentarily before disappearing.

Mariah went ahead as he heard the sound of hammering and the screaming of Mrs Mukluk. He stopped on the corner and peered around the wall to see what was happening. Outside the hotel in the swirling mist and lit by the street lamps was Walpole. He stood beside three neat piles of alligator-skin cases all initialled with the letters DZ. Zogel was standing next to his carriage as Lucius gathered up the cases and supervised their stacking on the carriage. Mrs Mukluk was being dragged away by two constables in uniform. A large crowd gathered in the hustle-bustle to see what was happening.

233

'What is it?' Charity asked as he lurked in the shadows.

'They're boarding up the hotel and Mrs Mukluk is being taken to the jailer's van. Zogel's carriage is there – he's leaving,' Mariah whispered as he looked on. 'There's Walpole and his men – Grimm and Grendel and –'

'And who?' Charity asked.

'He's standing by the door of Athol House. I can't be sure. Looks like the man from the Towers – the one who was speaking with Walpole.'

Charity edged closer to Mariah and peeked around the corner. In a brief clearing of the mist that came between fast swirls, he saw the man. He was dressed in his fine coat and silk top hat with a black cane in his hand.

'Bardolph,' Charity said in a whisper, recalling a distant memory and a face he could never forget. 'I never thought I would ever see him here.'

Walpole began to shout to make his voice heard as he read from the writ. 'I, Inspector Walpole of the town police, hereby give warning that as from this time the Prince Regent Hotel is out of bounds to all and sundry . . . and no longer the property of Captain Jack Charity, formerly of this parish and now deceased . . . This will be made law by the Mayor, Ebenezer Wolf, at the town hall banquet tomorrow night . . . Any person found on these premises will be prosecuted to the full extent of the law. I have men inside the hotel and guards on every door and they have orders to shoot.'

'Now it is all very clear,' Charity whispered as he pulled Mariah back into the shadows. Zogel's carriage rattled along the street, followed by the jailer's cart. Mrs Mukluk screamed to be released as she clung to the bars of the window, the fat driver giving no heed to her distress.

'What are they doing to her?' Mariah asked as the carriage rattled into the fog.

'She won't have gone without a fight. Doesn't like leaving the Prince Regent, thinks her son will come back and the only place he'll know to look is here.'

'Where is he?' Mariah asked as they hid in the doorway of the Italian coffee house.

'Lost at sea – believed to be dead. Mrs Mukluk won't believe it. The Prince Regent was the last place she saw him alive, before it was rebuilt. There was a small theatre. Twink would entertain the crowds with impressions. He took a steam ship to France that sank in a storm.'

'But she thinks he will come back?'

'It's what keeps her alive. Old Smutch fell in love with her. Sends her a card every Valentine's Day – she thinks it's from her son.'

'Look,' said Mariah as he spied through the dark glass of the coffee shop to the door of Athol House across the square. 'Grimm and Grendel are going inside.'

Finished with their business at the Prince Regent, Grimm, Grendel and Inspector Walpole went through the large grubby door into the tall, shabby white building of Athol House. Bardolph waited at the bottom of the steps and looked across the square at the mist-smeared facade of the hotel. He smiled in smug satisfaction and then turned and followed, and the door of the house was closed behind him.

'Bardolph. Never thought he would be in a town like this, Mariah,' Charity said as they took the long flight of stone steps that led from the Italian coffee house to the strand below.

'What does he do?' Mariah asked as they walked on.

'It is not what he does, but who he is. Bardolph is not his true name. Like Gormenberg he can change his identity as he likes. He is the Templar of the Society of Truth. When they need money or hear of some fine object that they could steal they send Bardolph. He is a scavenger.'

'Then why is he here?'

'Obvious,' Charity replied as they came to the bottom of the steps and watched the last steam tram of the night roll slowly from the beach up the side of the cliff on its iron rails. 'He has come for the Ghost Diamonds.'

'So they are here?'

'Possibly. Are you sure that it was in suite 217 where you saw the man?' Charity asked.

'Sure as sure,' Mariah replied.

'Then that is where we need to be. Suite 217. If we could find the diamonds before Bardolph, then we would be in a position of power,' Charity said quickly as they walked along the beach beneath the towering dark hotel.

'Even if we can get inside, Walpole's men could still find us,' Mariah said.

'They don't know the place. Imagine – we could hide anywhere. We could be in and out of the room as fast as light. My only concern is why they never searched for the diamonds straightaway,' he replied as the tide came near to their feet.

'There's a guard by the sea doors,' Mariah said as he pointed to a shadow far off along the beach. 'Walpole wants no one to get inside.'

'Then we'll have to find another way,' Charity said, looking up at the looming building that seemed to reach to the sky.

There was a sudden dull moan of the siren from the *Irenzee* anchored in the bay. It was as if it signalled the ship to wake from a sombre sleep. As before, the funnel and masts slid from the deck and a searchlight skimmed the waves as it scanned back and forth across the sea.

The ship's launch pulled away from the vessel and raced towards the harbour. The searchlight followed, illuminating its every movement. Mariah eyed its journey, pointing its path to Charity as it soared across the sea.

'Never seen a boat go that fast before,' Mariah said, watching the craft ease its speed as it reached the harbour.

'Looks as if it sucks in the water and forces out a blast at the stern,' Charity replied as he took from his pocket the miniature telescope that Quadlibett had brought from the Golden Kipper. 'Zogel and Lucius are at the harbour side,' he said as he peered through the lens. 'They're getting into the boat and –'

'What is it?' Mariah asked.

'It's Sacha and her father. They're with Zogel,' Charity said in disbelief.

'They must have been caught,' Mariah replied.

'See for yourself,' he said as he handed Mariah the telescope.

Mariah looked through the lens. The searchlight from the *Irenzee* lit the pier and cast dark shadows like black fingers across the water. There, on the steps just above the launch, was Zogel. Next to him was Sacha. She was with her father. They were both smiling. Lucius handed her a cork life jacket. She slipped it across her shoulders and tied it at the front. The dwarf squeezed her hand and laughed. It was as if they had been friends for a long time. Zogel shook her father's hand warmly. He led them both to the launch. Soon they were on board.

'They're taking them to the ship,' Mariah said as his mind raced to discover what could have happened. 'I heard Walpole saying that the reason they had kidnapped Sacha was so her father would do what they wanted.'

'Looks as if it is already done,' Charity said as he watched the launch get nearer to the *Irenzee*.

'Why would they do this – what is on the ship for them?' Mariah pleaded. 'She promised . . . I'm her friend.'

'We don't know what is going on. Zogel is a complicated man and can charm the birds from the trees. It could be believed that he has lied to them both.'

'Then we have to tell her – get to the ship and tell her, bring her back,' Mariah replied as he saw Sacha and her father step from the launch and on to the deck of the *Irenzee*.

Lucius and Zogel followed on. The launch was winched from the water and stowed beneath the enormous deck. The funnel and the masts slid back to their places until the ship lay in the water like a vast island in the bay.

'First thing, Mariah, is to find the Ghost Diamonds – then we can look for Sacha and her father. But we shall have to break into the Prince Regent and all the doors are watched by Walpole's men.'

'I know a way,' Mariah said as he remembered the *Piscis humanis*. 'I found a secret entrance. We should see Titus Salt. There is a tunnel from the Aquarium to the lagoon – it's where Otto Luger bred strange fish.'

'Then we shall visit the old dog and put an end to this skulduggery,' Charity said as a smile spread across his face.

[22]

The Porkpie Hat

THEY walked the length of the beach, covered by the shadow of the Prince Regent and the pall of mist that came in with the tide. As they reached the Aquarium, Charity saw two men by the museum. They stood in the doorway, huddled in their coats to keep out the night. He quickly realised that they were Walpole's men – their porkpie hats and long black coats were what they all seemed to wear. Charity walked ahead, Mariah following silently and keeping to the shadows, out of sight. Soon they had left the beach and were on the short promenade that led to the Aquarium and Pleasure Palace.

The door was locked and bolted. Mariah could see a faint glimmer of light coming from the office where Titus Salt lived. He tapped as gently as he could so that the police would not hear him. The dog growled as it stalked from the room and looked through the glass at the two dark shadows outside. It eyed Mariah as if there was something about him that it knew. It sniffed the air as he came closer and then jumped up to the door, its front paws on the glass standing higher than a man.

'Grub, Grub,' Mariah whispered as the animal stared at them. 'Go bring Titus!'

The dog seemed to know what Mariah had said. It dropped to the floor and ran off back to the office, only to return moments later followed by Titus Salt.

'Who is it?' he asked as he came closer, dressed in an over-large dressing gown and Egyptian fez hat. 'Can't a man have his sleep without being disturbed?'

'It's Mariah and Captain Charity,' Mariah said as Titus got to the door.

'You're early, always early,' Titus chuntered as he turned the lock and hurriedly let them inside. 'You weren't supposed to be here for another hour. I saw it clearly when I had the dream – saw the church clock, and you're an hour too soon.'

'Do you want us to go and come back?' Charity asked with a smile as they stepped inside.

'You're here now,' Titus replied as he fiddled with the belt of the dressing gown, trying to tie it into a tight knot.

'We –' Mariah said, but Titus interrupted.

'Want to use the tunnel to get into the Prince Regent?' He sighed. 'It's already known to me. I've seen it all. Ghost Diamonds is it, Jack?'

'That is yet to be discovered,' Charity replied as Titus walked ahead of them and through the doorway to his office.

'Tea first and then battle, eh, Jack? Wasn't that the way it always was?' Titus spoke happily as if recalling some fond memory.

'Long time ago and many miles away Titus Salt,' Charity replied as Titus put an old kettle on the stove. 'Does the future offer you any surprises with that far sight of yours?'

'It's a dim glass and only comes when others are in need. It's a Corinthian gift – I'm not your seafront diviner or charlatan. Wouldn't want to see everything – too painful to know.'

'But you saw we were coming and what we wanted,' Mariah said as he sat by the fire with Grub wrapped about his legs.

'You're both in danger. All I'll say as a warning is something I saw. Since I heard that you were arrested I could do nothing but think of you. Every time you came to mind, I could see a lion waiting to tear you to pieces. It was a dark creature with blood-red eyes. Something or someone wants you both dead. I've pleaded your case before the King of kings and for your sake I hope He heard my call.'

'I fear the same, Titus. We battle not against flesh and blood, but powers and principalities that work through human form. Nothing is clearer in my mind,' Charity replied as Titus poured the tea and stood by the fire. 'I have to clear my name and prove to the world that I didn't kill those people. The only way that can be done is if I find the true killer.'

'He's not far away, Jack. They have sent him for you. As we speak he searches the streets,' Titus said.

'Then we shall be about our business and the hunted shall become the hunter.'

'Like old times, Captain? Outnumbered – the enemy on every side – and still prepared to fight?' Titus asked.

'Isn't that when it's at its best? A fight isn't worth taking on unless there are seven of them and only one of you. It's the only reason worth leaving this land for – and you were one of the finest, Titus . . .'

Titus Salt looked into his mug of tea and watched the swirling leaves go around and around. It was as if he were no longer there – not in a dream or trance, but standing in the past. He could hear the sound of a battle far away as his fingers trembled. Titus said nothing but in his mind the sun had set behind the mountains and a squall beat against the land in fury.

'But when does it stop?' he asked quietly without looking up. 'I have left too many friends on foreign shores never to be seen again.'

'*No foes shall stay his might; though he with giants fight, he will*

241

make good his right to be a . . .' Charity sang softly as the fire light dimmed and Mariah stared into the darkening embers.

'Listen,' Mariah said as Grub pricked up his ears. 'It's coming from the Aquarium.'

From deep inside the Pleasure Palace came the faint echo of what sounded like singing. It wasn't a voice that Mariah knew and he couldn't understand the words, but he was sure it was singing.

'Can't be,' Titus said as he walked from the room and into the vast arcade, followed by Charity and Mariah. 'I can hear . . .'

Coming from the far end of the Aquarium was faint music. At first it sounded like the singing of a choir of high-pitched voices. As they got closer the sound changed to that of a shrill note pitching and falling.

'Someone's playing tricks,' Titus said as he pulled Grub close to him.

'Then they choose the wrong time,' Charity replied as he took the pistol from his pocket and cocked the hammer. 'I'll go around the back with Mariah,' he whispered.

Charity and Mariah slipped through the narrow gap between two large, dark glass cases that went from the floor to the ceiling. Each tank was braced with red-painted iron. Mariah stared inside. There in the murky black were the shapes of fishes and crabs swirling in the dark water.

'That's why I joined the army,' Charity said as if he could read Mariah's mind. 'Never liked dark water. You can never see what lies beneath.'

They could hear Titus walking slowly along the stone floor between the avenues of fish tanks and kept pace step by step. Charity held the pistol ready to fire as Mariah listened to the faint music.

'*Piscis humanis*,' Mariah said as he thought of the fish. 'Luger bred them. They look like people. It could be them.'

242

'It's the fish,' cried Titus Salt as he stared into the glowing tank.

Mariah and Charity slipped back onto the avenue between the tanks and stood with Titus. There in the tank was the *Piscis humanis*. It swam in small circles, its mouth out of the water. As it swam the fish glowed red, green and then bright blue. There was a gurgling sound that came from the large pipe that ran around the entire building. Mariah looked up at the large arches hung with vines. Small oriental birds danced silently through the leaves that wrapped themselves around each arcade. Before him the fish continued to sing.

'Can't be,' Charity said, his brow raised in disbelief.

'This is what was bred in the Prince Regent. Luger – or whatever he was called – brought them here. They change all the time. Sometimes I think they look even more human.'

'*Hu . . . maa . . . naa*,' said the fish eerily, as if it repeated what Titus had said, then it swirled from the surface to the glass and appeared to smile.

'Did you hear what it said?' Mariah asked, unsure he could believe his mind.

'A clever trick, Titus Salt – don't you get enough visitors here?' Charity scorned.

'That were no trick, Jack – that was the fish,' he replied, his eyes showing his own disbelief. 'I've seen them on a Sunday; they stay by the glass and listen to the visitors. It's as if they listen to what they are saying. Sometimes wonder who is on display. Told you there was something wrong with these things. I have a good mind to have done with them and have them killed.'

'You can't,' Mariah protested. 'They know what we are saying. Look.'

Together they stared at the tank. For a moment they could see their own dark reflections against the glass and then in an instant the water exploded in bright colour. All the fish began to sing. And as they called out they shone brighter, until the tank glowed so brightly that Charity and Mariah covered their eyes. The creatures rolled around and around, intertwining with each other as they sang. They seemed to be giving praise with a chorus of sound and uttering divine words that neither Mariah nor Charity nor Titus Salt could ever understand. The light grew even brighter as the fish swam around the vast tank of seawater and dived into the air above them.

Suddenly all went silent. The fish tank darkened and the *Piscis humanis* were gone. Mariah listened to the dripping of water from the roof and the chirping of the birds that lived in the vines. Titus looked at Charity as if they had been privy to something secret that should never have been beheld by the eyes of men.

From the look on his face it was clear that Charity didn't know what words to say next. He pointed at the tank. There, as if just appeared by some magic trick, was a single *Piscis humanis*. It was larger than the others, its face more human and its eyes dark and piercing. It had several long tentacles around its lips that touched the glass like a large catfish. It made the creature look like an army colonel with a waxed moustache.

The fish looked at them as if *they* were the ones on display. Its eyes searched each one of them as if it knew their hearts. Then it smiled and turned. In the second it was gone into the darkness of the vast Aquarium.

'They are like men,' Charity said. 'What was that madman doing breeding such creatures?'

'The *Piscis humanis* are just the ones that survived,' Titus replied. 'There were others that were so grotesque and wicked of feature that my eyes won't let me believe what I saw.'

'That man played with life and took on the Creator in his own task. I have a mind to bring the Prince Regent to the ground and rid the world of its memory,' Charity said angrily as he scanned the tank for another glimpse of the fish.

'They won't be back, not for a while,' Titus replied as he saw Charity's eyes searching for any sign of the fish. 'They vanish for days. It's as if they only come to the glass when they want to be seen. I once believed they could make themselves invisible and only appear when they wanted.'

Mariah ignored them both. He tapped urgently on the tank with his fingers and pressed his face to the glass. At first there was nothing. Then, as he tapped again, there was a faint glow that began to appear from the gravel bed of the tank. It came closer, translucent and pulsating like a ring of fairy lights. It then took shape. He knew this was the same creature that he had first seen when he had broken in to the Aquarium.

It came to the side of the tank and, just as before, stared him eye to eye. Mariah pressed his hand against the glass as if to touch the creature. The fish raised its long hand-like fin and mirrored his touch. The side of the tank began to tremble softly as if the creature purred like a gigantic cat. It then began to change in colour and slowly swam to break the water with its mouth.

'G . . . oooh . . .' it sung softly like a dove. 'G . . . oooh . . .'

'It's telling you to go,' Titus said.

'Why?' Mariah asked, not thinking he was speaking to a large fish.

'Da . . . ey . . . co . . . mm . . . fer . . . ya . . . ew . . .' it gurgled sweetly as it sang.

'They are coming for you,' Titus repeated. 'It thinks someone is coming for you.'

The fish looked at Titus through soulful eyes and appeared to smile. It shone bright red and glowed dazzlingly, shaking itself as the gills behind its human-like ears trembled.

'It knows something – perhaps it can sense the danger we are in,' Charity said as the fish quickly disappeared.

Grub shivered by Titus's side and then gave a low growl.

'Someone's near,' Titus said urgently. 'Go, Jack – Mariah knows the way. Lock the door behind you.' He looked at Mariah and nodded for them to be gone as Grub growled louder.

There was a beating on the door of the Aquarium and Pleasure Palace that shook the air like thunder. It came again, louder, and the doors began to split open and the glass crack within the frames.

Titus ran with Grub at his side. He could see shadows of men outside beating against the wooden door. There was a splintering of glass as the panel smashed and the door was beaten open. The yapping of a bloodhound heralded the chase.

Standing in the doorway were the two detectives who had questioned Mister Quadlibett.

'Titus Salt? It's Greaves and Readman, your old friends,' one of them shouted as he shone a lantern into the darkened avenue. 'We know you have them here. The bloodhound followed a thief and his companion from the Market Vaults. So no lying, Titus,' the man mocked. 'You know what happens if you lie to the police.'

Titus knew both of these men. They had come to the Aquarium many times. He walked on as calmly as he could, holding Grub tight to his side.

'There is no one here – you are wrong,' he said as the hound bayed and growled.

'Then you won't mind if we let the dog search the place?'

Before Titus could reply, the two detectives pushed their way inside and walked across the broken glass and into the Pleasure Palace.

'You'll find nothing here. I don't know who you are looking for.'

'Jack Charity and Mariah Mundi,' Readman, the smaller detective, blurted out without thinking.

'Fool,' cursed Greaves as he jabbed Readman in the chest with his fist.

'Ah,' Titus laughed. 'You hunt for the dead with hounds? Whatever next – searching for the man in the moon with a Cheshire cat?'

A scruffy old man in a tweed coat pulling an overweight bloodhound on a long leather leash came in from the cold night.

'My hounds can find anything,' he muttered feebly through his jowls. 'Even the dead.'

'Then search you may and I hope you find more than you came looking for,' Titus replied as he held Grub to his side.

'I'll leash up Burgho and walk him,' said the ragged man with the old dog. 'It's the only way I'll find anything in this place, it stinks worse than Titus Salt.'

Above them, a black macaw howled in disapproval, shouting out the words he had heard from the navvies who chewed tobacco and hid from their lodging houses on wet Sunday afternoons.

'It's dangerous to go on your own – there are creatures and I cannot guarantee your safety,' Titus shouted as the man walked into the shadow of the galleries.

'They're only fish,' said Greaves. 'Nothing to be afraid of, Titus – unless you're hiding something?'

Titus cast a glance up the long avenue away from the *Piscis humanis* and the entrance to the tunnel. He knew Greaves had seen him and looked again for good measure, this time allowing his eyes to tarry upon the large tank halfway along.

'What's up there, Titus?' Greaves asked. 'Is that where they went?'

'There's been no one here,' Titus insisted.

'He's lying, Mister Brough – let Burgho scent them out.'

The old man nodded at the detective and set off alone

towards the tank. The hound pulled him onwards towards the glass and sniffed the frame.

'Got something,' the man said as the hound skirted the side of the tank that led to the steps up to the gantry. 'Gone up here – you'll have to help me get the dog up,' he shouted as the hound scrabbled at the steps.

'Come with us,' the detective said, taking hold of Titus and dragging him along. Grub growled. Greaves slipped his grip and prodded for Titus to walk on ahead.

'You're making a mistake. No one has gone this way.'

'We'll decide who has made the mistake when we put you in Dean Prison for obstructing the police,' the detective snorted.

Titus knew he could not fool them for long. All he wanted was to hold the detectives back for such a time as to allow Mariah and Charity to get into the Prince Regent.

'I wouldn't take the dog up there,' he said as he refused to walk any further. 'No one has been that way.'

'You're lying. Mister Readman, get that dog and old Brough on to that gantry. That's the way they went, I know it.' Greaves laughed as he turned to Titus. 'Do you think I am totally stupid?'

'Not totally,' Titus replied as he watched the dog being pushed up the steps and onto the feeding gantry that ran above every deep and murky tank.

'I have something,' said old Mister Brough as Burgho found the scent of a creature. 'It's along here,' he said excitedly. Readman followed as the dog pulled Brough along the gantry towards a vast tank of still black water.

'Tell us who was here and where they are now,' insisted the fat detective.

'There is no one here,' Titus protested as the dog on the gantry sniffed at the water inches below.

'Tell me!' Greaves shouted angrily as he pulled back his fist to strike Titus in the face.

There was a sudden splash of water and a momentary howl as the bloodhound vanished into the tank, quickly followed by Mister Brough.

'What was that?' screamed Readman, just a yard behind Brough and his dog. He could see nothing but the rippling of the water beneath his feet. 'They've vanished!' he shouted nervously as he looked to the shimmering, black water below.

'What have you done with them?' the other detective screamed, his eyes flashing from Titus to Mister Readman, who stood terrified above the tank.

'I told you it was dangerous,' Titus protested too late as suddenly and without warning Readman was pulled from his feet into the bubbling, swirling black murk.

'Joe!' the man screamed as something dragged him deeper into the water. 'Help me . . .'

Greaves ran to the gantry, climbed up the steps and ran along the feeding platform.

'Don't do it!' Titus screamed at him.

'I'll be with you soon, Budd,' Greaves shouted as he ran. He quickly took hold of Readman's arm. 'It won't take you . . .'

Greaves pulled as hard as he could. For a moment, whatever had taken hold of Readman released its grip. The man scrabbled upwards, gripping the edge of the gantry, his clothes tattered and torn as if a thousand sharp teeth had ripped them to pieces.

'It's beneath me, Joe,' he said as he gulped his breath, but could say no more.

Just as he was about to be pulled from the water, a vast and terrible creature snapped a long tentacle across his back. The claws dug into him, pulling the man from Greaves and into the water. Then there was complete silence; even the birds that squawked in the vines that hung from the arcade had stopped singing.

Greaves looked into the water but could see nothing.

'You'll pay for this, Titus Salt. This is murder,' he shouted as he made his way precariously along the metal gantry towards the steps.

'I warned you. Told you it was dangerous,' Titus said, his words echoing. 'You didn't listen – when will you ever listen?'

There was no reply. As Titus looked up he could see that Detective Joe Greaves had vanished. All that floated on the surface of the water were the torn remnants of his porkpie hat and the collar of his grubby, faded white shirt.

[23]

Suite 217

THE door that led from the Aquarium and Pleasure Palace to the deepest regions of the Prince Regent Hotel had closed firmly behind them. Mariah had twisted the handle so tightly that it could be moved no further. Charity in turn had pushed the bolt as hard as he could so that no one could follow. They didn't know that their pursuers were dead, and that another of the late Otto Luger's weird creations had eaten its fill on two detectives, a large but old dog and an even larger and older Mister Brough. The creature, a strange cross between some kind of shark and an octopus, lay at the bottom of its dark tank, so full that it was unable to move.

In the tunnel, Mariah and Charity walked on blindly. They used their hands to trace along the wall. Each moved at a slow pace for fear they would fall upon some hidden precipice. Cobwebs and trailing strands of cavewort dragged across their faces like the hands of the long-buried reaching for life. Mariah took his phosphorescent torch and shone the beam at the ceiling. But it faded at once, leaving him doubly blind as the spark of light took away his dark sight.

It was ten long minutes before they had made any noticeable

progress. The tunnel became a twisting staircase that eventually found the light in what was once the storeroom of the magician Bizmillah. Mariah found the lanterns that had been left over from the performance of the disappearing pig and soon they found themselves in the lobby of the hotel. Charity was not sure if Walpole had placed any of his men inside the hotel. All he knew was that outside, at every door was an officer of the law.

Mariah led the way as they walked up the staircase and along the landing to suite 217. Their purpose kept them silent. Mariah wanted to find the diamonds quickly. In his mind he could see Sacha standing on the dock and smiling at his enemy. Lucius held her hand as they shared laughter. The spectacle made Mariah shiver in anger. As soon as he found the diamonds he would find Sacha, Mariah said to himself as he struggled in the turmoil of wanting to know why she was on the *Irenzee*.

Mariah was taken from his thoughts by their arrival at the door of suite 217. It was not locked. Charity pushed the door slowly and looked inside. All was just as it had been on the night Mariah had followed the thief from the hotel. The room was tidy. Nothing was disturbed. It was sprawling and vast and looked bigger than he remembered. It had once been several rooms that had been pulled together, with walls knocked down and ceilings replastered. Now it formed a peculiar suite that took up one corner of the third floor of the hotel.

Charity went to the window and drew the curtains as Mariah watched from the doorway. The hotel already smelt of sour milk and old newspapers. Since the guests had gone it had begun to fester and stagnate quicker than they could have imagined.

There was nothing left of Baron Hoetzendorf's in the room. It was obvious to them both that the room had been searched yet again and all the items put back in place.

Charity had stood in this room many times. Whenever a guest had stayed there, he had welcomed them to suite 217, the Prince Regent's finest room, with a bottle of champagne and Mister Bonnet's peculiarly good chocolates. But despite its extravagant design and lavish furniture, it had an icy chill. Not one that would be given from a cold draught, but the kind that hung in the air from tragic circumstances. It was as if voices from the past earnestly desired to warn those in the future of what had once taken place.

When Cordelia Troodle, a famous mesmerist and seer, had visited the town for a Gathering of Magnetism she had stayed but one night before the voices in suite 217 had driven her not only from the hotel but also from the country. She had run from the building screaming for her life, and having taken the first train to Liverpool had departed back to the Americas on the paddle steamer SS *Scotia*. What those voices had said, no one knew. But they had been sufficiently articulate to scare not only Miss Troodle but also several other guests since.

Despite this, many people booked suite 217 a year in advance. It had remained the most popular and the most expensive room in the Prince Regent. Baron Hoetzendorf's wife had insisted that no other room was grand enough for them.

Now it lay empty, colder than before, and the whole hotel was eerily silent. The sound of the distant steam generator was the only noise to give any suggestion that life continued somewhere in the empty building.

Mariah peered through a chink in the curtain to the square outside. He could see Athol House, its grubby door shut firmly as if to keep in its secrets. A Peeler stood outside. He kept his arms folded under his uniform cape, his half topper pulled down about his ears to keep out the cold. The man paced a yard each way like a ticking clock; he stopped at every turn and looked each way before ticking again back and forth.

'What do you think they are doing?' Mariah whispered to Charity who had started to search the room.

'Waiting for a time to come and look in here. They'll hang on until no one is about and then they'll be in to take this place apart.'

'How do we know the diamonds are here?' Mariah asked as he pulled the curtains back in place.

'We don't. Gormenberg used this room when he was pretending to be Otto Luger. I can only think he hid them somewhere near. He couldn't be far away from his riches. They were what gave him life.'

'Have you seen the Ghost Diamonds?' asked Mariah.

'Seen, never – but heard of them often. I can't understand why they were brought here. The Bureau of Antiquities has hunted for them throughout the world. Beautiful things, I hear. Cut from a diamond the size of a skull and divided into seven equal diamonds. It is said that if you stare into the centre of each stone you can see your own face on the day you die. That is why they are called the Ghost Diamonds . . .'

'And Gormenberg smuggled the diamonds into the Prince Regent?' Mariah asked as he looked about the room.

'No one knows. It was long before I came back. Smutch told me of a rumour. Everyone thought they were in the smugglers' tunnels and lost for ever. But they have to be somewhere very near.'

'Why would the Society of Truth need them?' Mariah asked as he looked under the grand four-poster bed that stood out of place in the centre of the room.

'They are like a spoilt child who will never share. The Society of Truth believes they have a divine right to every precious item in the world. What they cannot buy they will steal and what they cannot steal they will kill for.'

'But why?' he asked.

'They even kill their own when they have no further use of them. Two presidents of the Americas were amongst their number. The Society of Truth had Lincoln and Garfield killed. Shot dead by deranged madmen. They were honest men who declined the Society's invitation. Garfield was shot dead about the time the Ghost Diamonds vanished and Zogel set sail for Africa.'

Mariah sat on the large bed and for a moment held his face in the hot palms of his hands.

'I never thought that . . . I never could believe . . .' He struggled to speak; he felt like a mouse about to be eaten by a tiger. 'We cannot win against such people.'

'A fight here and a skirmish there . . . The Bureau of Antiquities will be a thorn in their flesh until they are destroyed – that is all what we need to do. One battle at a time. Remember Mariah, we are not alone in this fight.'

Charity looked up and smiled as Mariah stared at the ornate ceiling. His eyes followed the line of the plaster moulding that had been painted in shimmering blue and gold. A long vine branch took his gaze from the window to the centre of the room. It was woven with clusters of grapes and the occasional spider until it reached a crown at the heart of a six-pointed star. At each tip was a similar moulded coronet, and these somehow seemed out of place, as if they had been added later to the original decoration. The whole star fitted neatly into the space between the curtained posts of the bed. Whoever lay against the fusty pillows could look up and see the stars and coronets framed upon the ceiling.

The dim glow from the lamp cast a long shadow above him. It glistened against the faded gilding. Mariah stared and stared, wondering why someone should waste so much money on something only glanced upon in the last moments before sleep.

'It's like what Walpole has on his finger ring,' Mariah said with a sense of melancholy.

'What is?' Charity whispered as he looked up to where Mariah was now pointing.

'That star. I saw a design like it on Walpole's ring. Zogel had one the same.'

'The seal of Solomon – builder of the Temple and founder of the Society of Truth. I have seen the sign that Walpole carries, the square and compass. All part of their pinnies and party games . . .' Charity said softly with an air of contempt.

Mariah continued to stare at the ceiling. A shard of glistening light had caught his eye. It was like the slither of a silver fish darting through the waves on a dark night. As he looked he could see it shine and glisten.

'There's something under the plaster crown,' he said to Charity as he stood on the bed and reached up. 'Captain Jack,' he went on, unable to control the rising sense of excitement that swelled in his guts and took his voice away. 'It's . . . it's a diamond!'

Without saying another word, Mariah climbed the curtains that hung from the bed frame and balanced on the thick oak beams that joined corner to corner. Pressing his hand against the ceiling to steady himself, he reached out and took hold of the nearest coronet. He poked at the crumbling plaster with his finger. There, beneath the dust, was the smooth face of a diamond. He grabbed the crown and pulled hard. Like a loosened tooth it came away easily. Mariah slipped, twisted in the air and fell to the bed in a shower of plaster dust.

'Ghost Diamonds,' he whispered breathlessly, with a broad smile lightening his face as he looked up at Charity. 'You were right. Gormenberg had them all the time – right here above his bed.'

Charity took hold of the diamond in disbelief. It was the size of his fist and perfect in every way. He cleaned the coating of plaster from its surface and held it to the dim light of the lantern. As he gazed at the faceted gem he could see his own reflection looking back. Suddenly, like a misting mirror, it began to change. Gone were his bright eyes and there looking at him was the face of an old man.

'Ghost Diamonds,' Charity said in a voice at the edge of a whisper.

He handed the diamond to Mariah, who instinctively held the gemstone and looked within. He could see no manifestation. There was no change in its facade and no reflection.

'Did you see yourself when you were old?' Charity asked as he took the diamond from him.

'Nothing . . . I saw nothing.' Mariah replied.

'Must be the light. A trick in the way it is cut. Six more, Mariah. Six diamonds stuck to the ceiling where no one would ever dream of finding them. To think of it – Gormenberg had them near him and gazed on them as he fell to sleep. A clever man to think of such a way of disguising their hiding place.'

'In full view, so that even Baron Hoetzendorf looked on them as he dozed,' Mariah replied as he again climbed the large bed and clambered along the oak beams.

One by one he prised the diamonds from the plaster mouldings and let them drop to the mattress below. Soon they had all the diamonds. They nestled in the covers like a brood of eggs belonging to an extinct creature. They shone and glistened, begging to be adored.

'What shall we do with them?' Mariah asked impatiently as he and Charity filled a pillowcase with the jewels.

'Take them. I will ask for instructions from The Bureau. Isambard Black will know what to do.'

'I asked Sacha to tell Mrs Mukluk to send him a telegram,' Mariah said, not believing that what he asked had been done.

Sensing his discomfort, Charity was quick to reply. 'Already done. Mrs Mukluk would have sent it anyway. She is wiser than we give her credit and was told that if anything was to happen to me then she should tell the Bureau.'

'Will he come?' Mariah asked as a thin line wrinkled his brow for the first time.

'I would be surprised if he is not already here. Isambard Black is a man of many faces.'

'Then will it be over?' Mariah asked as if he faced the hordes of Hades.

'When Walpole is arrested and Bardolph is dead – then it will be over,' Charity said reluctantly as he looked at the concern on Mariah's face. 'If anything happens to me, you are to carry on. Hide the diamonds with Mister Quadlibett and wait for Isambard Black. He will take up the fight again and see it to the end.'

'I don't want to be on my own. I have only you,' Mariah said without thinking.

'And I you, but we shall keep these thoughts for another day,' Charity replied as he took a diamond from the embroidered pillowcase and looked at it again. 'We still have to find the killer and the reason why Zogel has come to the town. Our task nears its end but is not yet complete.'

'Light?' A sudden, sharp and unexpected voice from along the corridor. 'There can't be a light,' the voice said, the words almost lost in the shuffle of heavy boots against the carpet. 'The place is empty.'

'Walpole said he saw something in suite 217 – better check,' said another man who followed on.

Mariah looked at Charity. There was no way of escape. They were trapped. The brusque footsteps drew closer. A shadow was cast across the open doorway. Two men stepped inside the room.

'No one here,' one said as he cast the light of his lamp across the room. 'Walpole's seeing things. When did he say he was coming?'

'Tomorrow. Things to do, he said. Back in the morning, first thing,' the other man replied as he looked at the ruffled bed that by now was covered in dust and plaster. 'No point looking for evidence, not now that Charity is dead. Can't hang a dead man.'

'Not too sure about that – look.' The man pointed to a set of footprints edged in white powder that went from the bed towards the window. 'Someone's been here,' he said as he looked up at the ceiling and saw the plaster crowns had been torn from their place. 'He was right – a lamp.'

Hidden by the long sideboard was a smouldering lamp. A spurt of spiralling smoke twisted upwards to scent the room.

'Just been snuffed,' the man said in a sudden whisper as he looked about the room. 'Could still be here.'

The drapes at the window moved slightly and caught the gaze of both men. The older of the two pulled a short cudgel from his belt. He gripped it in his hand, ready to strike.

'Best be coming out,' he said as he raised his arm. 'Best be coming out as quick as you can.'

The drapes moved slowly as the breeze streamed in through the window. The man hesitated and then nodded to his companion as they both prepared their attack.

'Never give another chance, whoever you may be,' the man said softly as he took a step towards the covered window.

In a flash the man was on the floor holding his face. His companion jumped back, startled. The thud came again, even quicker than before. The crack of the diamonds in the pillow-case as they hit him echoed in the room.

'Run Mariah!' Charity shouted as they leapt from cover and dashed towards the door.

Mariah leapt the two groaning bodies that writhed on the floor. He jumped over the bed as if it were a horse fence. As Charity turned Mariah caught the smile on his face.

'Onwards!' Charity screamed as if he were leading a charge in the desert, the pillowcase stuffed with diamonds held close by his side.

The shrill sound of a police whistle came from the room. It blasted the alarm over and over seeping into the street below.

'They're on to us!' Mariah shouted as they ran together along the corridor and down the stairs.

'A copper on every door,' Charity replied, thinking as he ran. 'They'll be on us before we know it.'

'The cellar – the sea doors,' Mariah said breathlessly as he tried to keep pace. 'It's our only chance.'

'The balcony by the restaurant and then to the sea,' Charity said as he turned the corner of the landing. Far behind the sound of heavy footsteps followed them. They were relentless, evenly paced like the beating of army drums. As they came closer they gathered in number until they pounded as one.

'They'll catch us,' Mariah pleaded as he lost pace.

'Keep with me,' Charity shouted desperately in reply. He stopped and turned.

Mariah was gone. He had vanished. It was as if he had been snatched by the night. Something or someone had taken him. Charity ran back along the passageway. It was empty. There were no doors, no way of escape. Mariah had to be near, Charity thought as he searched for him. He pressed the walls for any sign of a secret place, knowing there were many passageways hidden in the walls that were still undiscovered. He looked back and forth in disbelief. It was then that he smelt a sweet scent of apples and roses. It came like a fleeting cloud and then was gone.

'Mariah . . . Mariah!' he pleaded hopelessly for the missing boy.

All he could hear was the sound of the beating footsteps coming closer. Charity waited, hoping that Mariah would reappear as quickly as he had vanished.

'Mariah - don't play tricks,' he said for the last time as the footsteps broke out from the twisting staircase and into the passageway.

Charity looked back. He could see the dull and distant shapes of several policemen getting closer.

'Ahead!' one of them shouted as they saw the man they chased for the first time.

The pursuers began to run. Charity ran, gaining speed with each step. He pushed through the doors and onto the balcony that skirted the Prince Regent above the cliff and the sea below.

'Take him!' a man shouted as the pursuers ran towards him, his voice almost lost in the gale.

Charity looked back. He had nowhere to run. Far below was the full tide. It beat against the sea doors. Waves broke upon the rocks. He gripped the diamonds tightly as he stood on the low balustrade. One of his pursuers reached out for him and grabbed Charity by the sleeve of his coat. Charity pulled against him as the waves ripped against the beach.

In an instant he was gone – falling faster and faster.

'No!' screamed the copper as he clutched a torn piece of fabric in his hand.

They watched as Charity fell towards the sea. A large wave rolled in towards the cliff face and swelled the water high against the rocks. Charity was gone – consumed by the darkness and the tide, lost without a trace.

'He's dead now,' said the peeler as he shrugged his rain-drenched shoulders and shone his lantern to the wind-blown sea far below. 'Twice drowned in the day,' he smirked. 'It was Charity for sure. Best be telling Walpole.'

[24]

The *Irenzee*

'IT won't be long before you can see me,' Zogel said as Mariah felt himself moving slowly from side to side. 'The chloroform should wear off within the hour.'

The words seemed distant. It was as if he had heard them in a dream. Mariah tried to open his eyes and lift his head from the hard pillow, but he could do nothing. His body was like lead. It was cold and numb. His hands ached from where they had been held in a tight spasm-like grip. When he breathed his lungs burnt. Slowly, very slowly, his heart beat in his chest and his neck pulsed nervously.

'Jack . . .' he said, asking for his friend.

'Quite safe,' Zogel went on in his Carolina drawl. 'He made a dramatic escape. Leapt from the balcony of the Prince Regent like a bird. My men were on the beach. They followed Captain Charity to the Golden Kipper. Well, after he had swum to the shore and struggled from the waves. I watched it myself. I have the most amazing telescope, it makes the night as clear as day. I'll take you on deck and you can see it. Tell me – why should he go to see a Mister Quadlibett before going to the Golden Kipper?'

'What happened to me?' Mariah muttered, his tongue parched like an old sole.

'Poisoned . . . Well, I should say anaesthetised. I have always had an interest in chloroform. It has become quite a habit.'

'Sacha, I saw Sacha . . .' Mariah said, stumbling over his words.

'She is here. My guest. Just like you. Some people were going to do her harm. I had to bring her here.'

'But you drugged me – you said you would help,' Mariah said, still unable to open his eyes.

'You wouldn't have come here freely, Jack Charity would have seen to that. The Bureau and I have never seen things the same way. He thinks I'm a thief.'

'Why kidnap me?' Mariah asked as he again tried to open his heavy eyes.

'I needed to talk to you alone. Ask you a question that I know will be answered truthfully.' Zogel shuffled closer to Mariah and whispered in his ear. 'The Ghost Diamonds – I believe you have them.'

'Is that why you came here?' Mariah asked, his hand beginning to shake as the blood rushed to his fingertips.

'Not at first. Shall I say I stumbled upon them?' Zogel replied as he sat in the high-backed chair next to the bed. 'I had some business with a few people. Unpaid debts to be recovered, that sort of everyday thing.' Zogel paused then leant forward. 'Did you find the diamonds?'

Mariah thought for a moment. He didn't know how to answer. His head was split with pain as his body came back to life. It was hard to think as he drifted between waking and sleeping.

'I don't have them,' he replied hesitantly.

'Captain Jack – did *he* find them?' Zogel asked.

Mariah didn't reply. He knew he should keep silent. Painfully he lifted his hand to his forehead and brushed away dried, crusted sand.

'I take it he did,' Zogel said as he rubbed his beard.

'Will you let me go?' Mariah asked.

'Will you tell me the truth?' Zogel replied.

'I saw Lucius at the Towers – you're helping Bardolph.'

Zogel laughed loudly. 'You are a wild one, Mariah Mundi. Lucius said he'd been followed . . . It *was* you. We help no one – especially Bardolph.'

'But you're a part of the Society of Truth,' Mariah replied.

'Did Charity tell you that?' Zogel asked, smiling to himself wolfishly.

'I saw the ring on your finger. It is the same as the one Walpole carries and he works for Bardolph.' Mariah groaned as he managed to open his eyes and looked at the room for the first time.

'Skull and bones, young Mariah, that is all I am. The Society of Truth isn't all it's cracked up to be. They think they control the world, but who controls them? I work for myself. Skull and bones . . . That's all you need in this life for real power.'

'They want the diamonds,' Mariah said.

'I know. That's what the deal was all about. I came to this place because of people who owed me money. I then heard about the diamonds. Bardolph thought that it was the Ghost Diamonds that brought me here. He wanted to strike a deal. Told Lucius all about them.' Zogel stopped speaking as Mariah tried to sit up. 'I love diamonds – don't you, Mariah?' He pulled the cuff of his crisp white shirt and twisted the gold linking chains.

The door to the state room opened and Lucius stepped inside. Mariah looked at him through eyes half closed. He sensed he was in a large, shadowy room. He could make out only the shapes of those around him and the burning light far to his left.

'Dedalus,' Lucius said softly. 'I think you have told him too much.'

'Not in the slightest, Lucius,' Zogel said with a grin. 'I wish to tell him everything, every sordid detail of why we are here.'

'Would that be wise?' asked the dwarf.

'Not at all. Wisdom is for the foolish,' Zogel replied.

'But the exchange? I have already sent word to Charity.'

'Has he replied?' Zogel asked as his eyes widened in anticipation.

Lucius didn't speak. He looked at Mariah and then to Zogel. He gave a gruff cough as if to clear his throat and then turned and left the room.

'Perhaps I'll get a chance to tell you more before you leave,' Zogel continued.

'I can go?' Mariah asked.

'There was never any doubt. You are to be traded for the diamonds. You are the one thing that Charity will not give up. It was when you said, "It's a family business" – the day we met – that's when I knew I had you. Thought then that Charity had a weakness and the weakness was you – his godson. Once I have the diamonds, then the *Irenzee* will be gone.'

'Do you always get what you want?' Mariah asked.

'Always,' Zogel replied as he curled his moustache with the tips of his fingers. 'That's why I'm the richest man in the world. The Society of Truth will have to wait for their money. To think – they expected me to take the diamonds to Notre-Dame in Paris on their behalf. Now I'll just take them for myself.'

'So that's what Sacha's father was going to do – allow the ship to leave without a warrant,' Mariah said as he focused his eyes. Above him he could make out the faint shape of a vaulted roof. He felt sick to the stomach and breathed deeply.

'You are one step ahead,' Zogel replied as he stood up to

leave. 'I didn't like the idea of them being killed. Pointless, really. I'm going to take them with me and let them go when the heat is off. She's a good girl – told me all about you. In fact, without her I would never have known where to look. She led us straight to you and told us how to get in the passage without being seen. Sacha has been working for me for quite a while.'

'Working for you?' Mariah asked incredulously, his words sharp and half shouted.

'Don't be so surprised. It's not a bad thing. How else did we know so much about the hotel? Can't blame someone for taking care of themselves, can we? I trust you would have done the same.'

Zogel began to walk from the state room with his arms folded behind his back. Mariah watched his every step.

'So when can I go?' he asked.

'As soon as we hear that Charity is prepared to exchange the diamonds for you. I have had to tell him that I will kill you if he doesn't do what I want. And he has been led to believe that it is Bardolph who is asking. So I do think he'll agree.'

'Won't Bardolph stop you?' Mariah asked. 'He wants the diamonds.'

'Bardolph is not my problem . . . He will be taken care of.' Zogel stopped as he got to the door and turned. His voice changed and he lost his smile. 'You have the free run of the ship. If a door is locked, it is so for a reason – leave it that way. Apart from that you can do and go as you please. I suggest you are not seen on deck. The ship is being watched.'

With that, Zogel was gone.

Mariah edged his way from the bed and gazed around the room. He still felt as if he was asleep. It looked more like the inside of a luxurious castle than the cabin of a ship. The bed was made of rich, dark oak and carved with frogs. The door stood open and he could see the long passageway that stretched out into the distance. To each side of him, pressed against the walls, were two large sofas, and on the walls were paintings of ships. There were no windows, just a light in the corner pinned to the wall on a swinging hinge. He could hear the engine far below. It reminded him of the Prince Regent. There was the gentle vibration that shook everything so that the whole ship trembled slightly.

He tried to walk. His feet were heavy. The deck moved with the waves, causing him to stumble. Everything spun in his head as the chloroform left him. Then there was a gentle tapping on the door.

'I couldn't tell you,' Sacha blurted as she stepped inside the cabin. 'I'd promised Dedalus.'

'First names, eh, Sacha?' Mariah snapped.

'It's not like that. You know Walpole was going to kill my father. Dedalus Zogel promised to help us – he said I should tell no one, not even you.'

'Fine thing that is. Get you from the castle, save your life and you run straight to him.'

'My father needed me,' she protested.

'If he were honest this would never have happened.'

'We can't change what is done,' she replied.

'You can't choose your family – but you *can* choose your friends,' he snarled. 'You lied, Sacha. You lied again and again and now I am here because you told him how to find me.'

'He said he wouldn't hurt you. Told me that you wouldn't listen to him. He had to bring you here. If he gets the diamonds then he'll be gone.'

'Can you trust him to tell the truth? All the man wants is money and he doesn't care how he gets it. For all we know he could be lying to us and working with Walpole to kill Captain Jack. Did you think of that before you snitched on me? You took him at his word. He's a liar – he's American.'

Sacha folded her arms and shrugged her shoulders. For so long he had wanted to see her, and now he wished she were gone from his life for good.

'It's all about money, Sacha. You father was prepared to cheat and look where it has got you. They'll still kill you – you can never come back here. When this boat leaves, you leave with it – for ever. The only way you can stay is if we find out who murdered the guests at the Prince Regent and clear Captain Jack – think about it.'

Sacha stared at the floor. She had no words for him. She knew he was right. Her father would have turned an eye and taken the money. A shiver ran through her until her foot shook angrily against the floor.

'So what will you do?' she said calmly.

'Get off the ship and find Jack,' Mariah said churlishly as his eyes dismissed her.

'But you'll be off tonight. I heard what Zogel said. If he swaps you for the diamonds you'll be gone,' she replied, ignoring his unspoken demand.

'The Bureau wants the diamonds and I work for the Bureau,' he said coldly, unable to look at her. 'Whatever I say you'll just go and tell him – so why don't you?'

'There's no way you can escape – it's impossible to get on the deck.'

'Zogel said I could go where I liked,' Mariah replied.

'But not through any locked doors. And every door on this deck is locked. We were brought down here and told the same thing. You're a prisoner.'

Heavy footsteps pressed against the floor in the corridor and a door slammed in the distance. Lucius stumbled in, ahead of a guard. He walked briskly, falling over his feet as the ship rocked from side to side.

'A slight change of plan,' he said to Mariah as he smiled deliciously at Sacha. 'Mister Zogel will keep you here until the morning and then you'll be free.'

Mariah wasn't listening. He stared at the guard. There was something familiar about his face. Although it was ordinary and in no way remarkable, the face of a man that could be seen across the world in every country and on every street corner, yet Mariah knew he had seen the man before.

He closed his eyes and held his hands to his face. In the darkness he could see him. It was the night of the explosions. Mariah was back at the midnight ball. There was Hoetzendorf and his wife. There was the waiter.

'I know,' Mariah said out loud, unable to keep his words to himself. 'I know –'

'What?' asked the dwarf.

'Can't think,' Mariah said quickly. 'Must be when I was poisoned.'

'Zogel wants to see you both in the dining room, by way of an apology. He has a surprise.'

Lucius gestured for them to follow. Mariah looked at the guard. There was no doubt. This was the man he had seen in the Prince Regent. It *was* him – *he* was the murderer. The guard was the man who had blown up the Ambassador and the others with hexogenamite.

Suddenly, what Zogel had said began to make sense. The bad debts had been settled. Hoetzendorf and the others had paid with their lives. Zogel had them murdered – but why? Charity would know why Zogel killed them and what linked them all together. He had to see Charity, tell him what he had found. These thoughts made Mariah want to escape even more. He could feel the panic rising in his chest as his heart beat faster.

Mariah tried to clear his mind as he followed Lucius along the oak-panelled corridor while the ship yawed from side to side. It smelt of caustic soap and beeswax. Through the small brass portholes that ran the length of the ship Mariah could see the outline of the town moving up and down. It seemed far away. The sea and sky were black against the lights of the town hall and the houses that gripped to the hillside beneath the castle.

'All is well . . . all will be well,' Mariah whispered to himself. Sacha turned and tried to smile at him. He caught her eyes for just a moment and then looked away, stiff-faced.

The guard walked behind them. He didn't speak, but just looked at Mariah as if he knew what he was thinking. Mariah bowed his head and followed silently through several doors and up two flights of steps.

Lucius unlocked every door and the guard locked them again as the procession went on. A door would never be left open. Mariah noticed the guard try every door after he had locked it, to make sure.

They walked in single file up yet another flight of narrow stairs. At the top they came to a small landing. It was dark. A small green lamp shone about their feet. Lucius mumbled to himself as he turned the key and pushed against the brass plate. The door opened and flooded the landing with bright electric light.

'Come in,' exclaimed Zogel loudly as the guard pushed Mariah into the room. 'I thought while we waited I could show you something of interest.'

Mariah looked about the room. It was like the inside of a palace. Fine Ottoman carpets littered the floors in between long sofas, and on every wall there was an electric light covered in a large glass shell. The colour of each light changed with the movement of the ship. In the middle of the room was a balcony rail that surrounded two wooden flaps edged in brass. Again, Mariah noticed there were no windows, just row upon row of tiny blacked-out portholes on every side. He found himself smiling with surprise.

'Knew you would like this place,' Zogel said quickly, as if he wanted to tell them a great secret. 'Even though I hate the sea, I love the ship. I was even thinking of having it built into my garden – but then again, Palmetto City has enough ships of its own.'

'Has Captain Charity agreed to give you the diamonds?' Mariah asked.

Zogel looked towards Lucius in the hope he would answer for him. There was a long, uncomfortable silence.

'I thought I would show you something that would interest you,' Zogel said. 'It's my latest invention. That's what I specialise in – inventions, things that make the world a better place.'

'Charity said all you invented was things to kill people and kill them quickly,' Mariah replied, his voice rasping with anger.

'A matter of opinion. If the guiltless Captain were here I would explain myself to him. Those are strange words from a man who has used my inventions for his own glory. I wonder if he has had a change of heart? What I invent brings wars to an end and stops the suffering of the unfortunates who get stuck in the cataract of greed. I provide a service.' Zogel smiled as he stepped forward and nodded to the guard. 'What I want to show you is not a weapon of war, but something I thought would distract you from the idleness of your temporary confinement.'

Zogel pressed a small button on the balcony railing and the two oak doors began to slowly slide apart. Mariah stared down, aware that Sacha had stepped closer to him. He could feel her breath on the back of his neck. He shrugged uncomfortably, not wanting her near.

As the floor opened the room was filled with a bright, deep purple light. There was a sudden hiss of steam as a platform in the cavernous room below came nearer. As Mariah shaded his

271

eyes from the brightness he could make out the shape of what looked like a wooden boat.

As it got nearer he realised that it had a roof with two glass domes at the front. The vessel looked like the face of a giant frog edged in brass. At the rear was a large propeller.

Zogel impatiently tapped the balcony rail as the machine came closer. He pressed the button again and the platform stopped.

'See – what an invention! An electric submersible, faster than a shark.' He laughed.

'For under the sea?' Sacha asked.

'Precisely, my girl. An invention of exploration and not war. What would Captain Jack say to that?' he asked.

'I'm sure you would find a way of using it to destroy your enemies,' Mariah replied.

'Sceptical as ever, young Mariah. I show it to you because that is how you will be taken to the harbour and that is how the Ghost Diamonds will be brought back to the ship. No one will ever know what has happened because no one will see.'

Zogel pressed the button again and the submersible slipped back into the hold and the doors closed.

'There is, however, one thing I forgot to tell your dear Captain . . . .' Zogel laughed as he spoke.

[25]

Ebenezer Wolf

FROM his hiding place in the small copse of yew trees by the side of the town hall, Jack Charity could see the *Irenzee* in the bay. The growing storm broke waves as high as houses over its bows. The long anchor chains trailed from the ship and into the dark sea. They strained as the waves grew and the swell became more intense. In the dark shadows of the trees Charity waited. He took a fob watch from his pocket and counted the seconds go by. The church clock reminded him of the time as it chimed the seventh hour after midday. All around the wind blew stronger, rattling the branches like sabres above his head and shrieking through the chimney pots of the houses on King Street. In the room two floors above him, a light came on and the figure of a man came to the leaded window.

Charity looked up. He wanted to be sure before he moved from the cover of the trees. Moving from under the branches, closer to the wall, he watched the man pull on his cloak and place a thick gold chain on his shoulders. The man looked younger than Charity, thinner and yet weary. His hand shook slightly as he fumbled for the clasp on the mayoral chain.

Ebenezer Wolf, Charity thought as he pulled the scarf over

his face, walked to the wall and began to climb the cast-iron pipe that went up through the canopy of yew trees to the roof. Soon he had climbed to the top of the town hall. A long stone balustrade circled the roof. Here and there thick glass skylights were wedged into the dripping grey slates. Charity pulled the first tile and opened up a small hole into the roof. He stacked the slates neatly before sliding inside. He had done this as a boy and remembered the way.

It wasn't long before he was standing outside a door in the darkened passageway on the third floor. A silver-white light outlined the door. Inside he could hear a man speaking to himself. The voice repeated the same words over and over, each time changing the speed and tone, as if practising to get the speech perfect.

Charity knew the man was alone. He reached for the door handle and turned it quietly, then stepped inside. He locked the door behind him.

The room was warm and dazzlingly lit with several candelabra filled with candles. A coal fire burnt brightly in a large marble fireplace. It looked to Charity like a grand office. There was a day bed and a wardrobe in the corner and two chairs by the fire. A large cluttered desk stood next to the window, and by the desk was a man. He was wearing a long red cloak with an ermine collar. Around his neck was a mayoral chain of links and charms.

'Say nothing,' Charity said to the man as he pointed the pistol at his head.

'I've got nothing to steal – only this chain. Is it worth the gallows for that?' the man asked.

'I'm not here to steal – just for you to keep your word. When I remove my mask you will not speak.'

'Agreed,' the man said nervously as Charity pulled the scarf from his face. There was silence as the man thought he looked at a ghost. 'Jack . . . You're *dead*!' he said, unable to believe who held him at gunpoint.

'Twice dead in one day, Ebenezer Wolf. But I am very much alive, dear friend. I need your help.' Charity put the gun back inside his coat.

For several minutes Charity told Ebenezer Wolf everything of the conspiracy. He spoke of the Society of Truth, Zogel and Bardolph. The Mayor sat in his chair and listened as he chewed his lip, one eye kept on the large oval clock above the door.

'If this is true, Jack, then no one is safe,' said Ebenezer as he tapped the leather on the top of the large desk that separated the two men. 'There is nothing I can do tonight – it is the banquet.'

'You will be asked to sign over the Prince Regent to a man called Bardolph. Walpole will say that I am dead. As you can see I am very much alive.'

'And a wanted man. They say you murdered your guests,' Wolf replied as he stood up and walked to the fireplace. 'I couldn't believe it – not Jack Charity.'

'An elaborate plot, Ebenezer. Three of the most influential people in the world murdered in one night in my hotel.' Charity then took a small, bread-like slice of hexagenamite from his pocket and placed it on the desk. 'They planted this in the Golden Kipper,' he said as he prodded the explosive with his finger. 'Smutch was wise enough to hide it away. A mouthful of this and death quickly follows. It is how they murdered Hoetzendorf and the others.'

'Was that Bardolph?' Wolf asked nervously.

'Baron Hoetzendorf and the American Ambassador were members of the Society of Truth. But I sense someone other than Bardolph had them killed,' he replied. 'I have to find Mariah and clear my name – but whatever happens, refuse to sign over the Prince Regent.'

275

'It may be harder than you think, Jack,' Ebenezer Wolf said nervously. 'Walpole has insisted I see him tonight. I don't think I can refuse. They have already asked me to sign the certificate of your death and hand over the hotel.'

'But you have to refuse. I am not dead,' Charity protested.

'It is only a matter of time,' Wolf said as he tapped nervously on the mantelpiece. 'Walpole will find you – he is bound to. He knows too much about me . . . If it came out . . . I was indiscreet – a foible of foibles, an idiosyncrasy that I thought would do no harm . . .'

'Just stall them until the morning. Please – for an old friend.'

'Until the morning and then it will have to be,' Wolf replied as he dropped his head and stared at the carpet. He couldn't look Jack Charity in the face. 'We all do stupid things in our life. The only thing is you never expect them to be held against you. I was trying to help a friend – and now Walpole has enough to blackmail me. It was injudicious, I –'

'Don't tell me what happened. Some things are best left unsaid,' Charity interrupted. 'I pray that by the morning I will have enough to put Walpole in prison. Then whatever you have done will matter not.'

'If that could be so, Jack,' he replied downcast. 'I would gladly swap your place on the gallows for my life.'

Ebenezer Wolf was about to go on when there was a sharp knocking at the door. He gestured for Charity to be silent and then pointed to the wardrobe by the day bed. Charity crossed the room quietly, opened the door and hid inside. It smelt of pine needles, snow and fur coats. He listened as Wolf went to the door.

'Ebenezer! Ebenezer!' came the voice from outside the room. Charity recognised Walpole's desperate screams. 'We have to speak to you before the banquet. It is of great importance.'

Charity could hear Ebenezer crossing the oak floor, the metal weights on the hem of his oversized cloak dragging clumsily on the wood.

'Just a minute,' he said as he slowly turned the key.

'You were talking – who to?' Walpole asked as he pushed his way into the room, followed by Grimm and Grendel.

'It was my speech for tonight. You know me, Inspector. Always nervous of these things. Ever since a lad at school.'

'I know you very well, Ebenezer. Far better than you would like the world to know,' Walpole grunted manically as he pulled his sagging cuffs. 'I hope the *business* we mentioned will be able to take place tonight?'

'Tonight?' Ebenezer Wolf asked anxiously. 'Tonight? Are you sure it would be best?'

'The sooner the better, Ebenezer, and then perhaps I will forget all I know,' Walpole replied as Grimm and Grendel kept watch on the door. 'I would be obliged if the little scrap of paper could be given your mark by midnight.'

'It will have to wait until the morning, there is much to be said and important guests,' Ebenezer Wolf went on. 'Come back first thing and it will be done.'

'If it is beyond midnight then know my tongue shall wag. By breakfast you will be out on the street and disgrace shall be a mantle on your shoulders,' Walpole whispered in Ebenezer's ear.

'Then we shall go to the banquet together,' Ebenezer said with a sudden and unexpected change of heart. 'I know what shall be done. Wait a moment until I get my speech from my desk. I shall have a police escort to the banquet – that shall protect me from any foul play. I shall be like Hamlet's father and this place shall be my Ellsinore. The law shall not be delayed and the insolence of office will soon be gone . . . Who would my burden bear? '

'Very well, my Lord Mayor,' Walpole joked sarcastically, not knowing what Ebenezer Wolf had meant. 'I shall even let you take my arm, right regal-like. Mister Grimm and Mister Grendel shall lead the way and I will introduce you to the Honourable Bardolph – he has all the papers. I'm sure you could be cajoled to sign them at the end of dinner?' Walpole said amiably as if he spoke to a madman.

Ebenezer Wolf cast a glance to the wardrobe and smiled as if to say goodbye. He reached to the desk and folded the parchment on which his speech was written into the shape of a long envelope. He looked up and tucked it into his jacket pocket. Turning, he looked once more towards where his old friend was hiding.

'*Oh juice of cursed hebenon – We have no friend but resolution and the briefest end*,' Ebenezer Wolf whispered as he walked away.

Walpole took Ebenezer Wolf by the arm and led him from the room so he could not escape.

Charity listened for the door to close and the treading footsteps to fade. Sliding the catch of the wardrobe, he slipped back into the world. He felt in his pocket for the slice of hexagenamite and then, when he realised that he had left it upon the desk, looked there. It had gone.

'Ebenezer . . .' he said, realising his friend had taken it. 'He cannot do this . . .'

Charity ran from the room to find him, but as he turned the corner of the passageway he realised he could go no further. He would be arrested – the Prince Regent would be lost. It would be his life for that of Ebenezer Wolf. All would be taken away, he thought as he gripped his hands into tight fists.

From the great hall he heard the clanging of the dinner gong. It clattered through the empty corridors of the town hall calling all to silence. Charity ran along the corridor. He knew the place well. To his left would be a door that would lead to the balcony above the great hall, and there would be shadows there in which he could hide and look upon the gathering below. In the darkness, he would work out a plan. Something in his heart told him that Ebenezer Wolf would eat the hexogenamite so that he could not be blackmailed.

Charity knew that if Walpole had the secrets of another's heart then it would not be long before he would tell the world. As soon as Ebenezer Wolf had signed the document and was no further use, Walpole would let slip some casual words and the secret would be out.

He remembered Ebenezer's sudden change of heart and the words he had said: 'I know what shall be done.'

Charity slipped through the door and into the shadows of the balcony. The great hall was filled with cigar smoke that spiralled in wafts of choking fumes from below. The dim glow of the candles formed crescents of light that surrounded each table. They were like islands set in a dark, impenetrable sea. On each chair, like decorated seals, sat the wise and mighty of the town. Every man waited to be fed as an army of skivvies fussed to fulfil their desires.

Charity didn't know what to do. There was no way he could speak to Ebenezer without being seen by Walpole. The Mayor sat at the high table overlooking the hall. Below him on the table next to the door were Walpole and Bardolph. The hall was filled with a hundred men.

Around each table the hubbub of conversation grew louder. Walpole looked about him uneasily. Grimm and Grendel sat with Bardolph in silence. Delivered to each table was a plate of goose, its long singed neck dangling over the side. One such steaming plate was processed across the dining hall and presented to Ebenezer like an offering. As each table took their goose, he nodded for all to commence the banquet.

Every man ate hungrily. Charity knew each one by name. They were the fat officials who did more for themselves than the people they served, the bankers and politicians who thought they owned the borough. Some were the idle rich who knew not the hunger of the streets around them. Charity knew if he were to approach Ebenezer he would be seen and arrested. Though his heart was broken he knew he had to stop Ebenezer from taking the hexogenamite.

Ebenezer in his ermine cloak ate in silence, his eyes fixed ahead as if he stared on a distant land. Every now and then he nodded as the man next to him spoke eagerly at his side. Ebenezer didn't reply. Charity watched as his thoughts tore his heart. He knew that to do anything would cost his life.

Suddenly Ebenezer got to his feet and banged upon the table.

'This is my last speech,' he said loudly, smiling at the surprised gathering. 'For that I am grateful. I have lived a lie and I was to be exposed – by the Inspector of Police and his companions.'

Not a man spoke as Walpole got to his feet. 'The Mayor is mad,' he shouted.

'Let him speak,' said a man in a blood-red fez hat.

'And that I shall,' said Ebenezer as he went on. 'We are caught in a time when good men are accused of bad things and bad men prosper. I was to be blackmailed –'

'Lies!' shouted Walpole as he vaulted onto the small dais and took hold of Ebenezer and tried to force him to the ground.

'Jack Charity is not dead and was framed for the murders. The killers are in your midst,' Ebenezer said as he pulled his hand from his pocket. As Walpole strangled him Ebenezer Wolf swallowed a chunk of hexogenamite.

'No!' screamed Walpole as he pushed Ebenezer away.

'If you have tears – prepare to shed them now – for death

will have its day.' Ebenezer clutched his stomach and gripped the walls with his stiffening fingers.

The crowd shrank back in silence as the swirling cigar smoke wisped to the high vaulted ceiling like a blue smog.

'Charity is innocent. May these be my last words,' Ebenezer said as he started to foam as the mouth. 'What I have done in my life should not be held against me. Walpole would have blackmailed me to say that Charity is dead when he is not – *he lives!*'

'Mad!' shouted Walpole as Ebenezer Wolf began to writhe on the floor. 'Mad and a liar!'

Without thinking, Charity leapt from the balcony to the dais below. Walpole turned. Charity pushed him from the stage to the floor and into the crowd of men. Grimm and Grendel jumped to their feet as Bardolph cowered behind them. Grendel drew a pistol from his coat and took aim.

'No!' shouted Walpole. 'Not here!'

'Will not one of you help this man?' Charity screamed as he grabbed hold of Ebenezer and tried to prise open his mouth and stop him swallowing more of the explosive.

'Too late, dear Charity,' Ebenezer sobbed as he coughed. 'Forgive me for this – I could not bear the shame. I know the judge of all will not condemn me as these men have in their hearts.'

'No, Ebenezer . . . It shouldn't be this way,' Charity replied as he cradled the man in his arms.

'Stand aside,' Ebenezer whispered. 'You know what is to come.'

Ebenezer Wolf gripped his stomach as the hexagenamite bubbled in his guts. Charity dived to the floor, looking for a way of escape.

'You're mine now!' screamed Walpole as he snatched the gun from Mister Grimm and took aim.

It was as he was about to fire that Ebenezer Wolf exploded. There was a blinding flash of light as a purple fire instantly consumed him. Walpole was blown from his feet. A ball of silver cloud then mushroomed to the ceiling filling the room with dense smog. A shimmering grey dust blew about the hall and fell like snow as Ebenezer's ashes were scattered by the explosion.

Charity seized his chance. He leapt from table to table as he ran towards the window at the far end of the room. Goose and port wine were scattered across the floor. The man in the fez reached out to stop him. Charity, seeing the shadow of the man in the mist, kicked a stuffed goose from its plate. The half-eaten bird hit the man in the face, knocking him to the floor.

'Stop him!' shouted Walpole as Grimm and Grendel set off in pursuit.

Walpole took aim with the pistol and fired into the mayhem. The bullets shot over Charity's head and through the window. One shot hit the stained glass figure of Alderman Periwinkle between the eyes. The crowd scattered. Grendel leapt from across the room like a demented deer as Grimm pushed through the screaming crowds of men who now clung to the tables for fear of being shot.

Walpole fired wildly until he emptied the chamber of bullets. In desperation he threw the pistol as hard as he could. Charity sprang from the final table towards the window. Covering his head with his arms, he dived through the stained glass. The portrait of Alderman Periwinkle crumbled as Charity burst into the night.

'Stop him!' Walpole screamed hopelessly as Charity vanished.

Landing on the sloping grass, Charity jumped to his feet. He knew he would have to run, and that nowhere would be safe. Walpole would have his men at the Golden Kipper before he could make it there.

Jumping the railings of the town hall, he ran towards King Street. Charity knew he would be safe with Mister Quadlibett. He looked behind to the dark shadows and slowed to a walking pace. The streets were damp and empty. He pushed his hands deep inside his coat and shrugged his shoulders to shake the chill from himself. He sighed, knowing his friend was dead and he was responsible. There was much about working for the Bureau of Antiquities that he hated.

As he turned into the long alleyway from King Street to the Market the enfolding darkness pressed in against him. He stopped for a moment and listened to see if he was being followed.

'Don't turn around,' a calm, heavy voice said as Charity felt the tip of a sharp blade press into his back. 'The boy for the diamonds – that is what we want. He is well – but if we don't have the Ghost Diamonds at midnight then we'll feed him hexogenamite and give what's left of him to the fish.'

'How do you know I have them?' Charity asked.

'Mariah Mundi – he talked. We know everything,' the man replied as he pressed the knife deeper into Charity's back. 'The graveyard, midnight. Come alone. The church door will be open . . . You have four hours. See to it you bring the diamonds.' His voice was a stern and urgent whisper.

'If you kill him then I will track you down and take your life in return for his,' Charity said bitterly.

He felt the blade move from his back. He turned. The man had vanished. Darkness was all around him.

[26]

Skull and Bones

CHARITY took the longest route he could find to Mister Quadlibett's shop in the Market vaults. Walking through the wet lanes, he stopped at every corner and waited to see if he was being followed. It was a surprise that there were no Peelers out on the crowded streets. News of the explosion of the Mayor was being passed from man to man. Traders with handcarts spoke of it with every sale. The tale was augmented with every telling until it was said that half the council had died in the conflagration.

Charity kept his face hidden with his scarf. He was covered in mud and his clothes were tattered from the tearing of the glass. He looked like a dirty, wet vagabond and was not out of place on such a dark night. He waited by the doors of the Emporium on Market Street. No one came this way, not after dark and not on such a night as this. They would stick to the East Bar with its chestnut vendors and beer carts.

From the doorway he could see the entrance to the vaults. Charity expected it to be guarded by at least one of Walpole's men, but from where he was he could see no one. A solitary gas lamp lighted the street. A thick, shimmering haze of rain fell constantly. Charity used his scarf to wipe the mud from his face as the water drenched him. He went several more yards and hid in the doorway of a derelict shop.

Footsteps echoed suddenly down the street. They walked quickly and were definite in their purpose. Charity pushed himself back into the deepest recess of the shadows. He held his breath for fear of being heard. With one hand he groped for the pistol in his pocket and made ready to fire. He knew he could just shoot through the pocket.

The footsteps got closer.

'Captain Jack?' asked a voice like that of a waiting beggar.

'Titus Salt,' replied Charity. 'How did you know I was here?'

'Seen it, seen it all . . . Bad things Jack, things you shouldn't face alone,' Titus replied.

'You've done enough – helping me could get you hanged,' Charity said as he stepped from the darkness and checked that Salt had not been followed.

'I know what's to come and I won't be hanged. Never saw it all – but know enough that you need help,' Titus said as he tried to smile.

'Then whisper as we walk and tell me what you have seen,' Charity said as he took Titus Salt by the arm and walked him down the dimly lit street to the doors of the Market Vaults.

As they stepped inside Titus finished speaking. Soon they were at the door of Quadlibett's Vendorium. Charity turned the handle and went in as if he was expected. Mister Quadlibett came out from behind the counter.

'Am I to be wrapped in tape?' he asked jokingly. 'And Titus Salt, the keeper of monsters – I haven't seen you in two years.'

'Fish keep me busy, Mister Quadlibett. Finding enough for them to eat takes all my time,' Titus replied.

Captain Charity locked the door to the shop and pulled down the blind. Instinctively, Mister Quadlibett dimmed the light and ushered both men through the narrow doorway to the room where he lived.

A warm fire burnt in the stove and as always the kettle rattled on the warming plate. Quadlibett nodded for them to sit by the fire as he got in his favourite chair and pulled the blanket over his knees.

'For the first time in my life I know the cost of having someone close to my heart,' Charity said with a broken voice. 'They have Mariah, and in exchange they want the Ghost Diamonds. I have no choice. Midnight, at the old church by the castle. I should go alone.'

'I insist I come with you – all I could see in my vision, Mister Quadlibett, was a creature with a metal skull that breathed fire. Consumed half the town. and I know in my heart it wanted to kill Jack . . .'

'Then we shall all go and fight this beast together,' Quadlibett replied excitedly.

'No,' Charity said. 'I wouldn't put you in danger. All I would ask you to do, Mister Quadlibett, is to meet the last train. I pray that the man I want to see will be upon it.'

'And what of me?' Titus Salt asked begrudgingly. 'I'm not letting you go alone.'

'Very well, but I cannot say you will be safe,' Charity replied.

'All will be well, all will be well,' Titus said, the flickering of the candle casting a dark shadow across his face.

'Do you have the parcel I left with you?' Charity asked Mister Quadlibett.

'Indeed,' he said as he got from his chair and rummaged behind the casks stacked against the door to the tunnel. He returned to the fire clutching the Ghost Diamonds wrapped in the pillowcase. 'I have to say that I did indeed look. Never have I seen such fine things – but there is something quite impious in their nature. It will be good for you to give them away, regardless of their value. The boy Mariah is worth every stone.'

'If you give them to Bardolph then more men will chase the Ghost Diamonds and lives will be lost,' Titus Salt muttered as he rubbed his hands in the heat of the flames. 'Greed is a strange thing, it makes fools out of the wise and murderers from the faint of heart.'

'That is why I thought they would be best in the hands of the Bureau of Antiquities – at least they would never be seen again,' Charity replied. 'Now it is time for us to be about our business. Keep safe, Mister Quadlibett.'

Charity wrapped his scarf around his neck and checked the bullets in the chamber of the pistol before slipping it back in his coat. He pulled up his collar and turned to leave.

'One thing,' Quadlibett said. 'If all fails, I will look after Mariah as if he were my own.'

Charity smiled and squeezed his hand.

'We'll see you again, Mister Quadlibett. I promise you that,' Titus Salt whispered as they left the Vendorium.

In the street outside the Market Vaults they heard the church clock strike eleven times. The rain had stopped, leaving the dark lanes sparkling as if crystals had been cast amongst coals. Titus Salt walked on ahead, his face to the wind that blew from the north. The town was deserted. It was eerie and silent. Titus stopped and let Charity walk ahead, each man taking his turn in checking to see if they were being followed. They turned the corner by the broken-down houses on to Rope Walk and passed by the charnel grounds.

Charity could see the whirling arms of the windmill blades on the cliff edge. They creaked as they turned, rattling with every gust. He went ahead, keeping to the shadows, as Titus Salt followed on behind. Every ten paces he would stop and turn. Then, stepping from the shadows, he would skip three paces to make up the distance between himself and Charity.

As they walked up the long hill the looming presence of the old church came into sight. At one end were the old ruins that stuck from the ground like the ribs of a long-dead animal. The lights of the houses on Paradise cast the shadow of bones against the walls. Facing them was the church and before it the graveyard.

Charity and Titus slipped quietly over the wall and were quickly consumed by even darker shadows. They made their way through the tall stones and sepulchre tombs with their doors and engraved walls. The shadow of the great church made the pathway doubly dark. Around each stone were piles of damp leaves browned by death and stinking of rot.

As they reached the solitary lamp by the west wall, they could see the door to the church was open.

Charity signalled for Titus to take a hiding place.

'Wait here,' he said in the faintest whisper. 'I shall go in alone.'

Titus could not protest. Charity placed his finger upon his lips to stop him from speaking. In an instant he was gone into the dark church.

Once inside, Charity stopped and looked about him. At the high altar a single candle burnt brightly. There was the smell of incense mingled with the damp fragrance of the old hymn books stacked by the door. Pools of water from the broken roof glistened along the aisle like the footprints of an ancient amphibian. The sound of the cascading drops echoed upward to the high vaulted roof. There was emptiness to the place, as if the angels had been long gone and no one had noticed their reluctant departure. The keepers of the stones had gone about their mumblings day in, day out, not realising that they were alone. In their wisdom they had kept the traditions made by men and forgotten the love that bound the place stronger than mortar.

Charity shivered as he listened to his own footsteps. He walked slowly between the rows of planked seats. He sensed the church was empty. Something drew him to the altar. He climbed the three steps and stopped by an old tomb of a faceless knight.

Tracing his fingers over its features he saw the nose had been shattered. The knight stared up at him in the shadows like a street fighter, a broken-nosed pugilist knocked down for the last time.

'Quite a place to end up,' said a voice from behind him.

Charity turned quickly but could see no one.

'Zogel?' he asked. 'I was expecting –'

'Bardolph and his pocket policeman?' Zogel asked. 'It's I who sent for you, Jack. I want the Ghost Diamonds.'

'How do you know I have them with me?' Charity asked.

'I have Mariah Mundi – a pleasant boy, but speaks too much.'

'He would have told you nothing,' Charity replied, knowing Zogel lied.

'He didn't have to. I had him snatched from the Prince Regent,' Zogel said and then paused. 'By the way, I no longer want to buy it. Bardolph can have it and turn it into a temple for the Society of Truth.'

'Thought that would be your ambition?' Charity asked.

'I am beyond dressing up and giving signs. The Bureau of Antiquities should keep you informed. Dedalus Zogel is now the Chairman of the Federal Reserve Bank of the Americas. The richest man in the world has his own licence to print money.'

'Is that why you had Lincoln and Garfield murdered?' Charity asked.

'I wouldn't use such a cruel word as that. They were in the way and so were moved to one side. Both of them foolishly asked for an inquiry as to who ran the bank. But he who pays the piper calls the tune. They didn't listen.'

'So – *you* are Skull and Bones?' Charity asked cautiously.

Zogel looked around and spoke only when he knew he was alone.

'That I am – the power behind the power as people keep saying,' he replied.

'So why do you want the diamonds?' Charity asked as he put his hand in his coat and held the grip of the pistol.

Zogel clicked his fingers. Two men dragged Titus Salt inside the church and pushed him to the floor.

'You should have come alone. Now I have Mariah, Sacha and this tramp. Strange how friendships can be our downfall.'

'Where's Mariah?' Charity asked.

'He's outside. As soon as I have the diamonds I will let him go.'

'How can I be sure?' Charity asked.

'Have I ever lied to you?' said Zogel sheepishly.

'Have you ever told the truth?'

'In all things,' Zogel said as he twisted the knot of his necktie.

'Then tell me why you had Hoetzendorf and the others killed,' Charity asked.

'Simple – they owed me money. They bought things and didn't want to pay. I had to make an example of them. Can't have people buying guns and not paying. Saw to it myself.'

'The hexogenamite . . . It was you who framed me,' Charity said as a cold draught shivered through the church.

'Simple, really, as I said. I needed them dead so I invited them for a display of the *Irenzee*. I pleaded to their sense of vanity. Told each of them they would be the only nation in the world to have such a ship – a submersible, a craft that can slip into any harbour undetected. Once they were in the hotel the rest was very easy. I was sad that I couldn't watch them explode. I heard it was quite spectacular.'

'You killed all those people because of money?'

'I would have killed them for less,' Zogel replied as he laughed.

'And you set me up so the evidence pointed to me?' Charity asked as he clicked the lock of the pistol.

'Not my idea. That was Inspector Walpole, a man with a sense of humour and a nagging hatred of you. Jealousy does strange things.'

'Prepared to see me hang and not to tell the truth?' Charity said.

'I was going to tell the police as soon as I was safely away that Walpole was behind it all and have him hang as well, but how things change.'

'And all for your own self-interest?' replied Charity as another shivering blast swept icily through the church.

'Then I take it we have a deal?' asked Zogel as he sat on an ornate chair by the altar. 'The diamonds?'

'Once I have the boy,' Charity said as he looked for a way to free Titus Salt.

'This is a done deal, Jack – there's no room for negotiation. It's how I say or not at all. I could take the diamonds from you now and kill you both,' Zogel said as he stared at Charity. 'It's my generosity of heart and colonial spirit that stops me from having you shot. The diamonds, Jack?'

'Very well – take them,' Charity said reluctantly as he threw the bag to the floor and watched the diamonds scatter across the dirty tiles.

Zogel bent down and picked them up one by one. He raised a diamond to his face and stared deep inside.

'Can't be – don't look a day older than I do now,' he said as he studied the ghostly reflection that twinkled in the diamond.

'Where's the boy?' Charity insisted as Zogel placed the diamonds one by one back into the bag and clutched them tightly in his hands.

'He's here, Jack.' The clear voice stilled the moment.

There was a rush at the church door as several men in long coats armed with pistols stormed in. Isambard Black stood in the shadows, holding Mariah close to him.

'Isambard Black and the Bureau of Antiquities – how interesting,' Zogel said as he laughed.

'And Commissioner Ritchie of the Metropolitan Police,' said a tall man who pushed through the flank of Bureau agents. 'We heard everything, Zogel.'

'Shame you'll do nothing about it,' Zogel said as he walked casually towards them. 'I would suggest that you let my men go. I will of course follow them, and the *Irenzee* will leave without hindrance.'

'You killed those men and you expect to walk free?' Black asked.

'Expect, no. Demand, yes,' Zogel replied. 'I have the girl, and if I am not back on the harbour side then she'll be cast into the sea.' He shrugged and went on. 'Even if you did arrest me I would be out by the morning. What I did was a military action against an enemy state. They were combatants of war, Commissioner.'

'Let him go,' Charity shouted, his words echoing through the church.

'At last – a man with sense,' Zogel quipped as the armed guards stepped aside. 'Sometimes there are no happy endings.'

'We can't just let the man go,' said Commissioner Ritchie. 'He murdered people. I heard his confession.'

'He's right, Commissioner,' said Titus Salt as he got to his feet. 'He would be out by the morning. Zogel is a diplomat of the Americas. No court in the land could convict him.'

'I'll take my carriage through Paradise and be gone from you. If you stop me, my men have orders to bombard the town and turn it to rubble,' said Zogel, his hands trembling.

Charity looked at Mariah and caught his eye. Mariah nodded, as if he knew what was to be done.

The police officers, Commissioner and agents of the Bureau stepped back and allowed Zogel to leave unhindered. His men picked up their guns and followed on. They were all silent and looked on as if at the departing of a funeral procession.

'You'll just let him go?' Black asked in his clear voice.

'Wait until you hear the wheels turn,' said Charity. 'Ready, Mariah? You know where they have Sacha?'

Mariah nodded and went to the door. He looked outside. 'The carriage has gone,' he said.

'Isambard,' Charity said without delay, 'I will meet you in the theatre of the Prince Regent within the hour. Take the Commissioner and three men. Once I have dealt with Zogel we have another rat to catch and Mariah will be the bait.'

Before anyone could reply, Mariah and Charity had run from the church. Taking the path through the charnel ground, they were soon running through the narrow lanes of the town towards the harbour.

[27]

The Night of the Fire Demon

THE horde of people that crowded against the railings of the harbour to look at the strange craft moored by the wall was several men deep. Others watched the waves breaking over the bows of the *Irenzee* in the bay. A wind blew spirals of sand along the promenade but still the babbling crowd looked on. Word had spread quickly of a boat in the harbour that could sail underwater. It was like a gigantic frog with goggle eyes and a brass mouth that could swallow eight men at a time.

Two hours earlier, the craft had appeared before three old fishermen. At first they had seen a strange green light under the rising tide and then, just as they thought the Kraken was about to appear, the submersible had broken the surface. Those who had come in the craft had left quickly. They were ushered through a small door into the fish shed, and then a darkened carriage had been driven along the promenade and up Paradise Hill.

Now everyone waited. As Charity and Mariah pushed their way through the crowd the door to the fish shed opened slightly and the uniformed figure of one of Zogel's guards looked out.

'Is that the place?' asked Charity as he held the scarf to his face so he couldn't be recognised.

'It was in there, by the nets, a small room – that's where they took her,' Mariah replied as he pushed a fat woman with a monkey face out of the way.

'And her father?' Charity asked as the woman squabbled, not wanting to let them by.

Just as Mariah was about to speak, the door opened again. The guard peered at the crowd as if he waited for someone.

'He's looking for Zogel. We must have got here first,' Mariah said as they broke through the mob into an open space near the door. 'What shall we do?'

'We attack, Mariah – we have been on the run for too long,' Charity said as he saw the paleness of Mariah's face. 'Leave the guards to me – you find Sacha. If we get separated, head for the Prince Regent and find Isambard Black.'

The door opened slightly. In the darkness, Mariah saw the rim of the guard's hat. Before the man could move an inch, Charity had jumped against the door. There was a dull thud, and the guard slumped to the floor. Charity pushed on the door as he took the pistol from his coat and stormed inside.

Just as Mariah followed, another guard leapt on Charity, pulling him backwards. Mariah didn't know what to do as the man struggled to get the pistol from Charity's hand. The gun fired three times in the air. The bullets ricocheted from the roof and around the baiting shed with its long tables and stink of fish. To his right was a pile of broken crab pots. Mariah took a long disregarded weight and struck the man across the back.

'Tie him, quickly,' Charity said as Mariah took a length of twine from a broken pot and wrapped it around the man's legs and hands.

The guard moaned as the twine was pulled tighter until he couldn't move. Mariah stuffed a length of rag into his mouth to stop him from speaking.

'It's this way,' he said to Charity, who took three bullets from his pocket and reloaded the pistol. 'There's a room by a staircase – they took them there.'

They sneaked quietly across the stone floor of the fish shed. The wind howled outside and the sea broke across the harbour wall. In the corner of the shed was a weighing house. It was a peculiar small shed within the shed. A metal chimney came from the roof and a fire burnt within. The shed was lit by an oil lamp that cast the shadow of the faded net curtains across the ground outside.

Mariah peered through the dirty window. Sacha and her father sat by the fire. He could see no one else in the room.

'Alone,' he whispered to Charity, who crawled to the door like a giant cat.

Mariah slipped the bolt that had kept them locked inside. He opened the door slowly as Charity kept guard. Sacha smiled as she saw his face.

'Zogel was going to leave us here and tell Walpole where we were,' Sacha said as she reached out for Mariah's hand.

'Where is Lucius?' Mariah asked.

'He went back to the submersible ten minutes ago,' she replied.

'Then we have no time,' Mariah said as he looked at her, wishing he could say that which he had wanted for so long.

'Go to the coastguard,' Charity said to Sacha's father, who sat shame-faced looking into the flames. 'Redeem yourself for what you have done. Tell them that the *Irenzee* must not be allowed to leave the bay.'

The man turned and gave a frail half smile as if the will of life had drained from him.

'He told me he would bombard the town if I didn't allow the *Irenzee* to leave,' he replied wearily.

'We shall see,' said Charity. 'Sacha. I need your help – will you come with us?' Sacha smiled at the note of sympathy of

Charity's words. 'Go with Mariah. Walpole will be in Athol House. Make sure they see you and run to the Prince Regent. Isambard Black will be in the theatre. He will know what to do. I shall go for Zogel and the Ghost Diamonds.'

They saw Charity turn and approach the door of the weighing shed. The shadow he cast crossed the floor and for an instant flickered on the dirty net curtains. Outside, Mariah saw out of the corner of his eye something move. It was small, compact and glinted in the light from the window. Then, as if it had been a dream, it vanished. Charity noticed the look on his face.

'What was it?' he asked, worried for the boy.

'I don't know. I think I saw something move. I can't be sure,' Mariah said as he drew closer to the window and peered into the shadows.

Sacha pressed close to him. Not so much to look as to be near.

The shadow came again, followed by the glint of light. This time it was further away, by the long flight of wooden steps that led to a gantry for drying fishnets.

'There is something out there,' Mariah said, sure he had seen a creature move in the darkness.

Charity cocked the pistol and pushed against the door. Mariah kept watch.

'It's by the wall, coming closer,' he said as a loud hissing noise began to billow from outside.

Just as Charity pushed the door open there was a smell of kerosene. It sprayed against the window of the shed and dripped from the roof.

'Run!' shouted Mariah as he pushed Sacha through the door and into the outer shed, followed by Charity and Sacha's father.

There was a sudden burst of light from under the wooden stairs. A surge of bright blue fire spurted through the air towards them. The weighing shed exploded as it ignited in red flames.

Mariah could see a creature coming towards them. It was the size of an ape. From what seemed to be its mouth it dripped fire. It had what appeared to be one large glass eye in the centre of a head that looked as though it were made of metal.

Charity fired at the creature. The bullet bounced off its head as it were made of steel. There was a wheezing noise as if it were gasping for breath. Then the dribbles of fire came again. Kerosene spurted from its mouth and suddenly exploded in a shaft of fire. The flames shot above their heads.

'What is it?' Sacha cried as the creature came closer.

'It's . . . It's a fire-starter – a weapon, made by Zogel,' Charity cried as he shot again. 'Bulletproof,' he shouted as they all ran from the fire demon.

'I think it's Lucius – he went back to the submersible,' Mariah bawled above the wheezing of the flamethrower.

An inferno began to engulf the building as smoke filled the fish shed. In the light of the encroaching fire, Mariah could see Lucius clearly as he got closer. The flames came like breath from a head that was made from a brass diving helmet. Upon the fire-starter's back was a large shell-like tank with a thin tube connecting to the helmet. Beneath was a suit of thick golden material that was wrinkled about the arms, and on its feet were black leather boots that steamed as he walked.

'We'll have to get outside,' Mariah said as they ran towards the door.

Charity and Sacha's father grabbed hold of the guard and dragged him outside. Already the crowd had moved away from the burning building. As Charity stepped from the building he was recognised. Angry voices were raised up in alarm.

'That's him – the murderer!' screamed a man so fat that he looked as if he had eaten the food of many men. The mob began to holler and bawl for Charity to be arrested.

Mariah and Sacha came out of the building and into the

night. The fat man made a grab for Charity and just as Mariah pushed him away the crowd began to scream. They pointed to the doorway in terror as if they looked upon the devil.

There, in the shadow of the flaming building, was the fire-starter. It stood like a dwarfed dragon gasping for breath. It sighed deeply. Mariah noticed that its hand pulled the handle of what appeared to be a pump.

'It's pressurising the tank,' Charity shouted as he pulled the bound guard to the safety of the harbour side. 'Get out of the way.'

The crowd began to panic. Hundreds of people started to scream as the fire-starter stepped from the building. The noise from the tank on its back began to get louder. It seethed and hissed as it took each step.

In the cold night air it sounded like the whirring of a parlour fan. It sizzled as it was showered with water from the breaking waves. Steam burst from the hot metal. There was a rush of air. Kerosene fired from its mouth and then exploded in flame.

The fire-starter walked towards the crowd. It appeared to be searching for Charity. If anyone came close it spurted short bursts of fire to push them back. The dark night and the black storm clouds were made as day by the gusts of flame.

Soon all the people were running. They screamed in panic as the blaze that engulfed the fish shed grew higher. Mariah and Sacha hid by the lifeboat house, the waves rolling across the stone landing and about their feet. They could see Charity outside the Golden Kipper goading the fire-starter to follow, always just out of reach of the flames. Sacha's father was nowhere to be seen.

'He's not there,' Sacha screamed as she broke cover and ran towards the harbour. Lucius turned slowly, the reflection of the fire flickering in the glass of his brass helmet. He seethed small droplets of fire as he looked at her running towards him.

299

The gurgling noise came again as the kerosene tank repressurised. Mariah saw Lucius force the handle frantically. The nozzle on the front of the helmet was re-lit as tiny jets of fuel shot through. He took aim at Sacha.

Mariah looked about him as the waves broke into his hiding place. There on the wall in a glass case was a fire-axe. Without thinking, Mariah smashed the glass with his elbow and pulled the axe from its mantle. He could hear Charity shouting to him.

'Do it, Mariah! Do it now!' His voice faded in the wind.

Mariah grabbed the axe just as Charity fired at Lucius. The bullet struck the back of the helmet with such a force that it knocked the dwarf from his feet. Slowly a pool of kerosene issued about him. Charity fired again. The bullet struck the same place to the inch.

The dwarf got to his feet and turned as Mariah set off to run across the pier. All seemed to go slowly. He could feel the blood pumping through his head as his heart beat faster. The sound of the wind and waves faded as he ran. He clutched the axe in his hands and raised it above his head.

Mariah could see no one but Lucius, Sacha and Charity. The screaming of the crowd was no more. In his mind he was alone as the seconds ticked slowly by. Pools of water splashed about him with each footstep. The dwarf got to his feet and turned towards Charity. The wheezing started again as the tank refilled under pressure. Suddenly the kerosene shot towards Charity, splattering the ground beneath his feet. The flame followed like a lightning bolt about to strike. Charity dived towards the harbour just as the fireball exploded.

Mariah ran down on Lucius. As he came upon him, the axe fell with all the force of his arms. It smashed the bottom of the tank. A small hole burst open. Mariah swung again and struck a blow to the helmet. The iron-wired tube severed. There was the sound of hell. It roared like a fire demon.

Lucius looked down as Mariah stepped back. The tiniest droplet of fire fell from the siphon. For a moment, Lucius looked Mariah eye to eye. Mariah saw the dwarf smile as if he knew what was to come. Lucius held out his hand as all about him was consumed in fire.

Suddenly a jet of flame shot out from the pressurised tank. Lucius shook for a moment before abruptly being propelled into the air like a rocket. Mariah looked up as he flew higher and higher as if he would never stop.

No one could hear his screams as they were drowned by the roaring of the sea. Lucius went skyward faster than any man had gone before. Then, in the twinkling of an eye, he was gone. A bright and blinding explosion rocked the promenade and shook the windows of the Golden Kipper. It broke the sky, brighter than the midday sun. The rumbling surged for mile upon mile like heavy thunder and the earth shook. The crowds of fleeing people looked up and gasped with amazement at the beauty of the explosion.

A crescendo of sparks fell to the ground like falling diamonds. Far out to sea the remnants of the fire-starter were scattered to the wind. Lucius was no more.

'I told you never to play with fire, Mariah,' Charity said as he brushed the wet sand from his coat.

'He would have killed Sacha,' Mariah replied as he dropped the axe from his shaking hands.

'You did well – saved more than just Sacha,' Charity said.

In the mayhem they were suddenly aware of the slamming of a carriage door.

'Where is he? Where is he?' asked Zogel frantically as he stepped from his carriage that had been hemmed in by the crowds.

'Who do you seek, Zogel?' Mariah asked before anyone else.

'I see you have escaped and I take it my companion is dead,'

Zogel said in a melancholy way as he looked about, not sure what to do next.

'I will take the diamonds,' Charity replied as he pointed the gun at Zogel. 'I will exchange them for *your* life.'

'Very well, my dear friend. The Bureau of Antiquities wins again. As soon as I am at sea I will have the *Irenzee* bombard the town.'

'That is a promise too far. Not even Skull and Bones would allow that,' Mariah replied.

'You train him well, Captain. He is so much like you. If I didn't know better I would say you were his father,' Zogel said as he walked slowly across the pier towards the submersible. 'Did you destroy my submarine?' he asked as the swirling smoke ghosted his appearance.

'Is that what it is called?' asked Charity.

'I had thought of under-sea-boat, but it didn't sound as romantic,' Zogel quipped. 'I take it I can still leave?'

'Without the diamonds,' said Mariah as he held out his hand.

'A boy with a golden tip to his finger, now *that* is interesting. Will you sell it to me?'

'I don't sell memories,' Mariah replied. 'The diamonds?'

Begrudgingly, Zogel handed Mariah the bag of Ghost Diamonds and scowled.

'Easy come,' he said.

'Easy go,' Mariah replied with a smile.

'Let me walk you to your craft,' Charity interrupted, pushing Zogel in the back to move him along.

'I will have to book in to the Prince Regent next year. I hear the food is very good. Baron Hoetzendorf said how much he enjoyed it – especially the sandwiches,' Zogel replied.

'We shall always be full. I will make certain Mrs Mukluk never returns your calls or opens your letters,' Charity said as he pushed Zogel further along the pier towards the submersible.

'Perhaps that would be a very wise thing. You could never win again and I would have to kill you like I did the others,' Zogel replied.

'I am the one holding the gun. The only thing that stops me shooting you is that I am an Englishman,' said Charity as he clicked the hammer of the pistol, ready to fire.

'I have outstayed my welcome. It has been a grand chase and one which I have enjoyed immensely. You have my permission to do what you want with Bardolph. He is beyond use, even for the Society of Truth.'

'Are you really the power behind the power?' Mariah asked. Sacha stood close by him, holding the hem of his jacket nervously.

'Only in this world,' Zogel said solemnly. 'We shall all come before a greater authority one day.'

'I think it is time for you to take to the sea,' Charity said as they got to the steps.

Before Zogel left, Mariah handed Charity the Ghost Diamonds. He looked inside: they sparkled as if they were jewelled eggs in a snug nest.

'I would have liked them for myself,' Zogel said. 'The Bureau of Antiquities will hide them away never to be seen or enjoyed. Such a tragic fate for things so beautiful.' They were the last words he spoke before he went slowly down the steps and got into the boat. A guard came from within and opened the hatch. Zogel went inside as the engine started. The craft cast off and shunted slowly through the calm harbour water towards the storm.

Zogel turned as they were just about to submerge and waved from the open hatch. From inside his coat he pulled an identical bag to the one in Charity's hand.

'They were for Bardolph,' he shouted. 'Identical in every way but made of crystal. He would never have known and neither would you.' He laughed.

Charity grabbed two diamonds as he dropped the bag to the floor.

'Look at them, Captain – can you see your ghost?' Zogel asked mockingly.

Charity stared into the diamonds. There was only a faint reflection. He crashed them together and watched as the cut glass shattered in his hands.

'Fakes,' Mariah said. 'He tricked us.'

From out in the harbour they could hear Zogel's laughter.

'Look further – there is a gift from me to Mariah and Sacha,' he shouted as he pulled the hatch on the submarine and the craft sank beneath the waves in the direction of the *Irenzee*.

Sacha searched the bag. Deep inside, wrapped in a silk handkerchief, was a miniature golden monkey. It was cast upon a small stone. For eyes it had red jewels, and about its waist was a belt of diamonds. Written on the stone were the words: *Where I fit – there will be more . . .*

Charity laughed. 'Sunwu – the Golden Monkey. Yet another legend.'

[28]

Bardolph Revisited

THE square outside the Prince Regent was lifeless. Far away, Mariah could hear the crowd that had returned to stare at the rats the size of cats running from the burning buildings on the pier. The dark sky was edged in a blood-red glow, and even on the other side of the bay sparks fell to earth like dying fireflies.

'You know what to do?' Charity briskly asked Mariah as he and Sacha hid in the ornate doorway of Alfie Tugwell's hair-dressing emporium.

'Take the letter and give it to Walpole,' Sacha replied as she rubbed her hands to keep out the cold.

'Then head for the theatre,' Charity added. 'I'll make sure the mannequins are ready.'

Charity then nodded and set off down the steps towards the beach.

'Will it work?' Sacha asked.

'Perhaps,' Mariah replied as he read the scrawled note once more.

'I never thought I would be with you again,' she said as she listened to Charity's footsteps running down McBean Steps.

'Thought my father and I would be on the boat and away by now.'

'Did you want to go?' Mariah asked.

'At first I did. But then I thought of the Prince Regent . . . and you . . .'

'I'm glad it has ended this way,' Mariah replied as he looked at her. 'Funny thing is,' he went on, 'I have hated myself for the things I said to you. I really wanted to hate you for what you did – but I couldn't.' Mariah smiled apologetically at her. It was the first time since he could remember that he had done so and meant it.

'I felt that about my father. He can be so stupid. So easily led.'

'Like us all,' Mariah replied as the sound of the collapsing fish sheds rumbled through the town.

'Zogel's going to just sail away,' Sacha said as she looked out to sea at the fire-red silhouette of the *Irenzee*.

'But he's alone.'

'Shall I come with you?' she asked.

'I have to do this by myself. Go to the theatre and when I come in remember the spotlight and the hoist.'

Mariah touched her hand. It was bloodless and cold. Sacha looked away as if it was more than a gesture of goodbye. He gripped the note tightly as he stepped from the shadows and began to run.

He was soon across the square. Athol House rose up out of the muddy street like a dark mausoleum. By the door, the Peeler kept pacing back and forth. He looked up as he heard Mariah coming towards him.

'Get Walpole! Quick – I have found the Ghost Diamonds!' Mariah shouted as he stuffed the note into the policeman's hand and ran back towards the Prince Regent.

For a moment the man stood and just read the words on the crumpled paper.

'Give it to him!' Mariah shouted as he turned. 'Inspector Walpole.'

Mariah stopped on the corner and from the shadows of the tram hut looked back. The Peeler ambled up the steps and through the old door of Athol House. He was gone for less than a minute before the door burst open and Walpole appeared.

'Grimm, Grendel, we can't hang about,' he said as he pulled his porkpie hat down to his ears. 'Mariah Mundi is in the Prince Regent and he has the diamonds.'

It was all that Mariah wanted to hear. He ran down the steps and into the hotel. There was the same old familiar smell. His stomach churned in excitement as he took the steam elevator up to the theatre and opened the door.

It was deathly dark. Only the mellow glow of the limelight lit the stage. Two ropes of thin wire hung down. Mariah walked across and clipped them to his belt. The door burst open.

'Better not be playing games with us,' Walpole wheezed as Grimm and Grendel followed him in.

There was a dull clunk as the spotlight cover opened quickly. A beam of pure white light broke through the darkness. Mariah appeared, cast in a crescent of light.

'The diamonds?' Walpole asked as he walked down the aisle towards the front of the stage.

'In exchange.' Mariah replied.

'What would a lad like you need? After all, the world thinks you are dead,' he replied.

'Information,' Mariah said as he wiped a bead of sweat from his brow. 'Why do you really want the Prince Regent?'

'The diamonds for that?' Walpole laughed as his face turned to ash and his eyes flickered.

'And my freedom,' Mariah added as he waited for the man to get closer.

'You are truly free – what could be freer than death?' asked Grendel as he followed on behind.

'So you have the diamonds – can we see?' Walpole asked as he reached the front of the stage.

Mariah pulled the bag from under his coat, pulled out a diamond and held it to the spotlight.

'See – is this what you are looking for?' Mariah asked.

Walpole was silent. He looked at the Ghost Diamond and then to Grimm and Grendel.

'Kill him,' he whispered in a sweet voice.

Grendel began to giggle nervously as he fumbled in his coat for the holster in which he kept his revolver.

'Give me the diamonds, Mariah, and you will go free,' Grimm said as he pushed Grendel to one side.

From somewhere far away came the sound of the whirring of a barrel organ. At first it was distant and soft. Walpole gave it no attention until the music grew louder. Mariah began to tap his feet in time with the music.

'Shoot him and take the diamonds,' Walpole said to Grendel.

Before he had time to draw his gun, Mariah had vanished. It was as if he had been snatched from before their eyes. Grendel stood for a moment and looked at the empty stage. He pointed his pistol to the circle of light cast on the floor. Then, just as he was about to speak, a sudden crash shook the stage.

From high above their heads seven mannequins had dropped to the boards. They lay in crumpled heaps, arms twisted as if they had been ripped from their sockets. Each wooden head tilted to one side as if held by a snapped neck.

'What kind of trickery is this, Mariah?' Walpole asked as he stood and looked on with Grimm and Grendel by his side. The music grew louder. As Walpole stared at the dolls, he was sure the mannequins began to move slightly. It was then that he realised that the face of each puppet was crafted to be identical to that of Mariah's.

At first Walpole thought their fingers twitched in time with the shrill notes. Grimm and Grendel looked on as Walpole moved to the edge of the stage, looking for the boy. Then one by one the mannequins began to move.

Suddenly, a doll jumped to its feet. It straightened its back and clicked its head from side to side until it fell into place with a double thud. There was a whir of a mechanical engine and the puppet began to dance. It was the size of a man and dressed as a sea captain. In its belt was a cutlass. With every beat of the music it clashed its jaw up and down and rapidly winked its eye. It was identical to Mariah in every way. Its hair curled and corked from its head and the tip of its finger shone gold. In the darkness of the theatre it was impossible to tell if it was Mariah; in the glistening spotlight the wires could barely be seen.

Walpole stepped back. Grendel aimed his pistol as Grimm cowered in the darkness.

One by one, the other automata got to their feet. Like the first, they creaked and groaned as their limbs snapped in place. Then, as if by magic, they too began to dance. Each one pulled the sword from its belt and crashed it from side to side. They leapt in the air in time with the music, barring Walpole from getting across the stage. They whirled like mad dervishes, spinning on their long taut wires and slashing with their swords.

'Won't be stopped by some dolls,' Walpole shouted. 'You got us here for the Ghost Diamonds and we won't leave until we have them. 'Grendel, kill the beasts!'

Grendel took aim and, as the puppets danced, pulled the hammer on the pistol.

'One of them could be the boy,' Grimm shouted suddenly realising that any of the automata could be Mariah.

'They're clockwork, ' Grendel protested indignantly above the beat of the music from the barrel organ.

'*Stop them!*' Walpole screamed as he held his hands over his ears, his face contorted as if in pain.

Grendel fired. The bullet exploded in the chest of one automaton. It stopped dancing. The sword dropped from its hand. Its head fell to one side. The body hung limply from the wires as the machinery groaned and whined.

The other puppets continued to dance as the music got faster and faster.

'One of them must be him,' Grimm shouted above the noise while Grendel's hand danced back and forth as he decided which one to shoot next.

'Don't shoot the lad!' Walpole screamed, unsure which, if any, was Mariah.

Grendel took aim and fired again. The bullet struck another puppet in the forehead, sending a shower of wheels and cogs bouncing across the stage. Like the first it whirred to a halt and hung on its wires as if dead.

'Another!' shouted Walpole as he sat in the front row, his head in his hands and unable to think for the screeching of the barrel organ.

Grendel shot again and again. Automata exploded with every bullet, stopped in their dancing. The music began to slow and eventually fade. Grendel reloaded the pistol as he fired and fired until there was only one automaton left.

'It could be him,' Grendel screamed above the sound of the dying music.

Walpole took a long harsh look, lifting the porkpie hat from his head and staring down the ridge of his long, sharp nose.

'It's a puppet – just looks like the lad,' he said after he had scrutinised it for several seconds. 'Shoot it – he's not here.'

Grendel took aim.

'It could be Mariah. If we kill him we won't find the Ghost Diamonds,' Grimm said.

Grendel's hand began to shake. He was unsure whether he should fire.

'Do it!' shouted Walpole as the spotlight began to fade and the theatre darkened.

The puppet danced quietly in the shadows at the back of the stage. It was as if it knew what was going to happen. It slowed in its pace until it stood looking at Grendel. Putting its hand in its pocket, it took out a shining diamond.

'Wait!' screamed Walpole as he saw the large stone in its hand. 'It's Mariah Mundi.'

The puppet jerked in its movements as its fingers slowly opened. Grendel kept the gun aimed at its chest, his hand shaking. As the puppet slumped forward, resting on its wires, the diamond dropped from its fingers and rolled towards them.

Grimm jumped on the stage and picked up the stone, holding it to the fading spotlight.

'A Ghost Diamond,' he said as the light dimmed until he was a brief shadow.

All was silent except for the rolling of three more diamonds that tumbled down the rake of the stage.

'Any more, Mariah?' Walpole asked.

There was silence.

Grimm walked across the stage and picked up the diamonds, stuffing them into the pockets of his long raincoat. He stopped and looked at the puppet in the shadows by the side of the stage. Reaching out with his hand, he touched the forehead. It was cold and yet vaguely human, as if masked.

'It's a mechanical doll,' he said as he looked back into the gloom of the theatre. From where he stood, Grendel and Walpole were indistinct shadows.

'You have the diamonds,' Mariah said from somewhere

nearby. 'You can have the rest when you tell me if I am a free man.'

'I thought you would ask for the life of your friend,' Walpole asked.

'He was innocent,' Mariah replied.

'Of course he was, Mariah Mundi. But someone had to take the blame. That was what I was ordered to do.'

'You? Ordered?' said Mariah as his voice echoed around the darkened theatre.

'I am just a cog in the works, just like your dancing dummies – I do what I'm told and in return have my own piece of freedom.'

'You danced for the Templar, Bardolph,' Mariah said.

'Many people dance for him. The world would dance for him if he had the chance,' Walpole replied.

'And you'll take the diamonds and give them to Bardolph?'

'Of course, and then we'll take this place.'

'Then Packavi will go free?' Mariah asked.

'He had his uses. Got rid of a problem for us in Whitechapel and did the same here. There will be some other city that needs its vermin eliminating,' Walpole replied. 'You will go free – he will not harm you now, I will see to that . . . Come out. I don't like speaking to the dark.'

Mariah took three paces onto the stage and made his way through the dangling corpses of the automata. He could see Walpole and Grendel below him in the front row. Grimm stood nearby, holding the wire of a puppet as if afraid to move.

It was then that Mariah noticed an even darker shadow behind him. It had the shape of a man with a hood cast across its face. A long knife was pressed against Grimm's neck.

'Don't be thinking you're going anywhere with those diamonds,' Packavi said as he held the knife to Grimm's throat.

'I wouldn't . . .' Grimm squealed.

'Give them to me.'

'Packavi!' Walpole shouted. 'Why are you here?'

'Orders. Just like you. Make sure you didn't mess things up – can't be trusted, the Templar said.' Packavi grunted, choking on each word. 'Taking them back and doing the job I came to do.'

'It's over – we have the diamonds, and the hotel,' Walpole insisted.

'Only when *he* is dead. We couldn't get his father but we can get him,' Packavi sneered as he pushed Grimm to the floor and walked towards Mariah.

'How many have you killed, Packavi?' Mariah asked as he stood his ground.

'Not enough,' he replied.

'Then I will not run. Take me here. I don't fear you,' he said as the madman approached within an arm's length and drew back his knife to strike.

In a blinding flash, the stage was flooded with light as two explosions fired from beneath Mariah's feet. They echoed about the room, and when all was still Mariah had vanished yet again, swallowed by the trap door.

Packavi looked at Walpole.

'He plays tricks with us,' the man screamed as he slashed the air with the knife. 'Bring him back at once.'

Before he could say another word, Mariah reappeared and ran onto the stage, a hook and wire in his hand. Packavi turned just as Mariah sank the hook into his chest.

'Now!' shouted Mariah.

There was a whirring of the winch above his head as Packavi was ripped from the ground and dangled helplessly above them all. Walpole clapped his hands slowly as Packavi dangled by the front of his waistcoat.

'Well done! What an entertainment! The boy vanishes and

313

reappears to save the day. What will he do next?' He licked his lips slowly. 'Mister Grendel – shoot him.'

'Not before I shoot you,' Charity said as one by one all of the theatre lights brightened. His face was steely grey, his eyes set towards Walpole. Mariah had never seen him look that way before. It was as if his hardened heart brimmed full of anger.

Walpole looked about him. There in the balcony was Captain Jack Charity. The pistol in his hand was aimed at Walpole's head. As he looked further he saw other men coming out from their hiding places. Sacha stood by a panel of switches at the side of the stage. Then the door opened and Isambard Black and Commissioner Ritchie stepped into the theatre.

'It's over,' said Isambard Black as he pointed his pistol at Walpole. 'Commissioner Ritchie is from the Metropolitan Division. We have heard your confession, Inspector Walpole.'

Walpole slumped back into a seat and stretched out his long legs and sighed.

'I thought a fat lady had to sing before it was over?' he asked quietly.

'Not yet . . .' The voice was that of Bardolph, who had Sacha in his grasp and was dragging her to the wings. 'Put down your weapons!' he shouted as he turned to Mariah. 'Give me the diamonds, Mariah Mundi, and I will allow your friend to live.'

Mariah looked at Charity and then to Isambard Black.

'Don't do it, Mariah. He wouldn't hurt her,' Charity shouted.

'Mister Grendel, take the diamonds from the boy. Mister Grimm, come with me.'

Bardolph edged his way slowly to the centre of the stage, dragging Sacha with him. Mariah could see the fear in her eyes. She whispered something that he couldn't hear.

'Take the diamonds!' Mariah shouted. 'They mean nothing to me. Just leave Sacha alone.'

'Very wise, Mariah Mundi,' Bardolph growled through twisted lips.

'What about me?' screamed Walpole as he realised he was being left behind.

'Disposable, Mister Walpole. The Society of Truth is bigger than us all and sometimes we have to make sacrifices.'

Grendel sauntered across the stage.

'Got the diamonds?' he asked as he stooped above Mariah.

Mariah handed him the bag of fake stones, hoping he wouldn't see they were only glass.

'Very clever puppets you have there,' Grendel said as he tapped the head of a broken automaton.

'I need Packavi,' Bardolph insisted. 'Let him down, Mariah,' he ordered before Grendel could finish speaking.

Mariah walked across the stage as Bardolph gripped Sacha tightly. He noticed a small silver derringer pressed into her back. She mouthed some words to Mariah again. He realised suddenly what she was trying to say.

'You'll have to stand away from the puppets,' Mariah said as he reached for a lever on the control panel by the side of the stage. 'They'll all have to be released if you want Packavi.'

'Just get him down, no tricks,' Bardolph quipped as he stepped back.

The stage beneath his feet sagged as he stood upon it. Bardolph didn't notice anything strange. He kept one eye on Mariah and the other on Charity and the agents from the Bureau of Antiquities.

'We'll hunt you down, Bardolph. There'll be no escape,' Isambard Black shouted from the back of the theatre as he hustled slowly forward.

'Another city and another name, is that not right, Isambard Black? The Society of Truth matters more than life itself. I will disappear like the mist in this barren place,' Bardolph replied.

There was a click as Mariah flicked the lever. Packavi was lowered and the puppets fell to the stage. Bardolph stood as if in the centre of a charnel ground. Packavi got to his feet and smiled beneath his mask.

'What would you like me to do with the boy?' he asked Bardolph, hoping he would allow him to kill him there and then.

'Take him,' Bardolph said in a constrained voice as his words were interrupted by a sharp clunk beneath his feet.

'*Sacha – NOW!*' screamed Mariah.

Without thinking, Sacha hit Bardolph as hard as she could and broke free. Before he could fire the gun, Bardolph was blasted into the air. Letting go of his grip on the derringer, he tried to scream. He somersaulted several times then crashed to the stage. The power ramrod flashed back beneath the stage with a hiss of steam as Bardolph writhed at Packavi's feet.

'Kill him!' Bardolph ordered, gasping for breath and unable to move. 'Kill them both!'

Before Packavi could attack, Sacha grabbed a sword from an automaton. In a move of her hand it flashed through the darkness. Packavi stumbled back, holding his stomach as he collapsed to the floor.

Sacha turned and smiled at Mariah. 'See – told you I could be trusted,' she said with a note of triumph in her voice.

The derringer fired. There was a muffled blast, an intense flash, and then Sacha trembled as if someone had run their finger down her spine. She stumbled forward, reaching out for Mariah, unable to speak. Then, as he ran to her, she fell to the floor.

Bardolph raised the pistol again as he tried to escape. Grimm and Grendel ran from the stage. Mariah dived upon Bardolph and managed to grab the hand and hold the gun to the floor before he could fire again. Agents leapt from the balcony to the floor below.

'Could have been different, boy,' Bardolph grunted. 'You could have been one of us – made up for your father's fear.'

With one hand, Mariah grabbed the wire from a mannequin. He pushed the hook under Bardolph's belt as he twisted the gun from his hand. Then, with a sharp tug, he pulled the counterweight from its holder high above them. The wire tensed as the weight fell. Bardolph was pulled from the stage. He was fired through the air, higher and higher. His screams echoed in the theatre until, with a sudden thud, they were no more.

A single drop of blood fell to the stage as Mariah cradled Sacha in his arms. He felt the wound on her back. The bullet had struck her shoulder, tearing a line through her skin.

'She'll be fine,' Charity said as agents surrounded them.

'It happened so quickly, I didn't know what to do,' Mariah replied.

'You have done well,' said Isambard Black as Walpole and Packavi were led away.

'Grimm and Grendel?' Mariah asked.

'Gone,' replied Isambard Black. 'It is better that way – no one will find out about us.'

Sacha opened her eyes and took hold of Mariah's hand.

'It was the best performance I have ever seen – they danced so well,' she said.

'Thanks to you, Sacha,' he replied.

As they left the Prince Regent Mariah sniffed the cold night air.

'They'll be no more trouble, Jack,' said Isambard Black as he led Walpole to the prison van.

'We can be open again in the morning,' Mariah replied as he stood looking across the road to Athol House. 'What will become of The Society of Truth?'

'All will be quiet for a while. Athol House will be sold and no one will ask any questions,' replied Captain Jack as he watched the door of the cart being slammed in Walpole's face.

'Bardolph mentioned my father – said I could have been one of them, it would have made up for my father's fear. What did he mean?'

'They had wanted your father to join with them. They knew to have a man like him on their side would have meant an ultimate victory,' Charity said as he deliberated his words.

'Did he?' asked Mariah.

'He would never darken the doors of such a place – called it the dangerous boys' club and if a man had to join, then life must be very sad,' Charity said as he patted Mariah on the back.

'But what about the power, the influence? Perhaps he would have –'

'He was an honest man and not one for subterfuge and intrigue. It would not have suited him,' said Isambard.

'How did you know where we were?' Mariah asked Isambard.

'Mister Quadlibett told me,' Isambard said. 'He met me from the train. I had received a telegram – in fact two in the same day. One from Sacha, the other from Mrs Mukluk.'

'From Sacha?' Mariah asked as he looked at Jack Charity.

'Sent from the post office on the pier,' he replied.

'So she did send it, Captain,' he said, now knowing she had kept her word.

'Are you sure you want to continue with this place?' Isambard asked as the carriage trundled away with Walpole screaming to be free. 'You can't put new wine in an old wine skin.'

'It works well for the Bureau and it still has many secrets to give up,' Charity replied.

'We have made enemies, Jack. Enemies with the memory of

an elephant,' said Isambard as he pulled his leather gloves over his chilled fingers. 'They will be back to haunt you.'

'Still, Zogel has the Ghost Diamonds and they must be worth going after?' Mariah asked.

'He will be long gone by the morning and it'll be some time before we see more of him,' Charity replied.

'The Society of Truth – do they really control the world without us knowing?' he said.

'Only when good men do nothing and the last agent of the Bureau of Antiquities is no more,' replied Isambard Black.